D0298804

989900478915 94

the RUBY SLIPPERS

KEIR ALEXANDER

the RUBY SLIPPERS

corsair

TELFORD & WREKIN LIBRARIES	
Bertrams	19/03/2014
GEN	£12.99

Constable & Robinson Ltd
55–56 Russell Square
London WC1B 4HP
www.constablerobinson.com

First published in the UK by Corsair,
an imprint of Constable & Robinson Ltd., 2014

Copyright © Keir Alexander, 2014

The right of Keir Alexander to be identified as the author of this
work has been asserted by him in accordance with the
Copyright, Designs and Patents Act 1988

All rights reserved. This book is sold subject to the condition
that it shall not, by way of trade or otherwise, be lent, resold,
hired out or otherwise circulated in any form of binding or
cover other than that in which it is published and without a
similar condition including this condition being imposed
on the subsequent purchaser.

A copy of the British Library Cataloguing in
Publication Data is available from the British Library

ISBN: 978-1-4721-0807-4 (paperback)
ISBN: 978-1-47210-811-1 (ebook)

Printed and bound by
CPI Group (UK) Ltd, Croydon, CR0 4YY

1 3 5 7 9 10 8 6 4 2

CHAPTER ONE

SHE stinks. It has to be said. Stinks to high heaven. No, worse, stinks like death. This is not just a smell, an unpleasant odour to be carried away on the next breeze, it's a stench, a pestilence that violates the space she enters and damns the air where she has been. The rest of her spells death, too: the funeral-dark clothes, head to foot, and the dry knot of hair which has surely been borrowed from a corpse, not to mention the skinny marbled wrists sticking out of her black shell, making her look like some great wounded bug dragging itself away somewhere to die.

She has the dog for company, of course. His name is Barrell – another great black thing, padding ahead of her. If you see him coming along the street, get away and downwind pronto before Old Rosa arrives. Why he puts up with her is a real mystery. She has never petted him, or made him stand on his hind legs for treats, or tickled his tummy. He has never known the restraint of a leash, so how come he never ran barking for the hills? Maybe he likes the smell and wears it with pride, like a doggy badge. All the same, you don't see too many other mutts running up to sniff his old balls. Even animals seem to give Old Rosa a wide berth.

Why the authorities have not taken it upon themselves to *do something* about the woman is another mystery. They could surely take her in, scrub her down, and dress her up and perch her on a floral chair in some nice old folks' home. But they don't. Maybe the neighbourhood possesses an unconscious collective wisdom and somehow they need Old Rosa to walk among them. This creeping intimation of mortality, accompanied by the dog and the once-tartan shopping cart, with its squeaking wheel so simply and eloquently mocking all the vanities that flesh is heir to. Memento mori.

So she is free to roam. Here she is coming along 98th towards Fifth. The dog is there at the kerb, mooning for the grass in the Park, slavishly looking back over his shoulder for the next intervention. With barely a nod, Rosa sends him on and steps straight off after him, looking neither right nor left. She's canny enough to know the police have already blocked off the traffic from the Avenue. People are out already – happy families and a few early-worm Paddies-for-all-occasions, huddling, flapping and stamping against the cold before the sun gets up. As Rosa hauls the cart up the far kerb, a little girl holding a green flag leans over to pat the dog. Rosa walks on, wilfully oblivious. She does not see when the child doubles over, retching, and she escapes the dagger of a look that the mother hurls at her back. Rosa has conditioned herself never to look back or to take account of the reactions of others. She just walks on, never turning to confront the chaos churning in her wake.

But all of these awful things about Rosa are far from the whole story. For within the cavern of her spirit, Old Rosa, the bag lady, carries a thing of infinite beauty. A secret, shining treasure.

■ ◆ ■

Michael Marcinkus shuffles out of the shop door, carrying a long pole with a brass hook, which he uses to draw down the tired striped awning from its recess. Rain or shine he does this; the weather is not the point. What matters is that these things are done and that they are *seen* to be done. It's the same with the striped canvas apron that he wears round his tubby waist. It's the same with the lettering, which makes a tarnished dawn across the window: Sunrise Deli and Grocery

Store. It's the same with the open/closed sign that must at all times give the correct message. And it's the same with the polishing and priming of the 'ridiculous' old weighing machine that, as his wife Grace has complained every day for the last forty years, takes up so much space in the doorway.

A small man shouldering big burdens, Michael straightens the chairs at the outside table, squints up at the cold slice of sun peeping out from behind the block and throws a glance in the direction of Fifth. Trade will be brisk today. In days gone by, the thought would have made him happy, but now that he is older and tireder it means the day will drag all the more. He flips the sign to open, wipes his feet, goes back inside to see that all is as it should be in a deli store preserved exactly as it was in the Twenties. Faded marble counters, big swishing slicers, grinders and ranks of knives. The stock itself – myriad meats, cheeses and fruits – all laid out on trays, set out on stands, hanging on hooks. Then there are the invisible but equally important things that give the promise of things: the cool, sad aromas of olives, garlic and anchovies; the warm, seductive invitation of coffee, oranges and spices. And all these items to be in their places at their appointed hours. Bread, bagels and bakery goods – in and arranged in their cases by five thirty. Ham, poultry, sides of beef – up from the cold room by six; pared, sliced and under the glass by seven. Cans, bottles and cartons – up from the cellar, tagged and onto the shelves by seven thirty. All of these separate things are part of the whole, and the whole must be preserved each day in the same way, because that's how it has been and how it shall continue to be. Articles of faith.

A blemished piece of fruit leers at him from an otherwise spotless battalion of apples on a stand. Michael stoops and studies it from all angles, his head twitching like a canary contemplating a seed. He tuts: the boy should have spotted that. He walks back into the store, ruefully holding out the apple for Grace to see as she mops the floor. Imperiously, he calls out, 'Benjy!' and looks towards the cellar door, where he knows he will emerge. Grace squeezes out the mop and sighs. She is less religious about these things. She's tired, too; she's been doing this for a lifetime now, and all she would like to do is lie on a beach in Hawaii for a month and watch her toenails grow. Fat chance. She watches blearily as Benjy clunks up the stairs and inches through the door, juggling a box of Wesseltoft's Luxury Cat Litter. Michael holds out the apple like it's Exhibit A. 'Would you care to explain?'

Benjy looks at the inadequate apple, shocked, as if it's a dead rat, then sticks out his bottom lip as if he's going to cry, which is the signal for soft-hearted Michael to back-pedal. Grace knows that once Michael is off his back, Benjy will go round behind the racks and laugh himself silly, and she doesn't blame him for this; he's a nice boy. She herself so often feels the same way about her husband. Why must he persist in being such a funny little man?

Michael continues, half-hearted now, to berate the boy. 'You have to be on the lookout for these things, young man. The devil is in the detail.'

Grace rolls her eyes. My God, so now we have St Michael the Evangelist! Why does he have to be so damn right and proper all the time? All these rules and regs on top of the crippling day. What do they gain by it? It's an issue, a real issue. Grace shakes herself out of her daydream monologue but already he has marched off to find the next abomination – some item wrongly shelved, or particle of dust gathering where particles of dust are forbidden to gather.

A brown-haired, dapper-looking man of forty or so walks in the door and waits meekly at the counter. With the turned-up collar and his mackintosh belt tied just so, he looks stylish, jaunty even. But look close enough and you'd see that his keen blue eyes are drawn tight and shuttered against the day. Grace, who has gone back to mopping the floor, looks up and calls out, 'A moment, please.' And then she yells for her old man to get up front. For the past five years and just about every day, this same nice polite man has been coming to the deli to have a coffee or buy some choice thing to eat. He has become a friendly regular, but still Grace does not address him by his name, which is James, and still James does not have many words for her, either, though each of them has nothing but kind thoughts for the other. Instead, he smiles and stands there until Mr Marcinkus comes shuffling up, wiping his hands on his apron. 'James, James, how are you? Macchiato, yes?'

James sits down at one of three stools just inside the door, while Michael busies himself at the espresso machine, a magician conjuring aromatic delights in a swirl of steam. He was in here only yesterday, and shadows have gathered inside James even since then, but the Sunrise always gives him such pleasure. Delis like this are rare now, so many of the smaller places having been gutted and ruined in the eighties and nineties, and the big downtown ones made over all fake and flashy. He takes it all in: the old-fashioned letters across the window, so beautifully crafted, and the mouldings, tired now and in need of TLC but retaining their Twenties charm. He adores the old weighing machine in the doorway, and above all he loves the whole mysterious interior – light in creamy marble counters; dark in mahogany, with curved glass cases held in flowing chromium and the vast array of products so abundant with their shapes, colours and aromas. More than once, it has occurred to him that the shelves here mirror in a more sensual way the shelves in his own workplace, the New York Public Library, both endeavouring to connect people with offerings from other places, to bring them closer to a bygone age. Yes, here time can pass, here he can be something more like himself.

As if to underline the fact, Michael strikes up, friendly and comforting, 'So, James, up and about early. Out to see the Parade?'

'I was on my way to the hospital.'

'Ah, yes, of course . . .' Michael can see by the new lines on James's honest face that it's a subject best steered away from. He brings over a steaming cup and sets it down, saying, 'I'm sorry, I should have realized.'

'It's OK,' is as much as James can say. How could he explain to this kindly old man that at this very moment all of his thoughts are calcified around one simple, horrible proposition? That as soon as he has finished his coffee he will turn out of this place along East 99th. Turn left across from the Park and walk two blocks along to Fifth and 97th. That he will then crane his neck to look up at the dark tower of the hospital, will take an elevator to the fourteenth floor and there enter an unnervingly pleasant room. And lying in this room he will find the beloved person who, as is the way of things, is likely this very day to die. This unspeakable knowledge slides round his guts like a blade. Death will soon come roaring for Paolo, his partner, and inside James burns to scream out at the wickedness of it. It would be so glorious to take hold of his dying lover, rip him from the web of tubes that have softened him for

8

the end and crash with him through the glass into the blazing corona of the sun.

But these are not the kind of things you say over coffee. James looks up and sees Michael gazing at him, all downcast. He takes a last sip, neatly replaces the cup on its saucer, lines up spoon and cup and stands down from the stool.

'Please give Paolo my best wishes,' Michael ventures, pointlessly, because James has already moved off through the door and back into a closed world of his own making. Michael sighs, slides away the cup and saucer and gives the spotless table a precautionary wipe-down.

■ ◆ ■

In a city built so high into the sky, people don't allow their vision to stray much above eye level. Only fools, romantics and children walk around with faces raised. For the rest of us, compelled by the daily grind, the must-gets and the must-dos, the sidewalk is the place to stare. But, if we were to lift up our eyes . . .

On a balcony, high up in one of those tombstone buildings for the rich on Fifth, sits a man in a wheelchair, the two fused into one, statue and plinth – the appearance so weighty you fear for the balcony's safety. Malachi McBride sits and glowers down upon the Parade as if it passes at his command, as if he could turn down his thumb and bring the whole teetering juggernaut to a halt. The beginning of a smile creeps like a seismic crack from the fault line of his jaw. But before it can take hold and climb to the upper reaches, he quickly bulldozes it flat, burying it in the jowly foot-hills. He wheels the chair round and heads back into the lounge; time for fun and games. A woman, an agency nurse, stands in the cold room watching the Parade too, on the TV. Inez is her name. Next to McBride, in her corn-blue frock, she looks like a tiny Madonna, stolen from a wayside shrine. But McBride shows no respect for her frail saintliness. With a hawkish jerk of the head, he makes his intentions clear.

'Well, don't it just make you swell up with pride.'

His words come out like bile, and Inez knows that darker, more poisonous stuff will follow. She turns away with a sad little dip – the eye contact thing – and struggles to keep the mask blank.

'We're all fucking Irish today,' he continues.

She closes her eyes and breathes deep. Of course, she knows why he is like this. He is sick; he knows he is going to die sooner rather than later (God willing and heaven forgive her!); and he is angry with his Maker. She braces herself to receive the next toxic secretion, but instead he tries a different tack: 'They show this stuff back in that tin-pot tropical fart of a country of yours, Inez?'

Inwardly, she stirs at this surprise tactic – when did he ever call her by her first name? – but outwardly she doesn't give a twitch, because he is looking for the smallest chink, a tiny drawbridge of tenderness she might let down, and then he will storm it.

'Hey, maybe the kids are watching right now, right there in Manila – if they show this kind of shit there. How are the rickety little coolie babies?'

How dare he strike her in the womb like this! Holy Jesus forgive him. McBride allows himself a sly sideways glance to see if she will react to his jibe. Inez bites her tongue, refuses to give him the satisfaction of her humiliation. It is at times like these, good Catholic though she is, that she would gladly see this man dead.

He makes the mistake of introducing a pause to the proceedings as he sits, staring her down, waiting for a new line of assault to open up. It becomes a bridge for her to cross. Meek but cunning, she seizes her moment: 'I think I go now and buy something nice for your lunch, Mr McBride.'

She walks straight to the door and takes her coat. He can't reach her here, and if he says something, she will pretend not to hear. McBride vents a snigger, a gloating celebration of his own wickedness, but he knows he's beaten – for the moment. Her hand on the latch, Inez takes in a great bucket of air to feed the sigh she'll let out with sweet relief on the other side of the door.

■ ◆ ■

17 Pinto Mews, Riverhead, Long Island sounds a good address, but it's no great place to live: a row of

apartments, box-square and drained of colour, like cartons that have been left out in the rain. It's the kind of building you would pass by a hundred times and never recall its being there. From inside, you would have to poke your head impossibly far out of the window to catch a view of anything more uplifting than the used-car lot on the one side, and the scrubby patch behind the run-down old theatre on the other.

Two women sit poles apart at either end of a table that serves every purpose. Siobhan King, a girl with merry freckles, hair like tangled brass and bright blue eyes that somehow do not belong to her surroundings, follows the Parade on TV. She is fix-faced, her eyes flickering side to side, as if impelled to memorize every face in the crowd. A TV guy burbles on all folksy about this proud platoon of officers and that happily marching band, but to her his voice is just a wasp trapped in a jar, so total is her concentration. Even so, one thing is really getting to her: the woman at the other end of the table. Her mother.

A handsome but overburdened woman, Corinne sits rifling through racks of display cards studded with cheap jewellery, all the time mumbling and muttering, 'Agate, agate, agate, amethyst . . . amethyst . . . Shit!'

Last week, at the Newton Harbour Monday Market, she sold so many of this particular semi-precious stone that she made her best profit ever.

'Shit!'

Now, the night before she is due to set off for the same weekly event, she discovers that she has cleared her supplies, forgetting meantime to buy in more of her bestselling line.

'Shit!'

It's not like her. She's normally so ahead of the game. But she has no choice, the stall is booked. She will just have to fall back on the agates, opals and moonstones that she knows do not sell so readily – it's that or risk losing her place altogether.

'Shit!'

Siobhan turns away from the TV and looks straight through Corinne, saying, 'Could you please be quiet, Mommy, and kindly do something about your language.'

Corinne looks up, caught out. At fourteen Siobhan has taken up indefinite occupation of the moral high ground and Corinne fells compelled to account for herself: 'You don't understand. I'm out of amethyst, it's Sunday night, and if I don't have the right stuff to sell tomorrow, I don't make enough even to pay for the pitch. It's catastrophic!'

Siobhan shakes her head with practised forbearance. 'Annoying; frustrating; a total pisser even; but catastrophic? Hmm . . .'

The superior manner of this remark unsettles Corinne all the more – not because Siobhan is being so damn high and mighty, or because basically she is right, but in reality because it confirms that her daughter sees their whole goddamn situation for what it is: the shabby apartment excused by bohemian trappings, the not quite respectable neighbourhood, and the whole shitty territory that goes with being a single mother making her own way by the sweat of her brow, always, always bogged down in tiresome details that mount up and weigh so heavy in the balance. Corinne steers the conversation to matters practical: 'Listen, if I have to get up and go at the crack of dawn, you'll just have to walk to the bus with Kelly.'

Siobhan rolls her eyes at this feeble tug of the apron strings, but secretly she is delighted. With her mother off her back the next morning, she will be at complete liberty to work her own wondrous plan, and won't that be so cool? Inwardly relaxed now, she goes back to watching the Parade, her beady-eyed search suddenly less urgent. Every year for the past five years she has followed the Parade, not for pleasure, not for the pomp and the ceremony, but in the dear desperate hope that one day she will catch a glimpse of *him*, standing in the crowd. Yes, she would surely recognize him – his face, the way he holds his head and the kind of clothing he would wear. She has only her hazy memories and one crumpled photograph to go on – the one she sneaked out of the bottom of her mother's drawer – but she would know him anywhere. In a way, none of that matters now, because tomorrow, or the day after maybe, she will go there, to the heart of the city where he lives, and she will not come home until she has tracked him down, and found him and won him back.

■ ◆ ■

Sure enough, trade has picked up, and Michael has never before set eyes on half the customers wandering in. So many saying, 'Well, just look at this!' and 'Oh, doesn't this just take you back?' It pleases him to greet these people coming from every corner; it gives him purpose to see them squinting through the glass, their senses awakening to the fine things on display. He loves to see them drift away from their busy routines, slowing down and finding the time to enjoy a coffee and a Danish, turn the pages of the newspaper, even fall into conversation with one another. It has long given him a kind of wistful pleasure to think about the countless people who have arranged to meet here at the Sunrise, to sit outside and eat bagels and sandwiches, or enjoy a smoke. It is as if he has played his own small part in their exchanges, the ideas generated, the projects born, the deals struck. He looks across at Grace, behind the counter. All very well for her to accuse him of running a museum, but is it so terrible a thing? After all, it was precisely because he had the foresight all those years ago to keep the place exactly as it once was that it is so very special now. If being a museum-keeper also means being a carer, a provider of comfort, a preserver of worlds, then it's a sad day when such a thing should amount to an insult.

Michael sniffs; Benjy is hovering at his heels, expecting no doubt to take his break five minutes early. He waves him on to go down and fetch more cartons, then wanders over to the cold-meats counter. A little girl jumps out from behind the counter where she has been hiding. Sylvie, his granddaughter, girl of his girl. 'Boo!' she shouts, and, 'Oh my goodness!' he exclaims, making a show of looking shocked to the core, all of a quiver and fanning his face. She shrieks again, delighted to have such fantastic power over her old grampa. Michael catches her, both hands on her waist, and hoists her up towards the ceiling – he is strong for a tubby little man, and he tilts her so she is nose to nose with him and giggling. His daughter Jenny is some-where out back. He lowers Sylvie to the ground. 'Here, honey,' he says, and hands her a Sesame Snap out of his top pocket. 'Now, what did your mommy say you should be doing?'

Although Sylvie can yell things like 'Boo!' and 'Hey!' and 'Ow!', and can giggle louder than a passing train, Sylvie does not yet have words, or at least she chooses not to use them. At the age of three it is, of course, her prerogative. So in answer to Grampa's question, Sylvie silently toddles off behind one of the shelves and brings back the colouring book she left there, holding it up for him to see.

'Ah good,' he says. 'OK. Oh look, did you do this? Was that really you?' She nods energetically, pride glowing on her face. 'Splendido!' he says, ruffling her golden hair and sauntering away from her to the window, where the brightness fades from his face as quickly as it had sprung. There they are again, across the street, just in front of the boarded-up entrance to the disused record store – the three black boys, loitering and gassing all the time and hopping on and off the kerb without a care for the cars – the tall one, the small one and the one who once worked for them and gave them pain. He glances over at Grace, who sucks her teeth. 'What do they want, just hanging around there every other day and doing nothing?' she says, drawing in a sigh. She's all set to dredge up more tired old complaints, but then she sees through the window the black ragged shape of a dog and is suddenly propelled into her own urgent exclamation: 'Michael, your eccentric relative is outside!' This prompts a shudder from Michael, who looks to see for himself and confirms that Old Rosa is indeed louring on the sidewalk opposite the store. His back stiffens, his lips purse and he gives a shrill whistle to summon Benjy, who magically appears, alert and ready – these minute actions part of a practised response to impending disaster. Michael raises an eyebrow of command, and Benjy, reluctant but mindful of duty, obeys. He wheels round, lines up with his master and marches stiffly in time with him to the door and out onto the sidewalk. There, he strikes his pose, keen and attentive, like a minor figure on a war memorial, as Michael raises a defiant hand and says, 'Stay right there, Rosa!' Rosa isn't actually going anywhere, but just saying the words makes Michael feel he is in control. Then, exactly as she has done for the past ten years, Rosa reaches towards him – arms stretching forward, hands open, palms up, as if he should go and embrace her. As if all would be well. This, he has never been able to handle. He cannot do it. And so, shaking his head, he ignores her. Out of the corner of his eye he can see the three black boys watching, sniggering from their safe distance. He drops his voice in search of a gentler tone, but it comes out weary and patronizing: 'OK, Rosa, send it over.'

With clock-stopping slowness, Old Rosa produces a rolled-up piece of paper and tucks it under the dog's collar. Michael watches with studied forbearance before issuing the next instruction: 'Let go the dog.' She hasn't in fact had a hold of the dog, there being no leash, but she says not a word. Instead she glares at him in her thick foreign accent. Michael hasn't heard his old aunt speak in fifteen years, but he knows how the words would sound: painful, with the vowels impossibly long and at war with the hard, clipped consonants – the whole effect comic and at the same time strangely noble. Barrell, apparently without prompting, now steps up to play his part in the dumbshow and plods across the street. Benjy shoots forward like a quarterback, snatches the list and scoots back inside the store, where it is his job to interpret the tortured handwriting and to obey the sentences that come from some cold, old foreign place:

1 small rye bread. Please to make sure that this was fresh today.
A large jar of dill pickel. I do not prefer the one from Hungary the one from Poland is much more to my liking.
Half a pound of smoke ham slice acord to existing arrangment.
1 ripe tomato but not to ripe.
For Barell a bone.

Michael peers across at Rosa, who bows her head, permitting no more communication. He turns away wearily, but then swings round again, unable to resist the words he has said so many times before: 'For God's sake, Aunt Rosa, take a bath, then we wouldn't have this performance.'

Even as he says it, he sees his words are wasted. She gives away nothing, not a thing – or was that just the glimmer of a smile? Michael blinks in defeat. Inside the store he sees his daughter standing protectively at the shoulder of his granddaughter, and his wife next to her, that same old stern look on her face. He feels as if he has somehow failed them all; as if he could have said something; as if he could have done anything at all.

He steals a glance at Rosa before turning back for the warmth of the store, taking his time, of course, to thoroughly wipe his feet at the door.

■ ◆ ■

And that is why the three youths are hanging there outside the record store: to be in place to witness, again, the cheesy old comedy show play out between the stinking old woman, the uptight grocer man and the wide-eyed shop boy. To them, it's a performance every bit as entertaining as the razzle-dazzle of the St Patrick's Day Parade.

The smallest of them, Floyd, is by nature likeable and easy-going. The huge one, Dale, is clumsy and strong but harmless, though not bright. It is only the third guy, Harrison, who is remotely mean and dangerous; but the worst of them stands for them all. If Harrison draws long and lethal on a cigarette, and spits in that terrible way that he does, they're a bunch of no-goods. If he curses out loud, they're a fearsome gang; and if Harrison by chance meets the gaze of a passer-by and is too proud to turn away and conceal the hurting years that have made him what he is, then that stranger is going to conclude that this is a hateful bunch of guys. A loner by habit, Harrison prefers to

walk alone, especially by night, seeking he knows not
what and finding whatever he finds. But there is still
enough generosity of spirit in him to be able to enjoy
hanging out with the guys, laughing about stuff and
taking some interest in what's going down.

The moment Rosa's sad figure has retreated away, it
begins: the worn-out old argument that has happened
as often as Old Rosa has come along this street and they
have been there – which is just about every other day.
They cannot resist, each taking his habitual position.

Floyd, who likes stories because they contain surprises, is quick to revive the legend that is the source of
their differences: 'She rich, I telling you. My old man
tell me this, since I was so high.'

Harrison, who hates stories because experience has
shown him that life holds no surprises, is fierce to deny
it: 'Don't give me no shit!'

Big Dale, as usual, is content to listen, nodding his
head, eyes growing wide on the meat of the quarrel as
the guys battle to outdo each other with their own versions of the living truth.

'She rich! That apartment she live in, man it stinks
and it's all shit an' everything, just like you would
imagine it, but she got big bucks in there too.'

'So who seen it, Bro? Show me the man who seen it?'
At this, even Big Dale can't resist chiming in, 'I heard
that. I heard that, too. I heard she got the money in the
mattress.' Which makes Harrison spit with contempt:

'So, like she tell every nigger this? Like I say, show me the man; tell me the name of the person who seen it, cause it sure as shit ain't so.' Floyd, though, sticks with his side of the story: 'There's people been in there, like nurses and social workers an' stuff. They say that once upon a time she been some kind of aristocrat an' stuff. She got a whole lotta money, that for sure.'

But it's Harrison who wins the day with a perfect one-liner: 'An' I got a crocka gold up my black ass!' The others crack up at this. Impressed by his unaccustomed turn of phrase, they concede the last word to him, and he heads off down the road, feeling pretty cool about himself.

■ ◆ ■

The hospital is just around the next corner on Fifth and still his inner fury is not spent. But James knows when it comes to it that he will bow his head as a nurse dispenses here and a doctor deliberates there, and that he will speak with a small, holy voice as men do at *times like this*, and that he will put on the meek, sneaky role he has been allotted to play. For it is a sad fact that no one has told Paolo that he is going to die, nor has Paolo ever come close to asking. So if, by chance, he has not yet slipped into the cold embrace of a coma, James has prepared himself to talk to his dying lover about small, sweet things that have passed in the hours since his last visit. How the rain came down like hushed cymbals in the night. How he forgot altogether to eat and never noticed the passing of time. How the marmalade cat from downstairs crept into the apartment and curled up on Paolo's vacant side of the bed. With each ephemeral phrase James knows that he will surrender Paolo to the great emptiness, and with each hollow utterance, something of the keen edge of his own humanity will be blunted.

In his savage preoccupation, James does not take in the weather, which, as it happens, is cold but sunny. Nearing the Park, he's oblivious to the people hurrying past him so eagerly: the mother with her unruly brood; the old couple sharing a thrilling squeeze of hands; the ramrod man wearing medals. And all of them sporting faces made vacant for anticipated pleasures. James simply is not prepared, then, when a fat, brassy blast of music bounces along the Park railings, shaking him from his private stone. And then he sees it.

'My God, the Parade!'

There it is, flouncing up the Avenue towards him. A teeming sea of banners and badges, of chests puffed like sails to fill tunic and tabard, of batons leaping like Masai competing for the sky.

Fine things are sometimes best encountered obliquely, when our senses are trained elsewhere: a beautiful woman glimpsed across a crowded carriage; a heavenly aroma beckoning from a rusty grate. Delights stumbled across can sometimes entice us from the hermit-cell of the mind. And so, all in a moment, James is alive with the knowledge that he is at the heart of a delicious thing. He stands in the bristling fuzz of people lining the sidewalk and gawps like a child. He catches the infection of smiles and laughs, as row upon row of heads go by, like coloured beads spilling from a box. Then he moves along with the thing, marries his own step to the serpentine train of humanity; marches with the drums and rides high with the pipes as they waft silkily along the bright avenue. What a wonder that a human spirit can, in the span of a sigh, soar from the darkest pit to the most rarefied peak.

Nor has James abandoned reality. In a few moments he will turn away from the Parade and continue his sober journey. But now he will be able to go into Paolo and – if he is not already gone – tell him that on the way to the hospital today he witnessed a fine, lovely thing. Indeed, he is duty-bound to take the glory of it with him. Maybe it will bring a smile to Paolo's harrowed face, or perhaps he will be in that place where words and gestures cannot reach. But either way, James is certain it will mean something, it will mean something.

CHAPTER TWO

M ARCINKUS the grocer goes out front to loosen up
and straighten out and swallow a coffee. The day
has been so-so but bitty; it's great to have Jenny's help
and to see little Sylvie, but when she and Benjy get
together it's like being in a kindergarten. Then there's
the question of Old Aunt Rosa. These frequent show-
downs are unsettling because, if the truth be known,
they make him feel guilty, and something in him still
longs to hear her speak, to recapture a trace of the
affection that had once existed between them. As her
nearest relative, it had fallen on him to come to the
rescue when she'd started to become strange all those
years ago. At one time, he and Grace had given much

to keep her on her feet and try to coax her back to the heady, happy life she'd once led. There had been kindnesses and high hopes, but each time she had relapsed until finally she had ended up like this – lonely and insane, pretty much. He knows that she has a bona fide condition. Syllogomania it is called: people who cannot throw things away, who hoard everything, their garbage even, and end up living in their own filth. He takes consolation in the fact that she has a recognized syndrome, but it never quite eases those guilty pangs.

Michael has seen people grow old. He has watched them struggling with seized joints, and slowing brains and memories blanching with the years. He has made a personal study of the phenomenon, doing his best to countenance the fact that he and Grace will surely go the same way. But what really gets to him about Old Rosa is how at eighty-seven years of age she is still able to keep on going with her stubborn rebellion. It must take a hell of an effort to remain so apart from the life of the city and yet to continue to walk abroad in it, repeating the tiresome routines it takes simply to continue to stay alive. It must take every atom of concentration, every last distilled drop of her willpower just to go out and buy bread in the morning, each step painful and empty of joy. How amazing, then, that she can at the same time keep the avenues of her senses so strictly closed off to the world. How exactly does she wake up each day, her mind moulded into the same negative cast? How do the molecules or electrical messengers, or whatever they are, in her brain stay fixed so doggedly around such cussed ideas? Why does she not simply fade away or disintegrate mentally, as so many of them do?

On top of all that there's the matter of the boy Harrison. Once he had been their shop boy, just like Benjy, coming in after school and at weekends. They had hoped the job would take him from hard-working kid to boy made good. But he had blown it, crazily, once, twice, three times over, taking things from the shelves, denying it even when they found the items in his pockets. Had he himself not bent over backwards to keep him on long after others told him to make the best of a bad thing and let the boy go? It hurts Michael to recall how Harrison had accused them of picking on him when all they ever wanted was for the boy to make a go of things. It was him, so pig-headed and twisted in his thinking, going out of his way to be anything but good, that had forced their hand. And in the end, what with Grace having gotten so weighed down with anxiety that she became ill, the kid had left him no choice.

He peers across at the record-store entrance. The youths are no longer there. He counts back through the years, surprising himself: more than three since they let Harrison go. Three years – my God, the boy is a man now, pretty much, and still hanging around

27

on corners, making nothing of himself. Michael slings back his head, drains the cup and goes back inside. The neat little Filipino maid woman is waiting patiently at the cold-meat counter. A polite, respectful person to serve. That's something nice in the day at least.

■ ◆ ■

The smallest room in the house contains the biggest and ugliest of truths. Just to haul his dead weight from the wheelchair onto the toilet seat and back again has become an ordeal that leaves Malachi McBride holed-through. And in between, there are the pitiful fumblings and spillings that slay him with the knowledge that he is failing by the day. He has grown fearful of this place. With its anaemic tiles and ghostly mirrors, the bathroom is as heartless as any church confessional. At every angle, he sees his alienation captured and cast back, dead-eyed in the glass. And his other senses play their part in the same unnerving conspiracy. Fragrances belonging to soaps and lotions bring to McBride's mind the sacraments, with incense in ghostly trails, turning his thoughts to mortality and, of course, to God: God the voyeur, the sadist; the mocking, sniggering bastard God! If he were a child he would cry and his mother would come and smooth away his tears. But there is no mother to come running, and this is a man who will not cry even in secret. He thinks instead about the true worth of the fortune he has amassed. What he wouldn't give just to be able to stand square at the toilet and piss into it, a man again. But no, he will not cry, he will not open himself to pity, and he would punish anyone foolish enough to offer it. The world must pay.

Rinsing his hands at the washbasin, McBride hears the click of the latch out in the hallway. The nurse-maid, Inez, has returned. Not even stopping to dry off, he spins the chair, flicks the lever and lunges the machine at the door, the kick plate slamming against a gash of wood in the paintwork that testifies to past injuries. The door flies open, and there he catches her, dramatized in shadows, wide-eyed like the heroine – or is it the victim? – in a silent movie. He knows that she will have stopped off at St Joe's on the way home to light candles and pray for everything under the sun. He is certain of it; he can all but smell the ghastly place on her, and it inspires him with words to shake her from her cosy Catholic notions: 'The day is fast approaching, my little rosebud,' he declares, giving a jolly little tilt of the head and oozing a terrible kind of delight, 'when you are going to have to wipe my sorry ass for me.'

A hair's breadth ahead of him, Inez hangs her coat on the door, turns smartly away and carries her groceries into the kitchen, prompting him to pump up the volume: 'When it's easier to slit your wrist than take a shit, you just have to start thinking!' Inez opens the refrigerator door and buries herself in domestic intricacies. Cheerily, she clucks away to herself: 'Now did I or did I not already buy tomatoes?'

McBride heads for the kitchen, even so, noticing in a glance through the living-room picture window how the Park seems ethereal in the spring sunshine. But it does not stop his onslaught as he rolls into her space: 'Do you pray for me, Inez? When you're down on your knees in the church, do you pray for me with all your soul?'

With a theatrical sigh and a shake of the head, Inez withdraws the salad tray from the refrigerator and places the tomatoes side by side with the newly bought ones. 'But there is much less than I thought of the lettuce,' she clucks, suitably irritated. From the corner of her eye, she can see that McBride has crammed himself into every inch of the door frame and will have the last word. She gives up on matters salad-related and turns, wearily, to face him: well then, let him say his worst. Naturally, he does:

'That is, of course, presuming that you are in posses- sion of an immortal soul. Because, come to think of it, Donna Inez, I have seen more feeling in a half-starved Mexican dog than I have ever seen in your slitty little eyes.' He prolongs the moment, keeping her trapped in his glare until at last she counters, quietly but bravely, 'It is very kind of you to show concern for my immortal soul, Mr McBride. But I think you should worry more that I am still here each day to follow after you and

clean up your shit.' He breaks into the devil of a smile
– the one and only of the day: 'Hmm, very, very good.
But you will be here, won't you?' He fumbles in his
cardigan pocket, and out comes a billfold, black and
potent in his squint hand. He scrunches out a sheaf
of dollars and drops it down on the floor in front of
her. Then he backs off, reversing the chair, the bulk
of him dwindling away to the living room and out of
sight. Inez watches, stern and frozen in her rectangle
of light, looking like a priest at the altar who has seen
off thieves. Disdainfully, she turns her head away from
the mound of notes in the middle of the floor. But the
contempt is mostly for herself – she will, of course,
conveniently tidy away that grubby heap before the
serving of lunch.

■ ◆ ■

James stands in front of the flower stall outside the
hospital. A pretty girl beams down from the counter.
He cannot choose between the silk-pointed purples,
the splashing whites and the star-spangled oranges.
His senses are drawn to the more colourful flowers, yet
he is wary of these scent-drenched attention-seekers.
They seem like so many high-kicking dancers taking
up the stage, while other, more modest blooms hide in
the wings. James has more of an eye for the greenery,
the stems and the stalks with their oriental filigrees and
interweavings. If anything he prefers the fragrance of

these humble supporting players to the sweet, cheap scents of the show-offs. There is something dark and ancient about them, with shades of melancholy, if such a word can be applied to vegetation. He really should get to know more about plants. There is a veranda to the apartment and one day, when all this is over, maybe he will wise up on it all and grow something beautiful out there.

James becomes aware again of the girl. Perhaps she would have an idea or two: 'What would be a suitable choice of flowers for someone who's in the hospital?' he asks. Straight away, she comes back, 'Well, sir, that would depend on the lady.' For once, James is in no mood to be coy on the subject: 'The *lady*,' he says, dwelling archly on the word, 'is the most wonderful man that ever lived.' The poor girl blushes to her roots, stammering out an apology that only makes James feel crass and insensitive. 'Not at all, not at all,' he reassures her. She has done him a favour by causing him to make private things public. Paolo and he were never strident about being gay, never desired to broadcast their love in theatrical kisses or hold hands in the street. But right now, it feels good to say it out loud and proud. 'Well,' she says, recovering, 'white roses? That's pretty good, I would say.' James mulls it over: 'You think so? OK. Roses it is then.'

■ ◆ ■

Ten blocks over, the St Patrick's Day Parade cruises towards the intersection of Fifth and St Laurence, just as Old Rosa arrives, the lightless, silent mass of her with the cart and the dog, drawn into the Parade's shining orbit. Mask-faced and parchment-stiff, she is surely indifferent to the pleasures of happy families, couples arm in arm and smile-high Asian tourists. But Rosa has known all of these sensations, and inside her mummified hide she is even now touched by sweet, invisible particles of pleasure, the charged ions of delight.

Her infant heart remembers marching to other tunes in other parades, though in an altogether different land. She remembers what it is like to be lifted high on your daddy's shoulders; to catch sight of your own pretty, plait-framed face in the melting brass of a euphonium; to feel the shudder of drums pass through you to the core; to bury your face in candyfloss and feel its sweet fibres fuse with your own hot cheeks. And Rosa still recalls with painful clarity the face of a woman arriving, young and dreaming, in the new country. She who once danced naked on an ocean-going yacht, defying the lightning to strike; she who has stood stiletto-high on the lid of a baby grand and sung to 500 people whose names have long since passed into legend.

In truth, Old Rosa has been all her life a woman of blinding passions and hopeless hopes. It is precisely because she is at heart so passionate that she has been able to sustain herself, so cold and unforgiving, in turning against the world. If she can never have again what she once had, she will never look back in the ordinary, foolish way and say 'if only' and then 'ah well'. If she cannot reclaim everything that was once her shining right, she will have nothing. So this, too, is Rosa: this terrible bat-like mass that sullenly dips its head and wades unheeding into the rippling flank of the crowd, ploughing its usual furrow of outrage, her only thought to cross the Avenue before the Parade swallows it up.

The St Patrick's Day Parade famously has no motorized floats, the whole thing going on foot, proud and purposeful: union men in their ranks, old soldiers, policemen, firemen, marching bands of all descriptions – any group whose glories can be stitched on a banner and waved up high. And it is Old Rosa's fate, as she steps off the sidewalk, to arrive on the roadway at the same moment as the one and only motorized vehicle allowed anywhere near the Parade. The official camera van – a long, low-slung flatbed truck – sails on, slow and unstoppable, to dock against the flapping wall of Rosa's skirts, throwing her over so that the back of her skull cracks audibly against the ground, raising a collective gasp of horror from the nearest spectators. Within seconds, this accident escalates into a tense, absurd drama as the broken bundle that is Rosa is overrun by a swarm of NYPD officers trained to the task. Some fan out to hold up the Parade, some form a barrier to keep back the crowd, and others go to Rosa's aid, the more valiant of them cradling her slumped body into a more dignified shape. In their Sunday-bright uniforms the cops are like so many overeager schoolboys, an impression that intensifies as Rosa's almighty stench declares itself and faces twist into infantile grimaces, at odds with the strong, silent aura of heroes. One officer, who is about to give some form of resuscitation, recoils from the task and staggers to his feet to save himself from passing out. Another man kneels down to give the kiss of life, but he is also too sickened to administer it.

Rosa chooses this very moment to come back to consciousness. The pearl-black eyes open in their leathery sockets and the scene spills into her vision: the gaggle of officers milling around, embarrassed, with one brave young man kneeling down knight-like to hold her hand. Sorrow creases his china-blue eyes. Incredibly, Rosa sees the scenario for what it is: the PD boys all dandified for their big day, but made to look like the Keystone Cops by a smelly old woman. It is, she decides, just plain funny. And Old Rosa, in her failing moments, starts to laugh – a high, girlish giggle that makes the officers all the more perplexed. Then her eyes roll back to white and she is gone. There is more than one sigh of relief from the cops, which is strange, because of course her smell lingers on, but at least it is where it belongs now: with the dead rather than the living.

Harrison, at this moment in time, has no care for the Parade; he intends merely to get across it, having business to attend to on the other side of the Park. But he stops short when he realizes the whole parade has come to a halt, with banners keeling to, a ship shorn of sails. Why? On the sidewalk, voices cut across each other and hands flutter in elaborate mime as people mesh together their different takes on the story to arrive at an acceptable whole. Half knowing what he will find, he pushes his way to the kerbside and reaches the heart of the hullabaloo. Cops everywhere; a bundle lying by the film truck, its face a waxy yellow grub in a black flower; the fat, black dog sitting panting by the shopping cart, tongue hanging out, head going side to side like a Christmas toy. Harrison's eyes swivel, too, as he sizes things up. There's none of death's deep mystery here, no sense of a soul departed or the presence of God, just grey-faced guys in uniform standing around giving out how they alone know how to handle this kind of stuff, moms tight-faced around their kids and the children themselves empty-eyed and licking ice-creams.

'So that's it. She dead. Too bad – time to move on.'

Harrison spits and moves on.

■ ◆ ■

James enters the ICU suite a shy child hiding behind flowers. He had meant to arrive bearing fine things and meaningful words, but between ground level and this high place, the courage has seeped out of him. It's to do with hospitals themselves, of course – the horrible reminder of going into such places when he was young, of being with his mother in death's waiting room. There are twenty paces and a door between him and the next unspeakable set of horrors to be endured, but as he finds the courage to continue forward, he stops in his stride, his eye held by a thing inexplicable. There, hovering in the shadows between the window and the door, is a young man he knows, but who simply doesn't belong here, and who by his down-turned expression and the timid manner in which he says, 'Hi, James,' seems to be fairly cognizant of the fact himself. It takes James a moment to square the familiar face with the unfamiliar circumstance. This is Jack from the library . . . your colleague, your junior employee, so why is he here? He cannot think of anything connecting this absurdly young-looking man to the two separated parts of his life.

'Jack, what are you doing here?' he snaps, unintentionally rude.

Jack stares back at him, allowing himself a wounded pause. With his diminutive stature and bland round face, he is a child left with no sweeties when the rest have seized the bag and rushed away. 'They wouldn't let me in. Not now, they said. Close family only.' He holds up his own large bunch of flowers, not white and graceful like James's but bright and multicoloured, a rainbow bouquet, intended no doubt to offer cheer. 'I just wanted to bring him these.'

James can only stare back at Jack's little-kid face, with the tiny nose so absurdly, optimistically upturned and, as always, reminding him so maddeningly of someone, though he has never been able to put his finger on it. But then he hardly knows the guy, beyond the fact that they work at the same place. In truth, he doesn't want to acknowledge this person in this place; he doesn't want to hear his childish breathy voice or hold his unsubtle flowers. But there is a question he simply has to ask: 'Forgive me, but I don't understand. I mean I didn't even know you know Paolo.'

Jack makes the same wounded pause before replying, which makes James begin to doubt himself, and when Jack speaks, he is made to feel guilty for having doubted him: 'But of course I do. From Woody's Bar – a whole lotta times.' He insists, faintly wounded but noble with it. Even so, James cannot remember ever having seen Jack outside of work. 'Such a great, great guy,' he adds, piling on the agony. 'Ah,' says James, faintly apologetic now and prepared to put the mystery down to the chaos that has reigned in his head for so long.

'No, no, it's me,' adds Jack hastily. 'Put me in a crowd – parties, weddings and the like – I just go invisible. Plain shy, I guess.' He visibly wriggles, doubly

self-conscious in the contemplation of his own gauche-
ness. He holds out the flowers again. 'Could you maybe
just give these to him for me?' And with this he turns
and rushes for the elevator.

James turns back, shaking his head, then smooths
himself down, ready to stand before the dreaded door
again. First, though, he looks right then left and gently
places Jack's flowers on the windowsill for someone
else to find.

■ ◆ ■

Paolo lies on the bed, stark and symmetrical as a jewel.
His two arms extended from his sides, palms raised,
like a saint beatified. Beneath the sheet, the sculpted
outline of his legs is arranged into the same religious
iconography. There seem to be fewer cables and tubes
than yesterday, as if they have fallen away, their cycle
completed, the sacrificial object sanitized and ready
for the final offering. Steeling himself, James inches
towards the bed. Never has he seen Paolo's pale face
look so spare. The sight stirs compassion in him, restor-
ing some warmth to his spirit. He leans over and says
softly, 'Sweetheart.' He imprints a kiss on Paolo's desert-
dry lips and draws back, expecting more of the empty
silence. But, wonderfully, Paolo's eyelids unmesh an
instant, giving the faintest glint of grey. James is ecstatic;
it is as if Paolo has just sat up in bed and smiled. He
holds out the flowers, saying, 'White roses . . .'

39

Paolo's breathing is faraway, infinitesimal, but James has read somewhere that the dying have heightened sensory awareness. Convinced that his lover is alive to the scent of roses, James's voice takes on a breezy note: 'I ran into the Parade on the way here. It was so . . . fine and dandy. It was like I was five years old!' He sits waiting, longing to see life in Paolo's eyes again. But then a voice hisses out of the dead space behind him: 'Sir . . . Sir . . . *Sir!*' He jerks around to see a white-frocked nurse – short, plump and middle-aged, but somehow childish, with her tiny cap perched on big strawberry-blonde hair and lipstick smeared crimson. Her eyes are wild as she stomps over and snatches the flowers from his hand. 'You can't bring these in here! This is Intensive Care!' It doesn't take much to make James feel foolish. 'I'm sorry, I didn't—'

'That's no excuse! Intensive Care – you can't read? There's sick people here!' she hisses, firing off a last poisonous barb, not knowing how close to his heart it passes, then stomps off. James reels; he's so easily thrown right now, and this stupid woman has violated their intimacy, bringing the world in all flat-footed. He doesn't know whether to laugh or cry, until the absurdity of it strikes him: sick people in a hospital? Well, that's news! It prompts him to share the joke: 'D'you hear that, Paolo? These flowers could make you very sick indeed; I could've . . .' The words die in his throat as he sees a tiny movement ripple across Paolo's sealed mouth! Instantly, his face is next to Paolo's, his fingers wrapped around the broken bird of his hand. James leans over, astonished to see lips that were rusted shut begin to prise apart. Paolo is trying to speak! It is the faintest rustle – no more than a sigh – but there is no doubt that, after all this time, Paolo has broken out of the void and has something to say that has a greater claim than death. James strains even closer as the words emerge agonizingly slow: 'I . . . love . . . you . . .' James feels the flutter of a hand inside his own. Words stirring again: 'Re . . . re . . . re . . .' Unable to haul itself over the impossible summit of the word, his face falls back to nothing, eyes and mouth scalpel-slits in a carved mask.

For James, though, the message is not lost. In his mind the words echo, urgent and fully formed: 'Remember me.' A last earthly request. James unwraps his hand from Paolo's and bursts into tears. He will not, *must not*, ever forget.

■ ◆ ■

Harrison sits on the bench under the big lonely tree and takes in the view. Safe. Whichever direction anyone came from, he would see them in good time. He takes out the joint, holds it up to eye level, reading in its smooth cylinder the craft he has invested in the making. He rolls it between finger and thumb and turns it to engage, his hand gliding machine-slow towards his mouth. White teeth behind dry lips close gently on the tip as he conjures a flame and draws on it, deep and easy, opening up the vault of his lungs to take in the last pocket of air in the world. First come the empty seconds, and then the release, the sleepy exhalation as crack steals silver across his senses. His amber eyes close, soft and dreaming; his mouth slacks to a wide 'O', and silky tendrils curl over the ledges of his lips to hang ghostly in the cold air. How hungry he is for this, how greedy for every last atom. If there is any magic in this world, it is here – begins here and so soon ends.

For the moment, though, his mind has become a vessel so clear that he sees into and through everything, and everything is complete. And all that was ever harmful and hurtful in life is replaced with a sure knowledge of things and a total command over them. Harrison knows he would only have to push, in the right way and the right place, against that big old tree and it would surely go over. He would only have to stand up and put one foot in front of the other and he could outrun the fastest thing on two legs. All kinds of pleasing notions materialize and evaporate with each stolen breath, and for all of ten minutes, Harrison is cool and easy with the world, because even a troubled person has a desire for peace and the knowledge that he, too, has the right to possess it.

But then something totally out of the blue announces

itself, and he sits up with a jolt, his child-eyes widening in surprise. For into the oceanic expanse inside Harrison's head has floated the biggest, bestest thought that ever came into any dude's mind, and it makes him say out loud, 'My God!' There and then, he decides he will do it – he will surely do it! He jumps to his feet, totally taken up with his big idea.

Here be the magic.

■ ◆ ■

The Parade has long ended, the rows of marchers melted away after the final surge at 86th Street, and the public spilling back through the floodgates of the streets to their quarters of the city and beyond.

He is just about to take off his apron and send Benjy down to bring up new stock when he hears Grace over at the front say, 'What the . . . ?!' He follows her gaze and is met by a sight so odd he actually rubs his eyes. There, sitting outside on the sidewalk opposite, occupying his appointed place, is Barrell the dog. Just sitting there watching them, his head dipped and motionless, his stare fixed and sorrowful, and not a sign, or even the faintest sniff, of Old Aunt Rosa. Michael steps to the door, with Grace scuttling up to his side. He stares at the dog, she stares at the dog, they stare at each other. It is all strange, unheard of.

'This doesn't look good,' pronounces Michael, crossing the road, a whole tangle of unhappy scenarios slowly slipping and twisting from the spool inside his head and looping into chaos.

■ ◆ ■

Harrison shuts the door on New York City and takes off his jacket in Goose Creek, South Carolina. The joke of it used to make him smile when he was a child, but now it has worn thin and he simply puts up with this place called home because he knows that it will never change so long as Great Aunt Crystal is alive, which will surely be a long time yet. It is nice enough, even if it was last done twenty years back, when Uncle Henry was still alive: all in blues and pinks to keep up the country look; cottage sofa and set suggesting solidity and comfort, with jolly old ornaments and southern prints under glass for tradition and good cheer. A perfect finishing touch is supplied by gingham tie-backs, to frame the city through the window and make it just another picture on the wall.

Jesus is here, too, of course. His image hangs above the piano – dreamy-looking, eyes raised to heaven, long-haired white man – surrounded by the family photographs. Generations of sad-but-smiling black people, some dignified by sepia, some bleached of colour. His holy face imparts dignity to their passing. Of course, none of this tells us that Great Aunt Crystal has no one left in the world – apart from Harrison, who is the source of her anxieties and the subject of her prayers. Nothing in this quaint preservation of a time and place that once was her world hints at the fact that she is penniless, housebound pretty much, and dependent on kind members of the congregation to take her Sundays to the Tabernacle. In each fretful week of cleaning and scrubbing, Crystal has just one allotted hour to make her prayers, speak in tongues and cleanse her spirit in the bosom of the Lord.

As Harrison comes from the hallway into the living room, Great Aunt Crystal enters from the kitchen, carrying a freshly baked cake and offering greetings: 'Hello, my honey,' she coos, ignoring his gruffness as he throws down his coat, pushes past her to the refrigerator in the kitchen and gulps down milk straight from the carton – all as if she didn't exist. It is her Christian duty to soak up the sins of others and offer serenity in return. She goes to the table and transfers the cake to a cake stand, all the while watching him sideways, avoiding unpleasantness, keeping things sweet. Somewhat needlessly, she announces, 'I baked a cake.' But Harrison just picks up the remote and flicks through channels on the TV. It is, of course, wounding to Crystal, and she has often wondered what he gains from these ill-mannered displays, consoling herself with the idea that young people are all like this these days. With a sigh, she starts to divide up the cake, following her age-old ritual: 'One for you . . . one for me . . . one for Henry.' Smart. She knows Harrison won't be able to resist saying how crazy she is, and she gets a reaction at last:

'Uncle Henry been dead ten year!' It's something, even if the tone is hurtful.

She goes to the kitchen, doggedly cleaving to the way of the righteous: 'Uncle Henry always loved my cakes.' She returns with a tea tray, pours two cups of tea and holds out a slice on a plate. Harrison picks up instead a neatly folded pile of ironed clothes she has left for him and makes for the hallway. But she hasn't quite given in: 'Have a piece, please.' She insists. He strides moodily to his room down the hallway. 'I don't want your fucking cake!' Crystal shakes her head, sharing her sorrows with Jesus up on the wall, who doesn't look in the least bit fazed. She arranges the cake plate, with both unclaimed pieces, in the middle of the table, knowing that he will take them later when she is gone from the room. Forgiveness, forgiveness is everything, she tells herself. After all, didn't she herself have such a happy childhood with loving parents, who worked their days, took their rest when their labours were done and who passed on when at last their time came? While he – oh, it was all so terrible. To have one parent pick up and walk out when you are five years old, that's cruel, shocking; but to have the other, but a year after, go off never to return, that is wickedness beyond imagining. That is abandonment. So, Great Aunt Crystal feels sorry for Harrison, and has often wondered if he ever felt sorry for himself. If he did, it might be a good thing: only when a person knows that they are broken can they offer themselves up to be fixed.

At this moment, though, self-pity is the last thing on Harrison's mind. In the storm-dark space that is his room, he peels off his top and gazes into the mirror. The last of the sun oozes in through the window, spreading a pale gold wash over his bare torso and casting him even more into the shadows. He stares himself down, hard and cold but alive to the moment, seeing himself the free spirit of his own making: he who dares. Slipping on a tan T-shirt, he goes to the closet, takes out a combat top and wraps himself in it, zipping it up to the neck. Then he pulls on a black beanie. With the collar of the jacket turned up to his ears and the hat pulled down to the same place, he is anonymous, eclipsed. It doesn't occur to him that the image he has made of himself threatens darkness and violence. Reaching down the back of the room heater, he draws out a long, slim army dagger, dark and lethal. Smooth and easy – it was bought to fit – he sheathes it in the thigh pocket of his pants, lowers his arms to his sides and stands stock-still and ready. But this is only the try-out. Today is too soon. Tomorrow he will go there and it will be so fucking sweet, and nothing, nothing can possibly go wrong.

CHAPTER THREE

BEFORE he set off for Old Rosa's place, Michael had the bright idea to fashion a leash from a length of twine. Science was in the making, Michael having observed that Barrell always walked ten feet ahead of Old Rosa, and therefore cutting the string to the right length. The dog has taken surprisingly well to it. So far as Michael knows, Barrell had never sported such a thing in his life, yet he seems quite happy with the arrangement, trundling along up front and allowing Michael to shuffle after him in his own sweet way.

The day has turned melancholy with the light, and the strollers and joggers who usually flit about the Park in numbers have paled away, leaving only the lost and the lonely. Michael goes through every permutation of possibility that might have separated dog from owner. Apart from the slim chance that the Parade might have parted them in some way, each one comes up spelling disaster.

Crossing Central Park West, where the sun lies slain behind grey battlements, Michael feels as though he is being swallowed up by forces dark and oppressive. He passes between the defiant facades and enters the dwindling street that leads to Aunt Rosa's apartment block. The dog picks up pace and the two arrive outside the building, noisily panting against each other like a misfiring steam engine. But then Barrell finds the energy to tug Michael into the hallway and they start up the stairs. Rattling back through the years he realizes, frighteningly, that it has been at least twenty since he and Grace were last here. It had been unclean and untidy even then, so he dreads to imagine what it might be like now. He stands in front of her door, which is solid enough, though the paintwork has peeled to a bygone colour in places, and presses the bell push, which is dead of sound. He raps smartly at the letterbox and stands back, respectful, for her to appear and take away his fears. Nothing. He raps again and then pounds on the door, growing more forceful as he allows himself to imagine her lying dead inside. 'Rosa,' he calls. 'Rosa, it's me, Michael. Open the door!'

Behind him, he hears locks being turned and chains

rattling. A black woman, wild-haired and carrying a baby, peers out from the apartment opposite Rosa's. Her door, like her eyes, is half open out of curiosity and half closed in suspicion. 'Can I help you?' she ventures.

'Sorry . . . Um, would you know if the old lady here is at home?'

'I wouldn't know nuthin' 'cept I seen her go out this morning. Ain't that her dog?'

'Yes it is. He came to my place all on his own. I'm related to her. You didn't see her come back?'

'Uh uh.'

'Are you sure of that?'

'Sure as I can be. You don't miss it when Old Rosa come passing by. Anyhow, I didn't know she had no relatives.'

'Well. Look, if you do see her tell her her nephew Michael came by.'

'I don't never speak to her. I give up on that years ago.'

The woman pulls shut her door, and Michael turns and heads downstairs again, dragging Barrell, who has got used to the idea of being home and dry. He doesn't think twice when a policeman brushes past them, going two steps at a time. Then the penny drops and he about-turns, allowing Barrell to drag him upstairs again. The man's arm is raised to knock when Michael calls out, 'Can I help you, Officer? If you're here about Rosa Petraidis, that is.'

'I am. And who might you be?' demands the officer gruffly. But before Michael can reply there comes a new rattle of locks and chains and the neighbour is at the door again, which is wide open now to give full vent to her suspicions: 'He say he a relative, but I sure as hell ain't never seen him before!'

Refusing to be goaded, Michael looks the officer in the eye and speaks up, quiet and polite: 'I am her nephew, her next of kin, and this is her dog. Has something happened to her?' The policeman looks him up and down, then turns to go eye-to-eye with the woman, until she backs off through her own door and he has Michael to himself.

'Yes. Yes it has,' he says. 'So, how exactly might you be related to her?'

■ ◆ ■

But she was not dead. She did not die. The truck ran over her, yes. And her head cracked terrible on the road, yes. And the eyes rolled back in their sockets and the officers fell back helpless. But within seconds an ambulance arrived in a dying howl, gliding into the tableau made by the policemen so still and solemn. And medics then sprang out, bristling with cables, and pads and interfaces; and having no respect for death in its rankness, ran across and sprang their searching shock three times over until, like the scene in *Frankenstein*, she came back with a shudder so terrible it might break her dead again. Then they eased a stretcher under her and carried her to the ambulance and slid her in and away, the siren now a high whining sentinel. And no one gave a thought for the dog, who sat there panting and stuck in his confusion, until the noise had died and the policemen had melted away and the staring, yapping people had folded back into themselves. At which point, Barrell the dog heaved himself, trembling, onto his haunches, put his head down to the world and lumbered away.

And so they rushed Old Rosa to the hospital, and took her in and deftly sliced through the matted carapace to release the bile-coloured armature of her body, and put it in a robe and trundled it into theatre. And figures in gowns came and pinned it with tubes and went inside its head and followed their unknowable ways. With slow, practised actions and incantations, the doctors introduced one mysterious instrument after another, probing and incising. And their voices rose a little and quickened as, at last, the unknown gave way to the known and the disorder of the beginning gave way to the symmetry of the end, and nurses fell to suturing and bandaging and the surgeons stood back, their work done.

So her body lies, fixed and substantial on the outside, but on the inside in that state where the thing we call self is so diminished it no longer knows how big it is or how small, or how dark or light, or even if it is dead or alive. And in that weakened state, the particles of thought and feeling that make up being start to fall like leaves and drift from their bodily bounds, radiating outward and away, beyond the reach of all the world and in step again with the unfolding universe.

■ ◆ ■

Grace stands in the doorway like Horatio holding the bridge, an unyielding barrier to Michael, who holds the dog tight to him. For twenty minutes they have stood like this, while he has conveyed to her every detail of what the police officer told him. She has stood with eyes wide to hear how the bizarre accident happened; she has winced to hear about Rosa's sorry condition, and has shaken her head ruefully to learn that they will have to go to the hospital the next day. And only when she's satisfied she has it all in her head does she turn her attention to the dog:

'So, the officer told you all this? And this was outside Rosa's apartment? So how come you come back with the dog?'

'Well, I couldn't not come back with the dog.'

'Really? So why didn't you give him to the policeman?'

'The policeman? How could I?'

'Michael, I wonder about you sometimes! We have no responsibility for this dog. So I suggest you take it somewhere right this minute!'

'What now? On a Sunday night?'

'There are places – the precinct – they would know. You shoulda given it to the guy there and then. Now listen, you gotta do something, Michael, or you got one big problem on your hands. And don't you dare even think of bringing that smelly animal in this door!'

Michael is a little crestfallen when she slams said door in his face. But then, suddenly thoughtful, he steps back from the doorway and off the edge of the sidewalk to get a better view of things. He surveys the Sunrise as if for the first time, then looks up at the sky – well, at least it's not set to rain. He gives Barrell a gentle tug, leads him down the alley by the side of the store, and ties him to a drainpipe. He slides out a layer of cartons and drops them flat on the ground. 'C'mon on, old boy, sit yourself here.' Michael is not at all certain that the dog will take to this – not if he's anywhere near as stubborn as his mistress. But Barrell does take to it. Immediately, he climbs onto the bed of boxes and sits with his head lolling. 'He'll survive the night at least,' thinks Michael. Later on he will bring the dog something soft to lie on and some meaty scraps to keep him going.

■ ◆ ■

James knows he should have gone back to work. He has taken liberties to be with Paolo and, considering that his line manager at the NYPL is an asshole and a bully, it will not be overlooked. For now, though, he sits on the couch and waits, drinking coffee after coffee, the curtains drawn, the dishes piling up, the shadows creeping over his face. It will not be long – the vital signs have said it, the evasive looks of the medics have said it, and Paolo's last desperate bid to express words confirmed that he knows it, too. As plain as day, he is going. He thinks of that last fragmented request, 'Remember me', and he thinks of all the ways that people have ever commemorated their loved ones, from Mount Rushmore to the Taj Mahal to park benches. But as soon as he has assembled these thoughts, he wishes them away – God, Paolo isn't even dead yet, and here he is planning his memorial. He turns and looks at his own reflection in the TV screen, seeing what he has become: a ghoul – empty, lonely and possessed of death.

■ ◆ ■

Corinne shuts the window on another tired dawn. Thankful at least that there is no rain, she takes her coat and gathers up her storage boxes stacked by the door. 'So, you're gonna be OK going in with Kelly, yeah?' she asks in as unconcerned a way as she can manage. Siobhan, at the battered table, stops short in devouring a bowl of Weetos. 'I'm not ten, Mommy. How about you? Are you gonna be OK, driving all that way and going to work all on your own?'

'Don't be ridiculous.'

'Exactly . . . ?'

'OK, OK.'

Corinne, made to look the fool again, gathers up her boxes, makes her ragged goodbyes and merges herself into the greyness of the day beyond the door. As soon as it closes, Siobhan wanders slyly to the window, there to watch Corinne load the boxes on top of the trestles in the back of the old station wagon. It is such a delicious agony, waiting, willing her mother to hurry round to the driver's door, anticipating the quivering of the exhaust and the dipping of the bumper that means the car is all fired up and ready for the road.

Siobhan sidles over to the phone, sits down, finds the courage to pick up the handset and dials. A pompous secretarial voice issues orders for parents to leave messages for due attention. Then comes a day-bright beep. An uncanny separation takes place inside Siobhan, and she is both fascinated and appalled to hear a passable imitation of her mother – weary and stoical, with the faintest rasp – delivered, magically, out of her mouth: 'Uh, hello, this is Corinne Harper. Um, I'm afraid Siobhan has a temperature and a very sore throat today. We both do as a matter of fact. And, well, we're waiting for the doctor right now. Hopefully she'll be all right tomorrow or the next day. I'll get in touch to let you know. Thank you. Goodbye.' She puts down the phone, dull and deadly, but then, realizing it is done, she flashes a whoop and a clap of the hands, topped by a cry of delight: 'Wicked or what?!' She gets up, throws on her yellow woollen jacket, rolls her bag across her back and marches to the door and out.

■ ◆ ■

Kelly is over at the corner of the road leading down to the bus stop. An older boy, Kelly's brother, stands shoulder to shoulder with his sister, but the minute he glances over and sees Siobhan coming, he lazily steps aside, shunning her company in the same old way. As she crosses over to join Kelly, Siobhan returns his cynical look with a resentful stare of her own. The brother – Siobhan no longer allows him a name – has always been 'off' with her, as if he has uncovered a hole in her that the world has yet to see through. And at this moment she is so totally consumed in her hot little deceit that it enters her mind that perhaps the brother really does possess some special insight into her iffy character. She has let Kelly in on part of the secret – that she intends to travel on the school bus only to get closer to the main terminus – but has kept the rest of her plans to herself. It took all of her cunning to swear her to secrecy without coming close to spilling the reason, and now Kelly is on fire with curiosity.

Even as the brother swings onto the waiting bus and they scurry down its shining yellow flank towards the door, she yammers at Siobhan for the lowdown.

'Where, Shibby, where? Just give me some idea, a tincy-wincy clue . . .' And when they are safely in their seats and the brother has checked in with his own pals in the back, she keeps up her whining: 'Please, please just tell me. Is it to meet a boy? Just tell me. Someone at least should know.' Frustrated still, Kelly is driven to more desperate tactics, letting out her fears in a sudden, dramatic whisper, her hands open like a scarlet fan in front of her mouth: 'Oh no! Don't tell me you're hooking up with some weirdo on the Net!' With a superior roll of the eyes, Siobhan lets it be known that she would never be so foolish, but that's as far as it goes. Only when they get off the bus and the rest, Kelly's brother included, have hightailed it for school, does Siobhan give any kind of hint at her mission: 'Listen, Kelly, I have to do this. It's a good thing, a right thing I owe to myself. That's as much as I can say.' She presses Kelly's arm, swings her knapsack and heads away. Defeated, Kelly heads along the well-trodden path to school. Only once does she turn to follow her friend's progress, but Siobhan has already flitted from view, lost in the hazy patchwork of faraway things lining the sidewalk, leading downtown.

■ ◆ ■

The bed that she lies on seems impossibly vast, making Michael feel all the more small and outside himself. The sight of Rosa's head, served up on a pillow in its helmet of bandages, and the insidious wheeze of oxygen from the cylinder, unnerves him even more. Looking over at Grace, stooped neon-pale on the other side, he can see that she, too, is disconcerted. And there is yet more strangeness in the way the prim nurse, who was earlier so soft-voiced and shiny-eyed, now stands there in a new guise, her back stiff and her voice mechanical as she recites her well-worn patter: 'Try, for example, saying things to her. The patient is in a coma for the moment, although of course we don't know how long that will last. It could be four or five hours only, or it could be weeks or even months. By talking to them, the idea is that maybe we can stimulate their consciousness. There have been many cases where recovered patients have repeated back things that people said when they were out. You could have a conversation – kind of comforting talk about nothing in particular – but include her, too, just like you would at any other time . . .'

This takes Michael well and truly into the land of the weird. The last real conversation he had with Rosa was more than twenty years ago. Since then, the most he has said to her is, 'Stay your side of the street,' or, 'Please, go take a bath.' Well, at least she won't require that kind of nagging any more, although he can still smell the faintest whiff of death's taint on her, despite the fact that she's been bathed and scrubbed and her ghastly clothes incinerated.

'Thank you,' squawks the nurse and marches away, leaving the two of them stuck for words of any kind, let alone conversation. Michael speaks finally, but only because he feels so foolish: 'So what are we supposed to say to her?'

'How should I know? Hi, Rosa, how's it going?'

'Don't be ridiculous.'

'Well, what am I supposed to say? I never had much to say to her and, come to think of it, I never wanted to neither.'

It pains Michael that Grace should carry even now the same old grievances against his old aunt: 'Come on, Grace, be charitable,' he urges her.

'What, because she got knocked down I'm supposed to forgive and forget everything she ever did?'

'No, because . . . because she's old and harmless now, and all of that business is long over.'

'No it is not. And that person lying there is the same person that did those things. And that person still has to explain one day why she did them. And then maybe I might find it in my heart to say nice things.'

'Don't be ridiculous. How is that ever going to happen?'

'That's right, it is ridiculous, and that's why I will not stand here another moment. Look at her, Michael. No way does she hear what we're saying. She's out of it. Gone. Tell you what, let me know the moment she sits up and says sorry, then maybe we can all get together and chew the fat about the good old days. Now excuse me, I have a store to open up three hours late!'

And she walks right out, leaving Michael standing there like a lemon. He is in no kind of position to go running after her, there are matters still to be sorted – Rosa's things, her money and keys and so on; he must stay and talk to the people. He watches Grace's bird-like figure flutter away down the corridor and has the same old sinking feeling. He prays she doesn't let her bitterness about Rosa get the better of her all over again.

Michael walks back to the bed, leans over the cushioned head and looks, truly looks, at Rosa's face for the first time possibly in his life. It reminds him of a chestnut squeezed hot from the husk: yellow, translucent, sort of, and imprinted with lines. He leans over and says in a half-whisper, 'Listen, Rosa, I don't have time right now, but I'll come back, depend on it. In the meantime, you lay right where you are. Stay right there and take it easy, yeah. I'll be back.'

■ ◆ ■

Siobhan sits on a bus-station bench. Smart girl that she is, she has shot-gunned the seat next to a together-looking woman who could pass as her mother. The bus is late, and she has grown empty-headed with waiting, her eyes wandering with her thoughts, around the dingy concrete arena, scored across with arrival bays. With

61

each circuit, the keen sense of expectation that led her here drains away a touch more. First thing in the morning and everything seems so limp and pathetic. There are people dotted around the place, but they all seem out of it, sitting either slumped or hunched or lolling against walls, each one of them somehow careless about who and what they are. On the bench to the other side of Siobhan, a woman jerkily sneaks a cigarette, while her little girl of three or so flops about, every ounce of her concentrated on sucking a lollipop. Just opposite the little girl and her mother, a fat old man sprawls behind *The National Enquirer*, while a large German Shepherd dog sits prick-eared at his feet, as if it alone is mindful of some noble purpose in their journey. For some reason, Siobhan is reminded of the tear-jerker movie where the two dogs and the cat take off across 1,000 miles and incredibly find their owner. It gives her a momentary feeling of warmth to compare *The Incredible Journey* to her own heroic mission, but then it occurs to her that the three lovable animals travelled across America, half dead and starving, on homing instinct alone, whereas she will travel the length of Long Island on the scheduled bus, after which she will snatch a bite in McDonald's or wherever before taking the subway to her destination. Even so, she reassures herself, it's kind of in the same territory.

Something nudges against her leg. She looks down

to see the girl-child looking up at her, lips plumped and cheeks sucked in, her eyes glassy with lollipop exertions. Siobhan smiles and leans in to her, but already the child has rolled down the length of the bench towards the next one along. Siobhan watches intrigued as the toddler comes to rest in front of the dog, who momentarily bounces on his haunches, his owner still totally oblivious.

The child considers a while, then takes the lollipop from her own mouth and offers it, warm and dripping, to the dog. Having no apparent fear of the animal, she jabs the stick at its fearsome head, all the while giggling with delight. The dog flinches and jerks its head this way and that, doing its best to keep out of harm's way, but the little girl presses on and will not rest content until she has inserted the lollipop into his mouth. She drags the lollipop along the dog's ragged jaw, bouncing it along the row of serrated teeth as though playing a xylophone. Siobhan watches with mounting fear. She can't believe that the fat man still hasn't stirred from behind his newspaper, and she can see that the dog is close, literally, to snapping point. She has an awkward choice: call out hysterically and draw the world's attention to the danger, or stay silent and anonymous, which is what a fourteen-year-old girl bunking off school and up to no good would be sensible to do.

But then all is saved when the bus squeals in, silver and hissing, from nowhere. The door flies open and passengers hop down, and the inattentive mom, suddenly a she-tiger in her instincts, sees her daughter with her hand practically in the mouth of a wolf and comes rushing over. She shouts furiously at the fat man, who has emerged from his paper sanctuary. He is none the wiser about what he is supposed to have done, but is left in no doubt as to his guilt in the matter.

'Asshole!' adds the mother as she scoops up her daughter, snatches the lollipop from her fist and throws it under the wheels of the bus. The man, indignant now that he comes to think about it, discards his *National Enquirer*, hauls himself to his feet and stands to meet the mother's accusing stare. Siobhan is riveted by the heat that's building up, but then the driver appears in the bus doorway, demanding tickets, and a line forms instantly. The fat man and the tiger-mother turn their heads in the same moment, like characters in some hammy musical, taking their cue for the next chorus. The mother plants the little girl down neatly on her feet, the fat man calls his dog to heel, and they both scurry obediently to their places in the queue, the whole angry thing evaporated.

Siobhan snorts, half in relief, half in amazement: people are so strange – shocking and funny at the same time. Then she stands, hitches up her bag and strides over to take her place, just behind the woman who has landed the contract to play the part of her real-life mom.

Michael turns in at the door, all breezy and putting on a good face, but one blistering look from Grace at the counter wipes the shine right off. Well and truly in the dog house, he hangs his coat, ties his apron and slouches towards the haven of the cold-meat counter. But he cannot resist making a throwaway remark: 'A harmless old lady, Grace.'

'Harmless? You fool, Michael. You were dying, all of you, and she stood by and did nothing.'

'But she was so young then; she didn't understand.'

'That's nonsense. She could have saved you and she did nothing.'

'I survived. Here I am, fat and happy.'

'It was worse than murder.'

Even as he shakes his head and smiles, tolerating her funny ways, Michael knows in his heart that this is not just the fretfulness of a stubborn woman. What Rosa did all those years ago was in some ways worse than murder, and it has always plagued him that, having made it to America before the war, Rosa could have helped him and his family to follow her, but she did nothing. His mother, Magda, had written to her sister, begging her many times over, but she made no reply. Of course she didn't know then that the Russians and the Nazis would come, one after the other, with such bloody vengeance, and none of them could have foreseen that it would lead to his father being taken away like that. But they were in hell, whichever way you looked at it; the whole world knew it, and any decent person would have reached out their hand.

An uneasy silence reigns for a full two hours between Michael the grocer and Grace his wife, as they carry out their daily chores, serving customers and filling shelves. For the first time in years, the two of them exchange not a word, not even through lunch, which is snatched in between orders anyway, and it is only when Michael hears the dog whimpering outside that any kind of get-out offers itself from the stalemate. Michael risks a glance in Grace's direction, hurries down to the cellar and comes up with a sponge, a bucket and a bottle of shampoo, which he holds up by way of explanation. He strides outside, unties Barrell from the downpipe and drags him to the side alleyway, where there is a faucet. The dog is all for escaping, but Michael, strong in his indignation against Grace, holds onto Barrell's collar, twisting it tight to the jaw and forcing the old beast to accept its fate under a gush of water and swathes of foam. Then Michael brings him round and ties him again to the downpipe, where he quivers and quakes like a cartoon animal, water flying everywhere, and whining like a baby. It is during this that Michael hears Grace's voice, sharp and rebuking as ever, but reassuring just to hear her return to her old habitual manner. 'Michael, it's not warm – you're going to kill the damn dog!'

'Nonsense, it's spring, pretty much. Five minutes and he'll be dry.'

So the hatchet is buried and soon they are on speaking terms again, with no more mention of age-old wrongs. He finds it in himself to tell her how the hospital provided him with Rosa's things, like her tattered old purse containing a pathetic sum of money. 'What about the cart?' she asks and, receiving no more than a shrug in reply, grows dismissive: 'Yeah, well, good riddance. Anything else?'

'Her keys.'

'Oh my goodness. Why give them to us?'

'We are her next of kin. Someone has to look after her stuff.'

'Does that mean we have to go there?'

'Just to keep an eye maybe, while she's in the hospital.'

'My God.'

'Yeah, well maybe we'll find Rosa's secret treasure.'

'Yeah, right.'

■ ◆ ■

The moment the bus is sucked into the gaping mouth of the Port Authority Bus Terminal, Siobhan is desperate to get away. The wait is agony. Why can't the people in front get their things and their kids together quicker? She would gladly have pushed them all aside if it didn't get her yelled at or slapped.

Jumping down at last into the great dead space, everything seems tainted – the walls, the pillars and the cracked plastic canopies. The buses themselves, which seem so sleek and gleaming in the daylight, look bloated and grime-ridden in here. And the people, too – penned like animals, restless to be led or fed.

She walks along a gangway, allowing herself to be shuffled in a wedge of bodies towards the far-off exit. The noise of engines, babbling voices and scrambled announcements is oppressive – one moment all muffled and underwater, the next wild and violent. In yet more waves, human beings seethe in and out of her vision. Suits, casuals and rags: people on their way to do business, people getting away to the country; people just going where they go. And more than a fair share of crazies, dancing to music only they can hear, or arguing with enemies only they can see. And in amongst it all, the lost, the lonely and, like her, the downright bewildered. Her grip is tight on her bag strap as the human tide swells finally through the exit, spewing her out into plain day.

■ ◆ ■

It's a relief to be on a street of any kind, but as Siobhan's eyes adjust to the light and her bones to the morning chill, she finds this one to be wide, busy and bound on both sides by imposing buildings with glass front-ages and half-glimpsed, stylish interiors. High on a plaque she reads, '42ⁿᵈ Street', and immediately associates it with the movie, the musical and a generally cool place to be. In a store window, she catches her own reflection: her beloved yellow jacket – how childish it looks, how out of place in such a grand setting. A signpost points to more wonders: a quarter of a mile on, Times Square awaits, and she glides in a dream into the famous precinct, the rumble of traffic falling away and the whispering brilliance of the place enfolding her. On the buildings are constellations of lights, with magical images shimmering, and news ticker-tapes flowing around the edges. Lining the walkways, so many people of every kind, with faces raised and fingers pointing. Siobhan greedily devours the sights – cafés and camera stores, sushi bars and souvenir shops, brimming with Big Apples and Statues of Liberty in every material from china to chocolate. She stumbles into a crowd gathered around an old black man on a box, with a banner proclaiming him as the prophet of the Church of the Divine Diocese of New Jerusalem. He rants that Manhattan is Sodom and Brooklyn Gomorrah, and some in the crowd shout and jeer, playing the part of heathen and disbeliever. All the while, Siobhan wonders why her mother has never brought her here. Why has she been starved of the crazy, dizzy rush of it? How has she simply accepted that the Gateway Theatre, Bellport, was just about as good as it gets in the way of entertainment? And to think that she had intended simply to jump off the bus, dive down in the subway and go to her destination! No, she will walk every inch, make her way north and take this in, drink this in, bring this whole great city into herself. She came from it, after all, and if she gets half a chance, to it she will return.

CHAPTER FOUR

THE afternoon goes off without incident and all is sweetness and light between Michael and Grace. She agrees to go with him to Rosa's after hours, trading it against a night off the following day to go and see their eldest, Jenny, in Brooklyn.

Around about three-fifteen, a young girl comes in, fresh and bright and looking not at all like a neighbourhood kid. An out-of-towner, he thinks right away, with the pack on her back and, what, fourteen, fifteen at most? Strange that she should be out of school and hanging around here on her own. He's even more intrigued when the girl drops her pack to the floor and goes and stands on the old weighing machine, watching

71

the pointer climb up the scale. This is strange; he can't remember the last time anyone actually stood on it. He has himself, once or twice, but only in private defiance of Grace's stated intention to have the thing removed. He watches closely as she hops off the machine and drifts down the rows, stopping at the deli counter, her eyes wide and roving. For all of ten minutes she keeps it up, studying the unusual ingredients and exotic arrangements. He slides behind the counter, supposedly to set out rollmop herrings but really to watch her sidelong. She looks like she's never seen anything like this before and then, out of the blue, she pops a question that certifies that she really never has. She goes back to the end, where she started, and points: 'What is this, please?'

'Uh, that is moussaka. A Greek dish; very nice. Lamb and eggplant cooked in a béchamel sauce.'

'I had moussaka but never like that.'

'It's the real thing. Would you like to try some?'

'Uh uh. No thanks. And this one?'

'Moutabel. That also is made from eggplant, with tahini and other things. It's Lebanese.'

'Vegetarian?'

'Are you vegetarian?'

'I'm trying to be.'

'Is that for reasons of health or for the animals?'

'Both,' she says. He spoons some of the moutabel into a tiny paper dish. 'Try some.'

'Oh . . . oh, I was just looking . . .'

'Here.'

She doesn't mention that she is only there to kill another fifteen minutes, because it's colder outside than in and it looked such a nice inviting place to wander into. But she takes the offering anyway, nibbles it and likes it. 'Go on, have some more.'

'That's very nice. Thank you.'

'My pleasure. Now, do you see anything you would like?'

'Um . . . Do you have any, um . . . Chinese oranges?'

'Chinese oranges? Sorry, no.'

'How about . . . chewing gum?'

'We don't sell chewing gum,' he says without any kind of expression.

'Ah well, never mind. Which way is Lennox?' she asks, hoisting up her bag again and heading for the door.

'That way.'

'Really? Oh I had it totally the opposite direction. Just as well I asked.'

'Just as well.'

'Thank you. I like your deli, by the way. It's cool.'

'Well, thank you. See you again some time.'

'Who knows . . . Bye.'

And so Siobhan goes, another quarter-hour success-fully consigned. She can see the grocer, watching her as she moves off along the street, but it doesn't bother

her. He seemed like a nice enough old guy and she's feeling pretty much at peace with the world right now.

Back in the Sunrise, Michael shakes his head, vaguely puzzled as Grace comes up carrying a mop and bucket: 'I've seen that face somewhere before,' he says.

'What face?'

'The girl; the girl that was in here.'

'I didn't see no girl.'

'No? Where was you?'

Grace sighs with the exasperation of one forced to spell out the obvious to one who ought to know, but doesn't: 'Well, first I went upstairs, then I went downstairs, then I came up again. Then I went upstairs again, then here I am. What about the girl?'

'Ah, nothing. I just know the face . . . Listen, don't forget to shut up early tonight to go to Rosa's . . .' This is quite enough to make Grace shudder to the core.

'Don't worry, I hadn't forgotten. Yeuch – it makes me sick to the stomach just thinking about it. And while we're on the subject, what are you gonna do about the damn dog? It's starting to rain in case you haven't noticed. He could die out there. I'm sorry, but he has to go.'

'No worry. I'm onto it,' says Michael, but he isn't onto it at all; he doesn't have a clue what to do about the dog. And of course it continues to rain, so he begins to imagine what it will be like to go round the next morning and find him dead. When Benjy turns up at five, therefore, it's out of genuine exasperation that Michael says, 'What am I gonna do about this darn dog?'

At seven o'clock, when it's almost time for Benjy to knock off, Michael receives his answer, for when he accompanies Benjy into the side alley to check that the cartons have been correctly folded – a fundamental part of the routine – there at the side is an edifice made of cardboard, a kennel, looking very much as a kennel should, with a pitched roof and a cut-out oval-shaped door. And Benjy has done all of this: fashioned it, folded it, cut and glued it into shape.

'Look what I did,' he says, proud of himself. 'He can live in it. Whaddya say?'

Michael is dumbstruck, not only by Benjy's extraordinary resourcefulness, but by the fact that the dog already seems to have taken up residence in it. He can see Barrell sitting inside, his head at the door, lord and master of all he surveys. 'Good God,' Michael says finally, and then, allowing a moment for sentiment to gather: 'That is wonderful.' Then, just as quickly nipping it in the bud: 'Now tell me, young man, if you had time to do all of this, what've I been paying you to do today?'

■ ◆ ■

Harrison strides, glides, flies along, his body supple

and strong. The mile across the Park seemed like twenty skips, and he didn't even break a sweat. He feels in every part of him tight, light and alert. Under his loose clothes, he can feel the beanie folded in his inside pocket, the knife shining and sheathed down the outside of his thigh and, in his sleeve, the heavy little slug of the tyre-iron. There isn't an ounce of fear in him; he has no need of it; he will not have it.

He arrives outside the block, on the opposite side, and notes the position of Old Rosa's apartment. There are her windows, unlit and with the filthy nets sagging on their wires. He came here once before, four years ago when the grocer sent him with deliveries – that's how good his brain is, to remember it from that one time to this day: second floor, left of the landing window. In the neighbouring apartment the flickering shimmer of a TV. The street is all but empty – just one distant silhouette slowly coming down, but no worry; he can be in and out quick as needs be.

The time is now. He crosses, goes in at the entrance, into near-darkness. The stairs are damp and dingy, just like he remembers, and as he reaches the first landing, he pulls his hat right down. His ears are alert: anyone comes up or down, he will hear them in time to back off. He skips up the last flight, pressing against the rails, his eyes peering over the top step. Under the door of the apartment opposite old Rosa's is a crack of light, and a peephole in the door is a tiny star. Right. He cannot make any real noise or spend any time going in. He puts his gloved left hand to his right sleeve end and draws out the tyre-iron. Just the one chance – jam it in by the lock and go for it. If it gives, he goes in; if it doesn't, turn and go, just turn and go. Excitement is in him, more delicious than fear. He takes three quick, fierce breaths, tiptoes to the door, gently forces the iron between door and frame, smiling to see it lodge tight. He levers it, at the same moment ramming his full force against the door, which suddenly flies open, taking him head first with it. He turns back and scrambles the door shut. His eye goes straight to the peephole. Nothing. Nobody comes to the neighbour's door, nothing stirs, no voices, and he can hear the TV going with people laughing. He is in. But the door sprang too easy; he opens it an inch and sees the latch is off – the door was never locked. On the floor is a hank of carpet material and he realizes it was there to wedge the door shut. Quickly, he places it back and shuts the door tight.

■ ◆ ■

James gasps horribly, his fragile sleep snapped, his waking harsh and devoid of all awareness. His eyes grate open to the dingy light and he feels the couch, lumpy under him, his body clammy in his clothes. It comes to him: how he came home and fell asleep and has been lying here an hour at most, though it seems an age. He turns his head to look at Paolo's picture on the mantelpiece and his spirits sink again. What is there to do but lie and wait?

Then comes a harsh buzz at the front door. Irascible, he pads along the hall: he has no time for anyone right now, and if this is some person selling charity art from Africa or a utilities salesman . . . The buzzer sounds again, longer and fiercer. He puts his eye to the peep-hole, sees the top of a tousled head and a blaze of pink brow. He throws the locks and opens the door. There stands a girl, forlorn and stooped, though her clothes are sassy. He blinks foolishly and stares back at her.

'Daddy,' says Siobhan, a seven-year-old again.

This isn't how she'd planned it: she would knock boldly on the door; she would shake her father's hand, or offer her cheek, depending on the reception. She would waltz into his apartment and be terribly smart and grown-up and overflowing with conversation. But 'Daddy' is all she can find it in her to say, and all she can do is stand there looking a total goof.

He is no better. 'Siobhan . . . ?' he asks, a complete halfwit, because now she is completely crushed, her head bowed and tears falling on her shoes. Such unbearable pain to think that he has never planned and imagined this moment, as she has done all these years. How could he have neglected to sit down and frame her face in his mind, to make allowance for how she might have changed? How could he not instantly know her?

'Siobhan . . . What are you doing here?' Again, his words come out horribly wrong. He means to express his own bewilderment, but she hears only an accusation. 'Daddy,' she says again, and this time her sorrow gets through to him and he finally summons something closer to understanding. Gently, he takes her hand and guides her into the apartment. When he turns back from shutting the door, he finds her blue eyes gazing up at him – more like the little girl he remembers.

James looks at her standing in his hallway, fighting to hold back tears, and it makes him contemplate his poor handling of matters so far. 'I'm so sorry . . . I really wasn't . . .' he gestures at the shadows, as if they could explain him and everything about him. Her eyes rove over the bland interior and back to him. He looks so worn out and shabby, far from the man she'd dreamed about. And there is something defensive in the way he says, 'Listen, sorry, I came home from work and fell asleep,' then hurries over to open the drapes.

She ventures into the bleary world he has wrapped around him, her eyes drawn through the drabness to daylight and the balcony and the tiny table out there with two coffee cups left facing each other. She sees the neighbourhood below, the neat little square with the little French fountain all dried up. And then, when she turns back, her eyes alight immediately on the mantelpiece. She ignores the small but exquisite Buddha head, the brass incense burner and other trinkets arranged there. She even ignores the cutesy portrait of her knee-high self. Instead, she fixes on the framed photograph of a dark-eyed man with a handsome, spiritual face . . .

James watches uneasily. The material world, which he has renounced so much of late, suddenly commands his attention: 'Do you want a coffee? Can I offer you something?' He visibly winces to hear himself sounding so limp and really downright camp, talking to her as if she were some visiting dignitary. She casts her eyes down and, to his relief, away from Paolo's photograph. But then her gaze settles on the door of the spare room – Paolo's room – the room no one must ever enter. He hurries over and shuts it tight, covering, meantime, with suitably polite enquiries:

'So, how did you get here? Don't tell me you came here all alone? Does your mother know?' Practicalities, loose ends, small things suddenly important. Her awkward silence lays her open. 'Oh my goodness!' he pronounces prissily, taking out his cell phone. This, then, propels her to jump up, inhibitions to the wind, and rush over to snatch the phone from his hand. 'Please, please don't do that!' she yells as he stands back amazed. Such wilfulness! An unaccustomed sense of pride rises in James's chest: so this is Siobhan; this is his daughter.

'Not yet! Please . . .' she begs, softer of tone.

'OK, OK,' he demurs, holding up his hands. Meekly,

she hands the phone back to him. 'I had to come here, Daddy, I had to. '

'Of course . . . Of course you did. Please, sit down. But Siobhan, you have to know, this is a bad time for me, a very bad time.' He gazes squarely at her, all his pain collected for display.

For a moment she is almost overcome but then snaps to her senses: Bad? How totally rock-bottom is this? She jumps up and lets it out: 'A bad time? You're having a bad time? Well what the fuck do you think I've been going through for the past seven fucking years?!'

■ ◆ ■

Barrell leads the way again. Michael and Grace trudge silently along the damp street. Michael's mind ticks over, unstoppable, browsing over the variety of nasty surprises that could lie in store behind Rosa's door. He spares half a thought for the legendary hidden treasure, but of course it's all just so much nonsense. The cost of clearing the stuff will most likely outweigh its value. Naturally, that cost will fall to them, as will the bill for the 'arrangements' when she dies, heaven forbid. It's a real bind; they are not strictly obliged, but decency dictates, just as it always has. Go back twenty years or so, they had been Rosa's only support. It was them who were forced to look on helplessly as her money had dried up, and her sanity with it.

And so, not even taking comfort in words, the old

man, the old woman and the dog trudge the streets and turn the corners until they reach the entrance to the block where Barrell suddenly takes up the slack and leads them to arrive, soundless, outside her door. Night is coming on by the minute and the landing light is heartless, so that each looks on the other and sees a grey old ghost. Michael takes out the key, inserts it into the lock and turns, but the door won't budge either way, and he rattles and shoves at it so hard in his frustration that it suddenly swings open. Grace bends down and picks up the carpet piece, holding it up with eyebrow raised and sighing – typical of the old woman to arrive at such a flimsy solution after the lock had packed up.

A terrible presence now comes upon the two of them. Even out here the smell is close to unbearable. Grace shakes her head helplessly; how did the neighbours ever come to put up with this? She looks pleadingly at Michael: No, her look says. No, they cannot possibly go in.

■ ◆ ■

They go via the Park, James seeking the wide open spaces and fresh air to carry away her anxieties and provide distractions, of which there are some: the usual joggers; animals calling from the zoo and a bunch of students over by the bridge making some kind of movie, with lights glaring and the runners all yapping into walkie-talkies and trying to look like they came straight from Hollywood. It's the coward's way out, of course, to distract her like this, but what else can he do? He knows he should call her mother, but the thought of speaking to Corinne after all these years is hideous and makes him jumpy. So for the moment he walks along with Siobhan, showing suitable fatherly interest and discovering the small and lovely things about his daughter that would have filled his days if things hadn't gotten so damned twisted all that time ago.

For her part, Siobhan is mad at herself for losing the momentum – such a fool for letting herself get carried away like that, and now she has to fall in with his small talk, although it would be mean not to. By the time they reach the zoo, she has shared with him her love of cheese, her abhorrence of anchovies, her passion for the colour orange. He has called her 'Shibby' and she has called him dad, although at one point she was bold enough to inform him that her mother some-times refers to him as 'the long-gone, no-good faggot father', and, unbelievably, he had laughed, which had endeared him to her an inch or so. But then she realizes that, so far, everything has come from her; he has given away next to nothing. So then, with the zoo behind her, leaning against the fence, she just comes out with it, her voice breathy but adamant all the same: 'Daddy, please tell me – the photograph, on your man-telpiece . . . who is that man?'

'Ah . . .' He would gladly run from this right now,

but sees that she will not be fobbed off. 'That is Paolo, Shibby. Paolo, my partner.'

She falls silent. OK, so it's no news he's gay – it was the cause of his going after all – but seeing the photograph and hearing him say these things, it's all suddenly quite shocking. 'Is that so bad?' he asks, so very reasonable.

'Where is he now?'

'He's in the hospital. Sick. Very, I'm afraid. I – I'm waiting to hear . . . It could be any time,' this said so gravely it leaves her with nothing to say but, 'Oh.'

'Look,' he says, forcing a lift in his voice. 'Ice cream, chocolate. Whaddya say? Run over and get some.' And he gives her money and sends her towards the distant kiosk, where people are lined up. Quickly, he bites the bullet, fumbles out his phone and dials, feeling himself shrinking with each strident ring. Then, there it is after all this time, that voice so cold and martyr-like: 'Hello?'

'Hi, Corinne. It's me. James.'

Silence closes around her, then: 'What can I do for you?'

'Well, it's Siobhan. She's here.'

Clearly, it's no surprise to her. She wades in: 'Do you realize how sick with worry I've been? I called the police!'

And that is how it goes. She is all tight-lipped and icy, outraged in the first instance to imagine him worming his way back into her life, and then hot and stuttering in the second as she realizes her little girl has come to no harm. She listens to him not a jot when he points out that Siobhan's arrival had come out of nowhere, that this is all entirely down to the girl's extraordinary determination. So all-consuming is her contempt for him that she pays no heed when James offers at once to rent a car and return Siobhan, insisting there and then on driving the whole way to collect her daughter herself. 'Keep your cell on,' she orders. 'And make sure we hand over somewhere neutral. I'll ring again when I get to the city.'

He puts the phone back in his pocket. 'Hand over somewhere neutral' – as if this was some sleazy drug-drop. 'Fuck!' he blurts out loud – he should have handled that better. But then he softens to see Siobhan strolling back up the path towards him, an ice-cream cone huge in her hand, and on her face a broad breezy smile.

■ ◆ ■

It's the dog who finally makes the decision for them. Before either Grace or Michael can come up with a solid enough excuse to sound the retreat, Barrell noses in the open door and for once throws his weight, yanking Michael into the apartment. 'Oh my goodness!' burbles Grace, as she scurries after them into the stinking darkness, but then there's a whimper from the dog, and an awful sound as Michael lands in something vile. 'Hold, dog, hold!' he gasps, fighting to hold onto the heavy animal. 'Find the light, quick!' Grace scrapes at the wall by the door, fumbling for switches. A light comes on, dim and inadequate, lacking the will to illuminate the fetid room. 'Stay! Stay!' yells Michael, now violently twisting the leash to hold the dog to him. Grace's eyes begin to adjust. All around, there are piled layers of discarded things. To head height in places it towers, a shapeless maze of garbage, possessions of every kind: clothes, objects, furnishings and unidentified rotting matter, all cut through with passageways that lead to awful ends. 'Oh no, please no!' pleads Grace, pulling her coat up over her face. The unholy stench is the worst thing of all. Michael sucks in air through his mouth, one hand cupped over his nose, the other braced against the dog, who strains towards a large, mouldy old wardrobe, picked out in a sickly haze of light, oozing in through two small windows in the kitchen area at the back. The wardrobe is an edifice, an outcrop in a clearing in an ethereal landscape. Inside it is Harrison. Crammed into one side of the boxy space, his head jammed under a shelf, he is gripped with fear, shuddering for air, sweat running down his face like it's springing from his eye sockets. The knuckles of one hand stand out white as his fingers twist impossibly around a flimsy little catch to prevent the door from swinging open. The other hand is fused around the handle of the dagger, its wicked blade at the ready.

Michael picks his way forward, noticing among the jungle of detritus old grocery bags, packets and, sometimes, bare remains of what once was food. Faded names and phrases on rotting scraps identify the products: Frozen Vegetarian Micro-Meal; Sea Spray Salmon Mousse; Moist Meaty Chunks for Man's Best Friend. It dawns on Michael that the whole thing is practically organic with decay, and he imagines it seething and alive, which indeed it is in parts yet to be chanced upon. He lets down his hand and braves the stench, allowing himself to be pulled in further by the dog, snuffling now at the wardrobe door. Michael studies the handle – yes, he could open this; it can't possibly be so bad on the inside – but then his eye is taken by things in the layers – old shoeboxes and document cases – and it occurs to him that there are family things here, under this pall of filth; things that bind him to Rosa. Something of his own history might be under all this. He pulls out an old framed mono-chrome photograph, still in good shape, of Rosa about fifty years back. He turns to look at Grace. Hunched at the door, hand at her face, she is beaten by the sheer magnitude of it. 'This scares me,' he confesses, child-like, holding the picture up for her to see. 'This was a life, Grace. To think that Rosa was once young and beautiful.' Grace peers at it, blinking to see a young and truly lovely woman. Michael becomes sad and philosophical; this hideous landscape says something not just about a crazy old lady, but about the two of them and everyone born to this earth, the whole damn shebang: 'Look at us, Grace,' he says. 'We were young; we had dreams – we were stuffed full of them.' But from Grace there is no more than a frightened rounding of the eyes.

Inside the wardrobe Harrison can hear the dog slobbering; he can even see the dark shape of its head against the pale crack of light defining the door. He can hear the grocer man wheezing and stuttering, and in his mind's eye he can see the fat little hand reaching for the handle. He raises his bladed hand to the door, so that when it swings open, one straight hard jab would take care of things.

'Oh my goodness!' Something has shaken Grace from her cocoon of disgust. 'Oh my goodness!' she says again. Barrell whines, but Michael pays no heed. His gaze is fixed on Grace, who steps away from her place of safety, spellbound, 'Look,' she says, pointing to the far end of the room.

Harrison is so rapt in the moment that he loses his grip on the catch and the wardrobe door swings open! He contorts himself, desperate to stay behind the side panel. Then he sees that the grocer man has let go of the leash and moved away. But Barrell is still there and still interested; he flops his old head into the opening, sees Harrison, gives a feeble yelp and pulls back. Harrison, close to panic, holds out a trembling hand:

will the dog befriend or bite? Barrell contemplates a second and licks the salty hand, and Harrison, seeing the grocer's back turned away from him still, pees his pants, literally, in relief.

From their separate locations in the room, Michael and Grace converge towards the window, where the drapes hang from the ends of runners, letting in pale spindly fingers of light. 'Look . . .' she says again, and points at a great heavy bookcase standing adjacent to the window, where light seems to gather and glow. Michael and Grace inch towards the foot of the book-case, like two children looking up at a fairytale castle. At the very top, centred and conspicuous, sits a hex-agonal gold hatbox. A look exchanged decides it. Grace pulls a rickety chair over and Michael clambers onto it. Reaching up at full stretch, he eventually manages to nudge the box and catch it as it see-saws on the edge. Clinging to a shelf with his free hand, he bustles it down for Grace to receive safely into her arms.

Harrison is mesmerized. Having gone so far as to stick his head right out of the wardrobe to have a ring-side view, he is on tenterhooks to see Michael at last lower himself to the ground and Grace carefully place the box on the chair. The hatbox looks such an elegant and luxurious thing. Michael shoots a glance at Grace, seeking her approval to open it, then prises the lid off, bringing into view a creamy silk lining that is fresh and new and so improbable in the surrounding filth. At once, the squalor of the room recedes as the box seems to draw the dusky light into itself and reflect it back into their gaping faces. With a gasp she lifts out the contents, knowing, as does Michael, exactly what these things are: a pair of lovingly made, red raised-heel shoes, shapely and covered exquisitely with sequins and topped off across the bridge with a neat, gleaming bow. The ruby slippers, whole and pristine, and seeing the light of day for the first time in a lifetime.

CHAPTER FIVE

THEY have moved on from the Park, both of them suddenly hungry. And where better than Pizza Heaven to brighten up a life? Conveniently for James it offers neutral territory again. Here, she cannot chance upon intimate things in the apartment that say so much about him and Paolo – the subtle messages encoded in things designed for the senses: books and music in the living room, soaps and candles in the bathroom, knick-knacks and pictures in the bedroom.

Siobhan has eaten well, the colour has returned to her cheeks and she is keen to get back to the really tricky questions that made her journey so urgent. Like how come he suddenly turned gay in the first place, after having been straight all those years, and being her dad and everything? But, hey, she's grown up enough to know about right times and places. She knows, too, that her mother will be totally uptight by now, and close to calling the cops – if she hasn't already done so. Seeing her glancing at the clock, James decides to break it to her: 'Listen, Siobhan. I called her, I called her already. It would've been wrong not to. She's on her way.' Gently, he tells Siobhan that she cannot stay the night, but that if she is willing and her mother is cool about it, they will see more of each other. She takes it on the chin, but it's far from mission accomplished and she *will* have her say: 'OK, fine. But just tell me one thing: why, in all this time, did you not get in touch with me, even once?'

He sits there, guilty as charged.

'You didn't even pick up the phone. I had no number for you, no address. Nothing. I had to trick Mommy to get your address. Seven years! You shouldn't've done that.'

He sits there, a little boy caught stealing candy – Pizza Heaven suddenly isn't so celestial a place to be. He leans in to her quietly, shamefaced, but her hard stare denies him any recourse to self-pity. So he pulls out the explanations: of how he was rejected, thrown out, branded vile and disgusting and a corrupting presence, and told never to show his face again. And when Siobhan continues to protest her simple need of him, he wades in, wounded, with how they took away his rights – the courts and the lawyers – left him with nothing and banished him. She just glares darkly and counts the seconds, making him shiver and squirm before saying her piece: 'I didn't banish you. I was seven years old; my father went away; that's all I knew, all I was told – apart from the fact that my daddy didn't want to be with us any more.'

'But that's nonsense!'

'Maybe, but it was nonsense I've believed all of seven years. Do you know, it was only a year ago that Mom ever got round to telling me any of the so-called facts.'

'That's unforgivable!' he finds it in his heart to say.

'You were unforgivable!' she outbids him. They sit there, silent in the gloom they have drawn around themselves, until at last she breaks out of it, taking up the menu again and declaring, 'The dessert better be damn good after this.' He cannot help but smile – at least she's inherited his sense of humour rather than her mother's.

■ ◆ ■

They are moving at snail's pace, the two of them shuffling along behind the dog – three lonely figures, shadowed by a fourth.

As soon as the grocer and his wife had shut the door on the disgusting place, Harrison climbed out from the wardrobe like a zombie from the grave, and leaned against it to think – a process not helped by the smell rising up from his pants, piss-pasted to his legs. One simple fact, though, stood out big and bold in his mind: these two useless old people had just walked out of the place carrying a box that wasn't rightfully theirs. And in that box was a pair of shoes that, if his hunch was right, were worth a whole shit-load of money. This was a pleasing thought, and it occurred to Harrison that he had just as much right to the pickings as they did. Stiff-legged, he clunked to the door, his mind made up to stick to these two people if it killed him. And that is what he told himself out loud to do: 'Man, you stay right there on their backs till you get what's yours by right.'

So now he follows them at a distance, halting as they halt at intersections, hugging the shadows whenever the dog stops to go sniffing. *I am stalking these people*, he thinks, *just like in the movies*. He feels alive and connected and excited about what has passed. He no longer gives a damn about his pants, wet, night-cold and smelling. No, he is too busy contemplating the possibility that he has stumbled onto something rich and strange. How weird that the ruby slippers should be kept in a place like that. The crazy old lady musta been some crazy young lady! But the money they must be worth, that isn't crazy, that is seriously serious, and, if he's got it right, these two people waddling along in front of him like a pair of fat old ducks are in possession of a fortune. Look at the old grocer, his arm round the hatbox, going along like he's out for a stroll. What makes them walk so slow? He can hardly stop himself shouting down the street for them to get a move on.

As they finally approach the darkened stretch leading to the Sunrise Deli, Harrison even thinks of running up behind them and snatching the box from their hands. It would be so easy: it's dark, he would be away in a flash, and who's gonna come after him? But then he sees people way down the end of the street and decides to bide his time; these shoes could be worth millions, and any cut of that kinda money is worth waiting for.

■ ◆ ■

It has not been easy. In the headstrong way of the young, Siobhan has tried to lead the conversation into trickier territory, but he has deftly steered her away from the embarrassing and the hysterical, by way of small subtle tricks, such as pushing the menu under her nose and asking her about friends and school, and by glancing now and again at the other diners, as if to say: Here we keep things light, here we are all smiles. After an hour of this, he flags, lacking the energy to sustain his pose. She sees him grow tense again, the sparkle gone out of him. It's really quite weird. Maybe he's thinking of his sick partner in the hospital, or maybe he regrets being so evasive. She even begins to feel guilty about bringing him nothing but trouble. But then it dawns on her: her father is afraid of her mother. Corinne is only minutes away, and when she arrives she will not be won over by his easy charm. If there is a scene to be made, she will play it to the hilt.

So now it's Siobhan's turn to ask harmless questions and smile as wide as her lips can be made to stretch. But all the time she's watching him watch the door, and the instant she sees his eyes shift sideways, she knows her mother has arrived. She turns to see the old station wagon pull up outside, its shabbiness an accusation, something else to make him squirm. He pretends not to notice as Corinne leaps out and sails across the sidewalk, red hair flying. And he keeps up his pretence even as she hurries through the door, weaving between the tables full of shiny happy people. Still ignoring the fact, he smiles at Siobhan and asks, 'Can I get you another drink?'

And then Corinne is there at the side of the table, looming over them both in her long coat, with a face like thunder. There are to be no niceties, no standing on ceremony: 'OK, Siobhan, time to go!' she barks. 'We have to go. The car is on the red zone.'

'But I'm not ready . . . !' protests Siobhan.

'I'm wai–ting!' Her voice cyanide-sweet, the sliding intonation threatening eruptions.

'I think maybe you should go, honey,' interposes James, all gallant and rising to his feet.

'I have to go to the bathroom,' announces Siobhan,

and jumps up and away. The second time she has gone, he thinks: necessity, the mother of invention. He sits down again, but Corinne remains hovering. A full minute skulks by. 'Would you like to sit down?' he enquires mildly.

'I don't have time,' she snaps. He fixes onto her flashing eye, stealing the initiative: 'Because the way things are, maybe we should, um, be discussing some matters . . .'

'Maybe not.'

'As a matter of fact, Siobhan would really quite like to —'

'Listen, you, keep away from her. Keep right away from the both of us, or I will have the whole damn —'

'Corinne, please, the girl is fourteen. It has nothing to do with what you or I —'

'And by the way, you don't even know her. A thousand things you don't know. Just coming here she ran a risk, did you know that? They have nuts here, nuts in the salads!'

'Nuts . . . ?'

'See how much you don't know? She has an allergy. By eating just one nut she could go into anaphylactic shock, and that can kill a person!' Over her shoulder he sees Siobhan heading back towards them. It would be so easy to give in and say nothing, but he cannot resist a final dig: 'This is absurd! If there was any danger, she's old enough and smart enough to know what not to eat.

She has her own mind now, which is precisely why you should—'

'What am I doing talking to this man?!' snorts Corinne and makes for the door.

He stands and walks over to Siobhan, who has kept back from them both. 'Well, honey, looks like the moment has come.' He shrugs and walks her to the door, bringing out his cell phone again. 'Listen, you have my number now and I have yours. Why don't we—?' The phone chooses this very moment to ring: a bright little Mozartian flourish. He looks at the screen, then holds it out to her as if it's a puzzle for her to solve. The word 'Hospital' is stark on the screen. The same four bars of music sing out insistently, while he stands frozen in a ludicrous pose, his mouth gaping and his finger pointing, looking like an old-fashioned tailor's dummy. She looks past him towards Corinne, who leans, broodingly, against the car, next to the wide-open passenger door, silently commanding Siobhan to go over and get in.

'Daddy?' she whispers, desperate to connect again, but he gives her not a glance – the call has claimed him, every particle. She watches, quivering as he says, 'Yes . . . yes . . .' all slow and dreadful. The seconds creeping by as she watches and sees the words take him over, one by one, like thieves into his ear.

Corinne calls out, crabbily, 'Siobhan – now!'

And there he betrays her – too dazed by what he has

heard to understand that by giving himself to this he took away what was hers; too staggered by the fearful news to see her eyes mist over, or even to notice when her angry mother marches across, grabs her by the arm and drags her to the car.

And that is it, they go, the teenager bundled off by the wounded mother; the old car coughing and juddering away. He didn't even say goodbye – just stood there in the doorway, far away again and unwaving.

■ ◆ ■

As the grocer lady rolls up the shutter and the grocer man unlocks the door, Harrison takes up his hiding place in the record-store entrance. Will they hide it down in the store, or will they take it upstairs to their apartment? The shutter slams down again and a pool of light appears below – a conspirators' light: so they are guilty about what they have done. Good: more power to him. He runs across the road, eager to see, to spy, to get closer to his prize.

Michael has started to shiver and shake, even though they are in the warm again. As Grace locks the door, he gingerly places the box on the counter, relieved to shed himself of his sinful burden. Grace, though, is less troubled by conscience. 'So, open it,' she says.

'Again?' he says. 'But it isn't ours.'

'What are you, a fool?' she splutters impatiently, and forces off the lid. She reaches her hand in and brings out a lilac letter, leaving the slippers untouched. 'It isn't ours,' he repeats pathetically, as she flourishes the letter under his nose. 'Whose writing is this?' she snaps back, showing him the scrawl on the envelope, which says simply, 'To Whom it Concern'. 'Well, hers, of course.'

'So who then is supposed to read it, if not us?' She reaches across the counter for a knife, slits open the envelope and slides out a letter on thin expensive paper. Michael glimpses the familiar old writing, as she unfolds the letter and peers at it, holding it right up to the end of her nose. She shakes her head and bares her teeth in irritation, unable to decipher the spidery shapes: 'My God, I think this is in Latvian.'

Michael, forced to play his part, takes the letter from her and scrutinizes the words. For some strange reason he has always been able to decipher Rosa's difficult hand.

'It's not, it's English.'

'Well, read it then.'

Michael clears his throat and tries to capture something of Rosa's voice in his delivery:

> *Here is written the truth of these shoes, which may be of import to whoever will read this, so I waste no time to explain. Many years ago, I was working in the costume department of the film The Wizard of Oz. If I may say so myself, I was young and beautiful . . .*

'For God's sake, cut the dramatics and just read the damn thing!' hisses Grace. Michael coughs and continues, more matter-of-fact:

> *There was a boyfriend, a young actor who had high hopes but was at the time a set-painter on the film. One day, we went back to the empty lot to be together (I leave you to imagine) in the shadow of the Palace of Oz. Even though it was a stage set, this was a magical place and we were together in the make-believe meadow outside the palace gates and it was oh so romantic. But I then saw beneath a Camelia bush a pair of the ruby slippers . . .*

Michael pauses for effect. Grace nods frantically for him to continue, as he does, with growing wonder.

> *They must have been left there by the props people. I myself many times had placed the slippers on Miss Garland's feet. But never did they lose for me their fascination. There were other pairs that had been made, and I knew that they would not seriously be missed.*

Grace raises an eyebrow, eliciting from Michael his own beetle-browed observation: 'Ah, but that means she—'
'Shush! Go on!'
  'OK, OK . . .'

And they have remained all these years since, in this box,
sustaining me in a cruel and unforgiving world . . .

Michael stops mid-flow, hoping to see some sign of
fellow feeling on Grace's face, but seeing nothing of
the kind, he waxes dramatic again:

The comfort I have received, just knowing that these
magical shoes are with me, has given me a warmth in my
heart, which has made me laugh when perhaps I should
have cried. You who read this have inherited the ruby
slippers. They will not mean to you what they have meant
to me, but I ask you please to allow . . .

His voice cracks, as in the moment he sees it all through
the eyes of a young girl with vivid dreams in a more
innocent age. Grace gives him a hard squinty look to
bring him back up to speed.

. . . To allow for the possibility that they may . . . bring
some good into your life.

He drops his head, musing over Rosa's wasted years.
He is just about to pronounce on the awesomeness
of it all when Grace pipes up breathily: 'Listen,
Michael, five or six years ago, I think it was, a pair of
these – I'm sure of it – they sold. It was on the TV;
they went for a fortune. I mean a very, *very* large sum

of money. A seriously large amount!' This seems to Michael absurd, but she is adamant: 'It was, it was, I tell you! Listen, these are the real thing!' But this only makes Michael all the more slow and stubborn in response.

'Hmm. According to this, these shoes were stolen.'

'Oh yeah? Were they now?' And now it's her turn to milk the moment. Michael watches aghast as Grace proceeds to rip up Rosa's letter and throw the pieces in the bin. She turns on him, strong and forceful, setting out the party line: 'The slippers came from our eccentric relative – given into our safe-keeping many years ago . . .'

'But we can't. She—'

'She came by them honestly. Judy Garland herself gave them to her, in thanks for her services and her kindness. And who can say otherwise? You said it yourself, Michael; everything is gone from us. Look at us.' He knows without having to look the weary desperation that is in her spirit – and in his – so long have they laboured under it. 'We need this. We deserve it,' she pleads, and he can see in her eyes a passion that has been missing for so long. But there is accusation in them, too, which makes him bow his head in submission. She shuts the lid and bundles the box into his arms.

'What am I supposed to do with this?'

'Take it downstairs and hide it. It won't fit in the safe.'

Outside, Harrison is pressed up against the window

– now pressing his ear to it, now squinting between the gaps in the shutters. He has caught some of the fervent conversation – enough to know that his hunch was right and the shoes are precious. And now he hears Michael's footsteps clacking over the wood towards the cellar door. He comes alert again and scoots round to the side alley. The wall here is forbidding and lightless, but the knife is in his hand again as he creeps along: he saw them take the dog down there, and he will finish it off if he has to. In the dense dark he stumbles against the kennel, wondering what the hell it is, until he smells the animal inside and hears it snuffle. Amazing – the thing has neither bark nor bite. But then, looking for the side window he knows to be there, he realizes the kennel is covering it and, bending to put his back into it, he shunts and slides the kennel – dog and all – off its spot.

Now he can see the narrow slit of the cellar window down at foot level, and yes, a tiny light is there. Harrison throws himself down and sprawls, his eye at the edge of the frame – so what if there be shit on the ground. He peers through the grime, his neck twisted round. He can make out stuff . . . just – the tops of shelves in a murky sprawl and the door frame over in the corner – but he cannot see to the ground, where the grocer must be. But then, bizarrely, something appears above the shelves: the top of a ladder. And then something new looms up, light and airy: a golden capsule, the hatbox, floating in space. Like a UFO, it seems to hover in mid-air, before shifting sideways and landing on the shelf-top with a puff of dust. Then, comically, the top of the grocer's head pops up, cut off below the nose, eyes goggling like something in a kiddie's cut-out book. Harrison can actually hear him, wheezing and spluttering as he pushes the hatbox further onto the shelf-top. It is beyond belief. Would they really be so dumb as to hide the ruby slippers in such a stupid way? Then the grocer man is gone, the ladder is gone and, with sudden nothing the light is gone. Harrison hauls himself up and dusts himself down. The smell of his own piss hits him and in a second he is cold to the core.

■ ◆ ■

He goes straight to the hospital. Siobhan, Corinne, everything that has passed this day is wiped out the moment he puts the cell phone back in his pocket.

He takes the elevator straight up to level eight, as he has done for the past two weeks. What do I do? he wonders. What do I say? He has mentally rehearsed this rendezvous with death many times over, but never properly got to grips with the savage detail of it. He pushes open the door to Intensive Care. The duty sister is at the desk. With a sad tilt of his head, he catches her eye and she leans across and squeezes his hand, a decent woman, his instincts tell him: 'I'm so sorry . . .'

'When?'

'Uh, around three. We tried to ring you, but . . .'

'Oh, God, I was switched off.'

'So, would you like – I suppose you were hoping to see him?'

'Uh . . . Yes . . . Yes, I, I suppose I should.' Of course, he must see Paolo. He owes it to him to make the final . . . witnessing. He braces himself for what is to come, expecting her to lead him through to Paolo's room, there to turn back the sheet and reveal him laid out. But all she does is go back behind the counter to consult her records. 'Well, it's up to you: you can wait and talk to the doctor, or you could go down there now.'

'Down there?'

'To the morgue.'

Such a brutal word, so blunt and unkind.

'Ah. Oh. Yes,' he stammers aimlessly.

He takes the elevator. Down, down it takes him, descending through the layers. Darkening. When he exits, two floors below ground, he finds himself in a godforsaken space lined overhead with a sprawl of ducts and littered with broken gurneys and cages stuffed with dirty laundry. The clutter clears as he walks the corridor towards the morgue itself, the colour draining away with each stride – ceilings, walls and floor merging to a grey emptiness. He arrives outside locked, faceless double doors, the word 'Morgue' printed stark on a sign. He pictures the cadavers, sheet-shrouded, labelled and neatly stowed away in cold drawers – death wrapped in banality. There is a grubby bell push on the wall. He presses it, hearing no sound, and hovers there a full minute, debating with himself whether to risk outrage and ring again or even bash on the doors. But then they open and a tired little man in a crumpled suit appears, asks his name and demands, 'Name of deceased?' James provides the terrible information and the man flits back inside, without comment and without any hint of human kindness on his face.

No one is in a hurry here, plainly. Ten more minutes pass; he tires of standing and drops into a battered canvas chair against the wall. He had entered the hospital clean and dignified, intending to manage everything calmly, but now here he is, slumped and done-for in a grubby seat in a vile corridor. He forces himself to sit up straight, his own humanness contracted to a hard shrunken knot. Five dying minutes follow before the door opens again and the little man pops out and dispenses words as if James has called by to collect an unclaimed parcel:

'Sorry, but access is denied.'

He can't quite take it in: 'I beg your pardon . . . ?'

'You can't come in here. Access denied. Next of kin only.'

'But I'm his partner.'

'Do you have a certificate of civil partnership?'

'No, no. We . . .'

'And you are not the next of kin?'

'Not in name, but—'

'Then I'm sorry, sir. Next of kin only.'

And with that the man steps back inside and ends it with the shutting of the door.

James crashes inside, sick to the core, sweat creeping under his shirt. Technically, he is not Paolo's next of kin, they never made such an arrangement, even in the last days. Pieces of paper, what need did he and Paolo have of them? All dignity deserted, James shuffles back to the elevator and up, chaos raging in his head as it halts for people to enter and leave at every floor. Somehow he makes it to the eighth floor again and stumbles to the counter where the ward sister is arranging satin flowers.

'They won't let me in there!' he blurts out, desperate for her sympathy, but her priorities have shifted. The bed linen has been changed and the record sheet with it – there is a new patient in Paolo's place, a new care package to be delivered.

'Oh dear,' she pronounces vaguely.

'Do I have no say at all?' He flops into a seat, his question answered by her silence. The sister is wary, her quota of kindness spent; he cannot sit there all day, taking up space.

'Maybe you should go home and rest a little. It would be for the best. *Really.*'

This solitary word laid down so flat and final that he jumps up, practically to attention, saying, 'Sorry. Sorry. I—'

'No problem,' she says with a professional smile, and he stumbles away, hands to his head and hunched over in confusion. But then he turns back to her: 'Oh, please, I wasn't thinking. I should take away his things . . .' She manufactures a pause, for the sake of decency at least. 'Oh, didn't you know? They already did that.'

The shock of it. He can barely look at her to ask: 'But who . . . ?'

'The family. His family. About five o'clock, it was. They came and took it all away. Everything.'

■ ◆ ■

Michael lies awake. At his side, Grace lies on her back, snoring lightly. He prods her gently in the ribs, and she rolls over and away into silky sleep. He is ablaze inside. How extraordinary this night has been, how totally weird and wonderful! He closes his eyes, seeing a shifting of shapes, vast and luminous, like clouds passing across the moon. The ruby slippers! No one could possibly know how much they mean – have meant – to him, long before this day. Michael's mind wanders now to a place that has lain unvisited in decades. A medieval city so quaint in the recall he can't quite believe it was ever real: the domes, the turrets and the cobbled squares, so dazzling in summer, so hushed in winter's snows. The war changed all that. Aunt Rosa had somehow gotten out of Riga and away to the States before the Nazis came. He was only three years old at the time. Along with the rest of his family, he suffered and saw his city turned over, leeched of any goodness. And, after, he joined his father, stumbling over broken buildings in search of anything that had stayed in one piece and could be sold that they might eat.

Michael Marcinkus, lying in his soft, warm bed with the heating gurgling lazily and his weary old wife sighing in her sleep next him, is suddenly struck, smitten by the realization that this is what led him to what he is, why he became the grocer, the deli-man, the purveyor of food in all its plenty. Tears come to his eyes. How real and powerful these memories are. How astonishing that they can still, after all this time, turn you in the guts and flood your feelings with sorrow.

And that brings him to another resurrected memory: a procession of Jews being led away by soldiers with guns raised, the eyes of the adults cast down, those of the children reaching out, bewildered, to find his own. His father had once told him that these same Jews had grown fat on the backs of people like them, but all Michael saw was raggedness, hopelessness, wasted people. It was what he and his momma became after the soldiers took his poppa, when they had been left to suck their own filthy clothes for nourishment and then within days fled with thousands of others before the Russians took the city. They begged their way onto the overloaded ship bound for they knew not where, and found themselves in Germany for reasons no one ever explained. Once they had disembarked, they clattered down the gangway and came out into a roped-off square, and were herded into ranks by guards who never spoke to them. Then, right in full view, they were formed into lines for medical inspection by nurses and soldier-doctors in white coats, kids gaping their mouths to spatulas and women opening their blouses to be explored.

After this, they had been assigned a destination and were given papers with the words DISPLACED PERSONS and BAMBERG stamped upon them, after which they were loaded into carriages whose windows were black with filth and there made themselves vacant and sat for countless hours as the clacking of the wheels beat up through the boards and pounded their bones. They came at last to a town, complicit in the night, and were led through hushed streets with monstrous buildings that glowered dark and damp, a grey chain of silent people. They were herded through a gate, behind which were great blocks like factories, in a compound that was a town within the town, and were billeted, eight to a room. They were with two other remains of families, but at least it was clean and dry, and food, such as it was, came at the same times every day, although hunger always sat at the head of the table.

And that was the way of it for all of a year, before one day he woke to a miracle: his mother shaking him from sleep – the excitement on her face, smiles he had not seen for so long – saying the Germans had left and the Americans were coming. Sure enough, when he went outside with the other children, there were no guards to be found. They ran full pelt to the main gates and heaved them open, daring each other to stand on the other side, though none but the biggest and bravest were bold enough. They stayed right there until, gradually, the whole camp came and gathered – a great chattering throng, which fell suddenly silent when they heard the roar of engines coming and saw the braver boys running back, shouting, 'Yankees, Yankees!' And sure enough they came in a great rolling convoy: smiling soldiers sitting on the bonnets of jeeps and leaning out of the backs of trucks, their helmets shining and throwing cigarettes and candy. To think these were the first Americans he ever saw.

Abject and wasted is how they must have appeared to those well-fed GIs as they stood there in the great compound for the roll-calls and hand-outs. But it was never to be so again, because now they began to understand that they would be safe – now the food started to come regularly and in good portions, and the medicine began to work and they were put into classes and had lessons and grew to know that they were allowed to give the wrong answers as well as the right, and could laugh and not worry about who might be watching. And this is how it continued for another year, until finally the chance came for them to go to America.

At last Michael comes to a bright memory among the dark: the movie. One evening, to remind the people that they too were human, the Americans set up rows of chairs, borrowed from a church, in the main square, and spread a huge sheet over a gantry raised between two trucks, and he had sat on his mother's lap and smiled at her and she had smiled back. Michael lies in his soft bed and remembers, painfully, what it was like to feel the outline of her bones – he had known even then that she was spent. The film they showed was *The Wizard of Oz* and it was all completely wild and beautiful. No one knew what the hell the characters were saying, although a man and woman who looked like professors in suits too big for them, since they had starved so long, stood at the side of the screen and barked out the translation, songs and all, in a totally mechanical way. They were drowned out by the soundtrack, though, and could only be heard in snatches. Yet it all had meaning, nonetheless: Dorothy's escape from a colourless world into a fantastic one; Dorothy's useless but adorable companions; the oppressed citizens of the City of Oz; the deaths of witches; the undoing of spells and the overthrow of bloated tyrants who turned out to be scared little men. It all had such meaning, such perfect meaning. And out of the whole dizzy mix, the sad, still presence of Dorothy, who was beauty and truth itself, and whose singing of that wonderful song said everything there was to say about loss and longing, even though the words were foreign. Dorothy, who found her way home with that cute click of the heels that belonged to the shining red shoes. How perfect a picture it presented, how neat and simple a trick to open a doorway to a better world. To have lived through terrible times and then to stumble across such a story told in such a place and time, and connecting so thrillingly to your experience – that is surely to know the meaning of meaning.

Michael's thoughts turn again to Old Aunt Rosa. It's odd how he had never truly connected her to the ruby slippers before. Of course he had known that she had gone west to LA for some time. He even remembers vaguely something about her working in Hollywood, but he had never properly taken it in, as if she had never been there for real. And now he berates himself for not having given any credibility to her life as a whole. She would have been only seventeen or eighteen when the movie was made. Strange to think that she had been so involved with the very shoes that had stood out for him, bright and blazing, in a war-dark square all those years ago. And it strikes him they must have had far more meaning for Rosa than they ever did for him. Why else did she keep them when she might have made a fortune from them? Thinking about it, it would be near blasphemous to even think of selling them now, especially as her death was no certainty. No, Grace is wrong in this, he decides, just as she is wrong about clearing out Rosa's place without a care. No matter how rotten the apartment might be, Rosa's history is there, hidden in all those old papers and, who knows, there may be things in there that might throw light on the darkness that has surrounded him all his life.

In a flash it comes to Michael: he knows what should be done with these shoes whose value is beyond value. He leans over and does something unthinkable: he squeezes Grace's arm to rouse her from sleep. Her brow knits and her lips purse in a half-woken snarl. 'Listen, Grace, listen . . .' He tips her chin so that her closed eyes face his, the lids twitching. 'Listen, Grace. We can't do this. They are not ours; we had no right. The slippers belong to Rosa and with her they must stay.' Her eyes are tight closed again, but he goes on, knowing she has heard him: 'Besides, we should think hard about them before ever letting them go. These things are symbolic; they stand for things. They should be put up for people to see. God knows how, but . . .'

Grace lets out a long, guttering sigh and rolls over to face the wall.

■ ◆ ■

Come morning, she has plenty to say on the subject. Two hours of argument already, and still it goes on. 'You have got to be kidding me!' she screams again, her voice louder than he has ever heard it. The neighbours must have heard every word: 'What need does she have of anything? She is dead, Michael, the woman is the same as dead! She will never go back to that place anyways, the authorities would not allow it!' So enormous is Grace's anger that she is heaving and quaking, her fury having raged since they got up, but showing no sign of abating: 'Fifty years, Michael. Fifty years is a long time, a long time to wait for that moment when it might just be OK, when it might just be safe to do what is normal for everyone else in the world to do – take it easy and retire!'

At least it had started quiet, and Michael has reason to hope that the neighbours didn't hear the tricky stuff about how the slippers came into their possession. Attempting to bring things back to the everyday, he reminds her that her coffee is getting cold. 'Fuck the coffee!' she yells, and bangs the table so hard it spills all over. 'Grace!' he clacks back at her, genuinely shocked – not once did she ever use that word! But she hurtles on: 'Because that is what we are going to do: retire. We are going to have the good things in life. The things that have been denied us: holidays, clothes, food that didn't come off our own goddam chuck-out shelf. Retire? I sure as hell will; you do as you damn well please!' And she throws down her mug in the sink, dashing it to pieces. She is getting far too uptight, too hot and bothered about it all, he thinks, desperate now for her to calm down before opening time.

'Listen to me, Michael,' she says in a last frazzled gasp, 'this is the last time I'll say it. We go on the way we been going, anyone works so hard so long, they die – die and go to an early grave! Look at me now and tell me you will not let that happen!' Her look is awesome, her eyes massive and brimming with tears, and he sees in her the passionate, good-looking woman the world once saw.

One last time, he tries to reason with her: 'If only it was so simple—'

'Which is exactly what it is: simple. Sell them! And maybe, just maybe, we won't drop dead right off and can get some of the things that are long overdue in our lives! How dare you put the needs of that evil, selfish old woman who woulda happily seen you dead, your whole family dead, before our own!' And with that she goes out the door and clumps down the stairs. Yet another first – he always goes down before her in the morning.

Michael looks heavenwards. He is going to have to rethink his whole position on this, bide his time, see what gives. For now, though, it's important to keep her sweet. He clambers after her and stretches out to her as she reaches up for her shop coat. 'Listen, Grace, listen,' he says, softly. 'I know we need to talk some more, but this ain't gonna be resolved here and now.

Look, tonight, you take some time out. Go over see Jenny, stay the night. Only promise me, keep this just between the two of us.' She looks at him, sniffing and dewy-eyed as he goes on playing the part of the wise old man: 'For God's sake, don't let them get involved – Karl and Dan and whoever – or we'll never hear the last of it.' She sniffs again, but is otherwise silent, her anger apparently dampened. 'Good,' he says. 'Good.' Taking her calmness for consent.

CHAPTER SIX

For three whole days James lies on the couch, his soul in the scales, hot anger distilling to thoughts dark and hateful of himself. The family, Paolo's people, have made it clear he is to stay away from them and therefore from Paolo. And so, having no one else to punish for what they have done to him, he punishes himself: 'Let me not eat for that is to love the world. Let my body fall away from the world. Let my beard grow, let my clothes be stained and dirty, let me stink.'

Friends have cared. Marcia from work rang morning, noon and night until, worried, she turned up at the door and was sent away unseen. Jack, too, knocked and called softly through the door to him and was ignored:

'I will lie in darkness; shut out light, shut out kindness. Let them drum like monkeys on the door. Let the phone keep ringing till it dies too. To hell with work, with friends and family; I will not be a father. Having no father, I can be no father. I will be a stone, hard and empty of feeling.'

Siobhan has not called, because he did not call her. A hundred miles away, she stays in her room, turning up the TV, lying lifeless, the door barricaded. For each day he lies in fire, she lies in ice, two people of one blood: the hurt of the one mystically communicating with the hurt of the other across the miles. And every day he turns away from the world and from himself, she hates him all the more, and in the end chooses to hate herself.

■ ◆ ■

Safe and invisible in the record-store doorway, Harrison sits on an old crate and watches, unblinking. The night has a damp chill about it, and staring into that dreary old store front these hours on end can take a person to a lost, lonely place. For now, though, he's feeling good about the way things are going. The past two nights he has 'cased the joint', standing on this very spot, doing no more than chewing gum and smoking, and now it's all there, safe inside his head. It has been brain-numbing stuff, and if nothing else it has taught him that he would sooner cut off both his legs than ever be a grocer.

Once more he runs through it: 7 p.m. – the shop boy comes up from the basement, carrying a whole stack of flattened cartons, takes them out front to the side alley and dumps them there. When he returns, Mrs Grocer hands him the mop, and he goes to it. She then hangs up her shop coat and goes upstairs to their apartment and starts to cook something nice and stinky for Mr Grocer, who likes fish. Soon as she is gone, Shop Boy puts down the mop, grabs the Coke and candy bar he stashed behind the shoe polish earlier, goes, where the CCTV cannot see, and sits down on the floor to guzzle them. By seven thirty, business being pretty much dead, Shop Boy starts to knock off. Then, just as he is going out the door, Grocer Man always pulls him up about the cartons, his voice ringing out clear as a bell, wanting to know if he has stacked them properly against the wall because: 'We can't have boxes just dumped willy-nilly in the alleyway.' ('Willy-nilly' – who the fuck is Willy Nilly?) Anyhow, it is at this point that the grocer man risks it, leaving the place unattended to take the boy round the side to inspect the carton situation. Seventeen seconds in the alleyway, at the last count – seventeen beautiful seconds when the two of them are clean out of sight. Yes sir, he deserves one big pat on the back for bringing this off!

A movement at the shop front brings Harrison bolt upright and excited: Yeah, here he is, Shop Boy, right now, staggering under the cartons round to the side, and

121

Grocer Man, not lifting a finger, deserving everything coming to him. When he sees Mrs Grocer take off her coat, all bang on plan, he knows it's a half-hour to action stations. It gives him all the more satisfaction to see the light come on up above as she tramps upstairs, and he starts to feel he is part of an unstoppable process gliding smoothly to its glorious end. He lights up a cigarette, cool as you like. So what if he is seen, don't he and the guys just hang out here all the time?

And now he allows his mind to wander – along carefully controlled lines, of course. Stealing the slippers is one thing, but turning them into greenbacks is another. Weird stuff like these shoes, it's gonna have to go through the hands of people who know other people, and a cut will come off each time. That's the way it is. Even so, a cut of a million is big bucks. Harrison moves on to the misty contemplation of what he would do with a quarter of a million dollars. In this he is not quite so realistic. In no time, he has conjured a big, swanky house with a pool and an annexe for Great Aunt Crystal. In the twinkle of an eye, he is travelling down to Coney with the guys in the next most desirable object of his fantasy, a big shiny Hummer. The imagination is a peculiar thing, and Harrison sees himself at one and the same time driving the wicked machine and getting high in the back of it, having fun with sexy women who simply cannot resist a cool black dude with dollars hanging out of his pockets.

It takes something out of the ordinary to shake Harrison from his daydream: an old yellow cab pulls up directly outside the deli and sits there with the engine running. For five grinding minutes he is left fretting and wondering if this is the thing that will throw his awesome plan. But then Grocer Man comes out of the door carrying a big old bag, which has appeared from nowhere. Then she comes out, and Harrison notices that she is wearing old-woman's Sunday best under a smart blue coat, with a brooch over her heart, her hair pumped-up and her lips all red. Then into the cab she gets and away it goes, with the grocer standing waving at the door. OK, so she's off on a night out, maybe to see that skinny mean-faced bitch of a daughter who sometimes comes round the place. Either way, all to the good: one less person to get in the way of things. This thing is going to happen; he has made it so.

He throws down his cigarette butt, takes out gloves and eases them on. He's pretty sure they would never go to the cops, but best take care. He pulls the beanie down under his hood, runs his hand along the bladed side pocket, feels the flashlight heavy in the other. From far-off St Dom's comes the striking of the hour. Can this be the moment? Seconds later, Shop Boy comes out, zipping his top, wiping snot on his sleeve, hits the sidewalk, picks up his heels. Shit, he's getting away! But just as he is about to disappear in the dark, here comes Grocer Man, sticking his old turkey head round the door, bang in the nick of time: 'Wait a minute, young man!' Shop Boy stops in his tracks and turns round, slow and heavy, cheated of his liberty. 'Hmm, are we not forgetting something this fine evening?' Harrison watches hungrily as, stiff and controlling, the grocer man reels the boy back in, beckoning with a crooked finger, like some cheesy old storybook character. Puppet and master, boy and man, line up and turn together for the alleyway.

Now, the moment is now! Breath-catching, heart-pounding, Harrison does it – runs like hell, runs like fury, across the road, into the doorway. He flies the threshold, trips and stumbles. Along the counter he goes, between the racks, between the cases, seconds ticking. The smell of bleach, cheese, bananas. Things flash by him; things in rows, things in colours. Easy, steady, take it slower. He comes to the cold store, frantic to remember: where's the door? There's the door – get it open! He grabs the handle, turns it, fumbling. He sneaks the door open, slips inside and gently shuts it. All falls quiet, cool and quiet – just the sound of his own breathing. All is stillness – dark and stillness, dark and nothing.

So they're his now.

■ ◆ ■

Harrison smiles softly in the darkness. Everything going just beautiful. Listen: there goes the shop door, the grocer wiping his feet on the mat – the damn mat that nearly had him over! Then footsteps, clattering across the floor like a train, followed by the sharp clack of the counter-flap. The grocer man back where he belongs. And now he can just make out the sound of the TV, *The Daily Show* and all the laughing. He slips the flashlight from his pocket, shining it away from the door, the beam bringing up the void. He sees he is on a narrow landing – a heavy stairway dropping straight down from it, with only a rope for a rail. It didn't used to be like this; the old stair must have rotted away. He counts the steps – twelve – and picks out the shelves spread below on the hard stone floor. Jesus, if he had run any further he would have gone right over. He angles the torch down onto gloomy rows of high shelves grey with boxes and trailing away in the dark. It reminds him, as it always used to, of those spooky underground tombs in horror movies. He turns in, gripping the rope to descend – not a clunk, not a creak – counting the steps until he feels cold stone beneath him. Down the gap he inches, pigeon-toed so as not to brush against anything. He arrives below the shelf, on top of which sits a million dollars in a golden box. Now to find the stepladder. He points the flashlight back at the stairs, then one by one down the rows. Where the hell is it? He tiptoes back to the shelf, takes hold of an upright, feeling its strength. Could it hold him, could the boards take his weight without giving way? He peers at his watch: twenty-two minutes to go. Easy now, settle down and wait. Gently, he pulls out a large carton – boxes of washing powder, the smell of it friendly somehow – and makes a seat of it. From this low position, though, the shelves loom all the more, like tombs. He shivers, craving the familiar and the ordinary, tunes his ears to the far-off TV, straining to hear it. Who they got this time on *The Daily Show*? Some crazy senator going on about guns, or some big wheel got caught with his pants down? Harrison relaxes, comforted by the pleasant fuzz of voices.

With a deathly judder, he wakes. Jesus, he has slept! He jumps up, tries to read his watch, but the dial is lightless in the dead black. Then a sound: a roll of steps above. Is that the grocer going out, or coming in? Then comes a weighty rumble, a jarring of wheels. He is bringing in the stands, thank God. Hurry, hurry, on with the torch and hurry! Sweat breaks on his brow; something crumples in his guts, the torch nowhere, not in hand or pocket; it must have dropped from his hand when he slept. Harrison pushes out his feet, scrabbling blindly in the dark, crabs right, crabs left, an age blind scrabbling. Then his foot rolls over something and he squats down, takes it and switches on the light, his hand tight-fastened. Hurry! The old man must not close the shop and lock the shutters! Harrison flies down the row, takes hold of the post – to hell with caution! Up he swings, up he clambers, feels the woodwork twisting and straining but holding. He reaches for the top, finds its dusty coldness, hoists up his face to see above the rim, both hands clinging. And there it is! Hanging on, one-handed, he stretches out his free arm, shuddering with the strain, until at last he has it. So, down he clatters, the frame creaking but holding, and jumps the last foot to the floor. And then it's to the stair and slowly up in silence. He reasons that the old man must be in the cold store, unless the door is already locked! He shunts open the door a crack, peering down to the counter and beyond. Nothing, but at least the shutter is not drawn. And there he sees it, the cold-store door half-open. So he is in there. Clutching the precious box, Harrison tiptoes quick, like a cartoon cat, comes to the door, ears straining. For sure, the grocer man is in there; he can hear him coughing. So now to dash across the doorway, run and risk it . . .

A funny thing happens: just as Harrison sprints for the gap, the door flies open and smacks him square on the forehead. Staggering back and looking faintly surprised, he drops the box, and then out comes the grocer, looking equally surprised, a big butcher's knife in his hand. Harrison puts his hand to his searing head, pushing back his hat and exposing his face to the old man, who asks, amazed, as anyone in the same situation might: 'What you doing?!' Again, despite the fact that here in front of him is the dangerous boy, all hooded and the hatbox lying on the floor in front him, he demands again to know, 'What you doing?!' And he raises up the knife, an exclamation mark.

Somewhat dazed, Harrison sees only the knife, a blade to slice flesh from bone. His eyes narrow: he hates this knife, he cannot take it, he will not, the old man raising it to him like this. 'Put down the knife!' he says, and takes a step. 'Don't raise no fucking knife at me!' Michael stiffens, heart pounding, his hand higher yet, but wondering if he could ever really use it. 'I said, put down the fucking knife!' Harrison's hand moves towards the dagger sheathed in his own pocket, but then he glances down and sees the hatbox lying on its side and empty, the lid fallen from it. The shoes have been taken from it! He begins to shake, all the anger that was ever in him rising and seething, every ounce of pain and hatred. The injustice of it – that this disgusting old man should have the slippers still and dare to threaten him with a knife. With a roar, he snatches up the box and, raising it up two-handed, brings it down on the head of the old man, who shields his head and instinctively retreats into the nearest space, which happens to be the cold store. In the panic of the moment, Harrison slams shut the door and throws over the flat heavy bar, forcing it behind its iron hasp. The old man shouts dumb in the glass of the door's soundless panel, his face written over, first with anger, then with unbelieving. Harrison, meanwhile, stamps the useless box flat, riding out the frenzy of anger that is in him, until at last it is spent and he can collect himself. Close to calm again, he pulls down his beanie, puts up his hood, walks up front, opens the door and turns out the light before letting himself out into the night.

And in the cold-store door, the framed contorted face is yelling all the while, far away yelling . . .

■ ◆ ■

So now the boy is walking, striding oh so fast, expelling from his hurting self every dumb-ass thing he ever did and every thing that ever gave him pain and every hateful person that ever put him down. He never meant nobody harm, but if somebody were to come between him now and what he wants, he would stand and fight and give them back the hurt that has been his. No two ways about it, he could kill if they tried to stop him. The days he spent setting this whole thing up, the time he gave, the watching and the waiting and the time-biding. Fuck them all!

Harrison is a confused young man and knows it, through and through, because everybody has told him so since he was five. And so he lives with it and deals with it in all kinds of complicated ways. The pain is still in him from the deli and he longs to shed it fast. Fool he is, for not realizing that they put the slippers in the safe, and fool to risk his hide over an empty stinking box. So fucking slow of brain and body – how could he be so dumb? Fearful thoughts come to him: will they let it go or will they come after him, the grocer man and his nagging wife? Would they dare to call the cops? He kicks a can, kicks it hard at a car, then kicks again, his foot arriving against the fender, taking empty pleasure in feeling the smooth, shiny metal give. Serve them right for having such a swanky thing when he has none. In all of this, not once does it occur to Harrison that a man is trapped inside a chiller and he's the only one who knows. His action was one in a whole bad bunch of actions and all those actions are tangled up with other people's badness. Striding and seething, he lights a cigarette, snorts dragon's breath. He wants a hit and wants it hard. Arriving at the Avenue, Harrison sees the Park gates shut. He runs over, sets his hands to the rail. He will cut across to his friend Finn, get some rock, and maybe later on he can get round to doing some thinking . . .

■ ◆ ■

'Come back! Come back! Come back here now, you fucking crazy, crazy, crazy—!' Michael yells. When all remains still and silent and he realizes the kid is not coming back, his anger turns to disbelief and he calls, pathetically, 'Stop this, goddam you, you can't do this!' And finally, he falls into deep amazement at the sheer cruelty of his fate: 'Crazy, crazy bastard!' Then comes a more primitive worry to set the blood pounding in his head and the breaths stabbing in his side – a fear of the deepest darkest kind, as it dawns on Michael that he is inside a locked cold store with the temperature at minus five. But he will not let panic get the better of him: 'Slow down. Calm down. Don't give way. Slow the breathing, let it go . . . Now, bring back the brain, make space to think. Just keep it, keep it so . . .'

The controls are outside on the wall, he recalls, and his best shot is to break the glass and reach through. On the floor is the knife, where he dropped it, the one object of any use. He takes it up and slams the hilt against the glass, smashing it clean out. He reaches through, straining for the control unit, but even with the knife in his hand he comes nowhere near. He retracts his arm and scans the space again. What can he use to extend his reach? Just sides of meat and hams hanging on hooks, carcases, dead-cold where he placed them, and wisps of vapour, his own breath held curling in the air, the beginnings of his own ghost. Ugly thoughts take shape: at five under, how long does he have? These sides of meat, four hours it took them to freeze. As he is a living, breathing thing, it should take longer, but maybe less if his brain starts to go. He should breathe slow, keep warm, but he's in his T-shirt, and he curses loudly to think that he removed his top so as not to get hot shifting stands. Heat goes from the head more than any other part of the body, he has heard. What was it, 30 per cent? Some fearful statistic? Fingers trembling, he removes the apron, rolls it loose, wraps it around his head and ties it under his chin.

The knife is cold already in his hand, and the thought leaps in him that the metal walls are all wrapped around with ducts. Maybe he could stab all the way through. Pierce just one and the freezer dies. He lifts up the blade and brings it over hard at the corner of the wall closest to the control unit. It doesn't give, but a dent is made. Encouraged, he swings over his arm in the same place. It gives, definitely gives, and looking closely he sees a tiny hole, though there is no hiss, no yielding of the machine. He aims for another spot – maybe, just maybe . . . He makes another mighty stab, but it ends in a jolt down his arm and a ping of steel: the knife is broken, the tip snapped off, gone brittle in the cold. He throws it down, appalled, the peril deeper yet in his guts. Someone will come by, surely, even if Grace is away. Someone will come along, needing milk or pasta or pet food and hoping for him to still be open. Yes, and then he will shout and all will be well. He stands stockstill, his ear at the hatch, listening for sounds: passing steps, a car, anything. He can just about hear distant traffic, he thinks, but nothing else. Even so, he will stay right where he is, keep calm, run on the spot and every ten minutes shout for help – starting now. He pumps up his lungs, pushes his chin up to the hole in the door and bellows as loud as he can, 'Help!' And then again, 'Help! Help! Help!' And he starts to run, a damaged bird hopping foot to foot. Someone will come. Surely they will – they cannot not!

■ ◆ ■

Time is the healer and the bad things have all fled. Harrison's dealer, Finn, who happens to be a nice guy, invited him in, which has never happened before, and they have spent the last hour and a half together, getting weightless and shooting the breeze. They have argued about who is the best hitter, Pujols or Mauer, and who is the sexiest singer, Beyoncé or Shakira? And after that they put the world to rights between them. OK, crack has a bad name, but it can make a person feel better about things, which is a thing that people simply do not understand. And all that shit about drugs damaging brain cells and stuff – nothing but politician talk, getting ordinary people insecure about themselves and making demons out of guys like them. They would do well to consider that so-called bad things in life can keep a man from doing far worse.

When at last Harrison is let out into the drizzling night, he feels good about himself and has worked up an appetite. He is almost looking forward to going back home, even if it means listening to Aunt Crystal going on about the old days and Jesus and stuff. She's a good enough soul after all, and can be a comfort. Just watch, she will have something 'plated up' for him, ready to go in the oven soon as he gets in.

As he takes the shortest cut for home, a smell of other foods frying seeps in through the rainy haze, causing him to glance across and take in a scene he knows so well he sees it before it is in sight. There, outside the day centre where the sidewalk widens, is the night kitchen of the Elim Tabernacle Pentecostal Church – a grand title for a battered old food-trailer and two trestle tables under a rickety canopy. One customer alone is there – a wasted-looking guy who, by his clothes, doesn't seem too far gone, but by the fact that he cannot sit up straight even to drink a coffee, plainly is. Harrison lowers his head to walk on, but then he sees a pretty black girl about his own age emerge from the side door of the trailer, carrying in her hand a bacon sandwich – the source of the aroma – which she places on the table in front of the man. She makes a homely remark, her voice round and musical in the night, hoping to bring the man to his senses – at least those required for eating a sandwich. Then she goes behind him to prop him up and even places the sandwich in his hand, guiding him to raise it to his mouth. Harrison watches fascinated: this girl cannot be for real; she is too young, too beautiful for this. He crosses the road and stands at the counter until the man, un-sensing of her kindness, slumps forward like a fallen statue, his forehead pressing the sandwich to the plate. She goes back to her place in the trailer, wiping her hands and smiling: 'Well, that's one way to keep your food warm.'

'What you doin' here?' he asks right out and as dumb as they come.

'What am I doing here? Well, I would have thought that was pretty obvious.'

'How come I never seen you here before?'

'How come I never seen *you* here before? Can I get you a sandwich?'

'I don't want no sandwich. Whaddya think I am?'

'I dunno – a nice guy passing by late at night who might appreciate a sandwich?' Then she smiles, to raise a smile from his own defensive face. And he goes on to tell her in no uncertain terms how he is no street bum; how the Elim Tabernacle is his Great Aunt Crystal's church, and how, a few times when he was small and she was better on her feet, he had helped out here. Like her, he had served up soup and slopped down tables, but then Aunt Crystal's arthritis got real bad and stopped her going and other things took his time. In all this talk of Christian fellowship, Harrison doesn't get round to mentioning his fondness for crack. Instead, he asks her name.

'Rain,' she says, with simplicity to match her beauty.

'Rain? Like what come outta the sky?'

'Like what's landing on your head right now.'

'Rain. Cool. That's cool. So tell me, why you do this?'

Slowly and thoughtfully, she answers the question she has never had to answer before. She explains to Harrison that she does this because of her faith, because she too belongs to the Tabernacle and has met his great aunt and thought that she was cute. Harrison smiles and falls silent. He does not mention how that same sweet old lady once stood by when Uncle Henry whipped him buckle-end first with a belt, and him descended from slaves. And how, when he had later questioned Henry's Christian kindness, she had shrugged and said, 'The Lord moves in mysterious ways.'

'But it still don't explain nothing. Like why you choose to do this over any other thing?' he begs to know, persistent.

'Because it's good and it does good.'

'Give good to people and they pay you back in bad.'

'Give good to people and maybe they will find some good inside themselves.'

He points at the folded wino: 'No way. Look at this guy here, you put food inside this man, he gets a free meal, that's all. Any money he can beg, borrow or steal from someone, he will use to buy more booze. And that's the way it goes. Believe me, I know.'

But her shining spirit is not deterred: 'True, it's the way it sometimes goes, but I believe, I *have* to believe that always in my life there is someone who needs me to be good, even if I don't know it at the time. It's why we have to do it.'

'We? Speak for yourself.'

'I speak for all. Believe me, there is always someone who needs us more than we know. If you stop to think about it, really think and shut out all the crap, you will see there is someone in your world right now who needs you, totally needs you to be good.'

He almost laughs out loud. As if he could ever do good in the world, as if there was someone who ever needed him. As if . . . then it hits him, a sledgehammer; it hits him and turns his smile to thunder.

'What is it? What's the matter?' She gawps as he swims back slowly from his mind's dark swamp and whimpers: 'How . . . how cold can it get . . . inside a refrigerator?'

'What? Is that some kind of a weird philosophical question?'

'It's a totally fucking real question. How cold is it inside a refrigerator?'

'I dunno. Cold that's for sure. But why—?'

'Could a person die if they was in a refrigerator?'

'I guess so. Yes, of course.'

'How long would it take?'

'To die?' By the fact that the lonely boy whose name she doesn't even know has turned practically white, Rain knows it's no silly joke. 'Hours, minutes – I have no idea,' she says.

'Shit!' he says, and takes to his heels.

■ ◆ ■

He gave up jogging on the spot a half-hour ago, his chest so tight and his legs so stiff and shaking there was nothing left in him to give. So now he falls back limp against the door, sweat creeping cold under his clothes and his ears ringing from yelling, though he has no idea if his cries reached through three inches of insulation. In his despair, he begins to hallucinate, the

walls closing in and the light from the bare bulb dropping down from dismal to tomb-dark. Even if by some
miracle someone comes, he has been delivered into
wretched places inside himself that he has never owned
to before. How pathetic he is, whining and squirming
– one moment calling out for some kind soul to come
and rescue him and the next hurling obscenities at the
same imagined person and every other hateful bastard
in the stinking world who failed to hear his cries.

His heart starts to race again, and once more he
works it down, slows his breathing to nothing, no longer
to think clear and stay smart, but just to have some
grip on who and what he is beneath the spiralling fear.
'Slow down!' he snarls at himself. 'The more it beats,
the more you die; the more you shout, the more you
die; the more you move, the more you – no, no that
can't be right. Oh God, which is it, what am I supposed
to—?' In the end, he gets so tangled up trying to have
a single clear thought that he simply has to let all his
thoughts go. And so, seizing in the brain by seconds,
Michael Marcinkus slides down the wall, surrendering mind and body, all of him, to the winter-hard floor
where thoughts that have been coiled up in him for an
age start to unwind and seep away.

And so he is taken from the frozen hell he is in
towards the other unspeakable time and place where
once before the cold came close to taking him . . .

■ ◆ ■

'Keep going, Mihails. This is how we find things. This is how we stay alive . . .'

He follows the rasping voice through the fog of time and sees his father, as large as life, a blunted hatchet in his hand, bringing it down as forcefully as his famished body will allow, upon a heap of rubble. Ice is everywhere – in the cobbles, iron-hard and treacherous; in the rubble suffocating under the weight of snow; and in the houses, what is left of them, hung with icicles and frozen to the last brick. Winter has stretched out its icy hand even here, across the vast stinking spit of waste that is the city midden. In warmer times this land has been their hope and their provider, but now it's seized by an icy spell, cast to cheat the starving of their last scrap.

'The winter will leave and the Germans with it.' His father smiles, the low sun in his face, making his ravaged features appear all the more dire. He looks like he, too, has been claimed by ice, in the straggles of his beard, in the glassiness of his eye and in the pallor of his skull-stretched face. 'It took the Russians and it will take them. Just you wait and see.'

The Germans will soon be on the run – that is the rumour. He has heard it on other tongues, not just his father's, so maybe there is truth in it. There has been a breakthrough, hundreds, thousands of miles away, they say, and the allies will come. They are like the sun, the Nazis, cruel and unforgiving for their season, but one day a new sun will rise to take their place, and they will fall out of the sky and be no more.

He turns, eyes narrowing against the same pallid sun that lights his father's face. He can look straight at it and not flinch, but even so it taunts with its faraway brilliance. So what if the Germans should fall one day? They are starving here and now. Everyone is. Why can the sun not lend them its heat and melt through this damn ice, so that he might find a potato or two, or the rotten end of a cabbage to take home to his poor suffering mother?

■ ◆ ■

Normally, the Park is full of phantoms for Harrison. He hates to cross it at night, the trees looming and reaching, the moody waters ebbing and clouds passing, moon-troubled. But as he runs at the very stretch, the ghostly things are no more than backdrops flashing by, and all the images of terror are inside him. He sees the grocer laid out stiff, shaped ice-hard for a casket. Then he sees him preserved forever in a frantic pose: the twisted face, stubs of fingers worn to bleeding where he flailed and scraped.

Vaulting the far fence and weaving between hurtling cars, Harrison prays unashamed, prays the horror story went a different way, that the grocer woman came back not too late and let her husband out, that the grocer has a special key for tight spots like this, that there is another door he didn't even know about. But as he runs the length of 99th, his mind is all stabbed through with self-reproach. How could he forget leaving a man in a freezer, a thing so real and shocking as that? How could he have walked off and just gone about his business? He must be crazy, insane, and all they ever said was right: no better than a space-wasting, mother-fucking crack-head psycho!

Turning towards the deli, seeing its frontage ever-sharpening out of its dark surroundings, he slows his step. Even in his urgency, fear winds him down. The shutter is still raised – she did not come back; the old man cannot have escaped; he's dead! Fear crawls cold around him. He ducks below the shutter, pushes open the door – how come nobody noticed? – and sneaks along, fearful, for the cold-store door. In all the darkness, his eyes are drawn to the centre panel casting out a sickly smear of light. The glass is out: there are the pieces. The old man must have smashed it trying to escape. Harrison half hopes to see the seething face in the frame, but there is nothing. He straightens up and steels himself to look through the stark hole. Nothing can he see but hams hanging and wicked hooks. He bows his head, rocking between the choices. It could not be simpler: walk away, let death be and hope it never comes back to haunt him. Or stay, open up the door, see death if it is there and hope against hope for life. He straightens himself, throws the handle and hauls open the door. Stepping in he sees no sign. Thank God! Maybe the grocer did find a way out. But then he spins round and sees it, there, that slumped heap, that bundle, neither death laid out, nor mangled horror. Marcinkus the grocer sits against the wall beside the door, his head, with the apron wrapped around it, flopped over to the side. His legs are stretched out before him, as if he were an infant sat down tired at kindergarten and gone to sleep.

Harrison pulls off the apron and squats to look into the face. The eyes are closed and the face is bluish-pink but not yet terrible. The signs of life – what would they be? Where should he look? He reaches for the neck, the jugular, puts two fingers there, as he has seen them do in the movies. No way of telling – his own hands too warm, too clumsy in this cold and with the savage pounding in his heart, his head. He tries the wrist – impossible yet to tell; lowers his head to bring his ear to the grocer's mouth – maybe he would hear breathing, but no. He forces himself behind the body, scoops it to him and drags it out into the store, which is warm, comparing. He lays the grocer down flat on his back and runs to the counter. There on a hook, a shop coat, a towel and a woman's coat! He rushes back, throws the garments over the torso, rolling up the towel to make a pillow for the head. Then he sets to, rubbing, massaging each limb, passing to it his own quivering fever, and all the time hugging at the corpse, gathering it to him for warmth and for dear life. After a while

he has to stop, short of breath. He hears something –
a living, moaning sound? Or is it just what happens
in the movies when a dead body is moved around?
He slaps the face this side, that. No good. He brings
himself full over and, taking breath for two, fastens his
own generous lips around the grocer's sagging mouth
– isn't that how they do it? – and blows and blows
again, and feels the pricking of the old man's bristles,
sees the swelling of the chest with his own breath. He
stops, looks for life, prays to the Lord and goes again in
measured seconds – one last try before surrendering to
the fact of death. Then, from deep inside the deathly
frame comes a shudder, then a jolt, and then a stuttering string of breaths: the corpse alive! Harrison pulls
back, eyes wide, and sees the grocer's own blue eyes
flutter open to catch him there in slow astonishment –
two men seeing each other in a moment they will both
remember for ever – Lazarus waking to meet the gaze
of his saviour and his assassin.

For the next five minutes not an action is taken and
not a word is said, the grocer stretched out, fighting for
every creaking breath, the frightened boy standing by,
transfixed and wondering, What have I done? Where
does this go? Astonished to see fingers twitching and
muscles flexing with new feeling, the old eyes blinking
as the numb brain comes alive to time and space, and
draws together the fragments of memory that had blown
apart. Harrison glances into the hateful freezer. A side

of beef hangs dead centre, and on the floor a fallen knife, the one the old man had raised at him. Then he sees it. Spidery capitals, scored crude in crimson into the hanging meat, a three-line poem shouting murder:

HARRISON DID THIS
BLACK BOY NOSE STUD
ONCE WORKED HERE

The old anger surges in him. He takes up the knife, slashing at the words to obliterate them, leaving a craze of lines in their place. A whimper comes from Michael behind him, struggling to prop himself up on an arm. Harrison runs out, hissing, his eyes flashing accusingly, 'You shouldn'a writ that! It was an accident! I didn't know what I was doing!'

At last the old man's lips shape themselves around words, pressing them, aching and separate, into existence. 'I . . . I . . . was . . . dying.' Harrison's fury melts to see a fragile man returned to life. Michael scrabbles like an insect missing legs, not feeling his feet as they fall away under him. 'Help me,' he gasps, twisted and shivering.

And so Harrison knows that the grocer will live and maybe, just maybe, he will not go to jail. He rushes to the counter and lifts out the chair. As he drags Michael into it, his cheek against the cold of the face, he has only one thing to say: 'I saved you. Remember that. I fucking saved you!'

■ ◆ ■

He lies in semi-darkness, a pool of light still spilling from the open freezer doorway. He heard Harrison's footsteps go out the door, heard it close shut, heard him bring down the shutter to shield the scene from prying eyes, heard the steps outside fade to silence.

None of it is real and belonging to any world he knows; he cannot yet fully connect the events that led to this moment. A full five minutes it takes to link the parts to the whole: the door flying open and springing the wide-eyed boy from nowhere; Harrison raging at the sight of the knife; Harrison wild, the hatbox raised above his head; Harrison, lips like suckers, clamped around his own. Finally, Michael begins to understand the surreal narrative into which, like a sleepwalker, he has strayed and played his part and come so close (again) to dying. And once understanding is in place, common sense also announces itself and Michael realizes he has to get himself upstairs – God knows how – and get himself under the covers. Summoning the will, he prises himself out of the chair, judders to the stairway, cranking the seized pistons of his legs to take the steps one by one, and then lurches under his own dead weight along the corridor and into the bedroom, where he falls like a toppled statue on the bed. Thankful to the bone, he pulls the covers over himself and surrenders to the great warm nothingness.

CHAPTER SEVEN

S T Dominic's Roman Catholic Church is not an inviting place at the best of times. The Victorian Gothic facade itself is grey and faded, and to pass through it from the brisk city into the vaulted gloom within is to make a choice between the bright world and the dark, to recognize death within life, and to wish to discover the reality beneath the world's glittering illusions.

James made no such choice. If it were left to him, Paolo's farewell would be held in a green and shining place, next to a rippling stream, in a sun-filled meadow. Such places exist – natural burial places or whatever they are called. Before the end, he had even allowed himself to imagine a send-off for Paolo, seeing himself as the main mover in the airy ceremony and the wake to follow. Both of these would be joyous events to strike a perfect balance and bring together Paolo's gay friends and family members. But it hasn't been left to him. In the past six days, not one of Paolo's relatives has been in touch, and he knows that he is not welcome at the ceremony in any shape or form. The truth is they have taken the whole thing from him, right from under his nose; everything that would have been within his power to mark Paolo's life; everything swiped away from him, including the body! All so that James could not claim any kind of ownership or leave any imprint of himself on what remained of Paolo.

It has taken every ounce of James's willpower just to put on his clothes today and assume a human appearance, consisting of black suit and tie, white shirt and cufflinks (though he would have preferred something more informal). But he has decided to play by their rules; he will give them nothing to confirm their ridiculous prejudice. As if he would turn up veiled and rouged, a grieving drag-widow awaiting her moment to throw herself wailing over the coffin? No, he has taken over an hour to dress, with immaculate attention to detail, his appearance so much the man. And so James arrives below the forbidding arch, under the eroded gaze of an angel, and enters the place, pale and shaking in his dispossession. At the inner doorway an usher hands out the order of service and directs mourners to their places: 'Are you with the family?'

James stares back, stricken, confronting the hideous truth concealed in the question, 'No,' is what he eventually mumbles, and is pointed towards the central pews. His eyes adjust to the amber light cast by inadequate clusters of candles, straining to fend off the encroaching dark. The church is close to full, and James shuffles into a row between a phalanx of backs in front and ranks of faces behind, stiff and pink, like flower-heads poking out from so many smooth black vases. He recognizes nobody. In how many different pockets of his existence did Paolo ever get to know so many people?

An organ plays, uncoiling a string of notes to wander the void as thin and insubstantial as life itself. At the altar stands a priest in a shining white cassock, but silent and bowed, the model for us all. Hanging shockingly behind him is the buckled image of Christ's agony. It takes an age for a minute to pass. James allows himself a sly turn of the head, eyes wandering to seek out familiar faces. Old friends will be here, he is sure, but dispersed among the many, as isolated as he is, and as Death would have it.

A sudden tumble of chords escapes the organ and becomes an avalanche of sound, swirling into the darkest reaches. The priest raises and spreads his arms for all to stand, and in comes the procession. An assistant priest leads the way, holding high a shining cross, and behind him, a boy in robes, swinging incense. Then comes a funeral director in a top hat, tied around with a black bow. With a dramatic backward lean, he marches a slow monstrous swagger, the metronomic ticking of a black cane across his chest with each fateful step. And then – cold claw to the heart – the coffin itself, carried by six bearers. James hasn't reckoned for it. How can it be? He has been so undone by the family's stealing of the corpse and their imposition of these grim rites that he had forgotten there would be an actual dead body. Dead bodies and funerals kind of go together, but he simply hadn't factored it in. The priest begins to intone and the coffin is set down in front of the altar. The six men peel away to their places among the family. So many to carry Paolo in death and so shamefully few that ever stood by him in life. He strains to see between the rows of heads; he must see it; he must force himself to look at the coffin, stark on the catafalque. How can his lovely Paolo possibly be inside that thing? It should have been a cream-white box splashed with huge corn-blue polka dots, a spray of sun, clouds and sky, a great bird in flight even – anything but this hard, dark thing, like a clumsy piece of old furniture, polished to a shine and put out for a quick sale.

Now it is all in the hands of priests with their liturgies: hymns to be sung and prayers offered. James sits, stands, kneels with the congregation and sings in the hopeless way that goes with funerals. He makes the responses in mumbles and snatches, all of these dredged up painfully from his own Catholic upbringing. And the eulogy itself – unbearable, brutally impersonal and making no reference to anything that Paolo ever did after the age of twenty-one, as if the rest of his life amounted to nothing. No mention of his successes and his wondrous flair as a designer. The cause of death is, of course, skirted around: an unexplained 'affliction' a sudden tragic end following complications. These awful evasions, as if Paolo had committed the sin of suicide, which in some minds it would amount to.

The tribute peters to nothing, and all glory is heaped on Father, Son and Holy Ghost. It dawns chilly on James that no one is going to speak out and recapture the Paolo that he and others know so well. If he had been allowed to arrange things, there would have been no end of friends to step up and bring to life again the real things, the moving things and especially the funny things that came from Paolo. There would have been music, too: Peggy Lee singing 'Fever', something from Cole Porter, and a fair share of Paolo's beloved Johann Sebastian Bach in among The Duke, The Count and The King.

As the service nears its end, James catches sight at last of someone he recognizes: Steve, Paolo's brother, who he once met in a bar, though little was said. Next to him are two shorter, older people, the mother and father whom he never met. Under any other circumstance he would see them as good Italians, good New Yorkers and no doubt good parents who somehow got short-changed through no fault of their own.

The words of the final blessing ring out, remote and comfortless. James's sense of banishment is so complete that he decides there and then that, unwelcome as he is, he will not go to the cemetery and join the family for the final committal to the ground. Paolo's sweet spirit has long since fled the scene, and James cannot bear to think that there will be no opportunity for him to express the tender things that he knows would come out hot and twisted if he ever dared to say them in such a place, in such company.

Leaving the church is purgatory. The brother and the priest have taken their stations at the door, hailing the mourners streaming between them. James lowers his head as he passes, avoiding the shaking of hands. Maybe the brother doesn't recognize him anyway. But he can't help overhearing the comments of others offering their respects, speaking in cleansed voices. 'That was beautiful,' says one. 'Lovely service,' offers another. Walking down the wide church steps, James starts to cry, no longer caring what anyone thinks, emptying himself of old bitterness but opening up new hollows. He weeps not for Paolo's loss but for the failure of the world to offer good things in memory of a good man.

A hand falls on his shoulder. He turns, confused, momentarily disappointed not to find Paolo's lean, wistful face, but discovering instead Jack's round face fixed on him, the eyes doleful, like a loyal dog's. Too defeated to express his annoyance, James soaks up Jack's bland condolences: 'You OK, James? It must be terrible for you. I saw you in there, but I couldn't get across to you. There were other guys from Woody's, too.' Caught in Jack's earnest gaze, James still can't make head nor tail of the guy. Jack drops his head to stare at his feet, saying bashfully, 'Speaking of which, we could go there now maybe – unless of course . . .'

'Oh no, no, I'm done here,' James insists, glad to draw the line between himself and this deathly place. 'I could use the company right now.'

■ ◆ ■

Pain being the enemy of reason, Siobhan goes through her cell phone again, every nook and cranny where messages might lurk undetected: the call logs, the text boxes and the voice mails. Nothing – not that she really expected anything. She removes the cover again and shakes the battery out, just in case. She knows she is being ridiculous but it hurts so much; it has been hell just to drag herself out of her room and back into ordinary life again. Siobhan barely notices when her mom comes skirling into the kitchen and opens the oven door, but when a swirl of smoke is released, the acrid snatch at her throat makes her hot with protest: 'Mommy!' Fumes are in her eyes and lungs, but Corinne is in too much of a hurry to apologize and cooking is always an unwanted chore.

'This oven is useless. And on top of that I am no kind of cook.'

Siobhan coughs fit to die – the more to make her mother suffer. But Corinne is unmoved: 'Ten minutes, Shibby darling. Keep an eye. And lay the table, please.' And she bounds out of the room to attend to some spinning plate elsewhere. Siobhan is in no hurry to leap to the task.

Nothing – two whole weeks and not a word. Not so much as a text! How could he do this to her? She throws the phone at the one soft chair in the room, and it bounces off and onto the floor. Her own father! He promised, took her number, wrote it in his own phone in front of her eyes and vowed to contact her the very next weekend! It is totally shabby and, yes, disgusting. She was forced to lie when her mother oh-so-casually 'wondered' if 'he' had been in touch at all – meaning, of course, that she knows Corinne is totally screwed up by the very idea that James could get to her, and is just itching to get something on him to show him up as the contemptible piece of work he is. So Siobhan has lied, telling her mom, of course, he had called her and the two of them had shared harmless daddy/daughter talk, and that he would ring again the week following.

So now she cannot even share her feelings with her mother; cannot get the rage out where it belongs. She asks herself, if she did share the truth with her mom, would that be such a bad thing? Why should she defend him when he can't be assed himself? Why shouldn't she betray him to her mother so they can both rip him apart and spit like witches over his good-for-nothing maggot-ridden carcass?

She cannot get out of her head that last sight of him before Mom whisked her into the car: him standing on the sidewalk outside Pizza Paradise, or whatever it was called, rooted to the spot with his phone, far away, like a lost boy for all the world to see. It was stupid of him to take the call like that, of course, just as she was leaving, but she knows it must have been to do with his sick partner, and, putting two and two together, well, it must have been kind of bad. She should, then, be a grown-up and accept that this is not a good time for him, as he had said. But the fact is she is *not* grown up and this is *not* just about how he let her down in the past week or so – it's also about how he's cheated her for the past seven years. Had someone died every week in his life? Had there been a whole procession of tragedies that had kept him away from her? And even if Corinne did throw him out and he was the scum of the earth, was he always so weighed down with sorrows that he never stopped to think about his simple duty as a father? After all, she needs him just as much as the man in the hospital needs him, the man who might well be dead for all she knows. And anyhow, why could he not at least have let her know? It would not be beyond him to ring or text and tell her that he would be back in touch soon as things looked up. That would be giving something, allowing for the possibility that she was there for him to share things with. But to say nothing, that surely said everything about his real priorities. Even worse, maybe it said that she was never truly in his thoughts in the first place, that for him she did not properly exist, even though she had taken the difficult and painful step to reach out to him.

Reflective now, she thinks that it's maybe all the worse because she'd actually liked the person she'd met, her father James. It would be easier after all if she had hated him, if he had been the puny creep of her mother's making. Yes, on balance, now she has had time to think about it, she had liked him. He was pleasant-looking for a start – shallow to think of such a thing but plenty of fathers were not good to look at and she liked his neat, likeable features, blue eyes and silky brown hair. She liked his quiet, easy voice, the evenness and good humour that added up to an intelligent and, well, OK man. 'Pleasant.' Is it the best she can say for him? She has had friends who were pleasant, and yet were vacant and sometimes as treacherous as cats. A father should be made of stronger stuff; he should be dependable, brave and above all true. She wonders if pleasant James might also have these things in him, but then who is she to say what a dad should or shouldn't be – she has been without one all this time. Still, she can allow that James might also turn out to be a good dad.

Corinne comes running back into the room, not quiet, not good-humoured, not pleasant, and dives into the oven again. 'Shit. It's gone way over. Why didn't you tell me?!'

Once again, fumes everywhere and Siobhan wheezing and hacking. Corinne grabs a cloth, fretting and fumbling to rescue the hissing dish, and burns her hand: 'Shit! Ow! Get the . . . Quick! Get the—!' Siobhan, simmering, slides over a mat for her mother to drop the dish onto. Her best intentions come to ashes. Corinne whines, 'Look at it. Don't tell me you didn't even lay the table!'

While Corinne runs cold water on her hand, Siobhan, sprightly all of a sudden, grabs cutlery and mats and lays them like a dealer with a hand of cards. But Corinne has lost all patience. 'You coulda done that before now!' Elbowing Siobhan aside, she slams the food down on the table. 'Look at it – ruined! Well that's what you get when you rely on other people!'

Siobhan is seriously pissed at her mom now: how dare she transfer the blame onto her! As Corinne scuttles back to the refrigerator in search of a salad, she cranks herself up, ready to spit: 'Excuse me, Momma, but—'

But then, right on cue, Corinne steps on the

discarded phone and skids, almost doing the splits as her legs splay comically and, with a demented shriek, she clings to the work surface to stop herself from going down flat. Siobhan laughs, despite her anger, and Corinne's attempts to haul herself up to a more dignified position are all the more hilarious as she keeps declaiming, tragically, 'It's not funny!'

Seeing her daughter in fits, Corinne is even more in need of a target for her venom: 'Damn phone. Damn, damn phone!' She shrieks and kicks it spitefully – the hateful handset, the contaminated thing, containing everything she detests: his influence, his presence and everything she wants kept out of their life together, for ever. What a dumb-ass thing was that, leaving it on the floor? She drags herself over to the table, plants herself hard in her chair and takes up a serving spoon. 'Well, shall we at least attempt to eat the burnt offering?'

How monstrous is this: the blame back where she first pinned it? Siobhan loses her smile; she was prepared to see the funny side and let it go, but now, seeing that her mother will not yield, she lets her have it with both barrels: 'Don't blame me, bitch!' this shouted so loud and sudden and unexpected that Corinne sits there, stunned, while Siobhan raves on: 'You're right, you're a useless cook. And there is nothing wrong with the oven, by the way, but you are a shit cook and this is total shit!' And with that, she marches to the door and out of the house.

Corinne takes a second to catch up with the state of play, then jumps up and runs over to the door in time to see Siobhan heading up the drive towards Kelly's. 'Christ!' she says to herself, baffled as much as anything. She looks down to see Siobhan's phone lying on the floor. Slyly, she shuts the door, picks up the cell, flops into the chair and carefully, painstakingly, presses the keys, trespassing into all the poisonous places he could have implanted himself: call log, text box, message box. Place by place, window by window, she searches for his sugary messages; his creepy overtures; his whiny, self-pitying voice.

Nothing. Not a sign. Strange: there are other bits and pieces of communication, mostly nonsensical, from Kelly and others. But from him, from James, or *to* him, there is not the tiniest jot.

■ ◆ ■

James downs a last drink. In a short while he will pull the shambling parts of himself together to go home, though not so unhappy as when he arrived. Everybody has been so wonderfully kind. They bought him so many drinks that he still has several untouched, lined up in a row at the bar. And Woody's itself: friendly and luminous, with long cinnamon-brick walls hung with jazzy abstracts. The guys, the regulars, have been so lovely. It touches him, as it has always done, just to look on from his place at the end of the bar, into the cosy space that opens out from there, and see them all ranged around the piano, singing their hearts out. He and Paolo couldn't hold a note between them, but they always loved to come here on Friday nights and soak it up. Some of the guys who sing here are pros – chorus-liners, names even, or were, once upon a time. It has always been intriguing, compelling at times, to watch a person just walk in off the street and take his place among fifteen or so other guys around the shining old baby grand, all poised and ready. And, in an instant, everything outside would be gone. It has been moving to witness that moment when, without a word, Rick the pianist would strike a chord, a couple of beats for recognition, and, as one, they would all start to sing. This was not just ensemble singing, one voice lost among many, it was each man singing to the pitch of his emotions, matching his own joy, his own sorrow, his own sense of what is true to the music. Beauty, truth and showbiz – a cheesy combination, but here somehow it was meaningful. 'There's a Place for Us', is the song of the moment. James has already been treated to 'Who Knows', 'Officer Krupke' and even 'I Feel Pretty', sung entirely without camp self-consciousness. *West Side Story* was way out in front his and Paolo's favourite musical, and it warms him to know that they sang it this evening for the two of them.

Jack, clearly something of a secret performer, has been in the thick of it since they got there – in among the rest and singing so naturally and at one with it all that James concludes that he must have been there all those times before. James squints blurrily at the clock: is it really that time already? He places his glass back on the bar and gets up to go. In a flash, Jack comes hurrying over to help him into his jacket. 'It was a shame about today,' he says. 'Everyone here loved Paolo. You know that.' That does it: James shakes his head and starts to cry, dropping back down onto his stool. For the next half-hour, it pours out of him – all the hurts and the injustices; how he had gone to the hospital the day after, trying again to see Paolo, only to find that *they* had already taken him away. 'The body, for Christ's sake; they took the fucking body!' How *they* had put the phone down on him when he tried to make contact. But worst of all, how *they* ignored what Paolo would have wanted, allowing no concession to the reality that the two of them had lived through all this time: 'That was cruel; that was evil; that was downright un-Christian,' he sobs to the uncomplicated youngster.

And, having got all these bad things off his chest, James moves on to the things about Paolo that no one ever really noticed, or had just taken for granted. James shares what he has never really shared with any other person before: the finely inscribed expressions of love that had passed between him and his dead lover and, at the end, the erosions that had reduced Paolo's spirit to its palest flame.

'It must have been awful for you,' says Jack.

Awful doesn't come close to describing how it has been. Even now, inside this warm, friendly place, he is staring into the void. But then, pulling back from the brink, he takes one of the glasses and slings it back. 'Have a drink,' he urges Jack while reaching for another. 'Or two, or three, or four . . .'

'Steady . . .' Jack puts out a hand, making James feel like a corrected toddler. Although they work at the same place, he hardly knows the guy, and now he begins to regret having revealed to him things that were sacred and personal.

Rick's nasal voice rings out from the piano room: 'This one's for Paolo!' and a blazing chord strikes up. The chorus close their eyes and begin to sing 'You'll Never Walk Alone' from *Carousel*. Jack looks across at James and, seeing James listening, enthralled, he hurries into the throng and starts to join in, bright and beatific, with the wash of voices. But when he looks up a few bars in, a smile already formed on his face to bestow on his sorrowful friend, of James there is no sign. He is gone; he could not remain so cold and hollow in so bright and friendly a place, and has slipped out and away into the shadows, where he belongs.

■ ◆ ■

Crazy days: thoughts tumbling and turning like particles inside a broken kaleidoscope, never settling into any shape that makes sense. Michael Marcinkus stands at the deli door, looking out at the street, but inwardly reliving, as he's done since waking, the terrifying events of the previous night. He has felt again the last desperate pangs that made him cut those words on a frozen flank, and that same sinking into submission as the cold closed around him like a vice and, inch by inch, squeezed his spirit out.

Not surprisingly, he's still dog-tired. He hadn't woken till an hour after dawn, and then he had to go down and start another day as if all was right with the world. The physical toll on him is bad enough, but what really shakes him to the core is that the Harrison boy should know about the slippers in the first place. How could he have known about the hatbox and what it contained? It has even entered Michael's mind that Benjy is somehow involved in it all, but that just doesn't add up.

Then there's Grace. She'll be back at nine and in no way is he looking forward to looking her in the eye; she has a knack for seeing through him whenever he's been up to something. So now Michael makes the superhuman effort to clear up the mess before she gets back from Brooklyn – sweeping up the glass, hiding the flattened hatbox behind Barrell's kennel, taking down the side of meat and hacking those dreadful scars into oblivion.

In readiness for Grace's arrival, Michael places himself behind the counter, keeping up as normal an appearance as he can muster. But when the taxi draws up, his heart almost stops, for there, sitting in the back alongside Grace, is Jenny, and little Sylvie too. Two pairs of eagle eyes. He wonders exactly what Grace has told Jenny about the ruby slippers – everything, probably. However, it's him Jenny's concerned about as soon as she sets eyes on him. 'Poppa, the state of you!'

'I came down with a sudden cold and took to my bed,' he says, a little hastily, though it was true enough! There's another hairy moment when Grace asks about the missing glass in the door. He explains it away casually, saying he had stupidly put the mop-handle through it, though by their raised eyebrows he can see it doesn't quite wash. Later on, when Jenny is out the back, Grace comes up to him and asks quietly, 'Michael, what happened here?'

'I told you,' he says, giving nothing away. 'And what about you? What did you do?'

'We watched *Casablanca*. I love that movie.'

'Oh yeah and what else? Did you happen to get round to talking about the slippers?'

'Michael. Really!' she says, meaning, *How could you possibly not trust me?* But her protestations are as half-hearted as his have been. And so they both agree, without saying it, to cut their losses and go about their chores. He is lifted a little out of his despondency by the experience of taking little Sylvie round to see Barrell in the kennel, so luminous is her delight. And he manages it through to lunch, despite Jenny asking him every five minutes if he's feeling any better, if he needs a hand with this or help with that, and if he wouldn't rather go upstairs and lie down. He does, in fact, agree to this, at least to go and eat from a plate and sit in a soft chair – another departure from the norm that doesn't go unnoticed.

All morning he's been plagued by their questions, spoken and unspoken, yet when he finally allows himself twenty minutes to flop out on the couch, it's the questions within Michael that keep rearing their ugly heads. Grace and he never had secrets, so why not just get the whole twisted story out in the open? The boy was dangerous and a criminal, and even if they didn't go the police, it needed to be faced up to. Just thinking about it now makes his head spin and stirs up a kind of nausea, in which all kinds of feelings are bound up: in the first instance, guilt about how he and Grace came by the slippers, and in a deeper sense, fear of how everything goes dark and rotten at the last.

As he comes down the steps, he finds Sylvie stretched out face down, wriggling and gasping as she tries to reach for something in the gap between the shelving and the floor. Michael squats to bring himself to her level – not too sick or too old to share in the excitement of a small child. But when she eventually extricates herself, she has in her arms the hexagonal lid of the hatbox, raising it up to him like a prize, with the lining turned towards him. A shade brusquely, he takes it from her, then glances right and left to ensure there are no prying eyes. 'Thank you, honey,' he says and tweaks her cheek. 'Do me a favour, will ya? Go along to the candy shelf and choose the bestest candy bar you ever wanted.' She looks at him, flabbergasted, in awe of the wonderful prize that is to come, but then her expression changes as she looks down at her knee and sees there a trickle of red. Glass – she has knelt on glass from the broken pane. Her face crumples and she begins to wail, bringing Grace and Jenny running. An almighty kerfuffle follows this, in which he is made to feel almost as though he put the glass there on purpose. He manages to smuggle the candy bar to Sylvie in the end, but by the time Benjy arrives for work, he is ready to crash out again.

Back upstairs on the couch, he finds himself reflecting on the many strange things that have happened in so short a space of time: Rosa's accident, then the robbery and being taken back to those terrible old times – let alone nearly dying – and all so painfully secretive. But he will not give up; if anything, all this suffering has made him even more determined to see it through; he will go back there, first of all to do what is right, and then to go through Rosa's things one by one, to find the missing bits of him and put himself back together again.

■ ◆ ■

Four days only since she went to the city and it feels like a year to Siobhan. It has all gone by in a daze. At first Corinne was wounded and chiding: 'You should've told me, Siobhan. It hurts me that you didn't trust me enough to confide in me.' And then she let rip with the black propaganda again: 'Well, at least you got to see what kind of a spineless creep the man is.' Of course she is hurt still, but Siobhan can't forget what she saw: that for all his faults, James is real and there were things to like about him amongst the things not to like. She feels better about the fact that she has been inside his home and seen Paolo's photograph on the mantelpiece. So, her father has a partner who is a man; he is gay. It doesn't seem so hard to say any more, she can live with it, and she has gone back to the ordinary way of things: going to school, seeing her friends, telling them how she went to Manhattan and why. There has been no comeback; she even went out on Saturday to the cinema with Kelly and the others, and there wasn't a smirk from anyone. Even so, the pain inside her will not just lie down and die. It has nothing to do with anyone else on earth, just him and her, father and daughter – about how she felt so small and childish and softly loved him, and then was told not to love him, and later was told to be hard and cold about him, and that he was never coming back and was never capable of being a man again. But her need is righteous; it demands to be satisfied, and she will take it up again as soon as soon as another chance presents itself.

■ ◆ ■

'Excuse me, where did you say you were going?'

Three people are lined up at the counter, but Grace just ignores them, shoots out after Michael and stands there blocking his path.

'You heard what I said,' he mutters.

'No, Michael, I musta misheard. For a moment I thought I heard you say you were going to Rosa's.'

'Just to do the necessaries, Grace. It won't take long.'

'Send in the clearance people and be done. That was what was agreed!'

Glancing back at the customers, Michael shakes his head irritably; she has no right to react so outraged and make her feelings so public.

But she will not be shamed into silence: 'Let it go, I'm telling you! All the crap in that place you could walk in there and never come out again.'

'Grace, listen to me, we're talking documents, papers, things that should be kept. Bank details, stocks and shares, who knows?'

'Stocks and shares? Since when did she have stocks and shares?'

'Since no one knows. That's why it has to be done. We cannot let these things go to the garbage. Go serve the customers, Grace, I won't be long . . .'

This he says right out loud and walks away, which has the customers all agog. Grace scuttles back to her place, red of face and simmering like a hobbled pot. He won't hear the last of this; she will not let this go. Michael is smarting hard as he goes round to the side alley, mad at himself for stopping to hear her out. He buttons his coat, takes the dog and sets off, under his arm a roll of garbage sacks wrapped around a hand shovel. A wind is shaping up all troubled as he scuffs along, shaking his head, oblivious to the tug of the dog. Really, Grace should know better, why is she being so damn intolerant? What really upsets him about it is that she's behaving as if Rosa was already dead and buried, when all the time she is lying in the hospital. Whatever her past sins, she is a human being who lived a meaningful life, and you don't just throw that away without preserving the best that was in it. In truth, he is at odds with himself over it all. What difference should it make to him if Rosa's crap was to go? The place is in a dreadful state, after all, and can hardly be left as it is. Also, if he is honest about it, there is something selfish in his need to stand up for Rosa, and he can't help wondering whether Grace would take the same stand if he were the one lying in a coma? That night at Rosa's he had caught sight of so many old papers and the like, some of them in the old language, and he has a growing desire to know them. If there is any light to be shed on things after all this time, Rosa's apartment is the only place on earth that holds the answers. A person should know their own history. How else could they ever claim to be complete? Michael's anxieties start to subside as he pushes on, and he even begins to look forward to the task: going through things, sorting them – things in and things out – it's what he does every day after all, just a little more unpleasant. He will start with the real crap, throw it into sacks and stack them to go. That way he can keep an eye out for papers and pictures and God knows what.

By the time he stands again, staring across the layers in Rosa's apartment, he has adjusted to the idea that, when he goes in, rottenness will spill, odours will spring and things will crawl. Big to small, that will be the rule. Furniture first, to its own heap, then all the way down to clothes, books and the black matter that once was food but has long since eaten its way through its wrappers and joined with everything else that was dark and sludgy. He ties Barrell to the door handle, pulls the shovel from the roll and peels off sacks: green ones for clothes, fabrics and anything that isn't too far gone; black ones for everything taking up space, like books and orna-ments; greys for everything foul and decayed. Through clamped teeth he sucks a hank of fetid air and wraps his arms around a pile of blankets stained piss-yellow. Into the sack they go. Spluttering at the mouth, his lips all slack and trembling, Michael takes up the shovel and thrusts it in, heaving in the spillage. He turns back for a second load, and a third . . . which is when it dawns on him and he pulls up, open-mouthed, astonished: 'My God! This . . . this is where it all started . . .'

Garbage people they called them – scum who lived on scum – their daily toil to crawl over and comb through the garbage heap that was the fallen city's rotten heart. The Jews had once lived here; it was their quarter, before they had been shipped out and their homes levelled. An estate of waste had formed where once there had been houses. And to it had come the rats, the dogs in packs and the human pariahs, like them, to pick their way across its contours, soft and giving in the warmer months and hard and unyielding in the winter. His father, Janis, was a simple man, in truth an ignorant one, who only dug and carried for his living at the best of times, who saw reality for what it was and made no apology for what he did. He was beyond caring about the smell he carried with him everywhere, or the fact that he traded in shit. They worked the garbage or they died, there was no other way; it was their daily lot to sift life from death, literally. And if they chanced upon more than was required for their own continuing existence, they set it apart for those who had the means to pay, and haggled and lied and wrung it out, hiking their price according to the degree of their customers' desperation. So they survived on starvation's crude capitalism, where hunger was the index and death the market leader.

Michael stands, reeling in the rank atmosphere of Aunt Rosa's room, his old head nodding helplessly. No wonder he had erased that awful time from his mind: it was for shame. And yet it staggers him to think that he could have stowed away in his forgetting so basic an experience, so hard a reality ingrained. Yes, he has been here before, and many times over, and all when he was such a little boy – another reason to have clean forgot.

■ ◆ ■

It is past closing time when he comes in the door. She looks up from the counter, where she has been smouldering ever since he left, sees the old battered suitcase under his arm and raises an eyebrow in place of words. He is in no mood for talk either: 'Later. I'll show you later. I'll go bring up stock.' He doesn't tell her how much pain he has endured, how prising open one terrible memory had brought to the surface so many others, how his own history repeated had left him exposed again and suffering.

At the basin at the back of the store, washing his hands over and over, far beyond need, Michael's mind is on ghastly things. He should be thinking of filling shelves with tagliatelle and sun-dried tomatoes, but instead he is seeing soldiers coming to the house and kicking the door in with their jackboots, seizing his father right in front of him and his terrified mother, and cruelly ripping him away. In the middle of putting sticky labels on jars of conserves, Michael winces to recall how, even as he was marched away his father had looked back and smiled, which only made his face all the more a skull and his body a corpse for a quick-lime grave. And he and his mother both understood, without recourse to words, that they would never see him again; they didn't need history to tell them he was gone for dead.

By the time Grace reminds him to go out and bring in the racks, Michael is drained. Sixty-five-year-old memories and they are fiercer and more consuming than those seeded only hours ago. But he does not say a thing. When Grace hangs up her shop coat and says, 'Time to go and rustle up something.' He smiles and says, 'Righty ho.' And when she says, 'What's in the valise, by the way?' He just says, 'Ah nothing, old papers and stuff.'

When at last he can hear her clumping up the stairs, he lifts the suitcase from behind the counter and opens it up. Inside are scattered sheaves of papers, all of them in a language he no longer knows, some letters and two photographs: the one he and Grace had seen on their first visit, of Rosa, glamorous and beautiful, and another, much larger, with words written on the back in the same writing: 'June '41 Monterey'. He turns it over and there is a woman in soft monochrome, naked – stark naked and completely unselfconscious. Waves are rolling behind her and she is on the deck of a yacht.

One foot is off the ground, her hands reaching skywards and her head thrown back with hair flying. It is as if she is matching her body to the elements, the whole pose abandoned, charged and yet not really sexual at all. Michael stares, eclipsing all the sullied memories of his ancient aunt, and sees that in the moment this picture was taken, Rosa was her natural self – she was free – and that as much as any image of her could be, this was the real Rosa. It must have been after she came back from California and took up with Gerry Clyde, the photographer, who must have taken the picture. 'Look at this,' he says to himself. 'Look at this; how did she go from this to such a sad old stinking person?'

'Are you ever coming upstairs?' Grace's voice cuts down shrill from above, shaking him from the story. With a sigh, he folds the sheets again, slips them back into a sheaf and into the envelope, then throws it in the case. He fastens the clasps, takes it round to the other side of the counter and pushes it to the back of the shelf below. It is his business, his secret; he has never really told Grace about his past before America, not the full horrible reality of it and how there was no innocence ever after. She would never truly understand because, even though she had grown a little sharp and cynical over the years, she had always held the belief in her heart, and still did, that there was good in the world to hold onto.

CHAPTER EIGHT

HARRISON comes out of Finn's place mad as hell. The last time he saw his dealer he was all smiles and high-fives. This time the guy had a bug up his ass, haggling over every grain, mumbling at him for off-loading small change and only too glad to see him out the door. He was feeling cool and mellow before he went in there, but now he feels mean and restless. It is only the thought of maybe running into her – Rain – that makes him feel anywhere near good. He has kept an eye out for her on his night-time walkabouts, and has come across one or two people at the night kitchen who knew her, but had no idea when she was due, and others who did not know her from Eve.

Tonight, approaching the stand, he is more hopeful. It's a week exactly since that weird night. Aunt Crystal always used to do shifts every seventh day, so her turn must be coming round. The night kitchen is busy and four or five guys are there with two dogs growling at each other and having to be held apart. At the counter is a married couple from the Tabernacle – weird how you can tell them, both pint-sized and dressed like for church. The woman flips things on the griddle, while the man splits burger buns. Harrison strolls over: 'Excuse me, but I was hoping to see a young lady who works here sometimes.' Smiles fixed, unspeaking, they gaze back at him. 'Her name is Rain.' They glance at each other, then turn their stares on him. 'Do you know her? Does she work here still?' There is a pause before the woman volunteers, very correctly: 'Rain is our daughter. She's studying at the moment and really has no time to be out.'

'Oh . . . does that mean she—?'

'And might I enquire who is asking?'

'Um, my name is Harrison. My great aunt is Crystal Parry.'

The woman's face looks blank a moment, then, as it comes to her, her face spreads to a smile: 'Oh, my goodness – Crystal Parry!' And then to her husband: 'You know Crystal Parry?'

'Crystal? Course I know her,' he replies gruffly. The woman points suddenly in Harrison's face: 'I remember you! You came to Tabernacle sometimes . . . Well how are you? Harrington, isn't it? Gosh you've grown! You shoulda said who you was.'

'We thought you musta been some kinda . . .' growls the father, and Harrison suddenly sees how he must seem to them – 1.30 a.m. in a place like this – it doesn't make him look like the boy next door; he'd better make it sound good: 'No, well, I was just – I, uh, come down to offer her a hand. Last time I seen her she was all on her own.'

'That was a mix-up. It shouldn'a happened,' mutters the mother, firing a resentful glance at her man.

'So you saying Rain is staying in these days?'

Here the father sees fit to bring the conversation to a halt, raising his hands and declaring: 'That's about it. You wanna see her, Sunday's the day. You know the place.'

■ ◆ ■

Yes, it's a relief to be ordinary again, doing ordinary things. All those days taken off seemed necessary at the time, but James wonders now if it didn't just drive him deeper into his own loneliness. What with the funeral itself and the soul-searching and the crying and the sending of thank-you letters to those who sent their condolences – sentences composed with care, all reasonable and elegant but never speaking to his own aching self. Not to mention the chaos: the forgetting of the names of days, the abandonment of routines, of waking, wrecked in one day's noon and prowling sleepless in the dawn of the next. And if that wasn't enough, the restless searching for a way to remember his beloved, which had led nowhere and still was not resolved. At least he had the common sense to let it go for now.

And so, all this behind him, James goes back to work. The way things have been, it's not so terrible to get up at a fixed early hour, to choose clothes to wear, already pressed and hung. To take breakfast – eggs, toast, coffee – allowing time and space to digest and gather things together and hear the national news, which fell away for all those months and lost all meaning. So now, to walk along the teeming street with unknown others, breathing in the spring air; to descend into the subway in common purpose; to hop on a train and give up a seat and hang on a strap – these unremarkable articles of existence adding up to affirmations. And then, as the carriage rattles in the tunnel, to gaze upon so many different faces, the permutations of race, age and experience written on them, the thoughts and feelings of separate beings turning in the orbit of every head, and to entertain never-to-be-answered questions: where did this person come from; where would that one be going? And what desires might be in this one's heart? To be possessed of such ordinary curiosity, that in itself is good.

But as James pushes open the heavy door of the East

Harlem branch of the New York Public Library, of which he is director, he comes face to face with his own hollow visage in the glass. Foreboding fills him, chasing away his sense of ease. For these two weeks, how did they manage without him? And why now should they need him back? And as for circumstances, will their show of sympathy be real, or will it mask resentments, dark, complicated emotions? James knows himself to be insecure, a child in need of pulling itself together, but at the end of the day, his anxieties are real. He lets go of the door, straightens himself and steps in, walks past the empty reading desks awaiting opening time, past the racks containing the day's papers, so shining fresh he smells the ink. Looking across, he can see Jack waving at him from the top of a ladder set against the high shelves at the back. And there at the counter, unpacking new books, is Marcia, his deputy and loyal friend, who gushes, 'James. Oh, darling James!' She comes around and plants a kiss and all is well. He takes comfort and later on takes coffee with her and all the other workers, with cookies set by for the occasion, shared between smiles and consolations. But as always there is the feeling that such delicate strands of harmony can be unpicked and easy lightness be outweighed. The library, like the city, is prone to forces prowling and sometimes slinking in at the wrong door. Even in this place of quiet reflection, chaos can enter and order be undone.

The first wave arrives at nine: those who rise early and are well into their ordered day: the respectable unemployed, the unjustly redundant and the retired – first-come to be first-served by quick-fire internet connection and newsprint hot off the press. Then, around ten, arrive the later birds, the more relaxed about their plight: self-styled students, researchers and inventors, those who once had solid purpose, but who now live in hope against a tide of hopelessness. Come eleven comes the third wave, the feckless and the dispossessed, there to surf for scandal, pore over sports pages and travel features – 'Fifty Best Bars' and 'Beaches to Die For' – crumpled columns idly thumbed by those who have never sipped at cocktails and haven't seen the sea in years.

A woman staggers in, fat and ragged and smelling of drink. Eleven in the morning and she is already smashed beyond reason. James groans out loud – this person is notorious for being disruptive, for singing at the top of her voice. He watches as she flops across a chair at the back of the reading section. He prays that she will just go to sleep; at least the snoring would be tolerable. But sure enough, within five minutes of coming in the door, the woman is top-billing at the Carnegie, opening up with 'Private Dancer' – this sung not so bad, but raw and fractured and all the more pathetic because she's singing for an adoring audience in another place and time. Straight off, this sets the regulars bristling. James sends Marcia over to reason with her, knowing she will not answer to a man. Nor on this day will she listen to anyone. By the time she has moved on to the next song in her repertoire – 'I Will Always Love You' – reasoning has given way to warning, and she is told to 'stop the racket or else', which of course meets with increased defiance. As the woman unleashes 'Jolene' upon the long-suffering library community, James has no option but to call the police, though done with a sigh, because he knows that it will take up to two hours for them to arrive. It's a long time for his readers to be made to suffer, her sad outpourings somehow tapping the despair that lurks in every human psyche. And even then there will be remonstrations with the officers, a refusal to go quietly, followed by lavish abuse for him and his staff, before finally they can remove her from the place. By lunchtime, he and his team will be worn down, and if there are other incidents, as is the way of it, by closing time they will all be on their knees, not so much undone by honest toil but by the daily infections of other people's pain.

James does not notice one more black youth sitting among the rows. Harrison arrived at ten forty-two, placing himself somewhere between the inventive and the indigent. But in truth he has not set foot in a library since he was in high school all of two years ago, and even then he wouldn't enter such a space unless they made him, and he never knowingly took down a book from the shelf. He is there when the drunk woman wanders in and starts her pathetic singing, but he doesn't give a damn. For today Harrison is on a mission: to find out all about the objects of desire that have consumed his thoughts since he saved the grocer's life. There has been time to take stock: no one has come after him, not police nor anyone else, which surely means he's off the hook. The more time between that weird night and now, the less likely anyone will be to pin it on him. Harrison has even spied on him in the past two days, strutting around in all the usual places and doing all the usual things. How could the old man know how close he was to death, or if he was in the cold store five minutes or five hours? How would he raise the evidence, except for a broken pane of glass, which he himself knocked out, and his own wild slashes on a hunk of meat?

Now it's all about the shoes. All is not lost. If what they said that night was true, he can make the situation work even better for him. He hits the keys: 'ruby slippers'. First thing he sees: 2,160,000 results. The next thing to catch his eye: 'ruby slippers stolen'. This gives him the real jitters. Paranoid, he checks over his shoulder, but seeing that all attention in the room is directed towards the wailing drunk, Harrison turns back to the screen. Clicking the link, he discovers that in 2005 the slippers were stolen from the Judy Garland Museum in Grand Rapids, Arizona – insured value $1,500,000!

But it's a mystery: how could there be two pairs if the stinky woman came by hers seventy years ago? He reads on to find that at least twelve pairs were made: four known still to exist – one in the Smithsonian. This is big stuff – a cool million and a half to be sure! Getting even more into it, Harrison uncovers all kinds of crazy stuff about the shoes: replicas for sale all over the net; some cheap, some at crazy prices! And theatre companies, cookbooks, jewellery – every kind of website you can think of, going on about how these shoes are magic and mean all kinds of shit to countless people. Most of it, as far as he can see, is put up by crazies – gays especially, who he hates. They all seem to be obsessed and have some kind of kinky thing going on about Judy Garland, who is the big 'gay icon', or so the writing says.

He looks up and sees it's gone twelve. An hour and a half he's spent wading through this stuff and never did nothing like it in his life – ain't he the scholar! The trashed woman is still there, and he can see the library staff whispering together and looking at their watches. He falls back into his own thoughts: *The Wizard of Oz* – something happy and sad about it at the same time. He remembers first seeing it when he was six. He kind of liked it – the funny characters, the wicked witch and the songs – but never was over the moon. It always comes around at Christmas and Great Aunt Crystal always tries to catch it. Nothing but sentimental, Uncle Henry used to say, but she never cared and tried to get him to snuggle up and watch it with her anyways, which always gave him a good excuse to leave the house.

As Harrison walks out the library entrance, two cops come striding up the steps in his direction. He holds his breath, but they don't give him a second glance as he slips by.

■ ◆ ■

Five days in a row, Michael Marcinkus goes to the apartment of Rosa Petraidis and sifts, shovels and carries, clearing the chaos that is outside him and within. He is Hercules in his labours, he is God making the world. And on the sixth day he meets a man there and pays him to take away the heaps of sacks and the worst of the furniture and the foul mattress from her bed. And he is left to take up mop and bucket and change the plug on the ancient Hoover and bring it screaming to life, taking away the last of the sins.

On the seventh day he stands in a room with a couch to sit on and a rug on the floor, and on the mantelpiece a clock whose hands move at least to give an approximation of the time. In the sleeping area is a bed, although wanting a mattress for the time being, but the wardrobe is back where it should be and a table is in the kitchen-space, with cooker and cupboards containing pots and pans and essentials. A person could live here; they could live with dignity.

He calls at the hospital on the way home, and stands blank at the foot of her bed, until at last the words come: 'Rosa. It's me, Michael. Listen, don't take it hard, but we went to the apartment, Rosa – just to clean, you understand, and sort out some things. And, well, there was things in there, a lot of it that was frankly unsanitary. It was a hell of a mess – you realize that? It was bad, Rosa, and, well, you just can't keep a place like that . . . Anyhow, some of it I had to throw, but only what was too far gone . . .' He drones on, feeling small, confined in spirit, afraid there is nothing in him worthy of saying, that his emptiness is no better than hers and that all his foolishness is somehow visible to the woman-corpse-alien lying on the bed in front of him. 'I tell you, Rosa, we can make it nice and clean and cosy. It's a fine apartment under all that and we can make it really nice. Maybe Grace and me, we could come round for tea and bring you something nice from the deli.'

Where do these words go, he wonders? How far do they reach? To his own ears only? This shell of a person, does it hear a single thing? Is any kind of mind in there? 'But listen, you gotta know this – the slippers, the ruby slippers, we found them, we rescued them, and they're safe.' Does any of what he's saying matter at all, or is he just a stupid old man talking to himself? It is so strange. A body is there: the dome of her head, the shell of her body and, inside it, the slowed clock of her heart – organs and parts in which a billion thoughts and feelings have sprung in their time, but lying now, silent and unknowable.

'Anyways, that's about it. It'll take me a couple of visits to get things shipshape, but don't worry, Rosa, it'll all be fine.' He stands back, his piece said, and watches and waits, just in case something behind those closed eyes might amount to a person who could also be watching and waiting. 'Ah well . . .' he says finally, and seeing no sign of anything in the petrified face, raises his hand, gives a little waggle of his fingers, as if saying goodbye to a child, and walks away, leaving the emptiness of her there upon the bed.

And yet something is there, something of who she once was – in her and of her and around her – the imprint, the dense but invisible traces of her being, the remembered energy of her contained in the void. And preserved, stored in that energy, is the order of her life, her story.

And this exists, too, in another place, for once, many years ago, when she had lucid moments among the crazed, when she had the benefit of time and space among the clamouring days, Old Rosa wrote her story down and left it in a place where even now it waits to be found and unfolded to he or she whose fate or fortune is to find it . . .

■ ◆ ■

185

Malachi McBride gazes out over the city that made him and in which he once had such purpose. He puts his hand square on the bench at his side, feels the coarse grain imprint on his palm. He reads the already faded plaque on the rail: 'Nancy Taylor, taken from us 2003. A woman who loved Central Park as she loved life'.

'Stupid woman,' he says for the ears of Donna Inez, who also stands gazing out at the great city. But even he enjoys going to the Park if it's bright like today, and he is not dead yet to passing things: the freshness of the air, the scent of pine. But he does not love life, not any more. There surely will be no one to raise a plaque for him, not this Filipino nurse-woman who he has cruelly used, not his own son who he hasn't seen in years. And what would it mean anyway if he were gone to worms? People are stupid and sentimental when it comes to death. Why are there so few like him, who see it for what it is – an ending and that is that – and who will not cry out for priests and be a hypocrite at the last?

'Onward!' he barks and lurches down the path, the maid ludicrously tripping along to keep up with him. Why does she even bother? Why doesn't she tell him to fend for himself for an hour or two while she goes off to feed the ducks or whatever pleases her? He is perfectly capable of driving himself along and doesn't need her to tuck the blanket over his knee and make him drink water from plastic bottles, so why should she bother?

The chair crunches purposefully along towards the nature reserve, arriving at the brow giving over the west side. In his largesse, McBride allows Inez to catch up and pause for breath. Beside them, two lovers are entwined on a bench. Spring, he thinks. Nature and its ruthless puppetry. The marionettes in question are a middle-aged man in a suit and a bohemian-looking girl, much younger, and they are kissing as if one of them is about to be led away for execution. Inez turns away, her gaze discreet to the end, but McBride, unabashed, manoeuvres the chair even further into their space and pronounces matter-of-factly: 'Rugged but dull corporate guy fucks uppity college chick!' There is a stunned moment, the lovers' lips still pressed together. But then they draw apart, staring dumbstruck at McBride, who gazes back, unflinching, and says, 'That is a hell of a bitch's brew in the making!' The woman is open-mouthed now in disbelief. Inez, too mortified to look either of them direct in the eye, crabs across and slams the chair forward and out of harm's way as McBride calls back over his shoulder, 'Close your mouth, honey, before something disgusting makes its home in it!' The man starts angrily towards him and Inez summons a strength beyond her stature to shove the chair over the brow – and away he goes, flying solo like a boy on a sledge. He has become wicked, she thinks, out of control, just as spoilt children can sometimes become. It cannot go on like this.

It has done James good, if nothing else, to be out in the bracing day, to feel the first touch of spring and exorcise thoughts that have recently set his mind into such a dark cast. He has walked the length and breadth of the Park, loving as always the idea of a wilderness-bounded square in the metropolis. And along the way there have been revelations: plaques and plates he has never noticed before, each, named for someone who had one day stopped living, but whose brief flourishing was now memorized in the growing of trees: beech and birch, plane tree and plum, and over there on a grassy loop by the pond, a tulip tree with its canopy of bell-shaped beauty.

Then there are the benches, some stout and useful, others fine and ornate. The inscriptions here are more direct, offering simple invitations to citizen, passer-by and tourist to sit and share what that lost person once possessed. 'Here was their favourite spot', 'This was a sight they loved', 'The view from here gave them joy'. And encoded in these messages, the deeper exhortation to stop, take pause and contemplate the way of things, the ever-reaping cycle.

James wonders how many of the people sitting along this path – the woman feeding pigeons; the bespectacled black man eating sandwiches; or the old man in the wheelchair and his nurse – have known the person their bench was named for. Would this be their daily homage to husband, mother, father, wife? 'Saul Liebowicz, died 1978'. 'Henry Ellinor, much beloved; 1990'. 'Nancy Taylor, taken from us, 2003'.

He quickens his step, keen to complete his quest. OK, so maybe he won't go for a tree or a bench, but something will come up. Around the keen sweep of path by the pond, he goes, climbs the shining steps and pays to enter the zoo's mock-colonial quarter. And as he drifts between the compounds and the disguised cages that house a thousand species, James learns from helpful notices that many of the inmates are sponsored. Could these animals say something in their yowls and screeches for the dead as well as for the living? Which of these would Paolo wish to be named for? If each of us has an animal alter ego, which one would neat, dark Paolo be – wolf-cub or wildcat, mandrill or marmoset?

He climbs to the highest point within the zoo, a concrete outcrop shaped and textured dirty-white to imitate the Arctic wastes. In his hand is a brochure, all about donations and bequests. He stops to take in the facts and figures of every animal worthy of a donor-dollar, from stick insect to hippopotamus. He is impressed to discover how the zoological people have harnessed science and nature to create conditions for new life: calf, cub and pup to be wondrously conceived and reared within these walls.

He looks down from the highest point at the animal continents spread out below him. Behind him is a great shapeless window of plate glass set in rock, fronting a large water-filled tank. Turning to look, he sees an adult polar bear appear up on a ledge, starting, as if to order, a restless pacing this way and that. And soon James's attention is taken away from the wider view and claimed by the time-tainted bear, so that he becomes lost in watching the demented animal as it thrashes side to side, then plunges down from sight, appearing in the tank to make an underwater encore of the same joyless and never-to-be-undone dance. Plain as day, this is suffering. Animal captivity syndrome, isn't that what it's called? To give money for a creature to be born and live its life forever yearning.

It's pretty much dark by the time James completes his round. He is tired and there's a chill in his bones. But as he comes to the bridge, something alarming happens: hurtling straight at him comes the iron mass of the wheelchair man. He is bang in its path and his heart stops dead, commanding his feet to do the same. The chair comes crunching to a halt and the man in it lets out his own expression of surprise: 'Well, well, well!' And then the nurse arrives, looking at them both, nonplussed, until James stops gawping and says unguardedly, childishly, 'Dad . . . What . . . ? What happened? I had no idea . . .'

'Of what, pray?' enquires the old man in his calm but cunning way.

'Of this . . .'

McBride looks at him with undisguised contempt. 'You look a little shocked, my son. Well, work it out. I sure as hell am not sitting here for fun.' James lowers his gaze – however undeserving of respect this man might be, it isn't nice to stare. But can he help it? The dad that James remembers was fit enough to row an ocean; the dad he sees before him now fills him only with despair – the jaundiced face carved with shadows and everything about him negative and dire. No wonder he's dumbstruck. McBride, though, is not stuck for words: 'So . . . time flies,' he chortles. 'And we're all full of surprises. How about you? What's new with you? Like, are you still a lousy faggot, or did you finally grow out of it?' James hears the nurse gasp to be witness to such casual malice. Outrageous, the old man is as outrageous as ever – cruel, as life has been cruel to him.

'Excuse me, but I think I have to leave,' James says, with as much dignity as he can muster, but his father is unrelenting:

'Ex–cuse–me. Just listen to the mincing little queer.' The nastiness of it, such vile mimicry, so hurtful – making a naughty little boy of him all over again. James walks away, staggers away, everything around him a blur, the old shame galloping inside. He gets to a distance, stops and puts out an arm to brace himself against a wall, his head bowed, his shame on show for all to see.

A still small voice speaks at his shoulder. Inez has followed him, broken away from her master to come and reassure this poor young man, who seems decent: 'Excuse me, I cannot help but hear what was said. He does not mean it. He cannot mean it.' James turns to face her, finding a little of his lost composure – enough to ask of her, 'Tell me, how long have you been looking after that man?'

'Nine months,' she says, all small of voice. 'Why?'

'Because then you know he means it. Tell me, do you care for him all the time?'

'Twenty-four hours, seven days a week.'

'Wow, you must have the patience of a saint. So, tell me about it, what has he got?'

James begins to gather himself and to breathe more freely as she tells him, discreetly and as quickly as time will allow, about his father's disease and how he might have a couple of years if he's lucky. She tells him also about his father's waning powers and his waxing mis-behaviour. And all the time, as she is telling him, she keeps glancing behind her to see how far the chair has travelled, until finally, when she sees it go out of sight, she scuttles away, saying, 'I'm sorry, I must go . . .' As she does, she raises her eyes, transmitting to him a look of kindness, a mother's gaze to a needy child, and turns and hurries away, leaving him there to pull himself together and find his way home.

And on the bridge, looking down on all this, stands

a figure, neat and inconspicuous. Solemn-faced, unblinking, Jack watches, privately sharing in James's sorrow.

■ ◆ ■

All the way up in the elevator, McBride is flushed and talking nineteen to the dozen – a spoilt brat notching up hits on his new catapult. 'How about that?' he yammers. 'Did you see him, that scrawny little piece of piss, that mincing gay? That was my son, *my son*, you understand?' He seems somehow proud of the pathetic fact, exultant, or is it simply his anger and disappointment coming out in such a strange and twisted passion? He turns his curiosity on her: 'You spoke to him; what was that about? Whaddya say to him?'

'I told him that you did not mean what you said.'

'You damn fool!' he splutters with laughter. She says nothing, fixes her gaze on the buttons lighting up with each passing floor. It alarms her to think that his behaviour during their walks has progressed from discreet asides to cruel insults openly directed at anyone who might unwittingly offer a red rag to the bitter old bull. Bad enough to abuse the lovers on the bench, whose privacy he so mercilessly invaded, but to talk to his own flesh and blood like that . . . the son he has not seen since who knows when? McBride himself has gone quiet, as if reading her thoughts. As the elevator doors open, he pronounces, almost reasonably, 'You think

I'm terrible, but I just say what other people think and never dare to come out with. Cripple's prerogative.'

First thing inside the apartment, she fills the coffee pot. He is in the living room, surveying the Park in its dusky glow. He is quiet now, she thinks, but just watch, soon he will start up again, no doubt picking on her family back home, making them out to be oriental trash when in fact she has brought each one up to be God-fearing and respectable. Every day he believes he can buy her off and all his sins will wind back to zero. His 'occasional transgressions', he calls it. God may forgive him, but she will not let him off so easily. 'The park was beautiful,' he calls out, uncommonly sensitive. And then following up with: 'What a shame the rest of life is such shit.'

She sets cup and saucer on the tray and plunges the cafetière, as he pours out more of his vileness: 'You know, if I were in your place I might be tempted now and then to just slip in a little extra something, something to . . . help me along, make it all go away. Wouldn't that be so nice?' Her hand freezes in the act. So, he is coming out again with this terrible talk. 'I wouldn't blame you. I deserve it after all.' She crosses herself against his blasphemy. He has taken to dropping these bombs now and then. It goes to show how wicked he has become.

But it isn't quite shocking enough to stop Inez from doing what next she does. Satisfied that McBride is safe in the living room, she takes a bottle of tablets, Oxycontin, his high-strength painkillers, empties three into a saucer and, with the back of the spoon, grinds them down. All his talking big about killing himself and her helping him on his way, it's all boasting and bluffing, of course, because he trusts her to be the saintly Catholic woman who never thinks such things. Carefully, lovingly even, she empties the granules into his coffee and stirs them in. Strong, bitter Arabica, just as he likes it. Three tablets only, but then he drinks an awful lot of coffee. Normally, he would be right about her being too holy to have such thoughts, but he should never have said bad things about her darling children, so far away, who she longs to hold in her arms. Can he not see that every time he hurts them it is unbearable agony to her? It is like taking poison.

CHAPTER NINE

A ND now, on a quiet Monday, late afternoon, neither windy nor rainy nor cold, Michael sits staring into space. Benjy has knocked off without any inspection of cartons because, for the moment, his boss has lost all enthusiasm for it. Michael sits at the cash register, not even watching TV, because that, too, has gone by the board. On a shelf under the counter is the one practical concession he has made to recent events: a gun, a snug forty-five, loaded and ready. Not that he ever expects to see the crazy kid again, though that is exactly what now happens. Whilst idly gazing out into the street, he sees Harrison walking straight towards him, large as life – the killing boy, the kissing boy, striding cool and casual to the door. His hand goes beneath the counter and rests across the gun. Harrison pushes open the door, wipes his feet, unzips his jacket like a friend just dropped by, and even nods at him in an everyday kind of way. Michael twitches to see how this will unfold, his hand curling around the pistol-stock, turning it to a more useful position. 'Hi,' says Harrison, as if catching up with an old friend. 'Now, listen to me . . .' And then, as cool as you like, he lays it down, sets it out – the situation as he sees it – how he knows that they have the ruby slippers and knows how much they are worth, and how the two of them are guilty as sin. But Michael's guilt is weaker than his anger at this boy: 'You must be insane. Insane! Do you hear me?' he yells, his grip tightening on the gun as he grows madder by the second. 'You nearly killed me!'

'I saved you!'

'You cheeky piece of—!'

'Listen to me. I ain't here to talk about that. I know what you twos are up to and I want my piece.'

'What the hell you talking about?'

'You know full well what I talking 'bout; the fucking ruby slippers, the things you two got hid away. That is what I talking 'bout.'

'I beg your pardon?'

'Don't fucking play games! I was there, you fucking old fool. Right fucking there.'

'What?'

'OK, listen now. Suppose, just suppose someone was already there in her stinking apartment before the pair of you ever got there. And suppose that same someone hid themselves somewhere, like in a wardrobe, and witnessed the whole sneaky thing. You getting with me?'

Michael is so much 'with him' he's practically having a coronary thrombosis, his hold on the gun limp now, his thoughts racing to keep up, his vulnerability sweat-drenched on his puffy red face. 'You mean . . . ?'

'Yeah, yeah, yeah. You starting to see how it is now.'

Appalling, unthinkable is how it is, but even as he stands there twitching, it's a kind of relief to Michael to know that someone was there to see them do what they did, even if it wasn't the Lord God.

'You stole them, man. It's simple as that.'

Harrison brays out loud to see Michael come over so busted. It's a full half-minute before the old man finally gets his act together enough to ask, 'So . . . what you want from me?'

'That's simple: seeing as I saved your life, seeing as we two are in the same business of stealing and stuff, I want my cut, man, and I want it fair and square.'

'And what is fair and square?'

'You and Mrs Grocer on the one side; me on the other. That come to fifty-fifty.'

Michael is suddenly back in the real world again and furious with it, because the boy's money-grubbing, so naked and dirty, shows up his own squalid actions for what they are.

'Now you listen to me,' he says, pointing his finger in Harrison's face. 'Whatever you think you saw, whatever you think is going on and whatever you think these supposed shoes are worth – for something to be worth something, it has to be for sale in the first place, and I don't remember anyone saying there was any such sale.'

'Don't fuck with me! There ain't no sale? You make sure there is, Grocer Man!'

'Get outta here!' rasps Michael, his eyes darting as he sees one of his regulars approaching the shop.

Harrison smiles and heads to the door: 'Don't worry, I'm outta here. You fucking sell them shoes or you fucking done for, old man.' Caring not a jot about the man coming in, he stabs his finger at Michael and has the last word: 'I saved your fucking life!' And brushing past the startled stranger, he storms out and away. Michael shakes his head and mutters, 'Crazy, crazy boy!' And seeing the customer's bewilderment, he turns his thoughts to things more in his power to command: 'So, what can I do for you today, Mr Halliday? The roast beef? Or can I maybe tempt you with the pastrami?'

It's not Michael's finest hour. For all of fifteen minutes he feels elated at having seen Harrison off the premises, but as time goes by, he feels more and more steeped in lies and deception, and curses himself for ever having allowed the slippers out of Rosa's apartment. Only an hour later does it occur to him that had he left them where they were, they would now be in Harrison's possession and nobody would have been any the wiser.

Trade is dead for all of the last hour before closing. Having little to do, Michael looks around for something to keep him gainfully occupied. He flips on the TV and just as quickly flips it off again – such a God-awful babble lately. But then he remembers an untied thread, and ducks below the counter to come up with Rosa's old valise. He opens it up again and settles down, still and thoughtful, to examine the contents. The last time he'd looked in here it was at the end of a monumental day and he had been exhausted; now he can go through it with a little more care and attention. Much of the contents is off-limits still – Latvian papers and documents – but there is an interesting thing amongst them: a yellowing but not ancient letter pad of fifty flimsy blue sheets, wrapped round by a rubber band. It's the kind of pad still used by people who wrote letters before the world stopped writing letters. There is nothing distinguished about it, except for the fact that the words on the cover are in Rosa's handwriting and in English. What makes Michael sit up, though, is the title: 'The Life of Rosa Petraidis'.

He reaches into his top pocket for his reading glasses, slips off the rubber band, flips over the cover and begins to read:

I was not always like this. I did not always live in filth. Once upon a time the world was at my feet.

Writing this I am in hope that words will come which I was never before able to say. The beginning is not so hard and this I write without pain. My name is Rosa Olga Petraidis. With my family I lived in Daugavpils in Latvia and was happy and was never allowed to believe that I was anything but loved. I cannot think of any one thing that darkened my days, although of course my country had been many times close to darkness.

I lived with my father, whose name was Andrejs, and my mother, Jolanta. She was very pretty and, of course, he was handsome, and both of them came from families with good standing, so they made the perfect couple. He had been at Conservatoire in Vilnius and was a player of piano and composer and always being around with important people in the classical music, and some of them would come to our house and play. It seemed all the time that we were much fortunate in our lives and that we would continue to be blessed with such good fortune.

At this time, me and my sister Magda, who was four years older than me, wore fine dresses and went to good schools. The idea that we would ever go hungry was absurd, and always there was love. But then my father started to be less successful for reasons that could not be explained, and the concerts and the commissions started to dry up. So he begins to play for cocktails parties and social occasions. But still, from this time I remember only good things, although my mother now was going out sometimes to work as a secretary. Through all of this my father was kind and gracious, and never once did I hear him raise his voice or let loose his temper, but upon occasion I would see in his eyes the sadness of the man who knows his time will not come and is in despair.

When she was nineteen, my sister Magda left the house and went to Riga to marry a man who's name was Janis Marcinkus, of whom my parents did not approve. He was in business, importing things, though it was never clear what. I remember him as a kind man, always smiling and making jokes, but it was true he was of a lower class and uneducated and was vulgar of speech, and therefore the marriage was frowned upon.

One Sunday, when I was twelve, my father was rowing me in a boat on a lake on a perfect day. If you asked me where was this lake or why we were there without my mother, I could not say. But as he was pulling on the oars, my Papa, he collapsed and fell down across the seats and I was unable to do anything.

202

And being unable to row, I fell into a panic, which made the boat go round in circles. When at last another boat came out, he was lying already dead and I was weeping and hysterical. From this moment it seems to me that misfortune came into everything for us, and it was strange indeed because the history of my country seemed also to decline from this time.

Father left us nothing, and all was turned about because my mother was now the struggling one, having to work like a slave, while it was Janis and Magda who gave the helping hand. They say that beggars cannot be choosers, but my mother remained hostile to Janis, and the more she seemed to despise his ways, the more she seemed to insist on the best in life, enrolling me in a convent school while she worked every hour God sent to pay the fees. And all the time we wore good clothes and ate good food from the best plates. After two years this became impossible and I ended up in a different school that was dirty and noisy, with other children who were rough and who made fun of me because I kept myself so apart from them. They teased me for looking down my nose at them, although it was not really true; I wished only to keep myself from their spiteful ways.

My mother was penniless now and moved to Riga where Magda and Janis were living. This was a city that was not kind to poor people. All around at this time there was money still, but not for us. She was yet an attractive woman and men were interested, but she was proud and always comparing them with a husband who became more perfect the longer he was dead. To me she became cruel and unforgiving with a harsh tongue, and she began to hold herself apart, as if I was to blame that my father had first been poor and then died. I think perhaps there was a question of her sanity, because there were many times she became hysterical over small things — a crack in a plate, a cushion on a chair out of place, although both the cushion and the chair were threadbare. So now we were a mother and a daughter living in the same house but in different worlds; she retiring into bitterness and self-pity, and me in my room secretly playing my father's old jazz records over and over. Among these were many of the American jazz — Armstrong and Sidney Bechet and Bessie Smith. They seemed to me to belong to a world that was full of life and colour, the music coming out so easy and rhythmical, but so touching to the soul. Of course much of this music came from pain and suffering, but I hear only the romance and the beauty of it, and I think it is this that first set my imagination going for America.

It was at this time I refuse to go to the school and started to go anywhere, doing as I wish because my mother did not keep check on me. I was rebellious in spirit, proud and intelligent, but also foolish and seeking out excitement to take away the emptiness. It

*is this that drove me into the wrong hands perhaps. I
cannot talk of this now and there is more to it than is
written, but just to say that in all this I decided for my
own reasons that I was unwanted, which made me to
break out and seek my own way in life.*

■ ◆ ■

'OK, so tell me, what the hell's going on?' Grace's
voice, hard as pebbles, shattering the crystal calm he
has been lulled into.

'Sorry, I was just . . .'

'What am I, stupid? You think I don't see, hear
nothing? I come up from the stockroom, I see you and
that no-good; I hear you trying to keeping it all quiet
but waving your arms and shaking your head, and then
he goes off mad as hell. I say nothing – just waiting for
when you gonna tell me yourself what is going on –
but nothing. And now I find you sitting here reading
God knows what when we shoulda shut up shop ten
minutes ago. What am I, Michael, did I suddenly cease
to exist that I cannot see the evidence of my own eyes,
that I am no longer worth taking into your confidence?
So, tell me, tell me now, what this is about, and don't
give me no nonsense!'

And that is it: he tells her. He can't keep it in a box
any longer; cannot keep it from this person with whom
he has shared every other part of his being. He tells her
all about the night he was locked in the cold store and

nearly died and how the boy returned and gave him the kiss of life, but then turned against him and delivered his ultimatum.

As Grace stands there reeling and disbelieving, Michael comes at last to the strange debt he feels towards the bad boy and, by the thoughtful silence Grace has fallen into, he starts to believe he has won her over. But when he puts to her the idea that Harrison should maybe receive a consideration of some kind, she erupts, bellowing to shake the shutters: 'Are you fucking insane?!' Even after her last outburst, Michael has never heard the likes, and so he tries to play it down: 'No, no, listen . . . between the two of us, we can just—'

'Don't you dare even talk about it! I won't hear it. This is gonna stop right now!' And this is what Grace now sets out to ensure – just as soon as she can get on the end of the phone without her husband overhearing her.

■ ◆ ■

'Oh, my gorgeous boy! My wonderful boy! Thank the Lord!' Great Aunt Crystal is so made-up with him that Harrison feels almost ashamed of himself; it's worse than taking candy from a baby. 'Of course you can come with me to Tabernacle Sunday,' she gushes. It is what she has hoped against hope for, prayed for every day over the past ten years. 'So how did you come to this?' she stammers, wiping a tear – an actual tear! – from the corner of her eye.

'I dunno, Aunty. I just looked around me and thought . . . Ya know how it is.' Such a good show is he putting on he should get a damn Oscar! Just pray God don't strike him down.

'Oh, sweet boy!' She stretches up on tippy-toes, frames his face in her hands and kisses it. Then she hurries off to get him 'a little something' from her pantry, while he smiles, pleased as Punch. He will get to see the girl Rain again and she, in turn, will see him in the best, blest, possible light.

■ ◆ ■

Sorry, Shibby. Loads on my plate, but better now. Get together soon, yeah?

His fingers flittering deftly across the screen of his cell:

Tried to call you but no answer. Everything OK? Love you lots, Dad.

He presses 'send' and sits back, relieved. He truly wants to make amends, to allow fresh possibilities to grow. Of course, he has no idea, and nor does his daughter, that Corinne has been intercepting everything. First she makes sure that Siobhan is in her room, or out of the house, or engrossed in her homework. Then she slips into the kitchen with Siobhan's phone, which is always lying around someplace. Finally, slyly and systematically, she opens up her daughter's message boxes, finds his messages and eradicates them, one by one – each and every whiny voicemail, every last self-pitying, pathetic text.

■ ◆ ■

Proud is not the word for it. Aunt Crystal can barely keep her feet on the ground as she floats in for Sunday Temple at the Pentecostal Tabernacle, her prodigal nephew on her arm. Scrubbed and smart, Harrison is all smiles and humility, the stud removed from his nose. Passing through the great glass doors, though, he feels genuinely nervous: if God wanted to strike him down, this would be the time and place and, more to the point, there are holy people here who can maybe see the sin crawling all over him and know him for what he is. It takes him back to when he used to come here as a kid and felt the same pangs of guilt just because he had broken a window kicking a ball. How much worse was this, pretending to be a believer just because he wanted to lay his hands on a gorgeous girl?

People are already up on their feet, testifying, shambling, shaking their heads and speaking in tongues as the minister speechifies at the front. Crystal leans on him as they walk up the aisle, her hand dainty in his, her prize exhibit on display. They squeeze into a pew as others brush by, eager to take their place on God's dance floor. A young man, not much older than

Harrison, approaches the minister and assistants take hold of him. The minister plants his hand between the man's eyes and he falls back like he's been zapped with a cattle prod. Then he's up on his feet, looking dazed and slurring out words that sound like a drunk Polish person Harrison once saw the wrong end of Broadway.

The choir strikes up and suddenly the place is all swaying and singing. It gives him time to allow his eyes to rove around the hall. There she is, up front and opposite him, with the couple he saw at the night kitchen. She stands a head taller and even more beautiful then he remembers, in a powder-blue dress that belongs to these days and the old days at the same time. The look on her raised-up face is sweet and real and loving of God; how could he ever hope to be near her? Maybe he should join the line of people waiting to get themselves zapped and fall into the arms of the Lord. On the other hand, maybe he should wait until people get together after the service and have coffee and cookies.

Harrison stays quietly in the pew, while Aunt Crystal gets so excited she takes herself to the floor and speaks in tongues, and even raises her hands and twirls around like a young thing. He, meanwhile, wears the face of an angel, sitting there all lit up and trying hard not to yawn. Every now and then he makes sure to call out a word or two, like, 'Oh, yes sir!' and 'Ain't that the truth', whenever the minister makes some godly pronouncement.

An hour or so later, when it's all over, Crystal folds his arm in hers and leads him to the back of the Tabernacle, next to the vestry, where elders and the like gather for refreshments. She makes a fuss of introducing Harrison to all gathered there and he puts on the perfect imitation of the nice home-boy who speaks when spoken to and listens with eyes aglow. When at last she does the honours between him and Rain's parents, they are all smiles and holding out hands: 'Hello again. And how are you since we saw you that night?' they ask, which surprises Aunt Crystal a little, but it is just one among the many momentary confusions she's grown used to living with. Harrison finds himself standing in front of the lovely girl this whole crazy charade is for. His eyes are cast down and he is truly shy as she reaches out her hand to him. How strange and sweet to be touched by the hand of the vision he saw in the drizzling night!

'Hi. How are you?' she asks, all light and breathy. 'Good.' His mumbled reply saying next to nothing. Such a deadhead he is again, unable to string two words together, whereas she is nothing but gracious: 'I was wondering if you might come here some time.'

He cannot speak for joy and misery together. She has thought of him, thought of him somewhere in her own time and space. 'Tell me – I forgot to ask,' she carries on, 'how did it go with your frozen man?' He looks at her blank-faced. 'That time you came to the night kitchen, you were talking crazy about how you could freeze to death inside a refrigerator.' It clicks at last. Here is something he can hold onto, something he can talk about: 'Oh, yeah, yeah. That was weird. A friend of mine kinda locked himself in a cold store, but he was good in the end – cool.'

'He sure musta been,' she flashes back. So, she's good for a joke too. Harrison really wants to be with this girl. He would go to church every Sunday for ten years and walk on coals to impress her and make her care about him. Which is why he brings her a cup of coffee, takes her to one side and, forgetting that he came in all humble, begins to talk. And in no time his words are falling over each other to clue her in on all kinds of cool things about himself – his music, his plans for life and his solutions to the problems facing planet Earth. And in amongst it all, he slips one humungous lie. He tells her that soon, by way of an inheritance, he is going to come into a very large sum of money, only he doesn't like to talk about it right now. Rain glances across at Great Aunt Crystal, who has latched on to her folks and is going nineteen to the dozen. 'Nuthin' to do with her – other side,' he whispers, but even as he says it, Harrison wonders what makes him come out with this stuff; he hasn't even had a sniff of the damn shoes yet and there isn't a penny to his name. Of course he knows what it comes down to. He's a poor black boy with a shitty past and no future to talk of. Who wouldn't boast and lie to get away from that? When Rain leans in and says, 'Money and possessions mean nothing. A pure heart has no need of a swanky mansion,' he hears the words but doesn't get the message. By the time the coffee cups are drained and the old folks are showing signs of moving on, Harrison has found out that Rain is pretty much grounded for the time being, studying for her exams. Although she doesn't offer her number or anything, it occurs to him that she volunteered the information, he didn't drag it out of her, so maybe she will see him again. At least she didn't tell him to get lost, and all the time they spoke together, she didn't once lose that awesome smile.

CHAPTER 10

H E returns home, bright and sprightly, the feeling of cleanliness inside him now, and a last rescued bundle under his arm. But the moment he sets foot inside the deli his spirit is dashed again, for there is Grace, hopping up and down and yelling in his face: 'God's sakes, Michael, ya forgot all about it, didn't ya? We was supposed to be at Jenny's a half-hour ago. Now, put all that crap down and go get dressed!'

A good old-fashioned Sunday roast, just the four of them and the grandchildren, given they had seen so little of each other since Christmas. That's what was said, but when they got to Jenny's place in Brooklyn, there were thirteen at the table.

Michael sees the betrayal coming in tiny signs: the relentless chewing of beef, covering awkward silences; the shushing of the children when they hardly spoke; the half-baked talk about the weather and the Yankees over apple pie and ice cream. No particle of conversation is allowed to flourish and direct attention away from what is to come.

When the kids are packed off to watch TV, Michael knows he's up for a grilling. He should have seen it coming. This past week has been difficult enough: clipped conversations, accusing silences at mealtimes, steely looks in the store, and at night Grace deliberately losing herself in the TV. He had hoped her anger would abate with time, but if anything it has mounted. He surveys the seven faces surrounding him. Jenny, sitting hand in hand with her mother. She always was a tough nut, from when he first saw her in the cradle, and as she herself is fond of saying, she 'don't take shit from no one'. It's true: she would always dish it before she was dealt it. Next to Jenny, her husband Karl, who happens to be a policeman – big, tough and uncomplicated, except today, when he has been painfully polite and held in check. Then there's kind Suzy, who has always been, secretly, Michael's favourite, and her man Dan, who happens to be a trucker – a couple who look good together and share a sharp sense of humour. Finally, there's pretty, practical June, who loves her poppa and never was one for confrontation, but who's now wearing to order a storm-dark face. Her husband Maurice, a pest-control agent, has the same expression. He, too, is easy-going by nature, but today he hasn't once cracked his tired old joke about he and Karl the cop being in the same trade. Michael feels a fool for not realizing it was all a set-up, and for walking slap-bang into it.

Jenny starts the ball rolling: 'So, what is going on with these shoes?' No polite overture, no show of interest in how the ruby slippers were acquired. Aunt Rosa is not worthy of a mention.

He casts a reproachful glare in Grace's direction. It was their secret and she spilled it; another first.

'Poppa, did you hear me? What is going on?' During the big, awkward silence that follows, Dan looks at the ceiling, Maurice drums his fingers on the table and June looks at the floor. So, they are all in on it. Well, he will not respond to their rudeness, will not just roll over and give them what they want. 'Come on, Poppa. Please . . . don't play games with us.'

'OK,' he says, drawing in breath for the fray. 'Perhaps *you* should tell us what is going on, since you all seem to know already!' He flashes an accusing glance at Grace who, fighting back tears, simply cannot hold her peace. 'I'll say it: your father wants these slippers to be a wonderful symbol of God knows what. He wants to put them in a glass case and make the world a better place. Abracadabra! As if that will make us both happy in our retirement!'

Grace's cold sarcasm stings him into indignation: 'One moment! I did not . . . That is not what I said—'

'It's exactly what you said! You wanna take what should be our comfort in our old age, our children's inheritance, and blow it. Blow it on this ridiculous idea that—'

'I did not! Not once did I—'

'OK, OK . . .' So now Karl intervenes, playing the role of the big-spirited guy. 'Let's hear what Michael has to say.'

Who are they to grant him his say? Who are they to 'allow'? Is this a court of law they are in? But then Maurice throws in his pennyworth: 'I agree,' he says. 'Perhaps Poppa should tell us exactly what he had in mind.'

'Hmph,' replies 'Poppa', stubborn to the last, but then Suzy joins in, speaking calmly, imploringly: 'Poppa, please just tell us what you want. Don't you think we all deserve to know?'

This weighs heavy on Michael. The last thing he wants is to go against his lovely, kind-hearted daughter. Sighing deeply, he draws himself up to present his defence:

'Well . . .' he begins. 'Well . . .'

It does not go well. They do not like his muddled story of fairytale castles in the old world, of wicked Nazis and starving peasants. They do not like his stubborn refusal to put aside his own tragic history. They do not like his ideas of symbols, dreams and magical meanings. They *do* like the idea of the slippers being worth a lot of money and they *do* like to imagine how such a sum could make him and Momma happy in their old age. And, without saying it outright, they also like the idea that one day, when heaven forbid both of them are gone, the same money, wisely invested, would bring them happiness when divided each to each, and after them to the children, the children's children and the children of the children's children. It is Karl, the man of law, who sets this biblical seal on the matter, and it is met with a solemn nodding of heads. Michael is left in no doubt as to where he stands. The question of legality is not even raised, and he knows that if it came to it, they would all stick to the story that the slippers were Judy Garland's gift to her faithful dresser, who then passed these precious things to kith and kin. The family's moral right to the slippers will not and cannot be undone. But still he will not give way. It's all very well to go on about what *they* deserve, but the one person who deserves anything in all this is lying in the hospital, and not one of them has mentioned her name. Damned if he will allow them to bully him.

'At the end of the day, it's for your mother and I to make the right decision, and I can assure you that we will do what is right and proper.'

A chorus of protest breaks out, so loud the children come running back into the room. 'As I say,' he shouts

217

above the babble. 'As – I – say!' and he hits the table. Silence falls. Michael simply loosens his collar, tugs at his shirt-cuffs, sits down and pours himself a glass of water, done with words.

All the way back in the cab they are not talking: she in her stony silence; he sitting up, stiff and self-righteous. As soon as they are back in the deli, she clunks upstairs to the apartment, while he hangs back, resentful. She can sulk as much as she likes. Laying down the law with one hand; stealing with the other. It's just not on.

■ ◆ ■

And this is how, after many complications, with another girl to give each other courage, I came to Germany, to Hamburg, which at that time was an extraordinary place and so busy and exciting for a young girl who was bright and full of hunger for everything that life can offer, and who was not afraid to wait at tables or to lie about her age. But also this was the time of terrible things in Germany. Hitler had come to power, with the Brownshirts like an army in the streets, with their flags and banners flying to show their strength. All kinds of rumours were going round about what they would do to Jews and foreigners and all they saw as enemies. Why I should come to Germany at this time is so great irony because this was the place that was nearest to

America in my imagination, the streets so wide and busy, the buildings so modern and people rushing everywhere. But soon I saw that underneath all this was cruelty and suffering, that for every man goes past in an automobile, another walks past in rags; that for every woman who passes by with her bag full of gro- ceries, another one sits begging in the gutter. So many people also looking out over their shoulder, either to make sure someone does not steal from them and they can eat that night, or to make sure they do not come to the wrong attention.

For this was the other thing, in the city there was always men go round like dogs in packs — the police go one way round, the Nazis go the other, and though they do not have proper authority, they behave like they own the city, checking identities, noticing when you do not speak good German, asking where you came from and where is your family. And this while they are looking at you up and down and leering to each other, making filthy remarks in the belief that a young Latvian girl cannot possibly understand what they are saying.

In many ways I enjoyed the life that we had, and it was nothing to sleep on a park bench or on the floor of a friend of a friend, but finding work grew not so easy, because people were not going out so much in the restaurants. It all changed when my girlfriend, whose name was Elena, all of a sudden she finds a man — one who mends shoes and is not rich, but always there is leather to stitch and heels to mend. And then, just as quick, she is gone with him to set up home and for all I know to marry. So now this is a totally different proposition, alone in the city, the winter coming and myself a good-looking woman. I did not mention this before but I was pretty since a child and fine of figure, and always my mother and father doted on me and everyone visiting and saying what a beautiful girl she is. But never I liked this because Magda, who was my elder, was not particularly good-looking and I did not wish to hurt her or make her feel inferior.

So now I am alone and, with the bad atmosphere that was growing, without comfort or protection. There was a man of my own country, I think it was the boyfriend of Elena who introduces us, and this comes at not the best of times when loneliness drives a person to foolish things and makes attraction when normally there would be none. His name was Felikss and he had a van, a small truck, though at this time it was parked in the street because the gas was sometimes impossible to find. He was a carrier, taking things for people place to place, and he knew everyone in the docks of Hamburg. This is where he had a small apartment, which was poor to look at but a home. And therefore I fell in with him and came to live in this place, sharing in a life that was hard but not terrible, and there were good people living in that quarter and no Nazis going round flying their flags and shouting, 'Zieg

Heil'. Also he was not unpleasant to look at and was a hard-working man who survived on his wit, though one day working and one day not, for the reason of the fuel. Like me, he was intoxicated with the idea of America, especially because he had a brother there. So we would lie in bed and talk about how, if we ever got there, we would walk along Fifth Avenue and go to see Fred Astaire on Broadway, and look down from the top of the Empire State Building.

Misfortune as I write before, it seemed to follow me, for now I learn that Felikss was half-Jew by birth, and this was exactly at the moment that the Nazis start to make reprisal against all Jews, vandalizing their stores and places of worship, gangs of thugs beating men and women in the street. And so many vile rumours and stories circulating about how the Jews are responsible for all privations we face day to day. At first we believe that Felikss is safe because he is only partly of the race, but then there is no leaving this to risk. The feeling is that worse things will come, so it is decided we must go. He has managed to have a full tank of gas at this time, which means he can travel 300 miles, which makes the decision very simple: we will find our way to Holland. That Felikss is in the docks and has genuine trade is the one piece of luck for us, because all he needs is papers and a reason to be travelling across the border. And this is where Felikss was so smart, because he now buys up with good money a whole consignment of rubber boots, a thousand pairs which, so he tells me, they cry out for in Holland but have so many in Hamburg. He finds a man in Amsterdam who is importer, and he offers to sell these boots at so low a price that the man cannot refuse. Thus the deal is struck and the man then supplies the details to the authorities and all is above board. Of course he discusses with me if I wish to go with him, but I was never in a position to say no. Felikss was my security, and in a way I was his, and we believed that if we could live free somewhere, maybe all would be good for us together. For me, besides, to remain in Hamburg was to place myself in loneliness and danger, for after the Jews, who would be next, and who knows what would wait around the corner?

It is true that sometimes good luck comes disguised as bad. And this, then, is what happened to me. I was six months away from home by now. Despite that the circumstance was fearful, the leaving of Hamburg seemed so simple it was absurd, and the weight on our shoulders seemed to fall away with each mile on the speedometer. Felikss was relaxed and happy and not in a race at all to make the drive. When I expressed to him the fear that they would stop us at the border, he showed no concern. The export papers were authentic, and if it meant that one more Jew slipped out the back door that would only be good riddance. And he was right; the border police stopped us and stood imposing with their guns and uniforms, their faces like hungry dogs, but it

came down simply to bureaucracy. They saw passports,
they saw papers, they went to the back of the truck and
saw rubber boots. They let us through and on we drove
in silence. And after we were in Holland ten minutes on
the road, suddenly Felikss pulls over and we both burst
out into laughter, and then into tears from the realiza-
tion that we were free to go wherever we wish. We went
then to nearest town that was called Groningen, and
in the best restaurant we ordered champagne and ate a
fabulous meal.

■ ◆ ■

It is a warm April day and the library is practically deserted, everyone gone to soak up the sun – on benches, beneath trees, beside waters – anywhere out in the fresh air. At lunchtime, having had a peaceful morning, James heads out himself. He goes around the corner to Frankie's and queues up to get himself a sandwich. Turning to go, he discovers Jack waiting a few places behind him in the line, and when he asks to join him James can hardly refuse.

They walk to the Park and sit there eating and looking out over the flat haze of the reservoir, not saying a lot until Jack strikes up, apropos of nothing, 'Did you find it after all? That special something?' Seeing James look perplexed, he clarifies: 'For Paolo – you were looking for something to remember him by. You told me in Woody's that night, after the funeral.'

'Ah,' says James, a little guarded. 'No, no, I still haven't made up my mind . . .' He eyes his new-found friend a little coldly, unable to remember having discussed this with him or indeed anybody. Jack, though, has plenty to say on the subject: 'I remember when my Aunty Norah died and my Uncle Benny didn't know where to scatter the ashes, and that was two years ago and they're still sitting on his mantelpiece.' He swallows the last of his chicken focaccia. 'That was good,' he pronounces, throwing the crust to the ducks. 'No, something will come, something will present itself, don't you worry.'

■ ◆ ■

A chatter of girls comes swirling out of the high-school entrance, their final examination done. Not allowing herself to get carried away with it all, Rain walks along, calm and collected in their midst. But she stops dead in her tracks all the same when, walking up to her out of nowhere comes Harrison, the boy from the Tabernacle, the boy from the night – she still isn't sure which he is. All wired and staring, he looks as her friends stream around him and away, glancing, coy and curious, behind them. She is far from easy about it, the way he just came up on her like that. Despite her annoyance, she is forced to be polite at least: 'Hi, how are you? What are you doing here?'

'I knew you went to this school. I didn't wanna go to

the Tabernacle again, with everyone, like, staring in on us all the time.'

'Sorry? I don't see—'

'I have to see you.'

'I hardly know you.'

'Then listen to me; let me tell you . . .' And then, for reasons she cannot comprehend, he tells her. There in the street, beneath a plane tree, with sunshine falling like splashing water through the new leaves, he tells her about himself, unpacks his whole life: how he was abandoned and then taken in; and then was young and good and then was older and no good, and is now what she sees: a washed-up individual. But still she cannot see the point: 'Why are you telling me all this?' she demands.

'Because you are a good person, and I really, truly like you.' And because maybe you can save me from myself, he thinks.

'So, what am I supposed to do about any of this?'

'Nuthin', I just want you to know what I am.'

'So don't tell me; tell God.'

'You sayin' you would maybe wanna know me if I did all those things, like gave up on stuff and just went and fell into the arms of Jesus?'

'It's an idea. His arms are open.'

'But you're prettier than Jesus and I wanna be with you.'

'Now I know you're crazy,' she says, shaking her head and turning to catch up with her distant friends.

'Please, please, let me see you!' he calls after her.

'This is crazy. Don't follow me, please!' she insists, and with that she walks away, leaving him there. Rain leaves Harrison where he is, scared and stranded on the island in the ocean between his dreams and hers.

■ ◆ ■

At four o'clock, when he would normally stay on to go through the daily tally, James takes himself off home: he will do a spring-clean while he has the energy, and at last clear those two unwashed cups from the table, then he will sit there in spring sunshine and eat a salad all alone.

As he walks along, James has no idea he is far from alone at the present time. For the moment James set foot outside the library, Jack, who had been working his way along the shelves, sauntered to the door and set out after him at a safe distance. He followed James all of a mile to Greenacres and 52nd, where he watched him go in the entrance to the block overlooking the little park. Marking enough time for James to climb the stairs, set down his bag, take out his keys and turn them in the lock, Jack then crossed the street and entered the building.

■ ◆ ■

Hauling himself up the last flight, James catches sight of a jazzy jacket in the darkness, sees her sitting slumped at the top of the stairs. For all of a microsecond the thought flashes in his head, Oh no, not again. He advances, wary of step, seeing her curled there, a sleeping animal, or so it seems until she leaps up, raging, 'I hate you! Hate you!' It is actually scary, here on the quiet landing, a figure flailing out of the darkness, shrieking at him like a banshee. 'How could you? How could you do this to me!' He glances around at the neighbouring doors and frantically beckons her into the apartment, 'Get inside!' he hisses. But she cannot stop herself; hell-bent on shedding herself of every last ounce of her toxic burden.

'Get inside! Please!'

'Ignorant, selfish . . . !' Seeing she will not stop her raving, he grabs her wrist and drags her inside, noticing that she offers no resistance, but at his touch disintegrates, her sobs coming in fierce convulsions. 'Sit down, honey, please,' he says, gently steering her into a chair, then giving her time, allowing for the crying and hyperventilating to stop. Satisfied she is calming down, he brings her a glass of water, but she thrusts his hand away, snarling, 'You didn't call me!'

'Yes I did!'

'You did not!'

'Siobhan, honey, I called.'

'You did not! You did not!' He assures her that if she cared to check she would see it, but she only demands to know why he failed to keep his word, and

227

calls him 'useless father' and even 'worthless piece of shit'. And he tells her that it is deeply shocking to hear her use such words at her age, and that she should be grown-up enough to know that there are other things in his life, tricky things, complicated things and projects he must deal with. But she is far from pacified: 'Projects!' she wails. 'What about me? I should be your project. Just tell me this, you were my daddy and you loved my mommy and you loved me and I loved you, so how come you just woke up one day and went off and never came back? Tell me, please, how did that come about?'

For James, this is, as it happens, the 64,000-dollar question. 'Listen . . . it happened; I don't know how. I'm not sure that these are things you would understand right now. I'm not even sure I understand. People change. The truth is I can't fully explain what it was. I mean, a thing like this, it wasn't just like choosing what shirt to wear. I guess, deep down, I was gay all my life, only I wasn't ever able to face up to it, even to myself – not with my dad on my case, that was never gonna happen.'

'But you married her, and that should be for love.'

'It was. I did love her – totally. You've no idea, Shibby, your momma was an amazing woman; she was wild and free and beautiful and always standing up for what was right. I loved her in every possible way. But you have to understand that there came a time when

228

the spark went out of it – for her as much as for me. In the end, I think, because your mom was so true to herself, it helped me finally to be true to myself.'

'So then you just got up and went.'

'No, no, no. It didn't happen like that. That's the point. You couldn't know it because you were small and had to be protected from these things. But the fact is your mother took violently against me when I came out. For someone who was supposedly tolerant of things, she took it out on me like it was personal, like I had found her wanting as a woman. It was none of that, but she got the idea in her head, and I tell you she was *deranged* about it at the time. Believe me, if your mother wants to be, she can be very, very scary.'

'That I had kind of noticed,' says Siobhan, planting one tiny seed of humour in among the thorny ground.

'Anyway, that was it; I was sent away. I was the leper. First there was a restraining order, then the custody hearing, which, no surprise, I lost. It was decided I was never to come near her again, or you – especially you.'

'I didn't know about that.'

'Right. And how was I to know you were never told?'

'OK, so when you went, did you go to someone?'

'No, Paolo was later. I was on my own for two years, and I was a mess. Remember, it wasn't only Corinne. My father had a ball rejecting me, trashing me to my face, sending vile letters. He disinherited me – and that's the other thing, he hated her as well, and she him, which is why you never got to see him. Honey, listen to me. None of this makes me proud. I wasn't strong, and I guess I felt sorry for myself, but the memories I carried of you were loving ones; you were the happy, beautiful little girl I lost.'

'And what about Paolo? What did he have to say? Did he know about me?'

'He did, yes. He said I should do everything I could to see you. He never stopped saying it, and I never stopped giving him reasons not to. I was a fool; I was afraid of Corinne, always have been, and I suppose I took it for granted that she would've made you hate me. Which I would understand if you did . . .' He stops mid-flow. This is the first time since she first arrived on his doorstep that he has genuinely sought her opinion of him.

Siobhan takes her time to seriously consider, then pronounces, 'Mmm. Part of me does. But not all . . .'

Outside on the landing, Jack hears every word of this, because, having sprinted up the steps and assured himself that the neighbours are safely inside their apartments, he has his ear virtually pressed to James's front door. So, James was once straight – a regular family guy, a dad bouncing a baby on his knee. He kind of likes that, though he doesn't have any time to ponder on it, because suddenly, from below, sounds come echoing up the hallway – voices and boots scraping. He darts back along the landing and skips up the next flight.

■ ◆ ■

Inside the apartment, the conversation has taken on a calmer tone, as Siobhan sits curled in a chair, listening attentively, her tears dried, while James states the remainder of his case, explaining to her how he knows his failings but will make amends, and how he is going to move heaven and earth to be a father to her. But then, out of nothing, she jumps up from her chair, crosses the room and throws open the study door. He rushes after her, but it is too late. She is standing there staring into the room, held back from entering by the otherness of it. Inside the room is a desk and a chair and Japanese prints on the walls and things left in their place on the desk: a pile of books, pens and papers and, spread out in the centre, a sheaf of sumptuous sketches, designs for a grand opera. For this is Paolo's study, and all of these things were of his choosing and have the effect he had intended them to have, which is one of balance and tranquillity and exoticism. The contrast with the rest of the apartment is quite startling, and Siobhan realizes, with a kind of wonder, that her father has kept these things just so – as if his lover has only just left the room.

'You shouldn've done that,' says James, meek but inwardly in a fury, pulling the door firmly to. An

231

awkward silence descends on both of them, from which they are saved when the buzzer sounds, loud and insistent, sending James hurrying to the door. Outside are two police officers, and James is horrified when, without so much as an introduction, the male of the two flatly demands, 'Is Siobhan McBride here?'

Admitted to the apartment, the officers take one look at the girl and right there, with James standing by looking foolish, they ring Corinne. The female officer confirms to her that they have located her daughter safe and sound, and asks what she wants them to do next. He can hear Corinne's voice fuming and crackling out of the phone as the officer informs her that they are in no position to return her to Long Island. The officer presents her final judgement, like Portia to the court: 'It's up to the family to get it together here,' even though, as it transpires, Corinne's car has broken down and refuses to budge from her driveway. Siobhan suggests, helpfully, that she would be happy to stay with James, but is told in no uncertain terms that she should go home to her mother where she belongs.

As soon as the officers have departed and they are alone together again, James tries a little clumsily to take up where he left off: 'Don't worry, Siobhan. I am your dad and I will be your dad.' He reaches out to her and she allows herself to be enfolded by him.

'Please, please do that for me,' she implores him.

'OK, OK,' he whispers back, though he can't help thinking now about how he's going to get her home 100 miles with no vehicle. He heads into the kitchen, nonetheless, with the intention of making something to eat, all the while thinking through the fix he is in.

In the middle of the scrambling of eggs, his cell rings. 'Hi, James,' says the wistful voice. 'How's it going?' It doesn't even occur to James to wonder how Jack might have acquired his number, he is so taken up with explaining how he is too busy dealing with 'a situation' to talk. And this provides Jack with the perfect opening: 'Oh, can I help in any way?' he enquires, as a good friend might.

'Well, put it this way,' says James, 'right now I have the small problem of having to get my daughter back to the middle of nowhere on Long Island, and I can't just put her on a train.'

Naturally, he is taken aback when Jack replies perfectly matter-of-factly, 'Oh, you should've said – I have a car.'

And upon learning that Jack is kind and crazy enough to offer to drive his daughter all the way home, James is grateful beyond measure. He hasn't a clue that Jack is at this moment in time right down there in the street, pocketing his cell and starting to run as fast as he can the two miles home to collect his car and get back just as soon as he can.

■ ◆ ■

Forty minutes later, father and daughter are standing at the roadside, looking at a big old beast of a car: a Sixties Thunderbird, two-tone powder-blue and cream. Sitting there, devil-may-care in the driver's seat with the engine thrumming and the sun glinting on the roof, Jack looks ludicrously small, more like a pilot in an airliner cockpit than a man in an automobile. Guiding Siobhan into the back seat, James couldn't be more indebted to Jack and thanks him for being a lifesaver. 'Least I could do,' says the reluctant hero, fresh-faced and smiling. 'You woulda done the same.'

By the time they are clear of the Brooklyn Bridge, the weather has changed. James sits up front alongside Jack, while in the back Siobhan drifts in and out of sleep. The wipers rise and fall hypnotically, scything and scattering a harvest of raindrops as the three sit in their spaces, separate yet bound together in silence.

A few miles from Upton, James calls Corinne to let her know they are near. As they pull up outside the house, he sees her standing in the rain, by the misbehaving station wagon. Soaked through, she is holding up an umbrella to shield an older man, a neighbour, who is scrabbling under the hood, trying to get the thing started. James wonders if this is just another performance, another act of martyrdom among the many. He gets out of the car slowly, wary of that which cannot be foreseen. Siobhan closes the door behind her, shivering as a sneaky bead of rain zips cold down the gully of her spine. Only now does it come back to her that she had argued violently with her mother that morning before running off to the city. So now she hangs back a little, with James leading the way, his eyes fixed on Corinne, who remains contained, her head unmoving and her gaze held by the unfathomable mysteries stored within the gaping hood.

'Hi, Mom,' ventures Siobhan, but Corinne just flicks her head – a quick, hard glance – and goes back to staring at the lifeless engine. James greets her, too, but receives not the slightest acknowledgement. The neighbour sighs, oblivious of the new arrivals, shaking his head in frustration. Corinne declares to no one in particular but for the benefit of all: 'We don't get this going, I am dead tomorrow!' Standing there in the rain, hair tumbling, cheekbones carved, her bearing upright and defiant, she looks, for all her misery, kind of magnificent.

'Can I help?' James offers, trying to be big about it. 'I shouldn't think so,' she snaps acerbically, remembering only too well his ineptitude with things technical.

'I know something about automobiles,' says Jack, reminding the world of his existence.

'I shouldn't think so,' comes the flat riposte, as Corinne wonders just what this absurdly young person has to do with her pathetic ex. 'What did you do so far?' Jack enquires of the neighbour, regardless. 'Checked the plugs, distributor; set the points. All good.'

'Coil?'

'Spark's good.'

'Right . . . Would you mind spinning her over a little, please?'

The neighbour gets in the car and turns the engine, which coughs and splutters in a losing battle for life. 'Timing,' pronounces Jack.

'Possible,' the neighbour perks up.

'Do you have spanners?'

'Sure.'

And Jack goes to, leaning into the hood, dramatic under the flashlight, the others all ranged around, their attitudes and positions suspended, lending their empty presence to the task. Jack wrenches here, ratchets there, twists things this way and that, and gets the man to try again. Nothing. Corinne raises a sceptical eyebrow – James's young friend is a dud by association. But then, amid fumbles and fiddles, Jack calls out again and the car judders into life.

'Wow!' says Corinne, her surprise not quite extending to gratitude.

James can't resist getting the edge on her. 'Not bad for a gay guy.'

'That is not what I meant,' she spits, and holds up the umbrella for Siobhan to join her beneath it. 'Come on, you,' she says. 'School in the morning.'

'Wait, Mommy,' says Siobhan, and she turns to James, whispering, 'Go on, ask her now; tell her how I can come and stay with you.'

It hurts him to disappoint her: 'Honey, this isn't the right time.' There is reason in this. Corinne has blanked James throughout all of this, making it clear that he remains nothing to her and – by extension – should have nothing to do with her daughter. He gives Siobhan a long hug and gently edges her over to her momma. 'Come on, Jack, let's go get a coffee somewhere,' he says pointedly. At this, a knowing smirk arrives on Corinne's face and she makes sure he can see her looking Jack up and down, curious to know exactly what their relationship is. James can hear the unspoken word in his own head – cradle-snatcher – and he's damned if he will hang around here a moment longer to disabuse her of her ignorance. With a rueful smile, he heads back to the car, waving again to his sad-eyed daughter.

CHAPTER ELEVEN

A WHOLE day has gone by and still Michael's mind is on the boy. He peers out past the deli's solitary customer and sees an orange pinpoint of fire quicken, drawing the darkness into itself. So, he is out there again. Crazy. He hurries to serve his customer and see her out. He rolls down the shutter and locks the doors. So many worries, he thinks. Apart from the crazy kid, the showdown with the family has left a bad taste in his mouth, and things are no better with Grace. It is all too much, and Michael has started to mistrust the people he loves and to feel a fool for ever having placed faith in them. After all, if you can't respect your elders for what they have been through, what *can* you respect them for? He will not just roll over and say that the experiences and the understandings that took root in him and brought him to America are suddenly of no value. On the other hand, he is not so mean and dictatorial that he cannot see their side of the coin. It is certainly true that trade has dwindled, and he is painfully aware of how he and Grace have both slowed down; how sometimes he has struggled to keep a grip on the routines and the particulars. He knows, too, from what she has said once or twice, that Grace sometimes goes to sleep wondering if she will wake up again, and that occasionally he is woken in the middle of the night by his own heart racing towards something terrible he can't even name. What if one day it raced away and never returned to rest? But these things are strictly between the two of them. By what right did Grace share them with others? And what right did they have sticking their noses in? It is starting to look more and more like naked self-interest.

Regardless of all this, he knows he has not been the same since the tussle with Harrison, and he has started to wonder if the things we imagine to be meaningful really count for much at the end of the day. Is it not, after all, the small things in life that get us through: tokens of warmth, simple kindnesses, a loved one there to put an arm around you at night or cook you a nice meal? Lately, of course, these have all dried up and Grace has been going over to Jenny's more frequently than he can remember her ever doing over the years – tonight being a case in point. Funny how the big philosophical questions in life can add up to so little if the person you love is no longer there to smooth your brow or plant a kiss on your cheek.

So now he starts to feel lonely, and creeping on the heels of loneliness comes guilt, for who is he to stand in the way of decent people and snub out their bright hopes? It would be so easy to just call them now and tell them to sell the shoes, sell the damn things and everybody would be over the moon. He goes to the safe for one last look, to set eyes on them once more and see if the sight of them will stir again the slumbering parts of him that once were so alive. Cold of thumb and finger, he turns the dial, hearing the tumblers fall in soft spindling clicks, a clock turning back. The door gapes open, iron empty. They are gone! The Harrison boy – how did he do it, for it must be him? As soon as Michael is calm enough to bring back together his scattered thoughts, he knows it cannot be so – the safe was never forced, the store never entered by stealth. Grace. She alone knows the combination; she alone would be in a position to do this! He pieces it together, sees how she must have bided her time quietly, calmly waited until he went to the cellar to bring up stock – that must have been the moment. He pictures her in her prim, careful way, turning her hand this way and that to the numbers, inching open the door so it wouldn't creak, and removing the shoes without a sound. What must have been in her mind as she then trudged up the stairs and hid them inside her overnight bag? What was she thinking when she came back down and kissed him and went off so completely casual, as if it was just another Wednesday evening? And in those few seconds, when she walked with shuffling steps to the door and climbed into the taxi, had it occurred to her that in her smiling goodbye there was such betrayal? Straightaway, he calls Jenny, who answers in a flash. It becomes a monumental effort just to keep his cool and sound calm and unflappable. 'It's me . . .'

'Hi Poppa,' her voice, matter-of-fact, pretending all is well but signalling the opposite.

'May I speak to your mother, please?'

'She's tired. She went early to bed.' He can feel himself cracking, giving way to his anxieties: 'OK . . . So tell me, where are they? What did she do with them?'

'This is not a good moment.'

'I said, where are they!'

'They are safe, don't worry.'

'Oh my God, how could you do this to me?'

'Don't shout, please, Poppa,' she says, and then tells him that the shoes are safe in a bank deposit box of all places. Nothing will happen to them, she tells him, without his blessing.

'This is terrible, shocking!' His voice rises to a scream. 'I am coming over this minute!'

And that, after slamming down the phone, is what he does: shuts up shop there and then, not giving a thought to the fact that it's two hours before closing time. He hurls the stands across the floor, skidding and colliding, with peaches splattering ripe to the floor, throws down his apron, turns the sign to closed, goes out of the door and hurls the rickety shutter down.

■ ◆ ■

When we got to Amsterdam, which was not far, Felikss had one more surprise, for he takes me to the city hall, to the office of the registrar and asks, in German, to be given forms that will enable us to be married. I was a little astonished at this, since he has overlooked to tell me this small detail and the word love has never passed between us. It is for good reason, he assures me. For here was a way we can go to America. His brother, who is locksmith in New York, was to sponsor him to go and take the same trade. But I say to him that I don't understand, that does not explain why it is good to marry, and he tells me that this can be my own passport to America and he wishes to repay all the kindness I have given to him. The marriage would exist on paper, but who knows, maybe it could come to love. Whatever happened, once we would be in America I would be free to do as I wished.

And so I went along with this. Within three days of coming to Amsterdam we were man and wife and within three months we were on our way, sailing steerage to America. It's cliché, of course, to talk about that moment of arrival in the city of New York. To gaze upon the Statue of Liberty, to look across at Manhattan gleaming in the setting sun, but this really was to be delivered into a fantasy that you have seen only in the movies.

So in the real world now we were met by Felikss's brother, Leonids, who was more American than the Americans, in the way he dressed and used the slang and is full of belonging to New York City. He refused even to talk to us in our own tongue and began at once to make us learn English. So then he brought us in a yellow taxi to the West Side, which is not the place of glamour and never was, but is only a walk away from the heart of the city, which is where we went to walk the first night. There it was heaven to look into the windows of department stores and drink coffee in Italian cafés and stare up at skyscrapers till our necks were sore. Even so, this was never going to put a roof over our head or food in our belly. And this is where things started to happen that did not go as I had imagined. Leonids had taken us to his own apartment, which was spacious and full of good furniture and fine ornaments, and there also was his wife, Martha, who immediately I liked and who was a real American of

American parents. But then he took us to the place he had found for us. It was right at the top of a tenement block in a noisy, dirty neighbourhood and was tiny, a room only with a place for a stove and everything else was shared, to include the toilet downstairs. It was not what I had dreamed, but it was a place where one could begin to have hope.

It was my wish that Felikss would wake every day and go bright and early to work with Leonids, but after only a week this was not so, and when I asked him he said that Leonids had agreed on paper only to train him but not to pay him — a detail which had not been conveyed to me. But then I see after that Felikss is not even being bothered to go one block to his brother, even to be trained. And then he tells me he does not much like to work with locks, that he is no good with metal and has not any feeling for it. So now it is I who is getting angry and saying it was not so long ago the Brownshirts would have him kicked to death in the street. And then it is his turn to hit back and he shouts at me, 'What about you? Why don't you train? Why don't you work? You can sew; you can be dressmaker.'

Much argument follows this, and eventually he agrees to go and talk to his brother again, but this time, when he returns there is a bruise on his face and he tells me in English — he was learning quickly — that I should see the other guy. It turns out that he and his brother *were in great argument, that the brother was saying that Felikss has let him down, that he was relying on him for help, that he has been used by him to gain a visa and he will go to the authorities if Felikss does not compensate him with dollars! This was unbelievable to me — that brothers should seek to profit from each other and even to fight fist to fist.*

■ ◆ ■

His finger has hardly left the bell push when the door springs open and Jenny is there, her look forgiving and forbidding at the same time. Even in his fury it occurs to him that she must have stood in this position for a while, perfecting her saintly pose. The voice too is soft with rehearsed compassion. 'Come on in, Poppa.'

'Try and stop me!'

'Don't be angry, please.'

'Me? Angry? What the f—!'

'Poppa, please. No cursing. Sylvie . . .'

'Send her to bed!' he yells and, striding into the living room, he finds Karl sprawled on the couch, his feet up on the coffee table, his head thrown back to a bottle as *The Family Man* crackles out of the TV. He sees Sylvie is behind the couch, solemnly playing with her dollies. She doesn't even break to look up at him. Under strict orders, he deduces – told to keep her distance.

Karl returns the bottle to the table, stretches elaborately and flicks out a lazy hand, saying, 'Siddown,

siddown.' A chair is there for him, but he will not sit down, he will not allow them to tame his anger.

'Siddown, Poppa,' urges Jenny, and then goes over to take Sylvie away to her bed, her half-hearted protest deflected in sly glances away from her and at him.

Some crass joke on the TV sends Karl into fits of laughter: 'Listen to this . . .' he snorts, laughing along with the canned audience.

'Listen to me! Someone kindly listen to me!' Michael snarls.

'Oh. Sorry,' exclaims Karl, tactically surprised, and seizing on etiquette, he removes his feet from the table and sits up. 'Can I get you a beer?'

'No you cannot. Where is she?' he says to Jenny. 'Tell her to get out here now!' This provides Big Karl with a cue to make his own display of righteous indignation: 'Hey. What goes on here?'

'Just tell her to come now, please.'

'Now wait a minute, whose house is this?' Karl does not like to be ignored by Michael. It rankles him to see the man standing right up to him, but with his face turned aside and paying him not the slightest attention. 'In case you didn't notice, this is my house and my room and you are shouting at my wife!' snarls Karl.

'Shouting? I hear only one person shouting,' roars back Michael. Seeing the warning signs, Jenny inserts herself between the two men. 'Please! Both o' you . . . Poppa, you better just go!'

'I ain't going nowhere!'

'Like I said, mister, my house, my room. You come in here on my night off and interrupt my favourite TV show—'

'Your favourite TV show! *That's* all that matters here? You interrupted my whole *life*! You stole from me, from my . . . my family. You took what was never yours to—'

'That's it, you're outta here!' shouts Karl and jabs Michael in the breastbone, nightstick hard, with his great stubby finger, so that Michael falls back, rubbing his chest. 'You any idea who you talking to here, buster?' he hollers, and over and over again he prods the unfeeling finger at the stubborn old man, all the time forcing him back to the door he came in at. 'Now get outta here, and don't come back until you feel like talking reasonable!'

Seeing the old man is practically out of the house, Karl turns his back on Michael and lumbers back towards his couch, message sent, job done. But before he can lower himself back down, a ball of wind rises in his gullet and spills out in an almighty belch. 'Pardon me,' he says, starting to laugh despite himself.

Michael, who has been on the verge of turning tail and slinking away, takes this as the ultimate insult: 'You bastard!' he shouts and sails across the room, leaping with wondrous agility onto Karl's broad back. Around the ox-neck he clamps his arms, squeezing for all his life and with not a care where it might end. It is an absurd sight, more in keeping with a cartoon comedy show: the big man, barking like a seal with a sore throat and thrashing his body this way and that, trying to buck off the round little pig-a-back man who just won't let go. And little by little, his own scrabbling hands fused to Michael's, Karl begins to sink.

Michael has not the slightest thought for the man who he is trying, without really knowing it, to kill. He takes no heed of Jenny's yelling, or her frantic scrabbling to prise them apart. He does not hear the wild laughter of Sylvie, who has sneaked down from her bed and thinks some kind of game is going on, and he does not even notice his own wife, who now comes padding into the room in her sky-blue velour dressing gown and pink fluffy slippers, her hair in curlers. Even as Karl slumps to his knees, down to the last gasp, Grace stares, baffled, at the scene confronting her, wondering how she had never before seen such passion in her man. Then, hearing Jenny still screeching like a stuck pig and Sylvie wailing and in distress, she slips into the kitchen and returns with a convenient object, a large well-used frying pan. High above her head she raises it and brings it down in a wide swooping arc to slam it home-run hard against the side of her husband's cranium, with a clang right out of Universal Studios sound-effects department. It does the trick: Michael sails away sideways and beaches face down on the carpet, while Karl topples over onto his back, spluttering and gasping, his hands at his throat.

'Oh my God!' squeals Jenny. 'My God, this is so bad! Poppa coulda killed Karl; Karl coulda killed Poppa!'

Grace looks down on it all. To the one side she can see Michael rolling over and groaning, his hand at his head; to the other there is Karl, his arms locked against the floor as he tries to lever himself up.

'Nah, I don't think so . . .' she pronounces, as calm as you like. 'I always dreamed about hitting him over the head with a frypan one day, but mine is too heavy. Now *it* coulda killed him, but this one is nice and light. To tell the truth, throwing that whack gave me more pleasure than I ever imagined!'

■ ◆ ■

Karl comes out of the kitchen, pressing a bag of peas to his throat and glaring at Michael, who is sitting bent over on the coffee-table edge, running his fingers over an egg-shaped bump on the topside of his skull. He is not pleased: 'You crazy bastard,' he says. 'This better not bruise. You forget I'm a cop? The only thing standing between you and a night cell is that you are Jenny's old man!'

Making much of being unimpressed, Michael looks Karl in the eye, brings his wrists together and puts them out ready to take the cuffs. A silent face-off follows, in which Karl snorts and puffs in his own performance of indignation, and Michael glares and glowers in his improvised show of self-righteousness. Grace and Jenny meanwhile just look on, shaking their heads at the insanity of it all. It is Michael who finally breaks the deadlock.

'OK, this is where I get up and go. But no way do I let this lie. Listen to me, Grace, we walk outta here now, and the key to the box comes too. You understand me?'

His words are aimed hard and unforgiving at Grace, but his eyes are fixed on Karl. As Michael walks towards the door, Grace at last finds her voice and speaks up obligingly.

'Sure I understand you, Michael.'

'OK, so come on . . .'

She looks at him all pitiful, then turns to face her daughter: 'Jenny, would you mind if I was to stay here one or two nights – let the dust settle?'

'Sure, Momma, if that's what you want.'

Karl is not slow to drive home the advantage: 'Sure. You stay here long as you like, Momma, and don't let nobody push you around.'

There is nothing left to say. The four of them just hang there in silence; Michael, isolated, defeated and waiting still for the Seventh Cavalry who are not going to arrive. 'OK,' he says at last and about-turns, like a sentry man at the end of his travel, and marches stiff-backed to the door.

■ ◆ ■

Every day there is a new consignment of books: as many
as thirty copies from the publishers or from central stock.
James enjoys dealing with them for a couple of hours
before things get really busy. First, there is the quick
scan of titles – the variety of them, the sheer multiplicity of ideas and experiences that they represent. Then
there are the more practical things to be done: removing dust sheets; covering them in film and embossing
the hard covers with the NYPL crest, not to forget
laminating in barcodes. All this is part of a process to
dress the virgin book and make it decent. Mostly, James
leaves this ritual to his staff, but once or twice in the
week he likes to sit himself down and enjoy the simple,
sensual pleasure of handling new books, their colours,
textures and scents, some spicy or gluey and natural,
some chemical and astringent. There is a childlike
pleasure to be had in stamping and sticking things and
cutting them out, and beneath all this, deeper, darker
undercurrents of appropriation and retention.

At break time, he sits with Marcia drinking coffee.
Through the glass in the door, he can see Jack going to
and fro, returning books to shelves. 'Our friend Jack,'
he asks, 'how long has he been with us?'

'Years – at least four,' she tells him, curious at James's
curiosity.

'No, it's just . . . I mean, do you find anything strange
about him, anything weird?'

251

'Beyond the fact that he's painfully shy, no. Why, what did he ever do to you?'

'No, it's not that he ever did anything, he just . . . Well, he turned up one time at the hospital, with flowers for Paolo, and I could've sworn they never even knew each other.'

'He must've done if he turned up there. What did he say?'

'He said he knew Paolo – both of us from Woody's Bar, where we always used to go, but I don't remember ever seeing him there.'

'People go to bars. Flowers, you say? Well, isn't that really rather touching?'

'Yeah, I suppose so. It's just I find him a little strange – creepy even. And that's the other thing; it's infuriating, he reminds me like hell of someone, but I just can't put my finger on who. Does he do that to you?'

'Not me. It'll come to you.'

After this James feels a little ashamed of himself for being so mean-spirited towards Jack. By noon the sun's rays are filtering, glorious, through the high windows, and he begins to feel lifted up on fine sensations. He will call Siobhan on Friday; he will surely keep to that. And he will call her at other times, when she least expects it and when he can most bring sunshine into her life. Then maybe Corinne will relent a little and grow more trusting. And he can hire a car and take his little girl on trips, driving out to the coast or up on winding roads to the hills. So taken up with this lovely prospect is James that all physical sensation runs out of him and he sits there, suspended, scissors in hand, until Marcia appears, leaning over him and muttering in his ear, 'Sorry, James, we have a situation . . .'

'Mmm . . . ?'

'A spitter.'

James surfaces from his dream of sea and sunshine. He looks up, baffled, then gets up and follows as she leads him over to the iron spiral stairway, up to the top gallery and along the balcony to the outsized art books. He can hear someone wheezing and hacking. At a table punctuating the walkway sits a dishevelled man, not old but made ancient by matted hair and layers of clothing darkened by dirt. In front of him is a huge hand-bound book, displaying over two pages Rembrandt's 'Anatomy Lesson of Dr Tulp'. But it is another printed spread that takes James's attention. Lying open on the floor is a library copy of the *Washington Times* and on it are pools of saliva and phlegm made by the man who, obligingly, as the result of his latest coughing fit, hawks up another mouthful and heartily deposits it onto the paper. 'Disgusting!' hisses Marcia, and quivers close to retching. The man shrugs, as if to say, what else can you do?

'Excuse me, sir . . . You can't do that. That's library property!' James feels absurd and childish saying this, and the man just shrugs again. James surveys the appalling mess.

'OK. Call the police,' he says sharply and makes for the stair. Marcia scurries along after him, but halts as James suddenly stops in his tracks and turns to stare again at the spitting man.

'What?' she asks of the shuttered expression on his face. 'What . . . ?'

Something inside James has stalled, something snapped. He will not do this; he will not call the police and wait two hours; he will not stand by and be a passive observer of his own unravelling. Marcia watches goggle-eyed as he strides back and positions himself behind the spitting man, then leans over and says, quiet and controlled: 'Listen, creep, get the hell out of my library or I am personally going to throw you over that rail!'

The man turns his head to see James glaring at him. 'Fuck off!' he says disdainfully, and slumps back down again. Marcia watches, disbelieving, as James moves in on the man, pushes aside the table, grabs his collar, yanks him to his feet and, not even giving him a chance to react, drags him to the rail, ready and apparently able, in his shaking fury, to pitch the man over his shoulder. 'No, no, no,' the man whimpers. Every pair of eyes in the library is looking up now. 'Please!'

'Ready?' asks James, drawing strength from nowhere. 'Please . . . No . . .'

James desists – lets the iron go out of his arms, and the man pulls his coat straight, rushes to the stairway and stumbles down in a riot of clanking. All heads are turned as he scurries to the door and out. Marcia is flabbergasted: 'My God . . . You wouldn't really have thrown him over?'

'I don't know,' James confesses in all honesty. Marcia watches, dazed, as he gathers himself, suddenly aware of where he is and who he is, the wildness going out of him and meekness returning. He shifts the table back into place, stoops to gather up the soiled paper. 'Let me do that,' she offers.

'No, no. I'll do it,' he insists.

Jack comes clambering up the staircase. 'Wow!' he says, surveying James in undisguised awe. Then, as James bends down to clear the mess, gingerly taking hold of the paper, intending to fold it over, a head-line catches his eye: RUBY SLIPPERS FOUND IN EAST HARLEM. GROCER STRIKES GOLD.

Everything changes.

CHAPTER 12

Mɪᴄʜᴀᴇʟ leans over the counter towards the reporter woman. Lucky for her she has a nice face and good manners, otherwise he would have lost it with her by now. 'OK,' he says with lowered voice, 'so you want the whole story. How it happened? How I felt when I made the amazing discovery?'

'Well, yes, exactly that.'

He thinks about it, drums his fingers, comes to his decision. Time to say it like it is: 'I never wanted no publicity. This all came from members of my family. I had nothing to do with it.'

'But . . . it was you who discovered the slippers.' The reporter had not expected so hostile a reception from the man who had made the lucky find, and she has no idea that her turning up like this had almost sent him into cardiac arrest. 'OK, Mr Marcinkus,' she continues, 'all I want to know is your personal take on it. I would've thought you'd be only too happy.'

'Happy I am not!' On a slip from the cash register he writes down Karl and Jenny's details and gives it to her. 'They gave you the story in the first place, they can tell you whatever they like. Now excuse me, I have customers to serve.'

'Well, thank you. That's very kind of you,' she says, heavy on the irony and halfway out the door. He stands there, his brain boiling in his head. How could they do this to him, knowing he was so opposed, and expect him to play along? Unbelievable! He looks down at the copy of the *News* she has left on the counter: GROCER STRIKES GOLD. How could they cook up all this nonsense and put it out as truth? As soon as there is a lull, he runs behind the counter and calls Jenny. No niceties, nothing – he hits her with it the moment she picks up the phone: 'What the hell d'you think you're playing at?'

'Sorry, Poppa, but there was no point in asking you.'

He can barely listen – the brass neck of her: 'No point? No point? What about decency, trust, honesty? That is the point.'

'We knew you would object, whatever.'

'Damn right I would object. This is bad. It's criminal! It could send us all to jail.'

'Really? The way I see it, there's only one person could make that happen and that person is you, and I don't think you're up for that, are you, Poppa?' He falls silent, and she puts an end to things: 'See? There was no point. You would never have agreed. Just cool off and take it easy. It'll all work out in the end. Goodbye, Poppa.'

■ ◆ ■

James sits in the sun outside Woody's Bar. It's the first time since Paolo died that he has come here after work, but with the weather so warm and giving lately, it's a real pleasure to sit drinking a cold beer among people of goodwill, many of whom remember Paolo with affection. In between chatting to people about things in the news – the crazy Koreans and the doomed Republicans – James muses over his day. Since his stand against the spitting menace, he has, like it or not, acquired a certain new status somewhere between blue-eyed boy and masked avenger. How strange it has been: readers in the library coming up to congratulate him, staff jumping to that bit quicker whenever he asks for a task to be done or a humdrum procedure to be followed. But at the same time his heroics are the source of embarrassment. He is a librarian, a harmless drudge, a custodian of books on dusty shelves, not of Metropolis City. He has no idea what came over him, except that he got tired of being always on the receiving end and

258

had felt ashamed ever since Siobhan told him bluntly to stop being a pussy. All the same, he must admit it feels great to be kind of a people's hero, and he mulls over in his mind whether he will tell Shibby about it all later when he calls, but decides against it. God knows it's not something to boast about. Strictly speaking, it was breaking the law, and if the man wanted he could press charges for assault.

While James is talking to a guy who's keen to tell him about his incredible log cabin in the Adirondack, Jack walks by, goes into the bar and comes out two minutes later, beer in hand. 'James, how are you? What a day, eh?' And in no time he is in with James and his pals, telling the tale of James's unbelievable act of valour But James is less interested in the praise being heaped on him than the fact that Jack is so uncharacteristically talkative and at ease with himself – the effect, maybe, of drink on a warm day. When the back-slapping has run its course, Jack produces a newspaper and opens it under James's nose. There again is the article about the ruby slippers. It prompts all manner of excitement, and soon there are any number of opinions being offered up, apropos the shoes and what they represent, from the philosophical – 'Well, there are many layers of meaning in that film, after all' – to the reverential – 'Just look at Judy in that scene: if ever there was truth and beauty in a song, that was it.' Amazing, incredible and fabulous are the adjectives of the afternoon and they only keep flowing when James casually remarks that he happens to know the grocer who has them. When he lets slip also that, although it had never really been his cup of tea, *The Wizard of Oz* had always been one of Paolo's favourites, Jack is seized by a sudden inspiration. 'That's it!' he exclaims, bringing about a charged silence.

'That's what?' says James.

'It's the answer! For Paolo – the thing to remember him by.'

'What are you talking about?' asks James.

'But you said yourself, it was his favourite. I mean, if I was looking and something like this came up, especially as you know the guy . . . I mean, to me that would be like a sign!'

And before James knows it, there are speculations going on left, right and centre, about how exactly one might strive to acquire so rare and valuable a prize. When one bright spark strikes up with the thought that it doesn't have to be one individual buying one thing but many clubbing together, there is an immediate response: 'Well, I would give a few bucks!'

'It's perfect, the perfect idea!'

Jack takes this as a cue to borrow a pen, tear a strip off the paper and rush around the establishment, coming back in five minutes with thirty signed-up names, which he thrusts into James's hands. 'Wow!' enthuses James, inwardly not at all convinced. 'Maybe there is something in it.'

Michael spends what seems like the whole afternoon on the phone telling other reporters to go away, and fobbing them off with Jenny's number. By four o'clock he feels even more tainted by the whole charade and even more to blame for Aunt Rosa, as if he personally had bulldozed her into the ground for death to claim her. And although all the increase in human traffic is good for trade at least, he knows it won't last; at the end of the day he'll still be sending Benjy home and dragging himself upstairs to the cold, lonely apartment, where there will be no meal waiting and the place shouting at him somehow in its emptiness.

It is, then, something of a relief when at about six o'clock, things having gone quieter, in walks James of all people, who he hasn't seen in weeks. But instead of coming over, James keeps apart, taking up a basket and setting off down the rows, netting items here and there. It's only when Benjy heads off to the basement that the old man takes his cue to come plodding over and make conversation: 'So, James, how you doing?'

'Ah, not too bad. May I have some of the Parma ham, please? A half pound . . . And some of the artichoke hearts.' So, the guy is not much for talking – understandable, considering. For the moment Michael refrains from engaging James in conversation, directing all his care and attention to the spooning of artichokes, the snug fitting of lid to pot. James smiles vacantly as

Michael slides the items across the countertop. But now, James takes up an unexpected tack: 'Listen, you've probably had enough of this, but I read in the *Voice* about the ruby slippers.'

'Goodness me; not again.'

'I'm sorry. That was thoughtless of me.'

'No, no, it's just been such a long day.' And, finding in James someone who has always shown a genuine interest in him and his life, Michael confides in James about the hard time he's been having. He omits the gritty details about his scheming family and his own questionable part in the affair, but one way or another he and James fall into a deep and meaningful exchange on the subject of the slippers, which seems to allow the two men to safely express their brightest dreams and deepest fears. James explains to Michael, in a muddled but sincere kind of way, how he has friends to whom the slippers mean much, and how, as a New Yorker of Irish extraction, he is European at heart and would love to hear more about Michael's personal story. And so, seeing as the man in front of him has always been a good customer and a kind person, Michael lets down his guard and begins to tell James the tale of his desperate days in the old world, and how a movie once flickered and danced on a white sheet, dispelling darkness and savagery, and became special to him.

It is peculiar, this intense exchange between two very different men that stops and starts, in between

Michael dashing over to serve customers as they arrive and leave. Benjy the shop boy, meanwhile, fills the shelves and mops the floor around them, as Michael rambles on and James stands rapt. By the time Michael reaches the end, describing how he finally lined up among the proud new Americans at Ellis Island, an hour has gone by and Benjy has long since checked out. At last, the story comes back from then to now, and James, freed from its spell, expresses his gratitude: 'That is a fabulous story. Thank you.'

'Just a moment,' says Michael as an afterthought, and ducks under the counter, coming up with Rosa's old valise. 'Look, this, apart from the slippers, is pretty much what was left.' He springs the lid of the case and James peers in to see the heap of yellowing papers with their grainy blocks of type and spidery scrawls as Michael rattles on. 'I can't make head nor tail of it, but it all goes back to Methuselah, far as I can see. I forgot mosta the language, you understand, and never learnt to read it, what with the war and being so little. To be honest, I been in half a mind to burn the damn things.' Squinting at one yellowed old document as he holds it up to the light, James is less dismissive. 'You're talking to a professional archivist here, Michael,' he says. 'Old papers are often more valuable than you might think.'

'I doubt it. Anyhow, most of them are in Latvian.'

James shuffles deftly through the last of the papers. A kind of intensity is in him and Michael senses a mind keen for these things and knowledgeable of them. James pulls out a sheet and flips it on the countertop – the photograph of Rosa naked. Michael had put it out of sight and mind, and now it comes as a shock again. 'Don't even go there!' he says, flushing to the roots. But James is intrigued: 'That was her? Wow!'

'Yeah, like wow!'

James is curious now about the old heap of papers: 'You know there are thousands of Latvian Americans in this city.'

'The weird thing is I never met one of them.'

'I was gonna say, why don't you give these to me and I'll have someone go through them?'

'You could do that? All that time and trouble?'

'It would be my pleasure. Given that or the fire, no contest. A half-decent translator could go through this PDQ and extract the necessaries.'

'Gosh. That would be very kind of you. I dunno what to—'

'Like I say, it's nothing.'

And then, seeing darkness falling and being embarrassed at the thought of keeping a man from his work, James takes his purchases to the cash register. But he is still curious of one thing: 'So, what will happen to the slippers now?'

'That's one hell of a question.'

'It sounds like you would keep them if you had the chance.'

'If I had my way and it was a different world, maybe, but my family . . . There are a hundred and one ways to spend the money, believe me.'

'It's a dilemma a lot of people wouldn't mind having. God knows what I would do.'

'Well, anyways, it's not totally in my hands, but that's life. I suppose in the end I should maybe let it go.'

'Well, letting go might be an OK thing to do.'

'Except sometimes you let go you fall off.'

James looks at Michael a little puzzled. Life is never simple, but here's a man who just struck it lucky to the tune of Lord knows how much – enough to put a smile on anybody's face – and yet he looks as though he's just gained the world and lost his soul.

Riding the subway home, the finer feelings that have been with James start to desert him. The carriage is packed to busting and he is rammed up against the window by a colossus of a man breathing loud and urgent and using his sleeve to wipe a slick of sweat from his face. All along the dingy walls are glitzy ads at odds with the grimy reality of the carriage. Here are people of every background and ethnicity, all leeched of colour, crammed, sitting and standing, in spaces, like so many factory goods in racks. People who started their day fresh and full of energy, but dispirited now, their best taken from them. All these thoughts lead James for some reason back to his father, a man who made a fortune by cynically playing on the weaknesses and habits of others, manipulating them with promises and percentages. And all the trappings he and his cronies enlisted to carry it off: grand buildings on Wall Street and all over the city, halls of marble, chairs of leather, executives in suits – the whole repertoire of stage-craft and dazzling words to entice ordinary people to set aside their honest doubts and seek instead quick, impossible returns.

A sharp voice, close at hand, snaps James out of his dark trance. A good old-fashioned lunatic has appeared, concave of face and absent-eyed. James averts his gaze as the man weaves between the weary passengers, preaching to anyone who will listen, which is no one, about the chemicals *they* have put in the water to make people have bad dreams, and how it's scientifically proven that more people have bad dreams now than they used to.

Suddenly – the gods really have it in for him this day – the train stops in the damn tunnel. Just stops. The lights dim and fall pitch-dark a full ten minutes before coming back on, but the train itself stays stuck. James groans along with the rest. At this rate he will be home hopelessly late, failing yet again in his promise to Siobhan. He should have rung earlier, but all that excitement at Woody's shook him up.

For a half-hour the train sits there, getting hotter all the while, and the madman ranting now about how they can make you have whatever dreams they want you to have: if rats you hate, it's rats you see – snakes, vampires, headless riders – whatever is your worst nightmare, they can lay it on you, just by sprinkling stuff in the water.

As he gets set in for the long haul, James runs over recent events: the shock of encountering his father, a wounded monster in a wheelchair; then there were his 'heroics' with the spitter. But, even in the contemplation of these things, he sees himself as an inconsistent person, at times strong and together, but too often indecisive and prepared to tolerate other people's crap. He should have stood up to his father for being a horrible old hypocrite and sent him on his way, instead of meekly falling away like that. His thoughts turn to Jack – how he has arrived in his life all of a sudden, popping up everywhere like Sir Galahad, and even now getting him onto this new slipper plan. Crazy, he thinks, but surely just a bit of pie-in-the-sky between guys with a few drinks in them.

When at last the train lurches onward again and he finally comes to his stop, James jumps out at a trot to ring Siobhan, so as not to let her down. But it's eight-twenty by the time he is safely inside the apartment, and when he rings, she does not pick up. At last her voicemail kicks in and he hears himself, the inadequate person again: 'Hi, Siobhan. Listen, I'm sorry; I got stuck in the subway, would you believe? But I've been thinking of you lots, and there's lots to tell you. By the way, whaddya say we take a car, get out together, go to the ocean or wherever? Anyhow . . . uh . . . I hope you're doing good at school and, well, ring me. I'll try again. Stay good, honey.'

■ ◆ ■

The next I know, Felikss is saying that he hates New York, that it is old America and he must go to the new, where a man like him who has talent can reap rewards. In no time he had concluded through his contacts to go to California. It will be like before, he says, he will drive a truck and will do deals as we have done with the rubber boots, only much bigger and always in sunshine. Washing machines, he says; there are washing machines which have these new spin dryers, and California is going crazy for them. Why he decided on washing machines I had no clue. All I know is that never did I see one in his possession. But what I do know is that all of a sudden I am sitting with him on a bus going 3,000 miles from one coast to the other. It is easy to wonder why I put up with all this and followed such a man with his peculiar ways. But who was I to argue? Remember that Felikss had taken us from the lion's den to the land of the free, which I cannot imagine I could have done for myself. Also, there was true tenderness between us, though not the deepest love. We came together, I think, because we saw the suffering and the damage that had been done to each other. In both cases dreadful things had happened, so we were bound together in sympathy and to give comfort to each other. We were Hansel and Gretel holding hands in the woods.

The sun shines in south LA the same as everywhere in California, except you do not notice it so much. This is where Felikss had brought us to, a neighbourhood where the houses were cramped and piled up, in those days, in slums. This was bearable for Felikss because he went out every day, supposedly for his new venture, so he called it. There was still some money, so I believed he could find a vehicle, however old. Every day he was talking on the phone to his contacts, so I could see no reason he could not make a start, supplying all these machines that people would kill to buy. But now it seemed he did no work at all, just smoking and drinking and waiting for the phone to ring, then laughing and making jokes with whoever called. Why the man who worked so hard when it was for his life, was so casual when it was for his fortune, I was never able to explain. When at last I complained to him one time too many, Felikss turned tables on me and encouraged me to take up work that paid more than peanuts. And so I learned to sew American fashion. I had acquired this skill from an early age, but the styles and the techniques were all different, and Felikss, who cannot find a washing machine to save his life, suddenly produces out of nowhere a sewing machine, a Singer Electric for me to work on. And this is how I become seamstress by trade, a thing I hated at first as it was so laborious for me. I only did it because I remembered my mother saying that there was always work for dressmakers.

It was not long after this that Felikss then went away from me, which was in reality a relief because he had become so lazy and, strange to say, possessive, and suspected me and began to behave in an absurd manner. This was especially ridiculous, because I was all the time in the house, and the only people I ever see are women who need dresses or alterations done to them. On the other hand, I notice that he starts to spend his time in bars, and sometimes stays out late, and so the faithful man becomes faithless. Again, I did not scream and shout. In truth, my world did not come tumbling down, because Felikss was not my world, and always it was known that the thing between us was not love. And when this is the case it is so much easier to let it go.

Then, one day Felikss went out never to come back. I knew this as soon as I woke and found him gone. It was for the simple reason that when I have gone to open the drapes, I find the Singer also was gone, and I knew that he had weighed up everything of our relationship and so concluded that here was a few dollars he could get back from it. I was not bitter and, as I say, I did not cry, but still I was alone and having to eat and pay the rent.

For this reason I consider myself fortunate that I was able to find work in a dress shop in this same area of south Los Angeles, which was only a short bus ride away. I was employed by a woman who was lazy, but not in the use of her tongue, and who stood over my shoulder all the time while I did alterations for people. It was hard work to take up a hem before a customer left the store, or turn a blouse made for a thin person into one for a fat one. All the time, I told myself that good fortune would come my way, and it is true that it did, because one day a woman came in looking for buttons — buttons only, because it was for costumes in a movie production. She wanted big, big buttons of many different colours, and I gave much help to this woman to find what she was looking for, and when she saw that I was quick and careful in the work I was then doing, she asked me behind the back of my employer if I was interested in work that was similar but more rewarding. And when she revealed the nature of the position, I hardly needed to be persuaded.

And so I came to MGM without even trying. Considering the circumstance, it was chance that took me to the studio and onto the set of a strange new musical film that was only just beginning, and this was called The Wizard of Oz.

I remember the first day I turned up at the studios, dropped off from the bus in the middle of nowhere, but then seeing this never-ending expanse of buildings.

Coming to the gate, I did not know if I was in a palace or a factory, because here there are Roman columns and grand entrances, but there there are just long, low, flat buildings, like warehouses, and soon I see there are lovely offices also, with windows looking out over fields in sunshine.

Jane Sixsmith was the name of the woman who had come for the buttons, and it was her that I was to meet. As far as I knew, she was in charge of costumes, but then I discover there are so many people in charge of costumes, but all in different ways. Anyway, she asks me to keep in her footsteps and watch all the time to see everything she does, for this is how I will learn my job. And she takes me down many corridors then out into the open, then into a huge, high brick building, which from this point I am told is my place of work.

Strange that the building that looked so huge on the outside, looked on the inside even more enormous! All around the walls there are scaffolds and stands of lights all lit up, and racks of costumes and tables of props and machines and trucks for the cameras. But then in the middle, where the eye is taken, is a great fairytale palace, which is all lit up and glowing green and reaching to the invisible roof. This was, of course, the Palace of Oz, and in other parts of this enormous studio are more extraordinary places I can see. There is a forest, and even a river with a bridge over it, and magical white houses. And right in front of me was a white horse, a real living one, which men are dabbing with paintbrushes to make it purple! But most of all it is the people that amaze me — so many and so different and colourful: actors and dancers and extras dressed like circus performers, dwarves — so many — who look like they come from children's dreams. Then there are producers and technicians and designers, with whom I now belong, and soon I am told that I must go from character to character, who is lined up by the rails waiting for adjustments to their costumes. And I must help each one, according to the need, with alterations, a tuck to hold a waist, a dart to take in a top, a quick stitch to take up a hem.

This was October 1938 and already I have been learning English for six months and improving all the time. The production has only just begun, but soon I hear from conversations that all is confusion, with an army of writers, but the script not even finished, with actors being replaced and people fired and hired all the time, even though this was only two weeks into the production. Turn around, people said, and a new director, or actor, or writer was there. And so every-where people were grumbling and moaning and the magical place was a scene of much discontent.

At that particular time, there was much disturbance surrounding Margaret Hamilton, who was the Wicked Witch of the West. She had been badly burned to her face and hands when they tried to make her disappear in a puff of smoke, and was in hospital and six weeks off set because of this. Of course the gossip and complaining that came from this was huge, especially as she was so good a person under the costume.

In all this turmoil I continued to be good and steady at my job and always managing to keep a smile. Why should I not? Dealing with actors was better than dealing with Nazis, and working in a painted paradise was better than going home to a slum. Jane Sixsmith was very impressed with me, because it must be remembered I was still so young, just eighteen at this time.

It was because of all this chaos and confusion that I then was brought to the most extraordinary fortune of all, for a dresser had left — run off with a production accountant — and Jane brought me into the presence of Miss Judy, as she first was named to me. She took me to her, where she was just sitting in a chair at the side. Because she looked in her blue dress so ordinary in among so many extraordinary characters, I was not properly aware of her starring position in the movie. Also, I was an outsider in America and so did not know anything about her.

So when Jane introduced me to her, suggesting that I can help her with her costume, I did not realize how special a thing this was. To me, she looked like a frightened girl, more scared by far than me. But this was the great Judy Garland and soon I get the picture, when people come running up, bringing script changes for her to learn, or making a fuss to adjust her hair and powder her face. I think that Jane was smart in thinking that I would be good for Miss Garland. We were two girls of almost the same age — she sixteen and a half, and I only just eighteen — and although we were so physically different — her being so tiny and me so much taller and big in the bones — we had much in common and seemed to get along. And so I came to be the dresser for Judy Garland, from this time until the movie was made, which was five months.

To me, Miss Garland was nothing but kind and quiet and would stand happily while I sewed her into her costume and later helped those lovely shoes onto her feet. This is how I remember her: sad and quiet but at the same time funny, because she had a gorgeous sense of humour. These two opposite things so often go together, for it was the same with me, and it was this that made us easy with one another. There were stories going about that she was proud and had tantrums, but I never saw them on the set, and with all the confusion, she was one insecure person among many. You would think that she might like me not at all, because I was tall and also good-looking, and, as I soon discover, she was dreadfully self-conscious for her own appearance. The famous Judy Garland would ask me, the dresser, did I think she was good-looking under this light or from this angle? And always I would reply that she was beautiful and how much I envy her. And this was true, for while she was not of classical beauty, her loveliness was from the inside and always shone through. She loved me for saying this and saw that I was sincere, but the sadness is she never seemed to be convinced of it. On more than one occasion she asked of me if I thought she had talent, which was absurd, and this was after I hear her sing that wonderful song and after she acts in front of a thousand people who all stop everything they do to watch her, and every one of them worship her.

It did not help that to play this innocent little girl, Dorothy, they pushed and pulled her body all around — to bind her breasts flat and put caps on her teeth, and make special rubber discs to press her nose and make it not ugly. To me it was unbelievable that they did this, but she told me from her own mouth that they did not think much of her looks and that she was third choice for the part. She had been called ugly duckling all this time and the great Louis B. Mayer had a pet name for her, which was 'my little hunchback'. This was incredible to believe, but others told me it was true. No wonder she was very insecure. But there was worse than this. In order to have her always able to work, they gave her drugs. The studio day was long at this time, starting sometimes before seven in the morning and finishing as late as nine at night. All that time heaping stress and strain on her, who was like a *little girl. I saw it only once when it was late and she wanted to be in her bed and demanded to have her warm milk and her little pill. And this is what they fed to her. I did not comprehend it at the time, but found out the truth of it many years later — that in the mornings they gave her amphetamines for energy, and at night, barbiturates to make her sleep. And all this to make a movie, a made-up story on a screen.*

CHAPTER THIRTEEN

GREAT Aunt Crystal has been 'over the moon' ever since Harrison told her he would 'kinda like' to go back to the Tabernacle with her, and once again it has given her joy unending to see him make himself clean and presentable to go to the House of the Lord.

Three days after he made his declaration to Rain outside the school, the nephew holds up his arm and walks slow and upright so that the old aunt at his side can shuffle, pigeon-toed, along the dusk-damp sidewalk towards the Tabernacle.

Inside, the lights are low to assist the outpourings of the soul, and if anything the hubbub is noisier than before. As soon as he catches sight of Rain, seated on the other side of the great mahogany horseshoe, Harrison sizes up his best vantage point. 'No, not there, Aunty,' he says, 'in here.' And so he insinuates his aunt and himself into a row right at the front and directly opposite the gorgeous girl and her parents. The zappings and babblings are well under way now and the dingy light gives him greater freedom to sound his soul, and in among some 'Yessirs!' he now floats up a few 'Well, rights!' and even an 'Alleluia' in response to the minister's rantings. And when Crystal pushes herself to the gangway at the end of the row and hits the floor twirling, he inches himself just to the edge. Closer to the action, he can see the people speaking in tongues, rocking their bodies and lifting their eyes to God, who seems to be somewhere up in the massive central chandelier. He looks across again before starting to sway and stumble on the spot, doing his level best to look like the Holy Spirit is in him. 'Abiba huala cooka,' he cries out, which sounds kind of right among the holy babble. He shoots a glance across to where Rain is standing so graceful, and catches her eye and sees her shyly cast down her eyes.

Afterwards, they go again to the social area, and eventually he summons the courage to raise his own gaze from the floor. She is there, laughing at her father's side. What a wonderful jolt it is to see her close up, bright and shining in that same blue dress. She smiles at him. He loves her, surely loves her, and his heart begins to thump. 'Could I see you a moment, please?' she asks, and leads him out of the back door and up the side path to the street. He follows in a daze. What is this for? My God, does it mean she feels the same as him, that she wants to tell him privately how much she would like to be with him? They arrive on the sidewalk, a little way away from the Tabernacle. 'This is for you,' she says sweetly, and deals him, as hard as she can, a single slap, her palm weighty on his face. It is so loud people turn in the street. 'Don't you ever come to God's house and pretend to be what you are not!' she rails. He stands there, childish, rubbing his face and smiling like a fool because he cannot cry.

'Now go back in there, and be kind to your aunty and learn from good people what it means to be good!' Like a schoolmistress, she stands ramrod-straight, pointing the way for him to go, accepting no other possibility, until he turns and walks, with head bowed, back towards the building.

■ ◆ ■

Such a sweet and gentle soul, Michael thinks to himself as she spells out the rest of her order: 'Yes, and some of the pastrami please, the usual amount.' Gracious as ever he is with this customer, he arranges the meat in the slicer and cranks the handle over, the heavy wheel turning in its slow scything rhythm, the slices easing into being, smooth and perfect of shape. Michael likes to serve this lady, the little Filipino nurse whose name he has never quite remembered but who always has a feeling of peace about her. 'Good,' he says. 'And would you like some of the . . .' Over her shoulder, he sees something fearful: a police car cruising smooth and silent into the window space, its tyre crunching against the kerb. 'Mr Marcinkus, are you all right?' she asks, all anxious. But he is already oblivious, and she watches in amazement as he glides out from behind the counter, feverishly wiping his hands on his apron. In the time it takes for the policeman to get out of the passenger door on the other side, Michael manages to pull himself together. So, the game is up. Harrison spilled the beans, and he must face it with dignity.

He stands dead in the doorway, ready to step forward and hear the charges against him and be led away. But when the officer reaches the door, he sees to his relief that it's his son-in-law, Karl. Relief is quickly overtaken by growling resentment, and he watches, cold-eyed, as Karl enters, his hat scraping against the door frame. 'Whaddya want?' The look on Michael's face has lost none of the reptilian hostility that was on it last time they met. Karl peers beyond Michael and sees Inez standing there, curious and concerned, but he is as reluctant to speak as Michael is to listen. At last, though, he finds it in him to squeeze out the minimum of words: 'I have to talk to you.'

'OK. Fine, so talk,' says Michael, blithe all of a

sudden, but Karl is not amused. 'What am I supposed to do here, say it right out in front of everybody?' Michael shrugs and motions him over to the window seat. Karl draws up a stool. 'A coffee would be nice.' Michael sighs and beckons Inez forward to the cash register. 'My son-in-law,' he mutters, as if it explains the strangeness of the situation. But she is too kind and polite to enquire further and busies herself with arranging the groceries in her bag.

'Ah', she says, and 'thank you' and 'goodbye', and is gone.

He goes to the coffee machine while Karl turns the sports pages lying there. As he brings over the coffee and looks at Karl, perched on the stool, Michael pretends not to notice the muddy streak, the faded line of bruises along his neck, just below the collar. For all of a millisecond, he allows himself to feel repentant, to feel sorry for the guy having such a time of it, trying his best to be reasonable when really he had every right to hit out at his cussed old father-in-law. Michael draws up a stool of his own, trying not to look at all interested in what Karl has to say. 'You know that the shoes are gonna be sold?' says Karl, just like that.

'I had noticed, since every reporter in New York fetched up at my door.'

'Yeah, well that wasn't meant to be.'

'You had no right.'

'*You* had no right to try and kill me. We all do things

we don't have the right to do. D'ya wanna argue about it?' And the two go eyeball to eyeball, until Karl sees fit to move matters on: 'Now, about this black kid been hassling you.'

'Since when did I say that?'

'Since your poor suffering wife said so. Anyways, it's taken care of; you don't need to bother your head about it no more.'

'I don't remember asking for your help on the matter.'

'You don't have to ask. All in the family, Michael. Just so you know. Now excuse me, I have to go. My partner is waiting.'

'Nice of you to drop by.'

'No problem.'

Michael watches ruefully as the cop car wheels round and roars away. Karl's eyes are fixed front; not once does he turn to look back in Michael's direction. And so he does not see the lonely old man stoop over and reach out his hand to steady himself against the wall, for into his head has come a sudden rush of heat and a swirling, swelling feeling that would tip him over. And there Michael remains a full minute until the heat goes out of him and the ground is in one place again. Wearily, he sinks onto the stool that's still warm from Karl's fat ass, and swivels around to peer along the shadowy rows. He senses the apartment above his head, creeping cold. The world is against him, yet he's no monster, so how come so many are lined up in opposition?

In his desolation, painful memories reel in his mind like a tuneless song stuck on replay: Rosa lying in her own dark place; the family all slack-mouthed and baying like dogs because he dared to dream; Harrison's face with the rage stamped on it as he held that knife up to him; and himself lying for ever on that floor, fused cold to the stone. The worst of it is Grace herself – staying on at Jenny's, clinging there for sanctuary, as if he had ever threatened her or shown aggression in their whole marriage, beyond raising his voice now and then. What does she fear would happen to her if she came home? That he would kill her and stuff her body under the floorboards? Does she not worry for him? Does it give her pleasure to think of him so cold and lonely? Once more he thinks of Rosa lying there senseless: it all started with her and yet she feels nothing – she is protected from the slings and arrows while he dies a thousand deaths on her behalf. And within himself, sitting on the stool he has hardly ever sat on, Michael makes his decision. Let them go, he tells himself. Don't stand in the way. Be neither right nor wrong. Let them go and if all hell breaks loose and people end up taking a fall, there would be no arguing he had not warned them. Let it be their problem.

■ ◆ ■

As she shuts the apartment door behind her, Donna Inez is automatically on the alert for the sound of the chair whirring into life, for the sound of his voice slashing and slaying. Nothing. So her remedy is going well. He has been so much quieter lately, less violent in temper and not so quick to hurl insults. He has complained of feeling drowsy and woozy and so nauseous he was sick several times and sleeping all the more. His mobility and mental capacity have also been visibly slower, which is, of course, in keeping with his disease. And she has arrived at the perfect daily dosage – for each tablet prescribed, one of her own little top-ups, which she has obtained from her own doctor to treat the arthritis that has lately sprung up so mysteriously. It is the best of all worlds: his nastiness contained, the onset of side effects not too sudden and the satisfaction of knowing that this will see him nicely on his way. It is a fact, too, that the more the Oxycontin takes hold, the more his illness has its way. There have been messes on the bathroom floor, humiliations that have made him lost and brooding, his helplessness almost touching, so that Inez has thought more than once of slacking off on her little extras.

He is watching the TV now in the sitting room. These awful programmes used to make him restless, spoiling for a fight, but now they hold his attention for up to two hours at a go. She can hear a syrupy sales-channel voice cooing and gushing over cheap jewellery. Before, he wouldn't have stuck with this kind of trash for longer than five minutes. He must have fallen asleep in front of it. Good. Less work for her.

■ ◆ ■

'Good,' says the voice. 'Now, listen . . .'

'How did you get my number?' jabs back Harrison.

'That's neither here nor there. Now listen, six thirty, down by the bridge next to the playground.' He weighs it up. There is authority in this voice, and he likes the way the guy gets right down to it, not at all like the grocer man. 'OK,' he says. 'So how come I don't deal with the grocer no more?'

'Do you want the money or not?'

'Yeah. But why you—'

'Good. Six thirty. Don't be late.'

■ ◆ ■

He goes through his wardrobe, looking for sporty clothing: T-shirt, baggy track pants, and the Nike bag, of course, to carry back the money. He likes the look of himself in the mirror. Yeah, when he has money to spend he'll wear this more, only more out-there and with plenty of real gold. And come to think of it, he will take sports more serious, have a couple of hoops in his garden and join a gym if he can't stretch it to have his own.

Great Aunt Crystal is overjoyed to see him so caring

of his appearance. She struggles to get up off her knees in front of the oven she has been cleaning, and looks him up and down: 'So, honey, where you going?'

'To play ball.'

'Who with?'

'Ah, the usual suspects.'

As the door shuts after him, she smiles broadly to herself: Goodness, the boy is coming out of his shell!

■ ◆ ■

And so Harrison turns up at the right place at the right time. The man had sounded reasonable and not unfriendly and when he had asked why they should meet there as opposed to anywhere else, the man had simply said over again, 'Do you want the money or not?' But now, arriving with the darkness, he suddenly feels not so good about rushing into it. And he is right to have these feelings, because out from behind a wall come two big men in dark practical clothing who, without greeting or explanation, proceed to punch, kick and pummel him to the ground. As they do this, not a word is said, not even to curse or to express their contempt of him. It's a technical beating, their kicks and punches carefully placed for maximum pain and minimum damage, to cause fear and distress but avoid real harm.

And when Harrison lies groaning on the ground, one of the men stands over him and lets go a shower of money, a hundred dollars in brand-new one-dollar bills, tumbling all over him and settling like snow, the just reward for all his pains.

■ ◆ ■

'Incredible,' says Steve.

'Incredible,' says Jack.

'Incredible,' says James, as they all stand back to look at the figures on the screen. And it is indeed beyond belief. The guys at Woody's did not forget Jack's big idea and they did not dismiss the notion of the memorial to Paolo as a naive fantasy cooked up by a few half-cut guys on a spring evening. Rather, James found himself swept up in a whirlwind of good intentions and willing hands as people decided they should go for it. The ruby slippers had meaning, and not just for them. And so their plans had taken shape: they would call on people all over America and ask them to pledge a single dollar and a dream, in return for a share in the slippers. Woody himself rang James and offered the run of his back room, and in a flash the guys came together to donate their nights and weekends.

'OK, time to eat,' declares James, and watches with quiet satisfaction as the others down tools and take up pizza. Jack is there, the mainstay, and there is Steve, an older, bearlike fellow who hardly has a word to say to his fellow man, but can whisper all kinds of poetry into a mainframe to make it sing. And there is Miles the musician, who seems to be able to do just about anything except get on with people. Between the four of them, they have in ten days got the whole juggernaut up and running, incorporated a not-for-profit company, begged, borrowed and stolen the hardware, and harvested returns beyond their imagining. The pledges have just poured in. Americans of every gender, age, colour and persuasion, snapping up their dollar shares in the Ruby Million – $800,081: that's what it says on the screen, and how close they are to the magic number. 'Hey, James, sit down and eat yourself,' calls out Jack. 'Well, I'm not that hungry, but I'll try the pizza,' jokes James, sharp as a tack.

As he sits quietly chewing, with high harmonies drifting in from the piano-room singers, James feels what it is to be human among humans and to know that laughter is as essential as oxygen. His father starved himself of it and look how poisonous he became. Corinne drove it out of her life and played the martyr and look what happened to her. James reflects with quiet satisfaction that this has been a good thing for him, and has in fact made him unafraid to be what he is: a gay man among gay men. He thinks, too, of the sheer multiplicity of human beings he has come across in the campaign, so many of them decent and kind, but so many others crazy to the hilt – the obsessives and JG nuts who think that just by wearing cheap imitations of these shoes you can blow up your own magic balloon and float away inside it. Then, with their own variations of insanity, were the rednecks and the queer-baiters, quick to send their ugly illiterate messages, saying how faggotism was a disease sapping the manhood of the nation, and how he and his kind should be put up against a wall and shot.

Schwartz, his manager, visited him personally to complain because the press flocked to the library, hot for the story. But even he had the common sense to acknowledge that all publicity is good publicity for the NYPL. James knows the visit was a warning, though, and for a few minutes he starts to dwell on hurtful things. Then Jack floats up a harmless little question: 'So, James, what you gonna say tonight?'

'Tonight?'

'Yeah, on *New York Now.*'

'Tonight?! Is it really tonight? Hell!' What a thing to forget. They had invited him on the TV station to tell the whole damn city about the Ruby Million and he had fallen in without a murmur. What had gotten into him, he who had always preferred to stay quiet and out of the limelight? He looks around at his companions in crime. Well, he can't send Steve, that's for sure, him taking a minute to complete a sentence, and certainly not Miles, who is as abrasive as a cheese grater, nor Jack, who is too much the child. Nothing for it, he will just have to go and do it, for Christ's sake. Nonetheless, he hasn't a clue what he will say, which is all too clear on his face, because Jack, by way of encouragement, says, 'You'll be fine. Tell it how it is – the facts, the figures, which are all great. And I could go with you, if it was OK?'

'Go with me?'

'Sure – if you want me there.'

'Well, I don't see why not,' he says mildly, but inwardly irritated that Jack should once again muscle in like this. 'But we should meet up there, if you don't mind. I need to go somewhere first.'

■ ◆ ■

The door opens and Harrison shuffles in, a walking corpse. Great Aunt Crystal lets out a godforsaken wail and drops the vase of flowers she has been fussing with

'Oh my golly gosh, what happened?!'

'Look at me, Aunty Crystal,' he whines, all attempt at pretence gone, all need for slyness and secrecy beaten out of him, along with the fierce desire that drove him to such trickery. Now he is like a child again, wanting the comfort that can come to a child. Crystal throws her arms around Harrison, and he allows himself to be held, feeling the bumps and bruises a little less cruel and deadening than they had been on his stumbling journey home.

'Who did this?'

'I dunno.'

'Call the police, we should call the police!'

He is not quite enough of a child to let her take him down this road. Instead, he tells her he went to the cops already but couldn't tell them anything because he hadn't seen anything, just a couple of men in the dark. And he tries to put her mind at rest by telling her it's bumps and bruises only and no real harm done. The motive was robbery, he adds, them having taken his sports stuff and all out of his bag – the same bag that's lying downstairs, behind the bins where he has stuffed it. (After the men stopped beating on him and ran off leaving him lying there, he had gathered up the scattered bills and dumped them inside.)

When Crystal has done bathing his face and fixing him a bite to eat and offering a prayer, Harrison drags himself to his room. And there he lies down, and turns over and cries, not because he is a baby, not because he cannot take pain, but because he has lost something he believed would change him and raise him up to better things. Everyone deserves for their life to come to something. Even a bad man can have good dreams.

■ ◆ ■

People always say how glamorous it was for me, to be in Hollywood, working on what was to become so amazing a movie, and that to be with Judy Garland herself and hear her sing was such bliss. It's strange that I never felt this at the time, and yet the more I look back, the more it has indeed become magical to me and belonging to a dream.

Of course this was 1939. In Europe the war was soon to come and there came terrible times. Magda wrote to me on only one occasion, after I had written many times before to her. She asked if I would help her family to escape because everything had become terrible. They were in fear the Germans or the Russians — they did not know which — were to invade at any time. My mother had died, which was terrible to hear, of course, and made me cry for days, and they were soon to be in starvation. Starvation. I did not know what it means — they were not in front of me for me to see. So often people say they are starving when their meal arrives late in the restaurant, and here she was saying they are desperate and telling me there is a way that I could help them from America.

She told to me that I should obtain work for Janis in Hollywood — just to get my bosses to write letters saying they are prepared to give him work as carpenter or electrician, it did not matter which one, because he will supply papers to show him to be essential worker. Of course, I know this is ridiculous, because Janis is just trader selling things and always full of fantasy. Also, who am I to go to studio managers and get letters, Mr Louis B. Mayer? No, I am new to the job and I am just a dresser, right at the bottom of the heap. It was ridiculous and also, now that I have to

293

say the truth, I had enormous reason to be angry with my sister and her husband, and because of this I do not really understand and I do nothing, not even to reply. Again I do not know why — maybe because I did not understand the power that was in my hands, or maybe because I could not imagine in my mind the terror that was happening in the peaceful country of my memory. Or maybe it was because I did not want to be coming to face again with things I had tried to forget.

So I did not take any action, even though I do not believe anything would have come from it if I did. Also, I was selfish, and for the first time in love and making friends and thinking only for each day, not of the suffering of others. But all of this later came on my conscience, and behind it all there was another, deeper shame. The truth is that I turned away, not even meaning to — not because I was cruel or desiring of revenge, but because I did not stop to think, and because there was grief in me and because really I was still so young.

I mention before that I was in love. This was a handsome young actor, Tom Shelden, he had only a bit part in the movie, but saw it as a stepping stone. He had been a stage painter but had big ideas. He came from a good family, of which my mother would approve, and he was so funny all the time — a big man and brave, but with the manner of a little boy, always being naughty but charming, so that you would shower

*him only with kisses instead of smacks. Much of my
father I saw in him — the charm and the courage. In
appearance he was like Clark Gable and just as manly,
but fair of hair with the same twinkling eye. It was so
true because I once had meet Mr Gable face to face.
But there ends the resemblance, because Tom could
not bring these qualities onto the screen and could not
deliver lines in a believable way. I know this because
they send him scripts for test, which he read to me, and
never they came out right and I could see that he would
not have success. So, it was the man I gave myself to,
not the glamour and money that might come to him.
It was for love alone and I could see all my happiness
in his eyes. And yes, it was Tom who was the man with
whom I went to the Palace of Oz when it was deserted,
and who was with me when I found the ruby slippers.
The events of this I write in another letter, which I
place separate to this account. Should you find this
you also find that story.*

CHAPTER FOURTEEN

Bored to the edge of reason, Siobhan flicks and flutters between chattering ads, hyperactive comedy shows and stiff-backed, stern-faced news blasts – babbling nonsense, all of it. She stretches back, idle-fingered, for a banana on the dresser behind her, and it falls to the floor. As she is crouching down, fishing and fumbling for it, she hears a familiar voice and looks up. There – impossible – on the screen is her dad in a blue suit, sitting legs crossed on a couch, jabbering away under the lazy eye of the chat show's host, who sits by, picking his nails: 'Well, the whole thing has been totally, totally beyond believing . . .'

'Mom! Mom!' she mews as James witters on, bright and eager. She has forgotten that Corinne is out, practising with the Newton Harbour Sound Collective – her 'weekly dose of choral tranquillity', as she calls it.

'It started off as a crazy idea, then became a not bad idea . . .' continues James. 'Then so many amazing, kind people came to us from everywhere, and it just kind of took off under its own momentum, and I knew it was a really good idea.'

'What is this?' she shrieks to no one but herself. As if for his daughter's exclusive benefit, James continues, warm and expansive, to explain the situation: 'We called it the Ruby Million so that it could be for hundreds, thousands of people from every place and every background, and nobody would have more than their share.' She watches in dumb fascination as he grows more eloquent by the second, settling to his story. Until, that is, the host – who up to now has sat easy in his chair, nodding his head and listening intently – suddenly leans in to James like a cardsharp and oh so calmly pops his killer question.

'So James, what is it about Judy Garland and the ruby slippers that gay people find so fascinating?' Thrown a little, James tries to keep it simple for the man, but it all comes out huffy and defensive: 'Oh no, this is not just for gay people. People of all kinds – every gender, age, religion, let alone sexual persuasion . . .'

'Yeah, but what is it about? I mean, why do gays

worship her? Is it about sex? In which case I don't get it; she was no Monroe.'

'I think you'll find it's many things: about ideals – people standing up for truth, innocence and the right of—'

The host is in the zone now, and he goes in strong for the pay-off: 'Or is it a kinky thing, like with the dressing up and everything?'

Sensing a disaster in the making, Siobhan yells at the TV: 'No, no, don't go there!'

James grasps for something solid to hitch himself to: 'Well, there's always some people who . . . but this is about anybody who would like to—'

'Yeah, but what I'm asking, I suppose, is why would any average red-blooded guy, or gal, give a damn about your campaign?'

And right there, right there on the screen, James visibly wilts, the whole goodwill thing between him and the host evaporating under the studio lights. Siobhan watches appalled as her father, wronged and wrong-footed, gives vent to his feelings for all the world to see: 'I . . . I don't think you heard what I . . . Why are we going down this line? What's it got to do with—?'

'Sorry, but I'm just trying to get to the heart of it. I mean, people out there are . . . they really do wanna know what it is with gays and the whole Judy Garland thing . . .' The host sits back, affable again. But James is on the edge of his chair, livid. 'I'm sorry, I can't go on with this,' he mutters.

Siobhan watches in horror as he gets to his feet, pulls off his mic and walks off the set. 'Oh my god,' she says to the bare walls. 'This can't be real; somebody tell me this wasn't real!'

■ ◆ ■

Harrison stands square at Finn the dealer's door, psyching himself up to reach out and knock. For sure he will do it – put it to them – there's nothing to lose. It takes an age for Finn to arrive, and when at last he does scrape open the battered door, instead of making his usual greeting of, 'Hey, my man,' he just stands there, blinking. And when Harrison tells him that he hasn't come to score but to talk about something cool, Finn just looks past him and tells him he has 'company'. The sly old skinny dog, thinks Harrison, but remains staring unabashed at Finn, his battered face conveying the urgency of his call, until Finn dives back in and returns seconds later, saying, 'OK, you have exactly ten minutes.' Following on Finn's heels, Harrison is a little put out to discover that the 'company' is in fact a guy called Curtis, a big black dude in a sharp suit, who's sitting lounging in Finn's miserable nothing of a back room, so laid-back and relaxed that he could be on Deck A of a cruise liner. He is in the middle of an unfeasibly long toke of a joint and pays out the smoke in a cloud, offering it on to neither of them, but demanding instead to know, 'Who is this guy?'

'Harrison. He's OK. Small-time but OK,' says Finn by way of a testimonial, and Harrison realizes that he is in the presence of someone a little more impressive than easy-going Finn. 'So whaddya want, Harrison?' asks Curtis, indicating by his manner that his time is short and answers should come quick. Given seconds flat to decide whether to tell this powerful stranger his secret, Harrison's first instinct is to go straight back out the door; but Curtis is clearly miles higher up the food chain than Finn, and Harrison needs to aim high. Yeah, the man's presence is fortunate, now he comes to think about it. 'Well,' he starts. 'I have this truly beautiful proposition, but I gotta tell ya the whole story. Then you can see why I look like this . . .'

They sit back and listen as he proceeds to unfold the whole tortured saga of the ruby slippers. He relates the ups and the downs and wildness of it, watching them watching him: Finn the skinny, button-eyed white man; Curtis, the formidable black man with luminous eyes growing wider and fatter on his story. Thus Harrison becomes conscious of himself as storyteller, his words forming and flowing into shape, expression arriving in his voice. Such a good job he's making of it, he thinks; he can see them nodding and smiling and willing it on. Convinced he has them hooked, he continues to tell them how he turned master criminal, and staked out the deli and went right in, and came up from below, and disturbed the grocer, fought him and defeated him, even though he had a knife. On he goes, describing how he later went back and saved the grocer's life and tried to strike a deal with him, which after all was reasonable, considering the grocer's guilt and his debt to him. He looks up again, expecting to see them nodding in agreement, sharing his outrage, but the two of them just sit there, calm and quiet, waiting for him to bring the whole thing to its end. As he moves on to the episode of his betrayal by white men unknown and the assault that was visited on him, Harrison begins to lose his composure: 'These guys, these two big guys, they fucking beat on me,' he says. 'Fucking punched and kicked me to the ground and threw a hundred dollars down on me – a hundred bucks that shoulda been two-fifty K!'

His story done, Harrison stands back, pretty pleased with himself. 'That's a cool story,' says Curtis, sagely and looking over at Finn.

'Cool,' says Finn. 'A little fucking weird, but cool.' They are clearly impressed, the pair of them, with what they have heard.

'I tell you it's true, bro, every last word,' says Harrison, smug to see them won over, but his smile is soon wiped away when Curtis asks, bluntly, 'So whaddya want we should do about it?'

'Well, look at it,' blurts Harrison, 'there's these two

fucking shoes laying somewhere right at this moment, waiting on someone to come along and just get in on them for like hundreds a thousands.'

'So we – you, me, whoever – we just go to the grocer, put the screws on him and he coughs up because he feels guilty and he has this big amazing debt to you?'

'Well, yeah. Because he stole them. And I was thinking, if the right people went to him and said the right things, and he saw they was like serious and could back it up, he would have to play ball. And he can't say nuthin' nor do nuthin'.'

'But he already did do something, like he kicked your ass.'

'That was the other guys.'

'Right, so who are the other guys?'

'I dunno. Relatives maybe.'

'And who has the shoes? Him or them?'

'Uh, I dunno.'

'So now we're dealing with the grocer and his wife, and the two unknown guys and his dog and his cat, and in addition to that, there's you, there's me and whoever else we would have to bring into this and divide it up?'

'Uh, yeah, well, I didn't really—'

'Like you thought it was so fucking simple.'

'Well it still is, kinda, ain't it?'

'No it is not. Look at me. This is what we do, me and him over there: we buy, we supply, we count the money. It's simple, we do it every day. This proposition of yours is not simple; it stinks, man. You would be dealing with amateurs, scared people, and you never know what they would do and who they would go to once the heat was on them. Who do you think we are, the fucking mob?'

Harrison can't believe what he's hearing: 'So you're saying no?'

'I'm saying, you just took a half-hour of my precious time when you were given ten minutes. So I suggest you fucking disappear right fucking now.'

'Wha—?' says Harrison, incredulous and a little slow on the uptake.

'You hear me?' yells Curtis, more than a little pissed. But Harrison just stands there stammering: 'I . . . I . . .'

'Go, H. Just go!' hisses Finn between his teeth and, seeing Curtis starting to rise out of his chair, he takes hold of Harrison's sleeve and outright drags him to the door. 'What did I say wrong?' whimpers Harrison, while Finn manoeuvres him through the door and says in fond farewell, 'Fuck off, jackass, and think about it!'

■ ◆ ■

The next half-hour is lost in a blur for James. Somehow, he must have made it to the men's room, wiped the make-up from his face, put on his coat, taken the elevator down and gone out through the heavy glass doors into the chilly night. Yes, Jack must have helped him to escape from the *NYNow* building, without him even

303

being aware, because here they are, him and the timid youngster, marching side by side along a darkened street unknown to him.

'It's just along here,' offers Jack, clarifying nothing, and hops up the steps of an apartment block. 'Come on, you need a coffee after that.'

While Jack goes off to make coffee, James sits on the little white leather couch and looks around the apartment, which is small but uncluttered, with not a single ornament or picture in view. All the same, with its soft lighting and carefully blended tones, it's an easy place to be, and James becomes more relaxed. Soon, though, his emotions get the better of him and he's plunged back again into the recent debacle: trapped in the gaze of the interviewer again, with his innuendos and sly, toothy smile. And so, preoccupied, James fails to notice that Jack is gone a full fifteen minutes from the room. It's only the sound of the door clicking open again that brings him back to the here and now. 'There,' says Jack, stepping primly into the room and holding out a mug of coffee, as if this somehow illuminates the shocking sight he has made of himself. James looks up, then stands in his astonishment. Gone is the shy, diffident young man, and standing there, serene and shining, is Judy Garland. Or rather Judy as Dorothy – the wide, smooth, yet vexatious brow, the round brown eyes, the snub nose, and, of course, the tiny crimson pout of a mouth. And Jack, as Judy – or

Dorothy – has worked other wonders, too, blending into his own strawberry blonde hair a silky pair of plaits. The pert, powder-blue dress is there as well, as are the bobby socks and a pair of replica ruby slippers, neatly pointing out from the heels, to round off the unmistakable embodiment of the girl from Kansas. 'Apparently I look a lot like her,' whispers Jack. 'Uh . . . yes, yes you do,' James finds himself saying. The alarm bells are going off, but bizarre though it is, the resemblance is striking and he can't take his eyes off her/him, or is it him/her? And now that he looks closer he can see how every tiny detail is there, down to each individual freckle, applied one by one to rose-pink cheeks. Jack smiles happily, fantasy and reality arriving together. 'They say I could make a living from it – if I wanted to.'

James takes a step backwards, feeling for an escape route: 'Right. I'm sure you could. Listen, though, Jack. Uh, I really do have to—' But then, in an instant, Jack is right up on him, his eyes fastened intensely on James's. This is it, the thing James has only just begun to fear might happen, but has no stomach to confront. 'You can hold me, if you like.' James backs away, his hands up, shield-like. 'Jack, no, please. I—'

'Please, James. Just let me say it; I have to say it: I love you.'

And James sees with absolute clarity that Jack has gambled all that he is on this one moment, everything in him subservient to James's wishes as the adored older man, and given into his hands. He should say something kind and forbearing and wise, but not a word comes to mind. It has been the most terrible day and it is far from over. 'I'm sorry, Jack. I should go now,' he mutters, shamefaced, and walks right past him to the door, knowing that there is no way he can stay and make things better, and no way he can go without trampling over the young man's pride. As he stumbles down the stairs, Jack's sudden rage reaches down the stairwell to him in a demented yowl that is a million miles away from the lovely Dorothy: 'You bastard! You led me on! You played with me, you fucking prick-tease!'

Scurrying down the street, clueless for direction but heading for lights far-off, James goes over the connected moments of their friendship. No way did he give out signs. For sure, it is all in the poor guy's mind, but he feels somehow to blame, although God knows how, and he resolves never to speak a word of this – to Jack himself or any other living soul.

■ ◆ ■

He arrives outside his own door, eager to keep out of his aunt's way, regretting that he had told her he was going out to see Dale and Floyd – God knows why he spun that lie. So now he stands, feeling exposed and lonely – humiliated by the dangerous Curtis, mocked by the weasel Finn – and he didn't get so much as a puff of a hit. He will get inside and slink to his room before she can bombard him with questions about how his day has gone and drown him in cakes and food. But when he searches in his pocket for the key, it is not to be found and, furious, he jabs at the bell push. She is there like a jack-in-the-box, the door flying open. 'Come on in, honey. Ah, you poor thing; look how tired you look! Aw . . . Take off that jacket and sit down. You're just in time for—'

'No, Aunty, I don't want nuthin'.'

'Nonsense, I made your favourite: stew.'

She has a hold of his jacket, trying to peel it from his arm. And now he just can't help himself: 'Let go my fucking jacket!' he rasps, irritated. On occasion she has been known to let this kind of language pass, but today she will not have it. 'Excuse me! No cussing, thank you! You know perfectly well, young man, we don't allow no—'

That's it, she started it, he will finish. He pours every last ounce of his energy into the words that erupt out of him: 'I said let go my fucking jacket, and while you're there, shut the fuck up! You can stick your fucking stew; I don't want your fucking apple pie, and take your fucking prayers to Jesus fucking Christ and shove the whole fucking lot up your fucking skinny old-woman ass! OK?'

Stunned, she sways on her feet, her mouth opening and closing like a landed fish, such sinfulness an impossibility. He stands over her, pointing in her face.

His teeth are bared and his body all of a-quiver, the crazed appearance of him telling her that she speaks at her own peril. She cowers beneath him, feeling his shocking power over her, until at last he puts down his hand and skulks away to his room.

All afternoon she cries, and all afternoon he sits with his head jammed against the head of the bed, his dirty boots up on the quilt, his thoughts cannoning between God and the devil, as he prays on the one hand to be released – to let the shoes go and come out clean – and on the other to keep on going, get his dues and make his enemies pay. And it is this constant collision of dark desires that finally sends him off to sleep. And when he wakes up with a start only a quarter-hour later, although it seems like six, he can hear her out in the kitchen, crying still, her heart all this time stricken with sorrow. I am sick, he says to himself. I am bad. But the demon is not yet dead in him: 'God take this from me,' he says in one breath, and, 'Fuck them all!' he says in another. If he can't have what was his to have, then he will take them all to hell with him.

■ ◆ ■

All of next morning James stays firmly in his shell. Marcia and the others tiptoe around him, hardly daring to speak. He makes it through to lunchtime, aware by now that Jack has not shown up for work and not sure whether to be relieved or concerned. He goes to Sergio's for lunch, where the waitress, an old friend, practically, tells him to carry on regardless. So what if people saw? For every person who saw a show on a two-bit channel, there's a hundred others who didn't. 'You don't understand,' he tries to explain. 'I've been a damn fool!' He hasn't told her about the close encounter he had with Jack, which made even more of a dumb-ass of him, and he doesn't want to go into how he has lain awake all night with the realization that he has been a victim of his own delusions in just about every way.

When he gets back from lunch, the first person he sees is Jack, up a stepladder, sorting outsize art books into order. It's as if he has positioned himself in the most conspicuous spot for James to see him, and his dress is particularly simple and sober – the message being that he is ordinary and at his work, although his eyes are firmly turned away, and neither man acknowledges the other's presence.

Later in the afternoon, James takes coffee in the workroom and is properly alone, a blessed relief, with no Jack to trot around after him and hang on his every word. Well, he knows now why the guy kept popping up all over the place; if only the penny had dropped earlier. 'What the hell possessed me?' he says to himself, thinking of Jack and the botched chat show, but also of his whole involvement in the Ruby Million farrago. Even as he is wincing at the thought, his phone rings, and there is Steve on the line, the one of few words, but sounding a little excited.

'Hi, Steve,' he says, a little wary. 'Wassup?'

'James, thought you should know. We just hit the mark.'

■ ◆ ■

It was after The Wizard of Oz that Tom started to get small parts in cowboy films and even learned to ride a horse. I thought it was such fun really and not too badly paid. And he was so happy, always saying to me, 'Howdy pardner,' and to other people that the work was as easy as falling off a horse. But never did his career get off the ground. At one time he tried to push me into the movies, saying I could be like Garbo, the new Garbo, but this was ridiculous, and after one dreadful test where my accent was to me a handicap, I did not go back and was happy, anyway, working in costume, so long as I had my man. Even if he did not have a great career, Tom had many friends, not only in the studios, because he came, as I say, from a well-connected family, and this brought us into many social occasions. As well as the premieres and gala nights, there was many wonderful parties where champagne flows like water, and we even were invited for weekends onto yachts right out into the ocean, which always I loved. This was when I was most happy. It could be said that I had no right to behave so greedy and selfish when before I had behaved so shamefully, but these memories were my comfort when others have been my shame.

It was mentioned before that my father was musi-cian. Well, some of his musical gift must have come to me, because I had a good ear and could sing well without any noticeable accent. And this is how I sang to large numbers of people, many of them famous, songs like 'Putting on the Ritz' and 'Night and Day'. It is hard to imagine that I should ever behave in such a way — even on one occasion to stand on the lid of a grand piano to perform. It seemed the sun was always shining on this life I had, and with all this I had for-gotten everything I had come from and my sorrows had gone away. Perhaps I am selfish, perhaps I am cruel, but it was only when the war came to America that I stopped to think again about my family so far away, but by then it was too late.

When war was declared, Tom did not even care at first to see other men go off to fight; he continued to try for parts. Eventually, when the fighting was all in the east, he signed up to fight for his country, but I noticed that it was only after his career did not go right that he became the patriot. I did not want him to go, but he asked of me to be strong and wait for him, and so I did. And when I did not hear from him for at least six month, I thought at first he may have perished and waited and waited to hear the news, but never it *came. As I was not his wife, it was impossible for me to receive information from the military, and his family was never approving of me. And so I was in the dark, until I hear from a friend, with such a shock, that he is alive and kicking and living in Chicago — and is besides married. This friend I shout at and give abuse, which I later regret. She supplied to me a number, and I call this, but as fate would have it, it is not Tom who answers, but the woman. I ask of her: 'Is your husband there, your husband Tom?' And she says, 'Yes, who's this calling?' So then I put down the phone. What was the use? What difference would it make now? The clock could not be turned back. Emotionally, this was a very bad blow for me, and I found it a terrible struggle just to carry on, because all this time I have waited for him and worked so hard to live and make sacrifice in the belief of his return.*

I think I truly loved this man, and even now I see his lovely face and lovely smile and hear the voice that could melt my heart but never make him a star. He will be long dead now, but if there was some magical way that I could meet him again, I believe that I would forgive him and still love him for ever.

Things become difficult for me after this — I was not happy in the studio any more and saw no point in it, and the films they make seem poor in the imagination and have no charm. For this reason I drift away from Hollywood, drift away from the world of fantasy to which I never really belong, and go back east and fall to all kinds of crazy behaviour, drinking all the time, which was never really before the case, and falling into relationships with men for whom I had no respect. Which is to say I had lost respect for myself and gone back into the careless place in me. Of this time I cannot find much to write, although it was a long time in my life, from when I leave Hollywood in 1942 to the time that Magda came, which was in 1947. Five years, yet there is so little to say. When the experience is so painful and of such sorrow, what is there to do but bundle it up small and throw it away.

It was when I was in Jersey City that Magda and Mihails came to me, although I do not know how they fell upon my address. It was the worst meeting in all my life, because Magda had lost her dear Janis and blamed me because I had not reached out and helped them. His death was on my head and who was I to argue? It was terrible: she spat at me, which I should have suffered, but I spat back and shouted, too. Never have I been so hateful a person. I did not know this was in me, and I drove them from my door. All this happened in front of darling Mihails, who was not then even in his teens and looked so young and trusting. I could see that he had come there wanting to love me, and now he was shocked at what he saw. I wished to stop and take him into my arms, but Magda was still screaming for my blood and telling me to take my eyes off from him. Even as I wished for them to stay, I was screaming for them to go. Both of us knew what really lay behind this argument, which was not the death of Janis, but neither was strong enough to say the truth.

For certain this was the end of any hope to come together as a family again, and I licked my wounds.

Among the bad I found one half-good man, a photographer called Gerry Clyde, who had talent but also a desire for drink, and these were always at war with each other. The worst of it was when I looked at him I saw a person on the same path as myself, and neither of us could save the other, which is not the best situation for making a life together. There were wonderful pictures that he had taken when he was younger, beautiful things of nature within the city, wild things among the creations of man, but these things were all of the past, and the free spirit that had been in him then was now smothered. Somehow, however, we stayed twenty years under the same roof — which changed, by the way, several times — and I end up with him in New York in the very apartment in which I write this history. I had long ago stopped being seamstress because no one wants hand-made dresses at this time, and became instead typist to pay the rent, then shop girl, then working as a cleaner, because I could not keep up any kind of appearance. So it goes, always downhill from here, but slowly. And I was

314

forever crying and complaining because I remembered the good times that had been mine. Twenty years to watch Gerry drink away all hope, and me sometimes to help him do it. In the end, I find out what it is like to be hit by a broken man and then kissed again when he saw what he had done, and this is what it is like for such a time, until one day he goes out and does not come back. This happened to me. He went from me — a bad man, no; a weak man, yes, but most of all an unlucky one, and because his misfortune happened from the time he meets me, it is me who is to blame. Of course he forgets to mention that it was in a bar that we first meet! And so I was left already down, already in growing confusion and desperation all the time.

What is madness? Is it something that we make for ourselves out of the chaos of our life? Or is it something that lies inside us, even before we are born? Or is it that both of these must come together? This cord that is stretched so tight inside us, and the burdens that we carry so heavy, one by one hooking themselves to hang upon the straining line.

So now I was more and more out of touch with things to cherish and a life in which to believe. I became strange and faraway to people, except by chance I come to know Mihails and his wife, Grace, because they have opened up the Sunrise store not far away. It was through them that I learn that Magda has died, and I wept then in front of him, but still I could not bring myself to explain the deepest cause of my weeping.

This I can say for them, that they reached out with compassion to me and hoped to give me help, but by then I was gone far away within my head and imagined only that they try to interfere with my life and, of course, there was this terrible thing between us that, in a better life, would bring us together, but in this life had always kept us apart.

For some reason, I was at this time starting to acquire possessions but throwing nothing out — keeping everything, even trash. First of all, these were things I thought precious and things that I believed I could make good. For example, there would be a dress and I would keep it, knowing I could alter it, but not having the machine to do so — illogical thinking like this. Later, it is not just clothes and ornaments, but everything, even to scraps of food that anyone should throw away. Of course it is crazy, and that is easy to see for those who are not crazy. In all these years there were times when I was not so crazy and could see clear as day what I had done, but then I had not the strength to do anything about it.

I entered then into great argument with the land-lord and neighbours and I turn away from them and anybody who could hurt me with the truth. Among them was Mihails — he more than anyone, as he had tried to help me most. Now and again I would feel the wish to go and unburden myself to him, and so many times I go to the store exactly to do this, and sometimes reach out to him, but never the words would come, and in the end I stopped from using words altogether. I remember going for a time for treatment and the doctors helped to bring me to reason, but always I fall back. How is it possible to see the silver lining in the cloud when always the rain falls on your head?

CHAPTER FIFTEEN

I T is the day of the auction. He will not go there, will not play their game. Trade being dead as a dodo, Michael has spent the whole afternoon cleaning brass, a thing he normally does once a year, strictly to schedule, but today he has polished and buffed and buffed and polished, directing all his venom into making something at least bright. At five, Benjy comes in for his shift and Michael gets him dusting and polishing, too, to make gleaming and perfect the big jars containing grains, beans and pastas. Business remaining slow, he takes Rosa's letter pad from under the counter, where he has kept it all this time. He has read it nearly to the end and has been astonished by the contents. The part where Rosa showed such awareness of her own mental condition was so harrowing that he has been unable to turn the page and read on. His own name has come into her story, and he knows from the lead-up that something monumental awaits. He cannot at this moment in time bring himself to take any more of it, not with everything else he has been going through. He puts the pad down on the counter and goes to the cold room for ham.

Later, hurrying towards the counter where at last a customer has appeared, he catches Benjy standing there, leaning over to peer at the letter pad. He swipes it from under the boy's inquisitive gaze and goes behind the counter, stuffing it in his inside pocket and gesturing angrily at Benjy to go get on with his work.

At about six, with the light outside failing, the store is soft with shadows, the new sheen of brass somehow drawing deeper the air of melancholy. Standing at the cash register, Michael looks up as a figure goes past the window. It is Harrison dressed in a shirt and jacket and with sharp creases in his pants. As he arrives, framed in the centre of the pane, he turns, makes a gun of his hand and brings it over, slow and deliberate, to point it at Michael, his head tilted and eye looking down the barrel. And then he passes on, a smile wafting across his features. Michael is neither scared nor troubled, simply annoyed: who does he think he is now – Clint Eastwood? He calls down the rows: 'Benjy!' And when the boy sticks his head out around a shelf: 'Did you just see that?' But Benjy just looks puzzled and grunts, 'Uh-uh.'

Before Michael has time to give it any real thought, the phone goes. It's the hospital and a woman with a sharp no-nonsense voice saying, 'Mr Marcinkus? It's about Rosa Petraidis . . . I think it would be a good idea for you to come over. We think she's coming round.'

'My God!' he says. Putting down the phone, he hurries down to find Benjy, 'Listen, stop what you're doing . . . No just leave it. I'll pay you anyhow. We gotta close.'

■ ◆ ■

The ward nurse outlines the developments in Rosa's condition: her eyes have twitched, her head moved – possibly. He asks if it means she's coming round, and is told that it could mean that, but it could also mean the opposite: sometimes patients rallied like this, and even had moments of lucidity, but then just as soon slipped away altogether.

He stands at the bed, straight-backed, and speaks assuredly now, in hope of her hearing. 'Hi, Rosa,' he says, as if she has just walked in the room. 'It all happens today, the whole damn shebang.' He stands waiting, as if she would know what he was talking about and would have plenty to say on the subject. Ten minutes go by, during which his mind drifts and flits between foolish things – how there is a smell of aniseed in the room, how he will maybe buy a hot-dog on the way home and have mustard on it – and serious things: how he will go to the fateful place and look his betrayers in the eyes, and how, if the worst happens, he will face his accusers. And now he finds himself no longer looking down in pity, but in need of consolation.

'Rosa . . . Rosa . . . Look, I gotta tell you this, I got us into one hell of a situation . . .'

And he confesses everything to her – about how they took her treasured slippers from her house, about the robbery by the crazy kid and him nearly dying, which showed how insane and ridiculous the whole situation had become. He tells her how people he loved and trusted had then made their move and taken things all into their own hands, and how he had betrayed her and wounded her and stolen her possessions and given what was precious to the devil, and all because of his own weakness and stupidity. 'Forgive me, Rosa,' he implores her. 'Look at me, old and foolish, but I never, never meant it to go like it did. It was all to protect what was yours.' He stands back, hoping against hope to see something, the faintest trace. Has he hurt her, he wonders? Has he sent her spirit racing to the precipice? There is no sign of any expression, no change in breathing, or in the luminous tracery of her heart on the screen. Nothing.

Just as he's preparing to take his leave, her eyes twitch, a tiny tug, the black slits of them contracting with a glint of moistness between the lashes. And there is a sound, a muffled grunt behind her closed lips. He leans, urgently, over her, taking her waxy hand in his and whispering, 'Rosa, it's me – Michael.' Something subterranean forms in her faraway brain and finally inches, broken, over her crusted lips: 'Mi–hails . . . Mihails . . . My darling Mihails.'

■ ◆ ■

Already, before James has entered the bristling triangle, it is in his senses: a droning sound somewhere, coming through the haze of rain. As he heads into Times Square, the sound becomes a thrill of voices joined in song. A crowd is gathered at the base of the Walgreen Building, and in the heart of it a huddle of guys are delivering a sweet, melodious chorus of 'Somewhere Over the Rainbow'. A light in the sky filters down through the drizzle, causing James to look up at the buildings opposite, and there he can see Dorothy's wide, hope-filled face splashed across a screen of stone and glass. Passers-by stop in their tracks, all in awe of ethereal Judy and her heavenly choir.

James lowers his head. He had been hoping for a more restrained affair, something he could approach quietly, conclude promptly and leave gracefully. But it is not to be. Rounding the corner, he is staggered to see a line of people stretching all the way to Seventh! He had not reckoned on it, but some of them immediately recognize him from the publicity, and as he walks past he finds himself glad-handing all manner of complete strangers. There are people wearing 'ruby slippers' T-shirts and hats, and indeed a few of both sexes wearing replica slippers. But there are other people, too, more ordinary in their ways – little old ladies wearing their childhoods on their faces; couples and families and groups all blessed with the same collective smile. James wonders, somewhat uneasily, if Jack might be somewhere in the crowd, another apparition of the blessed Judy, or was his cross-dressing for private viewing only?

He comes to the doors, bronze and imposing. He can hear people murmuring to each other, 'Look, it's that guy.' A young snappy-suited guy in charge of the line gives him a respectful nod of the head and holds back the throng for him, not bothering to examine the pass James is holding out, but instead beckoning to another guy, who now holds the door open and gestures respectfully for James to enter.

■ ◆ ■

Michael Marcinkus, a tired and confused old man carrying the heaviest of burdens, gets on a subway train and finds himself alone in a carriage filled with schoolchildren – girls, all of them, most five years old. He imagines them on their way home from the zoo, where they have laughed at penguins and stood fearful of lions. Two teachers are going up and down keeping an eye on them, but the kids are quiet and contained, mesmerized by the jumble of light and shade rushing past the windows, or gazing at the colourful posters, all sitting there, sober and silent and adding to the world inside their heads. Inside Michael's head there are worlds, each of them occupied by dark and painful things. And during the next few minutes he visits them: the world of treachery that has divided him from his loved ones and made him solitary; the world of cruelty beyond fathoming from which he escaped all those decades ago, and the world of an old woman's sorrow, which he has just walked away from.

Sliding his subway ticket into his top pocket, his finger comes to rest against the letter pad in his inside pocket. He can read this now. Nothing more can hurt him. He pulls it out and opens it to the last few flimsy pages . . .

■ ◆ ■

It is important to understand the meaning to me of these wonderful slippers. They were the very first things that I kept and put away, never to let go, the first of the hoarded things. And yet, when I took them, it was not because I saw them as any kind of treasure. At that time they were never so magical or special, just pretty objects that made me smile to look at them. It was the rest of my life and how it took so many sorrowful turnings that made them so mean‐ ingful to me. So, they were just a pair of shoes and not even valuable. *Several pairs of them were made for the production and nobody had any idea at the time of the tremendous significance that would come to them. And certainly they did not fit my feet, which were size 7, while hers were size 2! No, they were just things that anyone could admire for what they were and for the skill which had gone into making them. That Judy Garland herself had worn them also was meaningless. To the producers she was no more than 'B List' before this movie — an actress good for playing children.*

But if the slippers were hardly to die for, why did I take them? I suppose it was because Tom and I had gone to the studio that Sunday for so intimate a reason — to make love in the fairytale palace — and that when we found them, it was as if they were a gift to bless the love between us, a beautiful pair of shoes for a pair of young lovers. Even now, when I think about the ruby slippers, it always takes me back to Tom, who was my one true love. And all my happiness was around this time. Two years only in all my adult life when I was allowed to have around me beautiful things and beautiful people.

Later on, it gave me such a shock when I discover how the value of them has gone sky-high, how history changes everything — a war goes by; a new age comes; a president is assassinated and an age is gone. A star is born, a star fades, a star dies tragically. And suddenly this crazy movie in which you played a tiny part becomes meaningful for millions of people all over the world, and the star of it, who was just a frightened little girl, she becomes a legend. It terrified me all those years later to discover that they even display a pair in the national museum and people pay money and queue for hours to see them. To think that there were times after I went from Hollywood when I had thought to destroy them and cut out the memories of good times because they were never to come again.

And so the ruby slippers did come to have great meaning for me. For the further away those times have gone, the more rich and vivid they have become in my memory. And the more my mind is unable to keep hold of small details from today, the more I can remember perfectly those long-ago places and people and all the things they said and did.

For a long time now the world has become weary for me and people intolerant and unfeeling. Just to drag my body around to eat, drink, sleep and stay alive. But truly it has given me comfort just to keep these shoes inside a box and no longer even need to look inside, only to remember that once there was love and beauty in my life. So, perhaps, the slippers have become for me a token of this: that always there is something beautiful that awaits us all and will be forever shining. Let no one take this from me.

Michael looks up. Only one stop to go, then he can walk home from there. He closes the pad, thinking of the poor old woman: Let no one take this from me. But this prompts another thought: the memory of Harrison going past the deli window, making that gunman gesture. Suddenly it comes to him what it had meant. 'Jesus Christ!' he says to himself, rather loudly. The heads of the teachers switch round to glare at him and he shrinks back in his seat, embarrassed and apologetic for being such a foolish old man. As soon as the train stops at the next station, he goes flying out the door in search of a line to take him where he now must go.

■ ◆ ■

Siobhan sees it all for what it is – the whole Oz and Judy thing with the singing and the massive projections. She smiles despite herself. But she will not be distracted from what she has come there to do. She brings her gaze back down to street level, catching sight of herself in a store window. Yeah, at least she looks the part this time – the brown velvet jacket over the powder-blue roll-neck top and the grey jeans below. Cool. She looks across, sees the snake of people all colourful and excited. She goes along the line until the auction-house doors are in sight. Deftly, she slips in behind a stately old couple and in front of two guys under an umbrella.

Fifty or so yards shy of the entrance, a murmur ripples through the crowd and a voice comes down the line behind her, saying over and over, 'Thank you, thank you.' Instinctively, her head drops, her cheeks fired red. Her father! He is moving along, grinning, pressing the flesh like he's a film star! As soon he is safely past her, she stands up on her toes to see him reach the doors. Behind her, one umbrella guy says to the other: 'Isn't that the Ruby Million man?' And she feels warm and cold about it at the same time. She knows there is good in these outpourings of approval, and yet she resents her father for giving so much of himself to people he has never met, whilst allowing so little for her. She turns her head away, feeling foolish all of a sudden: what the hell is she doing here? Who cares whether he gets the damn shoes or not? But then she comes back, firm to her purpose.

Just twenty places from the front, Siobhan sees that people are holding up passes to an absurdly young guy in a flashy suit, standing guard near the door. Some people are being waved through by him, while others are being turned away. This she hasn't planned for. A woman stands there arguing. She makes God knows how many protestations, but the sentry-man just keeps saying, robotically, 'Like I said, the places are taken.' When at last the woman turns away, defeated, others behind her also shake their heads and drop out of the line. But Siobhan seems to take strength from it and carries on against the flow. Nothing, nothing will stop her. She walks right up to the guy, smiling wanly and saying, totally matter-of-factly: 'That's better. I feel so much better.'

'Uh, sorry?' he says, already hassled off his feet and now not sure what to make of this latest annoyance. 'I went out, remember? I went out to get air because I wasn't feeling so . . .' He looks at her, suspicious but conscious of others hovering behind, intent on stealing their way in. 'I'm with my father,' she rattles. 'James McBride; he just went in.' She glances behind her, seeking support among the crowd. 'You know, the Ruby Million man.' This brings about much murmuring and nodding in recognition, but still the suited boy stands his ground: 'I don't remember . . .'

'God, this is crazy!' she yaps, looking beyond him, as if seeking to catch the eye of someone higher up the food chain. With an intolerant shrug, she appeals once more to her supporting cast, most of whom oblige by looking suitably pissed. 'OK. OK.' Choosing the path of least hassle, the boy gives way and stands aside to admit Siobhan, who clumps towards the door, bridling in mock annoyance. But the moment the door opens to admit her, the hardness goes out of her and she whispers to herself, deliciously, 'I am in.'

■ ◆ ■

Michael runs, trips, stumbles towards the place, clutching his collar at the throat to keep the rain out, to shut everything out. He is closed to everything except his absolute need to get there and get inside. And yet he cannot help but notice things: the sweet singing and the images diffusing down through the drizzle. And for the briefest of moments he is startled out of his indifference by the towering vision of Dorothy's wide face – eyes, nose, lips all turned up to heaven. As he hurries past the dwindling line of people, a minuscule pulse of pleasure passes through Michael. Even in his closed-off, wilful state of mind he cannot set himself against the happiness of others. As he turns the corner, a sudden squall of rain flies chilly against his face and he longs to be inside, where at least it will be warm and dry. The rain seems to be falling harder here and umbrellas are going up. He can feel the droplets collecting in his wispy hair and dripping down to soak him through. He peers up at the sky, the tiny luminous patch of it, formed by the building tops so distant and beyond reach. Picking up his step, he hurries up to the front of the line, where he takes an instant dislike to the stripy-suited youth holding back the throng. It's the kid's swagger – the way his thumb is hooked over his waistcoat pocket, as if he's about to pull out a watch and chain; the way he stands there in his path, his head cocked out of the shirt collar that's at least a size too big; Michael bristles at it all. 'You have to let me in,' he says, muted but blunt. 'I am the owner.'

'The owner of what?' demands the youth snappily.

'The ruby slippers,' he mumbles as inconspicuously as he can. The youth looks Michael up and down, taking

330

in the grubby, faded look of the man; the hair splatted thin to the head and the cheap old jacket tucked over the heaving gut. 'Check it out if you must. My name is Michael Marcinkus,' he says and stares back with such intensity that the youth is compelled to raise a hand to attract the attention of an older man in an even stripier suit. A flurry of bad-tempered muttering breaks out around him, those standing in line growing resentful at this new hold-up. In the end he has the bright idea of producing for ID his battered old grocery wholesale card with the near-illegible signature. Now the second guy goes away in search of an even higher authority, and before he knows it there are three guys in rank order of stripiness, peering at his particulars. After an agony of deliberation, consensus is reached and the third man indicates for Michael to follow him to the huge bronze door, which opens smooth and soundless.

In his bewilderment, and with the guy hurrying him along, Michael sees it all in a blur: the grand atrium with soaring ceiling, the chandeliers and shimmering screens with images flowing over them like silk, and all the people hurrying to the far doors. Unspeaking, as he has remained through all of this, the suited man escorts Michael across, pulls open swish doors and they are in the auditorium, which is vast, soft underfoot and champagne-tinted. But when he looks down at the rows of sober-suited, serious-faced people all gathered in the congregation, Michael is overcome, sweat-hot in the

331

sudden warmth, his knees stubbornly locking at the prospect of going to sit amongst them. But his minder is in no mood to tarry: 'Right, so I'll take you to your seat . . .' Michael just stands there, rooted to the spot. A few rows down he can see a free place at the end. 'There would be great,' he pleads. There at least he can remain unseen. 'Fine,' says the man, rescued from a chore much beneath him. 'Have this, please, with our compliments.' And turning on his heels, he thrusts a glossy catalogue at Michael, who stumbles down to claim the vacant seat. His weary frame supported at last in soft yielding velvet, he lets out a great sigh, releasing all the anxiety that has dogged him en route, and it is only now that he can really start to take it all in – see the people sitting eager and expectant; hear the stir of voices, so hushed and reverent. It really is like a church. So thinking, Michael's eyes are led to where an altar would be in such a place, and he sees where the curved rows of chairs slope down to a long wooden stage, served at each end by a short row of steps, and having at its centre the auctioneer's stand. On a plinth, in pride of place behind and above the stand, is an open oyster shell, completely realistic in its appearance, except that it is three feet high. His eyes narrow to take it in: the shell open so that one half is raised vertical, its gorgeous rim of mother of pearl reflecting rays of light. The other half is tilted on the plinth and houses an interior of folded silk, and on this, sitting on a pink velour cushion, are the ruby slippers, crimson and luminous – and magical to those who have come seeking magic. To Michael, though, it is all quite shocking. The effect of seeing them all lit up and fancified is nothing but false: Rosa's treasures, removed entirely from the trials and sorrows that brought them to this place.

His thoughts returning to present dangers, Michael scans the rows, until at last he finds the face he has feared to see. There, almost in line with him, twenty people over but just a row down, is Harrison. The doom-bringer. He is bent over in his chair, an idle smile on his face as he fiddles with his cell phone, both thumbs paddling. In the amber light, a faded bruise shows across his cheekbone and a graze faintly trails down his nose. At least no one is with him, thinks Michael. Perhaps it was all just bullshit after all. But his unease won't go away. To look at him, Harrison's appearance is careless and casual in the same old way, but in this place and in these surroundings, there is something unspeakable in his detachment, and it fills Michael with a foreboding that sends a shiver down his spine. He allows his gaze to wander further afield. To either side of the room, smart, efficient-looking men and women take their places behind computer screens, reaching for headsets and handsets, clicking into contact with clients in faraway places, whose names are marked under a row of clocks telling the time in Houston, LA, London, Tokyo, Moscow.

A distinguished-looking man with swept-back silver hair and a gold waistcoat under his rich blue suit climbs the stand and taps the microphone. A hush falls over the audience, who have grown bold and more noisy. But it's a false start and the man goes away again. Michael opens the catalogue, wondering how much a classy thing like this would cost to produce. He turns the pages and finds a centre spread of the slippers on a silk cushion, vivid and glamorous. He looks at the page, then up at the real things. All smoke and mirrors, but they sure know how to whet the appetite.

Three rows down, in the line between him and the slippers, another face flags up on the edge of Michael's vision: it's the girl who came to the Sunrise that time. She seems more grown up in the clothes she's wearing today, but it's definitely her. She is sitting halfway down in the rows, but she is staring at a point way up front, and following her gaze he sees James sitting there, contained and unmoving. Of course, that is why he recognized her. She must be James's girl! So how come she is not sitting with her papa? How strange.

The auctioneer mounts the stand again, an assistant at his side. This time, they mean business. The hubbub dies down; something clenches in the pit of Michael's stomach and he finds himself wondering what on earth it will all come to.

'Ladies and gentlemen, we start tonight with a sale of film and theatrical memorabilia, among which is an upright piano once belonging to Count Basie, and a pair of—' A salvo of applause breaks out but the auctioneer wades on, undeterred. 'Thank you, ladies and gentlemen . . . A pair of ruby slippers worn by Miss Judy Garland in the film *The Wizard of Oz*. Beginning then with lot number one: a collection of theatrical programmes dating from the year 1883. Very well preserved with some light foxing; a collector's item. Who will bid me on this?'

And so the auctioneer gets it going, brisk and businesslike. Michael settles back in his seat. It hadn't occurred to him that there would be all these other things to be gone through before the main item.

With growing fascination he starts to observe the bidders and their little ways, from the blunt raising of a hand, to the grand gesture, to the merest twitch of an eyebrow. The lots tick down until over a hundred have gone under the hammer. According to the auctioneer's tone of voice, this is all routine stuff, but the prices are incredible: programmes going for hundreds, posters going for thousands and a pair of gloves that belonged to some actress he never knew raising $5,000!

After an hour and a half of one unbelievable thing after another, the fall of lots grows tedious. Michael zones out, and instead contemplates the awfulness that has brought him here. He puts his hand into his pocket again, wondering if the rain has got through to the fragile letter pad. He pulls it out and sees that it's in good shape – a little damp around the edges, but otherwise unaffected. He finds his reading glasses and puts them on: yes, why not, this would be a good time. He should get it finished now, for all the pain. He finds his place again and begins to read . . .

Bound by the spell of words, he comes to know the heart of Rosa's wildest joys and the pit of her deepest sorrow. He peers over the rim of his glasses. He scratches his head in confusion. He reads again what he has just read. And then he exclaims, loud enough for those around him to hear: 'Holy shit!' Still in disbelief, he takes up the flimsy sheet to read it a third time and check his eyes are not playing tricks on him. 'Holy shit!' he repeats, inaudible now because the enormity of it all has hit, winding him and leaving him stunned until an urgent stir in the room brings him back to himself. At the centre of the stage, the auctioneer is standing straight and panning round to take in the audience. His voice seems to become more rounded and penetrating as he begins: 'Lot a hundred and eleven: a pair of ruby slippers, authenticated by Warner Brothers and in perfect condition. These shoes were worn by Miss Judy Garland in the celebrated movie, *The Wizard of Oz*, made in the year 1939 at MGM Pictures, Hollywood. Who will bid me? Starting at three hundred and fifty thousand dollars . . . Ah, yes – man on my right, three hundred and fifty thousand. Three hundred and sixty? Good, three-sixty to the woman at the back . . .'

And so it goes: the bids climbing by tens of thousands. At five hundred thousand, Michael sees James raise his hand for the first time. The auctioneer acknowledges him – 'the man centre front' – and despite his determination to remain detached from it all, Michael finds himself willing James to see off the competition. He glimpses over at Harrison, no longer playing on his cell but slouching in his chair and looking down with that same knowing smile. It is as if nothing in the room is of any consequence to him, as if he knows exactly what will happen here, as if he has it somehow in his control.

At $550,000, James drops out awhile, leaving others to hike the price to a new mark. A man at the back in a green jacket slugs it out with a bidder in Hamburg, who by his invisibility and remoteness brings new mystery to the proceedings. At $700,000, James takes up the bidding again. There is a stutter as the green-jacketed man drops out, leaving the auctioneer in search of a new player. James's hand remains in the air, ready to wave away the next call. The auctioneer's voice shifts a touch, uncovering a new seam to be tapped: 'New bidder right in front of me: seven hundred and fifty thousand dollars.' Here, James's head jerks round in a double-take straight out of a cheap TV soap. Michael looks over and sees, right at the foot of the auction stand, a wheelchair with the great bulk of a man poured into it, and it is at him that James continues to stare, his eyes fixed and glassy, as if his brain has jumped ship.

'Against you, sir. At seven hundred and fifty thousand dollars . . . Do I have any more bids?' The auctioneer sounds almost bored with it. Michael can see people close to James looking at him in alarm, one of them even tugging at his sleeve, but to no avail. Michael wonders what's going on and turns to study Harrison, as if to find some kind of explanation, as if he should be the source of all ills.

'Seven hundred and sixty thousand . . . More bids please.' A woman at one of the desks nods; they are off again, a new tack opened up. 'In Rome, then, at seven hundred and sixty thousand dollars . . .'

Straight away the wheelchair man bids against her and it goes in a sudden flurry, the price tag rising swiftly, the numbers rising from the unbelievable to the astronomical. The audience is in raptures, willing the game to new heights, and so it climbs before the woman at the screen lowers her head and Rome is gone. It is all with the man in the chair.

'At eight hundred and sixty thousand to the bidder below me. Are there any other bids? . . . Well then, ladies and gentlemen. Going once . . .'

Michael sees the wheelchair man sneering at James. He sees James's girl start to get to her feet. And he is staggered when he notices the kind and pleasant Filipino nurse sitting alongside the wheelchair, her face pale and impassive. It seems to Michael that a darkness has gathered in that tiny pocket of the room. The spotlights are blazing bright, but a shadow has swallowed up the light. He has seen bad before, too many times, been trundled over by it and swept away. He knows bad when he sees it.

■ ◆ ■

Everything falls away. James sinks to the place where he was sent whenever he was wrong, whenever he was hopeless or chicken-shit, or just plain bad, and the words rang out, ice-cruel: 'Go to your room! Go to your bed! Go where I don't have to look at your pale, pasty face!' Shame was the commandment and his duty to obey, to lie cold and lonely under its weight, never to measure up to his father's expectations. Yet, he is no longer a child. He is a man, and it was all so long ago now. The coldness no longer smothers him as much as once it did, so despite the ancient shame that is heavy upon him, James hears the words spoken out loud and clear and for his benefit – 'Going then at eight hundred and sixty thousand dollars' – and the nearness of things returns. He feels the marker clutched in his hand and the presence of the woman in the seat next to him, so that his body comes back to him, his eyes opening to the light, his ears ringing with a shock of sound. 'Fight,' says his blood. 'Fight,' say his limbs, feeling themselves warm again. 'Fight,' says his brain, coming in clear and sharp, his bright eyes bringing into shape the man with the hammer raised above his head. And James summons his petrified arm to unlock and raise itself, pivoting mechanically into the air like the pointer on an old-time train signal.

'New bid from the man centre left.' The words ring out clear, incised by a chorus of gasps. The flame is back in James now. It will be a straight fight between him and his dad, who glares at him now as though they are the only two people in the room. 'Nine hundred thousand to the bidder in front.' And so it goes, bid for bid, McBride edging slow and canny towards his endgame, James holding on firmly.

'Nine hundred and eighty thousand to the bidder in front.' This is it. James quivers with the intensity. He feels the audience are with him. 'Are you still bidding, sir? Can I hurry you, sir? Nine hundred and eighty thousand, then, to the bidder below.'

The tension stretches near to breaking point as James raises his hand. 'One million. Here, at centre left, a million dollars!' A gust of applause reaches James's ears, where there should have been a gale. Somehow, the audience has divined that something deeper and darker than the rule of money is being enacted.

'At one million dollars then . . . Any advance?' James braces himself, forces himself to turn his head and look directly at his father, whose face wears an expression of unaccustomed serenity.

'At one million dollars . . .' A murmur takes hold in the room, the audience wondering whether the bid will stand or whether the game is up. James deflects his father's stare with a defiant smile, and even manufactures a smug little snort.

'Are there any more bids, then? Going once at one million dollars . . . ?'

There follows a cold, empty waiting, while McBride shifts in his chair. Could it be that he is thinking better of it, that he has become suddenly aware of the monstrosity of his actions? Seemingly lost in thought, he lowers his eyes, then raises them again towards James and lazily raises his hand.

'One million and fifty thousand dollars, then, to the man in front. Do I have another bid? One million and fifty thousand dollars. Can I see another bid? Might you still be in the bidding, sir? Last chance now '

James stares into space. The seconds that follow are vile, decimating – the ruby slippers lost, gone to him who least cares for them or deserves to possess them. The auctioneer sighs prissily. 'Going once, then . . . going twice . . . going three times . . .' With undisguised relief, he lifts the hammer to its height to bring it falling down . . .

'Just a moment!' says a voice, strong in the silence. A man comes down the centre aisle, like a hawk dropping. The audience clamour for a view, but soon falls quiet. There is something powerful and dramatic about the way in which the man, who is tall and grey-suited, approaches the stand. And there is authority in the firm but polite way in which he calls out, 'Excuse me, sir,' and beckons the auctioneer to him, engaging him in hushed, quick-fire conversation. Then, on the heels of suspense, comes sensation. Because the man then turns and raises his arm, and out from the wings come two uniformed officers who, following their captain's pointing hand, go treading like unwanted children in a room full of adults. All eyes are on them as they head for the end of the front row, where a little old lady rises under their command, like a plump bird on thin legs, and is then led by them, blinking and slow of foot, back into the shadows where they have come from. Then another woman, younger and wirier, goes racing after them shouting, 'Shame on you, shame!' The auctioneer, forgetting himself, takes off in the same direction, leaving his assistant, struggling in her shy breathy voice, to keep everyone in their places.

Confusion reigns.

'What is this? What the hell is going on here?' snarls McBride, who fires up his chair and surges off in pursuit of the policemen, the auctioneer and his scurrying entourage.

CHAPTER SIXTEEN

S HE saw it all, from the moment her father sprang
to life and took up the running, till the moment he
fell, a wounded hero, brought down by his enemy, his
nemesis – isn't that the word? She knows, of course,
who he is; a part of her knows, although she cannot
join the jumbled clues together. She came here to
punish him, to force him to see her, yet it pained her to
see her father brought low in front of all these people,
staring at him round-eyed like sheep. Her instinct had
been to run down to him, to shout and scream at the
dumb onlookers to make them scatter, to tell him to
carry on fighting.

She looks at him still sitting in his seat as the hall

empties to a dying murmur. No, she will not go to him and fall weakly in with his emotions; she has done that one time too often already. Can he not see how he has made a fool of himself and a victim of her? *Seven years.* He cannot just slip aside and stick his head in the sand. She will make him deal with this whole thing, once and for all.

■ ◆ ■

James sits in the great blanched emptiness of the hall, the stage lights dying, drawing in their silky magic. Working lights go on, harsh and unforgiving, to bring porters scurrying noisily to sort the lots and bear them away. On the stage, a police officer stands by as a pair of black-suited, white-gloved porters stand on twin stepladders and reach up in choreographed symmetry to bring down the oyster-shell, slowly treading down the steps in time with each other. Each plucks out a single slipper to wrap it in cotton and place it with its partner in a grey metal security box. Items of evidence.

He stands at last, pulling on his coat; but his hands freeze in the middle of fiddling with buttons as zooming towards him comes the contraption containing his unholy father, with his sad Madonna-nurse following. He comes to a halt by his son's side, turning on a dime to face him. With a voice strong and terrible he makes his harsh pronouncement.

'You know what? I don't give a shit. Whatever comes

out of this, you lose. I would have paid to see that!'
And skewering his son through with a mocking eye,
he wheels round again and fizzles away, his worst
done. James stands there, lost and pathetic, then he
raises his sorrowful eyes to see, descending the stairs
grave and ghost-like, Marcinkus the grocer. This man
understands what has happened here. He knows what
a vengeful father looks like, and a broken son and all
the sorrows that can come. But as he reaches the floor,
level with James, Michael gives only the barest nod
in his direction and continues towards the wings and
the corridor beyond, as if something awful awaits him
there. James watches until the old man has gone out
of sight, and then it rises in him, the anger and the
shame. He throws down his programme, along with
the redundant bid-marker, and goes hurrying from the
place.

■ ◆ ■

Michael had witnessed it, every significant moment, and
had from the first sensed Harrison's hand at work in it all.
When the auctioneer looked up and the detective strode
out and broke the sale, he knew that this was justice. He
had suffered to see them lead his tiny wife away in dis-
honour, with Jenny scurrying after, furious at such cruel
humiliation. But yes, it, too, was justice of a kind.

When the auctioneer had hurried off and confusion
had brought the audience to their feet, he had seen

Karl and Dan, big, brave men that they were, making for the doors, pushing and scrabbling like children, and running for the hills.

And when he stood to make his way to the front, he had seen the girl walking straight towards him, away from her father, her face pale and fixed. He stood in the aisle, ready to stop and say hello. But on she went, like a sleepwalker, brushing his shoulder as she passed by. Then he had seen the wheelchair man roll up to James and heard the old man's voice bellow, ugly across the space, and had seen him spin and sail away, the Filipino nurse padding after. It is strange. Without knowing anything about any of them, he has understood everything that has passed.

Now Michael stands in front of the door with the word 'bureau' on it, engraved in brass. He swallows hard. God knows what will follow from this.

■ ◆ ■

James is running, haring along Seventh, overtaking the last straggle of people retreating from the sale. He can see it ahead, the ghastly contraption, and so he shoots past, wheeling round into its path to make it stop. And now James stands almost side by side with the nurse as he leans over the man who all his life has eclipsed his sun. 'Listen to me, you damn old monster. You think you got me? Got me dead in front of the whole world? Well, guess what? You did nothing. Look, I don't give a damn! So you got the shoes and you thought you got me scared and pathetic, just like you did for forty years. Look at me. I'm shit, right here right in front of you, worthless faggot shit!'

Inez is aghast and elated as she watches James, oblivious to the world, fix his arms rigid to the chair's rails, the man in it stiff of face and body. 'So whaddya say, Dad. Wanna hit me? Wouldn't you just love to hit me right now, in the street, in front of everybody, and I won't say a word? Here . . .' James actually takes hold of his father's hand and pulls it to him, touching it to his fresh white face. Still nothing from the old man, his hand limp in his son's. James has gone beyond reason 'C'mon. *C'mon*. Go on, have a pop!' His voice is loud and urgent now, and people are stopping. It hardly looks good – a healthy young man standing over an old man in a wheelchair, haranguing him.

But James is absolutely lost in a place of hatred and pain: 'I can't believe you never actually hit me when I was a kid; God knows I deserved it.' He stays there stock-still, holding his father's eye with his own. 'Well, say something, old man! Maybe it woulda knocked sense into my head and I woulda been something, a regular guy just like you, and never woulda turned into what I am, a hopeless queer!' Seeing his father so unresponsive, James actually kicks the wheelchair, kicks it full against the footplate so that it skids sideways and McBride's lifeless foot jumps up in the air. Shocked into action, Inez steps forward and gently puts her hand on James's, which seems to bring him back to himself and he watches now, his anger replaced by fascination as she stands between him and his father, obedient to his command. The old man sits there, unmoved and unmoving, eating up time, until at last his twisted hand creeps along the rail and crabs itself around the lever. As the chair nudges forward, Inez turns to offer James a look of regret and sympathy, but then seeing the chair gathering momentum, she turns away again and scuttles off after her patient.

■ ◆ ■

In all the splendour of the place, it must be the plainest, shabbiest room they could find for the purpose. A cheap table and four hard chairs, looking all the more dowdy against faded walls. The lieutenant of police sits judge-straight on one side of the table, reading out loud the deposition so far taken. On the other side, Grace and Jenny sit side by side, the mother hunched and the daughter stiff and defiant on the edge of her seat. Jenny's lips are pursed and her eyes dagger-sharp, although below the table, her two hands cradle Grace's own tiny paw to provide comfort. The detective spells out each sentence with painful precision. Grace's head nods, unceasing, seemingly hanging on every word. Inside, she is in a whirl of agitation born of her own shame and of the fear that cramps every breath and muddles her mind so that hardly a word makes sense.

As soon as the lieutenant has finished reading, he lays it on the line: 'Listen, Mrs Marcinkus. It doesn't matter whose name the sale was in, or whether your husband was in agreement with you or not. I am here to investigate a felony, which is the taking of a thing from a place where it belongs to another place where it does not belong. And I am not satisfied that you are telling me the whole truth here, about how these shoes came into your possession. Especially since you have told me two different versions of the same story in the past half-hour. On the one hand the old lady, Rosa, gives them to you and your husband years ago, and on the other she gives them to you only weeks ago – only at a time when she is lying in the hospital, in a coma, incapable of speech, as she is to this day.' He pauses to allow Grace the full effect of his all-seeing eye. Jenny can no longer keep a lid on her indignation: 'Leave her alone!' she cries out pluckily. 'In case you didn't notice, my mother ain't so young neither, and now you got her all confused. Don't say no more, Momma. He only wants to tie you up in knots!'

But Grace is less quick to hand out brickbats. 'Please, Jenny,' she murmurs. 'The man is only doing his job.'

'Thank you, Mrs Marcinkus. That's right, and you would do well to remember, Mrs . . . ?'

'Chainey.'

'Mrs Chainey – to keep your peace, unless you want

349

me maybe going into your part in all of this.' He waits until Jenny sits back, well and truly put in her place, although her scowl has not budged, then raises his voice a notch: 'Now, listen, you wanna be left alone? I can leave you alone any time you like – alone down at the precinct, alone in a night cell, until the prosecutor decides where to go with this. Believe me, this here is the easiest way, but we're already outta time. So please, just tell me how it is. Tell me a story to make me happy; allow me to believe that everything here is good and above board. And then we can check it out and tear up these pieces of paper and all go home to our beds.' He looks hard and long at her again. She looks sideways and sees that Jenny is out of all resistance. Delivering herself of a deep sigh, Grace opens her mouth to speak. Then the door opens and her face falls lifeless again. A police officer walks in and leans over to whisper in the lieutenant's ear. 'Sure, sure,' he says and looks up, smiling unaccountably at Grace, who throws a startled look at Jenny, who simply sits there, glaring beneath her brows.

The officer goes back out of the door, and a few seconds later it opens again and in walks Michael, all dishevelled-looking and wringing his hands in front of him as if holding an invisible hat. 'Come in, please, and sit down,' says the lieutenant. Michael takes one look at Grace, sitting there terrified under the detective's all-seeing eye, and rushes over and throws his arms around her. She flips her shoulders, quaking, with sobs coming loud. Jenny gets to her feet and embraces them both, yammering, 'Momma, Momma, Momma . . .'

'This is awful, horrible,' mutters Michael, fighting back his own tears. The lieutenant stands and stretches, as if this is an everyday kind of scene, and then wanders outside to speak to his two officers. When he comes back in, the storm has subsided, and he waits again until the two women are back in their seats and three pairs of eyes are on him. 'OK, everybody, so who wants to go first?' he asks breezily, not really expecting a sane answer. 'I do,' says Michael. 'Then please sit down,' says the lieutenant civilly.

'Am I under arrest?'

'Not yet, you're not.'

'Then I will stand.'

So Michael stands and unburdens himself of the truth that has troubled him all this time. He explains, calmly, as though it had happened to somebody else, how the ruby slippers came into their possession, how they found them amid filth, how they took them to the deli, how decisions had been made that eventually brought the ruby slippers to auction. As he unloads himself of all this, Michael can see Jenny and Grace sinking into their seats, their faces ghastly white.

'If all this is true,' says the detective, 'then a crime has been committed.'

'Not necessarily,' says Michael.

'No?' For the first time there is surprise in the man's voice, and this increases as Michael now becomes prey to his emotions.

'You see . . .'

Grace looks over, baffled to see her man stammering so to get his words out.

'You see . . . it, it so happens that Rosa Petraidis is my mother.'

'*What?*' gasps Jenny.

'Excuse me?' exclaims Grace, flabbergasted. Michael stands there looking a little foolish, as if he has just farted at a funeral.

'Really? Tell me about it,' says the lieutenant, looking at Michael with new eyes, as is everybody in the room.

'That's it, she is – was – my mother. And what is more, she died this day.' He looks at them in turn: the detective eager for the truth, Grace in her state of confusion, Jenny in her cold hostility.

'Now, this is on my shoulders, me alone. Please,' he addresses the lieutenant, 'take me wherever it is you have to take me.'

■ ◆ ■

James gets out of the cab and walks, drained, towards the entrance of his apartment block. Ten yards from the door, a voice calls brightly from one side: 'Hiya, Daddy!' He turns to see her, sitting on the wall of the disused French fountain, all dappled in sunshine and looking happy in an odd kind of way, with a jolly beret on her head to go with the jacket. 'Siobhan?'

'Hiya, Daddy,' she chirps again, takes a candy from a bag she is holding, pops it into her mouth. 'How are you today, Daddy?'

'What . . . what are you doing there?' he asks falteringly. He can't quite come to terms with what he's seeing – it belongs in a dream.

'Oh I dunno, just . . . sitting,' she says, wheezing a touch, and pops in another candy.

He steps towards her as she munches away, all childlike and delicious, with cheeks shining. 'I don't understand. How come you . . . ?' Then he sees that the bag of candy is a bag of nuts, half empty. Openmouthed, he stares as she smiles insanely back.

'Poor . . . Daddy,' she says, a touch slurred now and holding out the bag for him. 'Would you like a . . . ?' The hand just flops away and Siobhan's eyes roll to white as she keels over and lands on her back in a bed of leaves inside the fountain. He runs to her, but she is gone in shock, blue and wheezing like wind in a bottle. He spins round in the street, looking for someone, anyone – not the smashed man on the bench; not the old woman sweeping outside her house. He runs fifty yards to a woman carrying a poodle and breezing along clack-heeled. 'Quick, ring nine-one-one ! My daughter – she's gone into ana . . . anaphylactic shock.'

'Oh my goodness. What is that?'

'Just call them. Please!' And he rushes back to Siobhan, literally scooping her floppy body out of the fountain and into his arms. With his thumb, he prises open her eyelid. The pupil is a big black moon. He is gazing into his daughter's eyes. It was never meant to be like this.

■ ◆ ■

All this time since, McBride has been quiet, as meek as a lamb. They went home just as soon as they could get away from his son, who had been so wild and passionate in his rage. There, he went straight to the living room, put the TV on blaring loud, and she has heard nothing from him since. For a full three hours he stayed silent in there, the TV on, the ads sounding like chimes each quarter-hour.

So astonished is Inez at his muteness that she neglects to prepare his coffee in her special way – today, perhaps, he does not deserve to go to hell. Of course, she does not forgive him, even so. It was wrong what he did to his own son, humiliating him like that in front of everybody. She had even prepared herself to speak her mind to him over his shocking behaviour, but the son had taken his own actions and delivered his own retribution. For this reason she is in fear that sooner or later McBride will rise up and vent his anger and his shame, and that his vengeance when it comes will be terrifying.

It does come, while he is eating dinner that evening, but it is less of a storm and more of a dark brewing. 'So, how do you feel, knowing that we mighta lost the ruby slippers?' he asks, the old slyness in his eyes. She sits there unanswering, knowing full well that the shoes have no meaning for him, representing to him nothing but other people's delusions, their possession offering no measurable gain. 'Well, were you not looking forward to seeing them?' he demands again, and for once she responds without fear: 'The ruby slippers? As a matter of fact I was not.'

'What's the matter with you? I am asking you, oh saintly one, if you ever wanted to see those wonderful fantasy shoes that would have brought magic into our dark, miserable little lives and cured us of all ills.' So, he will try this trick again, her religion the bait for his godlessness. She responds in kind: 'Only God can do that.'

'Well he didn't make such a good job of it so far!'

'It would have been nice see them,' she ventures, 'but I don't understand why you would pay so much and go to so much trouble only to wound your own flesh and blood.'

'Aren't you the spunky one today?' he smirks back at her, surprised that she has so perfectly understood his motives. 'But what if "my own flesh and blood", to use your quaint expression, is a confirmed sinner? And that is according to the Holy Bible, by the way.'

'But it is wrong to punish a person so many times for one sin.'

'Well aren't you just full of it today? But at least you acknowledge that it's a sin.'

'But maybe not so enormous a one.'

'To quote a wise teacher: that is for God to decide.'

Suddenly, he is red-faced and panting, his head dropped like a broken bull.

'I . . .' he rasps, trying to straighten himself. 'I . . .' His face twists, sweat springing on his brow. 'I . . . feel—' and over he doubles, a fierce spasm smiting him in the side.

'Oh my gosh!' she gasps as he slumps forward, in danger of tipping the chair, for this now will surely end in another place altogether.

■ ◆ ■

She's not in bad shape as it turns out. Getting her there quick was a good thing, and the medics got the reaction under control at once. Even so, the deed itself was shocking – pure attention-seeking, of course, but then she had every right to seek his attention; it was her need, her nourishment and there was nothing trivial about it. He wonders that he is so resilient right now. Only a few hours ago he had felt that he could take no more, that the gods had played their cruellest hand. And yet here he is now, feeling really quite philosophical. Of course, it is because he finally got to be in control, and cast out at least one of the demons that had scared him half his life.

Right on cue, another one of these very demons appears in his line of vision: flying through the automatic doors, his ex-wife, looking wilder and more fearsome than he has ever seen her. James jumps up as she peels away and rushes to the reception desk. He plucks up courage and hurries over to her, saying, 'She's OK, OK. The worst is past.'

'Oh. Thank God . . . really?'

'Sure. They're dressing her and giving her drinks and stuff, giving her time to recover.'

'Thank goodness!' And she actually puts her hand on his shoulder to steady herself, though just as soon she takes it away, realizing her slip. It has gotten very weird all of a sudden, the wildness on her face replaced by the scared look of an infant. Why does she not scream and shout and name him as the source of all her woes and blame him for practically forcing the nuts down her throat?

Emboldened, he assures her quietly, 'They got to her in good time, she's OK, she's through it now.'

'Oh, thank God!' She sighs and begins to cry. Now he really doesn't have a clue what to do next.

'Go through,' he says. 'I'll wait here.' He points the way and she goes to their daughter. While he is putting coins in a coffee machine, his cell rings. It takes him a while to recognize in the faraway voice his father's

Filipino maid, who just launches in, saying, 'It is your father. Please, he is very sick. He is in the hospital.'

■ ◆ ■

What feelings is he supposed to have? To see his father lying like this on a hospital bed, a warrior-king stretched on the lid of a medieval tomb. Convention says that he should be forgiving – the man who wronged him but is flesh and blood after all – but James can take no solace in such sentiments; the feeling is not there, it cannot be summoned for show. Until the confrontation earlier, he had always gone in fear of his father. Even as a child, when his young dad was easier and more gentle under his mother's pacifying gaze. It was always the sheer bulk of the man, the savage energy that filled it, that left him in shadow: his father was sporting while he abhorred sport, competitive while he shrank from competition, acquisitive while he showed no desire for possessions.

If James is not yet ready to show forgiveness, he can at least sense the sadness of things that happened which never should have, and of happiness denied, which in turn caused so much pain. And this is what it comes to – this fallen person stretched out, the gathered mass of him reduced to the faintest trace and present only by turns as he ebbs in and out of consciousness, in and out of pain, and in and out of what is human and what is not.

James turns towards the foot of the bed and sees Inez, the nurse, who was so good as to show him kindness when his father was so cruel. He at least owes it to her to show common decency: 'How long now has he been like this?' he asks.

'A day. Twenty-four hours, more or less.'

'What? He suddenly just keeled over?'

'Not exactly. He was having dizziness and nausea, but I thought it was to do with his sickness.'

'Has he spoken?'

'Oh yes, he can hear; he has said things. You can talk to him.'

'And how long did you say he had been having these other symptoms?'

'That's hard to say. It's all mixed up with his condition. A week or two maybe.'

'Strange.'

And it is strange. A nurse has already taken James to one side and pointed out to him that his father's collapse is not typical of his condition and that tests will have to be conducted. He tells Inez to go home and get some rest while he will do the same.

■ ◆ ■

Back down in the ER, he goes through to his daughter's cubicle. Corinne is sitting there in a chair, while Siobhan, in her own clothes now, sits on the bed, swinging her legs and looking pale but otherwise all right. She looks at him sheepishly, a smile still lingering on her face. 'Sorry for what I did,' she says, as if she had just dropped a cup on the kitchen floor.

'Can I speak to you a moment, please?' asks Corinne, looking at him stern of face and then leading the way briskly to the corridor. Shuffling after her to the main door, a tremor passes through him – his old fear of her. Outside, she turns on him: 'I don't know how to say this.' And then she simply bursts into tears, her handsome face crumpling under her anguish. 'I'm so sorry,' she stammers. 'So sorry . . . I was petty and jealous and childish and just mad . . . and . . . and God knows what made me do such a thing!'

'What?' he wonders, seeing the tears take hold of her again. 'What did you do?'

She tells him how she let the bitterness and anger get the better of her; how she had stolen into Siobhan's messages and wiped out every trace of him she could find and had behaved in so vengeful a way. Strangely, he is neither mad at her nor resentful. 'I understand. This wasn't a petty thing, a spiteful thing – this was years of suffering, years of pain and insecurity, and I played my part in that. Please, don't cry; don't blame yourself.'

And she does stop crying and she does stop blaming herself, at least to his face, and they get to the point where she is able to ask him whether her mascara is all smudged, and he is able to tell her that it all looks fine. Eventually, the two of them are in a position to walk back along the corridor to Siobhan, who sits there looking chipper enough and only a little mystified as to why they both went out of the room.

Out in the darkness, on the way to the car, Siobhan finds herself walking between her father, silent on one side, and her mother, silent on the other. It takes her back to long-lost times and, like a five-year-old, she swings her arms in time with theirs, a bridge spanning their separated hands. 'What am I gonna do with you two?' she says. 'I mean, you're as bad as each other.'

James looks on as the battered old station wagon backs out of the parking bay, and remains watching as the tail lights fade from view, Siobhan's stark silhouette in the back vanishing with them. He knows now that nothing stands between him and her, and that there is nothing for him to hide behind, either.

■ ◆ ■

Michael peers out into the mournful dawn, beyond the paint-peeled window of the boxy precinct room, beyond the grimy porch with the tattered old posters and the ghastly yellow light swinging in the draught. A taxi is at the kerbside, waiting. Even at this distance he can hear the motor running.

'OK, mister,' says the sergeant, bringing him back to formalities and producing his belongings from behind the desk. Michael runs his eyes over them and the sergeant puts pen and paper on the counter. He scribbles his name against 'Items Returned': his jacket, his belt, his billfold, his glasses in their case and Rosa's precious letter pad.

He sits in the back of a taxi as the city awakes, scattering cluster-bombs of light to kill the gloom – windows in the buildings bursting iridescent to life, cars gliding in to make one serpentine organism, their halogen headlamps fusing to one dazzling shock of light. Thankfully, the driver is in no mood for talking, his whole attention tied into hypnotic Arab-sounding music that oozes tinnily from the cab. Now at last Michael can sit back in a soft seat and reflect on what has passed, and what might come. The night-cell bed has done him no harm, his bones and joints no more aching than ever and the breakfast was bearable. At least he can get back in time to open the shop and get back some order into his life.

Michael has begun to fully understand it all: the woman he was raised by not his true parent at all, and the 'eccentric relative', as Grace would have it, his birth mother. It is strange and tragic, the story she has left behind her. Harrowing, really because at the end of the day, all the cruelty and evasions in it were unnecessary. He takes the letter pad from his pocket and retrieves Rosa's last words so that he can properly take them in and tie his grief to them again . . .

■ ◆ ■

So now I come to the end of my story, but must go back to the beginning to reveal what before I did not say. To write this I feel myself free at last, and know that I am able to confront my shame, for that is what was hanging on me all this time, nothing but shame.

Early in this story I relate that I went from the house in Riga of my mother, Jolanta, who was already widowed, but I did not give the whole reason. In 1936, at the age of only fifteen, I made a terrible mistake: I was going to where the river comes to the harbour and there was a café full of musicians and poets — I am drawn to these people who are so intelligent and artistic and full of life, and noticing especially how the poets are so much the better-looking. And I meet a Russian who is poet — you have to understand that they were not all bad and sometimes there were friendships and more. And this is what happened to me. Love and sex I did not understand at all, and so before I knew what it mean to conceive I become pregnant. Of course it was then a dreadful thing. My mother was not very religious, but we were respectable and in the church, and it was therefore looked upon with shame. Also I was young and did not understand what it means to be a mother; I did not realize I had rights of my own. Soon I start to grow bigger and did not know where to turn, for fear and shame was to come on the family. But then for good fortune, my sister Magda and Janis, who had tried for five years but were childless, come to me. They offer to take the baby, and the result was that I agree to hand the child to them, and they are to bring it up as their own. I was sworn by them to tell no one, to live silent with my secret and go away as far as possible. The child was born in Christmas 1936 and his name was Mihails Bendiks Petraidis. After this he became Marcinkus, the name of my sister and her husband.

To those who ask how I could do this — to let a baby go, to go far away and live a different life — I say this. Live my life; go to the places I went; suffer what I suffered; endure the good things and the bad; then come back and tell me what I should have done. There was a time I dearly wished to tell Mihails all what is written here, but I came to believe, after my mind became unsafe, that I no longer could, because the mother he would find was not a good mother, not even a whole person. The shock of the discovery would be worse than the lie.

This story will be found perhaps when I am dead. The truth can be perhaps a comfort after the reality is gone. What is there left to say? To Mihails I say, I love you, and I pray to God and Heaven that my story will bring something better to your life than it has brought to me.

Rosa Petraidis

■ ◆ ■

He sits there, dreamy with the music. Four times he has read this part of the history, but still he feels devoid of any meaningful emotion. By any standards her story is tragically, shockingly sad – enough to make the angels weep. And yet *he* cannot. What is wrong with me? he wonders. I should be crying my eyes out but I can't.

The sun is fully up by the time he gets out of the cab. He looks at the dusty window and sees the Sunrise sign, faded with age. For some reason it always brings a smile to his face, even now. He chose the name itself but never knew why. How many times has he stood here, outside the Sunrise at sunrise. His world: solid and knowable and comforting in its familiarity.

He peers through the window into the darkened store, looking for signs of life, wondering if Grace is up and about, wondering if she is there at all.

CHAPTER SEVENTEEN

HARRISON is there, outside the convenience store. Just when she is walking back home with her messages, he arrives out of nowhere and stands in her way, staring terrible at her, his face all bruised and swollen. Rain's anger is hard and sharp this time. How in heaven's name did he know to find her here? And how dreadful he looks. For all her annoyance, she forces herself to be polite: 'What happened to you?'

'Don't ask.'

'I don't get it. What are you doing here? This is not funny; it's awful!' She is practically yelling at him now, such is her fury. 'No, it's not cute, it's not nice. Stop

366

looking at me like that! How in hell did you know to find me here?'

'Are you gonna stop shouting?'

'OK, so I'm quiet now – so tell me.'

'Because I stood outside your house two days nearly and waited,' he says calmly and really quite proud of himself.

'You did *what*? Are you crazy? You stood outside my house and waited till I came out? That's stalking!' she screams.

'You're shouting again,' he says, for once the quiet one.

'Damn right I'm shouting!'

'I did not stalk you. I waited to see you. And then I followed you because I care about you and have to tell you – I have to say what I have to say.'

'If my father saw you he would whip you, I do believe it, he would stand here in the street and whip you!'

'Well he ain't here, thank God, but I am and so are you. The thing is, I wanna be with you, to listen to you and care for you – don't ask me to say why – and do things right and be a better person.'

'This is just nuts!'

'No, it ain't. Please, please, just hear me out.' Now at last he tells her the really tricky stuff about himself: the whole story about the ruby slippers, from the smelly old woman to the frozen grocer, and the beating he took for daring to believe he could share in the stolen magic, and the pain and suffering he has endured because what is rightfully his was taken. It all comes down to one big, crazy, sorrowful story, and she starts to feel his sadness and to make sense of things about him that hadn't added up before. If nothing else, he has been honest and told her difficult things about himself, and that at least makes him more of a man than she had first thought. He allows himself a smile, relieved at least that he has got this far unscathed, as if her hand had never exploded against his face and made him see stars. But she is far from sweetness and light. 'Why are you telling me all this?' she starts. 'Don't tell me, tell God. Go to the Tabernacle and tell Him. That's the first thing you should do, and when that is done you should let go the money, lose the money and be happy.'

'I don't have the money, that's the truth. Just a hundred fucking dollars. What, I should give that away too?'

'That especially. And by the way, don't curse around me. It was blood money. Lose it, get rid of it. Nobody should keep what gave them pain.'

'I can't do that. It's like saying money is bad, period, but money is money – like you should never want it.'

'Then we have nothing to say to each other. Please. There is no point in this conversation.'

■ ◆ ■

It is beyond a joke. James should be at work, but instead he's sitting in this hideous corridor waiting for the God Almighty doctor to get back off his rounds and he's three quarters of an hour late already! If it wasn't urgent, if the old man hasn't taken a turn for the worse, why did they insist he come? Ringing him at seven in the morning when he had had so little sleep. Didn't they know he was here for hours last night when they could have spoken to him at any time? They'd better have a damn good reason for all this trouble! Glancing at his watch and growing all the more jittery, James tries Siobhan again – a long shot – and the phone rings on and on, and still no sign of the damn quack! Seriously rattled, he calls work and speaks to Marcia, who is 'overjoyed' to learn he is still in the land of the living and 'ecstatic' to hear from him again. Just as she is starting to really wallow in it all and tell him how 'frantic with worry' everyone has been, he spies the doctor walking towards him: Dr Benedetti. He looks like a Benedetti, tall and thin and sort of ascetic; it must be him. And so he pockets the gushing woman and stands to meet the impassive man, keen to display outrage at being messed around like this. But Benedetti has no time for petty nonsense; he steers James into a side room and poses the question that has been vexing him: 'Mr McBride, certain irregularities have come to light concerning your father's condition. The tests show that he has ingested, over a significant period of time, something like three times the recommended dosage of painkillers.'

James struggles to take this in. 'Three times the dose? What does that mean?'

'It means he is very, very sick. He has liver damage, kidney damage, severely reduced red cell—'

'My God, how did it happen?'

'I was rather hoping you might have an answer.'

'Me? I don't see him. Hardly ever.'

'You are his son?'

'Sure but . . . long story. You should speak to the nurse; she's with him twenty-four hours a day.'

'Ah.'

'Just tell me again; this has nothing to do with his illness?'

'Nothing.'

'And he took three times the normal dose and now he has organ damage?'

'Yes. It's serious . . . Mr McBride.'

'You mean he's going to die?'

'I'm very surprised he's still alive.'

'God . . . Does he know?'

'That he's dying? Possibly. I tried to find out from him how it happened, so he must have some idea. And of course he's aware that he's not feeling so good.'

'Did he say anything?'

'No. That's why I want to know what happened here.'

'You think he took them deliberately?'

'It's what we need to find out. Usually in cases like this, we would call the police. Except by then the person is usually dead.'

'Really?'

'Really.'

'Jesus. Can I see him?'

'Please go ahead. Maybe you can find something out we couldn't.'

James stands at his father's hospital bedside. Looking down he sees, in the carved, sallow face, everything that ever made his own life dark and solemn. It is hideous to be alone in a hospital room again with a dying man without a trace of tenderness to wrap himself in. McBride lies there, propped up, a mechanical man, wired to monitors, plugged with drips and in a shut-down state that's far from sleep. There is the sound of breathing, but it comes from a machine releasing morphine in its own cycle of slow, sad exhalations. James looks into his father's flickering eyes and for some reason remembers his long-dead mother. He struggles to find something to say – even with his father's evil behaviour he should try and find some decent words. When McBride speaks first, it catches him off guard: 'What . . . are you . . . doing here?' The voice, slow and breathy but connected still to the same reptilian brain, the half-closed eyes still full of intent.

'You . . . you're not well.'

371

'Ain't . . . that . . . a fucking fact!'

'You took painkillers.'

'So . . . I am told.' His head flops away to the side. James presses on still: 'What does that mean? Listen to me. You have to tell me. Did you do that? Did you overdose on purpose? Because if you know something and are capable of saying it, you must say so now.'

The eyes close and James thinks he has gone away again, but suddenly Malachi McBride begins to laugh – as much as a dying man *can* laugh – a throaty cackle sawing at the air with his eyes closed and twitching. Whatever the joke is, it isn't that funny, because now the eyes flash open again, as if alerted by a sixth sense. 'Well . . . here comes the star . . . of the show!' And she just walks into the room, arriving at the foot of the bed: the saintly figurine, hands clasped in front. James looks at her, staggered. She gives a little twitch. Her eyes are bright and hard, knowing the truth is out.

The dying man is not done yet: 'Gotta . . . hand it to you . . . that was a damn . . . good murder.' He gasps and falls away again. James, meanwhile, draws himself up to his full height and glares down at her. 'Not here,' she says, almost inaudible, before he can find his next words. 'Not here.'

■ ◆ ■

The first thing to hit Michael is the clean, sharp and oh-so-familiar smell of disinfectant floor-wash.

372

'Michael!' she calls out from where she is mopping. 'Go that way – *that way* – it's dry there already.' Grace: no-nonsense and practical to the last. He exhales in relief, and the first smile in a week rearranges his crumpled features into something softer and smoother. He goes to her and she comes to him, and they kiss and she strokes his cheek and tells him she is sorry, and he holds her to him and tells her not to beat herself up over it. 'No, Michael, I won't, but this was all my doing. Mine,' she insists. 'But now you sit down and have a good hot coffee, and when you're feeling up to it, tell me everything.'

So Grace comes to know the appalling and enthralling truth about Michael's birth. Two cups later, she knows, too, that they are safe from the reach of the law, him having satisfied them that Rosa was his mother and that there was no real charge to answer to. As for the original theft of the slippers, it was in another time and place and no one could ever come close to the truth of it. 'Well, I guess that makes us lucky,' she says, for once philosophical. 'We had all this heartache, but at least we didn't go to jail.'

'And we still have the slippers.'

'Well, yeah, but I ain't so fussed about them right now,' she adds. 'Looking back, I kinda got it wrong. That goes without saying. But at least I didn't take off and hotfoot it outta the building. Like certain others we don't care to mention.'

'I know. I saw them go. How did Jenny take to that?' he asks.

'I'd be surprised if she didn't throw Karl outta the house. Anyways, what about you? You must be in sore need of some rest.'

'Not really. Too much to do . . .'

'Poor you,' she coos when he tells her how he spent the night in a cell.

'Not a bit of it. I slept, didn't I? And I can't remember the last time I did that in my own bed.'

'Ah, come here,' she says fondly and kisses him, only to spring away beetroot-red when a customer walks in.

'Here we go, then,' he says.

'Here we go,' she says.

Home again.

■ ◆ ■

In the hospital cafeteria – with children playing at one end, with people seated at tables wearing kind hospital faces, and with bright primitive paintings on the walls – Inez proceeds to explain to James how she set about ending the life of his father. They are, of all things, drinking coffee. Quietly and calmly, she tells the story that starts with the terrible old man mocking her beloved children and spitting out blasphemies, which then moves on to the 1001 private cruelties he has visited on her across the years, and that ends in the finale that James knows only too well: the public mocking and scourging of his own son. There are no tears, no rise and fall in her voice, just a plain account: the dates it started, the dosages she gave, the progress of symptoms. No defence is made; no justification attempted or apology offered. So calm is she that James starts to wonder whether she is mad, or evil, or actually a vessel of the Lord, who has been known, after all, to send his messengers to strike sinners down. He decides that she is not mad or bad. Her love for her absent children is heart-rending and she herself so sorrowful and self-effacing. He recalls the time he almost threw a man down the library stairs and was all the better for it, and more courageous, as she has had to be, in an upside-down kind of way. Yet he knows it is his duty to go to someone in authority and put the facts before them.

'What will happen to me?' she asks humbly. He imagines her in a courtroom, where her impassive manner would be portrayed as the face of evil. He imagines her in a prison, where there will be sinners eager to make martyrs of saints.

'Go home,' he tells her. 'Go home and wait there. I don't know yet what will happen to you.'

She leaves, her head bowed, slowly walking towards the elevator. He drains his cup and takes the stairs down.

■ ◆ ■

James stares at his old man lying there, withdrawn again to nothing. If he never woke up it would perhaps be to the good. James leans over and quietly speaks, in as kind and reasonable a voice as he can muster. 'Look, I know I have no right to say any of this, and I know you will be angry and hurt for the things I said to you, but please, you cannot let this woman, Inez, who you have made suffer, go down for this. She will go to jail, her life will be destroyed and her family too.' He reaches out and takes hold of a clammy paw. 'I do not wish you dead. If it was in my power to stop this, I would, I promise you. But I cannot, and you have to face it in your own way – send for the priest or whatever it takes. Make peace with yourself, but know that there are still things that you can change.'

He crouches down and whispers urgently into his father's ear. 'Tell them, Dad; tell them it was you: you took the tablets, you stored them up, you kept them by and you poisoned yourself. This is in your power to do. Tell them, and spare her and her family.' James stands up straight again and waits to see if he was heard, waits until at last the old man's spirit stirs, climbs up out of its dark lair, the lizard eyes glinting behind the lashes.

'Murder – is – murder.' The sound of his voice dry, ancient, portentous, but James does not fall back in awe. 'Well, you'll just have to live with it,' he says softly and walks out of the room. He makes straight for the

376

desk and tells the nurse to call Dr Benedetti – his father has something to say.

For the longest of all hours, James sits in the waiting area. He has no idea which way it will go. He cannot, and does not really want to, bring to order the shreds of thought spilling inside him. He wants only for release: to be free to close his eyes and dream everything away to nothing.

■ ◆ ■

Benedetti wakes James from a doze so deep he almost falls off his chair. The doctor leads him into the side room again and informs him that he just heard from his father's lips a full account of how he had for some time planned and carried out his own extinction. Through all this, James can see from the way one of Benedetti's eyebrows stays stubbornly raised that he does not quite buy into it, that there are questions remaining unanswered, such as why would a man kill himself over weeks instead of minutes? But he does not linger on any one of these things, he just tells James that he has noted down everything that Mr McBride has said and will pass it to administration, who may wish to take it up with the relevant authorities. Then off goes Benedetti's bleeper, whisking him away into his pressing day.

Outside the hospital, the wind is blowing in gusts through the trees in the Park. James rings Inez. He hears her scared voice lilting and fading among the wind and the traffic. He tells her that he thinks it is going to be all right. But by now it has all caught up with her and she starts to go to pieces: 'But what shall I do? I have killed somebody.'

'As far as the hospital is concerned, he did it himself. The doctor heard it from his own mouth.'

'You do not understand. That does not take it from my shoulders. I should confess.'

'In church? God no. They will give you absolution and tell you to go to the police. And then you would go to prison. Your children need you more than the American justice system, Inez. If you need someone to confess to, try me. He was my father. I am the one who should forgive.'

■ ◆ ■

When it comes to it, Malachi McBride does not call for priests; he does not call for anyone. The nurses and the doctors decide between them that his time is near and send for his son. And not too long afterwards, the son comes and stands at the bedside and is quiet and respectful. The man in the bed is only just possessed of breath, and the son reaches out and takes the hand of his father. And soon after, the hand of the father curls and tugs a little in the hand of the son, and the hard lines of his face melt away to make the face of a man remembering better things and knowing better things again and sinking willingly into better dreams. And then it falls away to nothing, the breathing and the spirit with it. The last unseen part of the organism that was Malachi McBride crosses the final fragile span of time and is gone.

James goes home. He sits in a chair facing the window, his eyes half closed in the sun. There is no place inside him for any thought or feeling or care. He will sit, just sit . . .

And in the state which he now falls into – something between a dream and a meditation – Paolo comes to him, wearing a white shirt over blue jeans, sits on the arm of his chair, gazing at him with his dark bright eyes, and says:

'Really, James, this can't go on – punishing yourself like this, suffering for nothing. Your father was foolish, but you are ten times more so. To honour me, you searched so desperately for a beautiful thing. But already you had found it. The red shoes would have been out of this world, but there were simpler things you passed by without noticing. When you walked in the Park, that was a beautiful thing. When you looked at trees and looked out at the shining city, that too was beautiful. But the most beautiful thing you did was to look into the eyes of the daughter you had not seen for seven years. And even then you did not properly understand. So now, having found her father and put herself in his hands, *she is in pain. Of course it is complicated, but how was an uncomplicated mind to understand this? To her, it seemed only like punishment, and she did not deserve to be punished.*

'Look again at your world; look at what is there and what is not. Make room for what is right. Take away her pain. That in itself is sufficient to remember me by.'

James sits up in the chair, awake and aware that this was no ghost, but astonished that such wisdom could be latent in him, so complete and eloquent. He stands up, certain of purpose, goes to the mantelpiece, to the porcelain incense holder there, and takes from it a key. He walks to the study door and undoes it from the closed-shut state in which it has lain since Siobhan's last visit. He stands at the centre of the room and slowly turns on the spot, taking in the world between its four walls. He muses for a moment, hand to chin, then goes and leans across the desk, reaches out to the most beautiful of the Japanese prints and removes it from the wall.

Time to get her room ready.

■ ◆ ■

'Look, Michael, take it easy for five minutes. Sit down and read the paper for God's sake and slow down. I dunno what, but all this week you been going like the Pacific Express. You gonna have a heart attack; you gonna drop down dead you're not careful.'

He takes her up on it, drags himself to the window seats and picks up the paper. He feels tired after all, dog-tired, although he has worked no harder than usual and Grace has been nothing but kind and considerate and determined never to put a foot wrong again. It makes things worse in a way, that she is so resigned now to his will, no longer so much as mentioning the shoes or the money; no longer complaining about her aching joints and her ringing ears and her throbbing head; no longer holding out for her time in the sun, but soldiering on, getting from one day to another in the old accustomed way.

Yet he, too, has been reluctant to talk about it, for in his heart he has been slow to forgive. Oh yes, he has allowed her to believe the worst was behind them, that they had a scrape from which they were lucky to get out in one piece, and that all is patched up between them. But in his heart, he has not once been able to say he can let go of the resentment that burned so hard inside him it made him leap on a man's back and try to strangle the life out of him. They say that God forgives whatever – well, that may be, but *he* sure isn't up to following that act.

Around seven, just as they are bringing in the stands, Jenny walks in and hangs there drawn-faced in the doorway, looking so dreadful that Grace instantly runs to her. Michael knows from Jenny's manner at least that there is no cunning in her sudden appearance. When at last they are all three in the same room upstairs – he in his comfy chair and the smell of cooking wafting from the tiny kitchen – Jenny pours out how hard a time she has had of it, what with Karl firmly in the doghouse, she lonely in her anger and the coldness in their bed. 'It was horrible what happened over the slippers, and the guys behaved abominably. And if you must know, I regret some of the things I said. But that's not to say I think you were right at the end of the day. Nobody was totally right in this. Nobody comes out smelling of roses. Nobody.'

■ ◆ ■

James goes there because these things must be done. He goes half thinking that she might have upped and gone, fled while the going was good. Inez opens the door to him, looking frailer and older – only a day gone by and she has aged ten years. She knows, without him saying a word and despite his dignified manner, that McBride is gone. She invites him in, but she is shaking: he is the master now and she the shameful one. She offers him a seat and apologizes – for still being there, for not giving herself up and cheating justice of its right. 'So you see, they didn't come to arrest me. And I did not go to the priest. I thought of my children, as you told me, and I have waited to give you my confession, which you also said to do.'

'I didn't mean it so literally. Besides, you made your confession in the hospital.'

'Yes, but nobody has said if I am forgiven.'

'Well, of course. If I hadn't forgiven you, I would have gone to the police, and if I hadn't—'

'If you don't mind, Mr McBride, I would prefer to hear it with my own ears.'

'OK then. Mrs Garcia – Inez – I forgive you. You are forgiven.' Even as he pronounces these words, James is uneasy with himself. There is something flabby about it – to play the liberal do-gooder, when in fact there are within him more primitive emotions crying out for a harder kind of judgement. Strangely, it is she who comes out with the more unforgiving viewpoint. 'I cannot be allowed to get away totally free,' she declares in all conviction. 'I give you power over me. If one day you become angry and decide I am to pay, that I must to be punished, then so be it. I bow my head.' She stands there, her head actually bowed. After all the recent shocks and high emotions he has somehow withstood, this seems in its own way the most disturbing thing of all and he is keen to get back to safer territory. Ordinary things. 'Now, listen hard to me,' he says and takes out of his pocket an envelope. 'In here is money for your ticket home. That and enough to live on for a month or so.' She looks at him, astonished, as he holds it out to her and lays it on the line. 'You take it and you go – today, tomorrow. Don't leave it any longer.'

'I can't possibly,' she protests, falling silent when she sees he will not give way.

'That is all I have to say. The next time I come back, you won't be here. Now, I have to go.'

As he is on his way to the door, she rushes over and opens up a writing desk, bringing back a foolscap document to hand to him. He studies the title printed in heavy black gothic on a faded grey-green cover: 'The Last Will and Testament of Malachi, Thomas, James, McBride'.

'Oh my goodness,' he says, turning the cover.

'Take it with you,' she says. 'There are other things, but not so important. You will find them once I am gone.'

He walks briskly down Fifth now that he is in a more lucid frame of mind. The light is kind and golden, and the air a blessing on his face. He runs through it again. All proper and legally stamped; his name as the beneficiary of his father's will. He puts the brakes on his own thoughts, actually slowing his step. Of course, it's entirely possible that another, subsequent will might have been made, but then why would this one have stayed in the drawer? He had always assumed that he was cut out of his father's will to the very last dime, possibly even long before he ever came out, and yet this will, made twenty-five years ago, has remained in place. How could it be that the late, great Malachi McBride did not change his will as categorically as he had changed his heart? Surely the Republican Party or the Gun Club would have been far more deserving?

He crosses the road, goes into the Park to claim the nearest bench and sits down to study the small print. Fishing in his inside pocket he finds a solitary cigarette in a crushed pack and lights it, his first in a year, and allows his half-formed thoughts to float with the smoke. Had the old man always kept alive a hope that he would make good with his son? Perhaps he even truly imagined that being gay was just a phase, that he'd be saved by some true-blue McBride genes lurking somewhere in his puny frame. Maybe because the old man was so competitive, he always saw the actions of others only in terms of their opposition to him. Like a ghastly game of trumps: I call you a chicken-shit, idle no-good, and you go one further to be the screaming, limp-wristed queen. As if such things were a matter of choice and could be made simply to spite another person. He stubs out the cigarette only half smoked, the taste and sensation of it sour and invasive. The facts are the facts: his father died and he has inherited a considerable fortune.

CHAPTER EIGHTEEN

Six guests only are at the funeral: Michael, Grace, Jenny, Suzy, June and her husband, Maurice. They fill up two rows; the rest remain glaringly empty behind them. Between them they cannot raise a single god to preside over Rosa's consignment to the flames. Michael can still remember how his mother had taken him to church when he was little, but then when they starved and his father Janis was dragged away, there was little to thank God for. In the end Magda had taken God to the grave with her. As for Grace, she was always too down-to-earth ever to make space for the Almighty in her life; the three girls left God and all his dominions behind with their school books, and Maurice, though he was brought up Jewish, at least nominally, is none too fussed on the matter.

For all the solemnity of the occasion, Michael is at odds with it. He doesn't like the way he has felt in the past two weeks since Rosa died; he doesn't like it that the principal emotion he feels towards his birth mother has been one of anger. The fact is she had kept the truth from him even to her death, and has in a sense cheated him of the satisfaction that could have come from a little honesty. At the same time he is discontented with himself for being so cramped and ungenerous in his thinking: the woman was afflicted, damaged by what she had been through; how could she ever have been expected to do the reasonable thing?

The service is led by a professional, a business-like woman in a dark suit, who wears the badge of the Independent Order of Funeral Conductors. The chapel is plain but light and spacious. Ella Fitzgerald is singing 'Blue Skies', a song Michael had come across three times over on old vinyls among Rosa's demented collection. There is a single posy on the coffin to match the lilies, exuding subtle scents to direct the mourn-ers' sensibilities heavenwards. Michael stares at the coffin, implausibly small and neat on the catafalque and containing within it the relics of so turbulent and complicated a life. The conductor starts in, glowing but reflective, as if she had lived next door to Old Rosa, saying how she was essentially good and decent, though troubled, and that she'd had so interesting a life. Michael has omitted to tell the woman about Rosa's actual relationship to him, and, as the funeral speech goes on, it seems a rather glaring oversight. All the same, he is glad of it; it's a raw thing for him right now, and he can't handle putting it out there for people to make a song and dance over. So the high-point of the eulogy is Rosa's time in Hollywood; how she rubbed shoulders with the great and the good and how she had once been the handmaiden of none other than Judy Garland. This is the perfect moment for another musical tribute and, of course, it's Judy singing 'Over the Rainbow'. And it is this, after all the shocks and surprises and trials that he has been through, that finally gets him, perhaps because it is so simple and true. Michael, who had feared feeling nothing, sheds tears, while Grace squeezes out one or two of her own to see her old man so affected.

The final moment comes as the coffin glides away, the low doors sliding open. The cue for this is provided by Gene Kelly breezily delivering 'Singin' in the Rain' – another gem found in the filth – and as it turns out, a little misplaced in the circumstances. Everyone manages to keep this observation to themselves, only Maurice and June sharing a sly smirk.

Emerging onto the terrace outside the chapel feels surreal. A party of Orthodox Jews is sprawled across the area, which had been filled only by sunshine when they went in. A coffin is there, big and black on its cart, apparently ignored by the mourners, who stand around in groups, chatting away like nobody's business; the males with side-locks and shawls and huge hats perched like water jugs, the women with their blatant wigs. Putting his arm across Suzy's shoulder, Michael looks back though the windows of the chapel. A man is there, using a long pole to reach high up and hang high on the wall a huge Star of David in place of the cross that had been there earlier. Funerals to order, he thinks to himself, and a god for every purpose under heaven.

James sets out downtown, determined to walk every step of the way, his senses keen for every sight and sound. Along by the railings of the Park he goes, glimpsing the sky through a veil of leaves, joining his footsteps with the tourists and the out-of-towners.

Past the Gallery he cruises, where people really do come and go, talking of Michelangelo, and on he strides, further along, across from the zoo, where a road-gang tames the highway – the catch of hot tar in nose and throat, the rattle of jackhammers, the snarling and yelping of traffic captured and protesting, and, all but subliminal, the screeches of caged animals.

And in the concourse that opens out to mark the bounds of the Park, James sees the skateboarders, now huddling in a mass, now hurtling apart, a splitting star. Soon the city begins to narrow down and huddle up, taking his vision from wide expanse to looming tower. The people themselves are more workaday now and more about their business: shoppers laden with their prizes, workers hanging outside offices to draw on cigarettes. Turning into West 32nd, James encounters in a stone's throw a grand old woman walking a cat on a leash; a man hunched, begging, on a step; a hot-dog seller stepping from one foot to the other in his winter habit, even though it is spring, and a platoon of students bent under packs but craning to see to the top of the Empire State.

Here is the magic, he thinks, here on this ordinary journey. Look at them: each one inside themselves and at the same time looking out; people containing every degree of joy and every shade of sorrow, and all chasing the magic, searching for something beyond them, when all the time the people themselves are the magic. Theirs for sure is the wonder that never could be captured in something so insubstantial as a pair of shoes.

He comes to Sixth and 32nd and stands in the entrance of a department store, where, on a high classical frieze, heroic figures look down fiercely, demanding those below be worthy of entering. Glass doors draw apart in silent judgement and James steps inside. Through Cosmetics he goes – the heady scents and goddess-girls – steps on the escalator and is carried up to new realms. At the top, the soaring stairs still at his feet, he follows signs to Beds and Bedding. He walks between the stands and comes to Quilts and Covers, all in racks, all in sets. He walks along, his eyes scanning the shelves, puts his hand to the soft cotton, imagines her curled up under it. A soft, sad smile is on his face. Powder-blue, orange and pink, these are the colours he will choose; seventy-five dollars the price to pay for the simplest of joys, to give to someone what it pleases them to receive. So fine a thing, to give this to them.

And see their eyes light up.

■ ◆ ■

It's Wednesday, late afternoon – always the quietest time, when custom can be counted on the fingers of one hand. He says to Grace at the counter, 'I gotta get some fresh air.' She looks up as he takes off his apron and goes to the door; since when was he ever into that?

Michael walks in the city for no explicable reason, a thing he has not done in thirty years. He goes the length of 99th and stands small beneath the buildings, looking towards the Park as the traffic swishes by, scattering his thoughts to other times and places. He crosses the road, arriving in a space that has gentler sensations, with sounds and shades merging into one. He skirts around the reservoir and down the flank of the museum, and walks to the centre of a vast island of grass. Standing straight and still at the hub, he hears the traffic whispering distantly now and somehow friendly. He could be in the middle of the widest ocean, or lost in an endless desert, and yet he is in the city, feeling the frontiers of his spirit expanding to its extremities. And he feels no other need except this: to stand still in this moment in this place.

On he goes, walks right across the Park, arriving with the dusk at Strawberry Fields, where he sees the memorial, a mosaic on the ground, with people in ones and twos, standing motionless and wondering. He has never been here before, although it's been here all this time. 'Imagine' says the word in the middle of the mosaic. Yes, he likes it, come to think about it, and they were kind of right about the whole peace and love thing as well.

He sits down on a bench facing the lake, allowing ordinary thoughts to come back into his mind and connect him to the material world again. Only that morning the auction people rang to tell him that the sale could go ahead. Of course, it meant that soon he and Grace would come into a large sum of money, but when he tried to talk to her about it, she backed off; the whole performance at the sale room had made her afraid even to think about the damn shoes again. He will have to deal with it on his own. The power is back with him now, and the decision of what to do with the money is his alone to take. Should he ignore the family's wishes and cut them out for their cheap, greedy behaviour? Or rise above it and be forgiving. Since he found out all about Rosa and him, that's pretty much how he has started to feel about it – merciful, godlike even, above the petty scheming of others. The revelation has made him stronger. The news was shocking but the ending of mysteries has made him at peace. Now that he has got over the worst of their treachery, he can look on them and see them for what they are and still have room in him for kindness.

When he gets back, she is already wheeling in the stands. 'I thought we could shut up a little early,' she explains. 'Then I can do a nice juicy steak with all the trimmings.'

'What did I do to deserve that?'

'Don't even ask.'

'Sounds good to me,' says Michael, having no heart to protest over closing early. But before she can head back out, he stops her with the most solemn look and says, 'Listen, Grace, listen. This is how it should go: four households – the girls, Jenny, June, Suzy, us – a four-way split, no questions asked.'

It takes a moment or two to get through to her, and for a smile to dawn on her harrowed face: 'No? Are you kidding? What about the guys?'

'They did wrong, but you can't punish them over and over for the same thing. They're just people after all, and they all have to carry on going in this crazy great damn city. No, we get our little ticket to happiness, they get theirs and nobody gets to argue with nobody. Whaddya say?'

'What can I say?' she says, when at last she properly understands what is being suggested. 'Perfect, nothing but perfect!'

■ ◆ ■

Sky-blue, that was good, that was right for this visit, this returning. The jacket fits her trim and chic, the cream jersey beneath and her curls springing electric under the white beret. Upright but easy, she sits in her seat, eyes gleaming to see the insubstantial world flashing past. People are all around, they in their places, she in hers. Gone is the time of pretending, of camouflaging herself among others. Her mother stood on the platform to wave her out and her father will stand at the other end to welcome her in, and hold her and take her into his city.

And so at last the train cruises into Grand Central Station, the world slowing down to substantial again. As she steps off the train her eye alights on him, standing there with his hand raised, and they greet each other and walk together into the city, feeling the slow giddy turn of its ancient hub.

'Wow!' she says, when she sees how the room has changed, the drapes bright and floating and the walls brimming with light. And the city is there, too, in a different way – the same old view down to the fountain and gardens beyond, but alive now with May blossom, bringing the promise of summer into the room. 'Oh look at that!' she gasps, following his coy glance towards the table and seeing its bold chequered cloth painstakingly laid out with tableware that's groovy and funny and grown-up at the same time. But it is the mantelpiece that holds her attention most and does away with words. Buddha is moved, she gathers in a glance, to a recess in the bookcase. Paolo is still there, but shifted to the far end. And right there is her own infant photograph, blown up and newly framed.

'You must be just about ready to eat,' he says, drawing her smile to him.

'You bet,' she answers.

'Me, too. I'll see what I can do.' And with that he dives into the kitchen, knowing exactly what he can do, because he has bought it all in and planned it for days.

'Can I help?' she calls through.

'Tell you what, while I get all this together, you think about places we can go later.'

And they do go to places and enjoy doing things together. And early Sunday evening, after she has slept two nights in her lovely bed in her lovely new room, and after they have done the Statue and done the zoo and done their lazy share of daytime TV, he walks her to the station and sees her onto the train, the last link to make the circle.

■ ◆ ■

As he is walking back from the station he gets a call: an out-of-state number he does not know. 'Is this James McBride?' enquires a hazy voice. 'The Ruby Million guy?'

'Well, yes,' says James.

'Good,' drawls the voice, 'because I have something you have to see.'

'Really? And what would that be?'

The voice grows a little sharper: 'I'm speaking to you all the way from Salt Lake City.' As if this should explain things. 'Can you get mail right now, where you are?'

'Uh, not at the moment. Why?'

'Like I say, you have to see this. How soon till you can get hooked up?'

'Uh, a half-hour maybe.'

'Good.' The lazy drawl is back in place. 'Soon as ya can. You are so gonna be into this . . .' The voice slides away, the line gone. James looks at the screen, mildly bemused. Weird, but he doesn't give the call much thought. There are 101 other niggling demands on his mind, paramount amongst them being what the hell to do with the ruby slippers. The saleroom people had called him only the previous day, the auctioneer himself confirming that the sale was safe. Of course he had been somewhat surprised to hear that the old man had died, but the fact remained: Mr McBride had bought the shoes. James had expressed surprise at this, wondering if the hammer had actually fallen before the sale had been stopped – he could not remember hearing it hit. The man had been absolutely adamant: they had CCTV and had played it over to check. No doubt about it, the hammer had fallen; wood had arrived on wood, as he was welcome to see for himself.

Back at home, he collects his papers together for the next day, writes down his tasks, packs his briefcase and tidies up now that Siobhan has gone, loading the dishwasher, thinking of food they have shared and memories they are making. He starts the washer, and soon everything is humming and swishing and whirring around him. He throws a meal in the microwave and goes over to his laptop. Among the spam and chatter, one email stands out:

FROM: Kenny Chopra
SUBJECT: The Great American Picture Show

A video file is attached. Curious, he clicks it. The head and shoulders of a man materialize on the screen. 'Hi, ahm Kenny.' The same see-saw voice from the phone, out of a sallow face, the eyes dulled with disaffection. He could be twenty-five; he could be forty-five, with his lank thinning hair and dirty orange T-shirt. 'You better be ready for this,' the voice slithers in again. 'This is ma secret store.' The image scrambles and then rights itself to focus on the rust-scabbed door of a lock-up. Then it all goes giddy again as Kenny's other hand reaches in to grab a handle and the door scrapes open to black. 'One moment . . .' A strip-light goes on, showing the interior grimy and bare, apart from a heap of broken plasterboard in the middle of the floor and a row of metal racks running down one side. 'Now, come right along here . . . just over here . . .' Kenny pans the camera along a dusty shelf where there are grease-black tools and dingy cracked storage tubs crammed with rust-fused screws, and brings it to rest on a rectangular heap, neat and symmetrical among the decay – six old-fashioned khaki shoe boxes in two stacks of three. 'Just look at this,' says Kenny, and his hand enters the frame, removes a box and sets it apart. 'Now, ah can't tell you every detail right now, like as to where this all come from, but imagine if you will ma surprise' – the hand peels off a rubber band holding the lid to the base – 'when first ah set ma eyes' – the hand now fumbling at the lid – 'on these little beauties.' A layer of tissue is teased aside, revealing a pair of ruby slippers. 'Prime condition,' oozes Kenny, as though he is trying to offload a second-hand car. 'And, believe me, gen-yu-wine.' These last three syllables as long as a train. The camera focuses on the label on the end of the box. 'Ruby Slippers,' it reads, '*Wiz of Oz*. MGM '39. Prac. Mod. Feldman's Bespoke Footwear.'

'And what is more,' Kenny lilts as he arranges the

other boxes side by side and removes their lids to expose to view five more pairs of the exact same appearance, 'six pairs, my friend. Each one good as the last. Cool, don't you say? V cool.' Now the camera comes back to Kenny's wasted face. 'Hang around,' he says and, just as the screen goes blank, adds, 'Ah'll get back to ya.'

James has viewed all this in total silence, and so he continues for a while after the video has ended, his face as blank as his thoughts. It takes time for it all to sink in, and it is only the ringing of his cell that stirs him sensible. Kenny again: 'Ah see you got ma li'l picture show.' Still James says nothing. 'You there, James McBride? You hearing all this?' Kenny is getting annoyed now, but before he can redeliver his question, out of James's mouth comes a shuddering, spluttering sound. 'Mr McBride, you OK?' he whines, but James is oblivious, having begun, heartily, to laugh, abandoning himself to the sheer joy of it. Even with Kenny yelling down the line for him to 'listen up!' and 'get serious now!' James pays no heed and simply ends the call, first presses the key to disappear the man, then throws the phone to the ground and continues to laugh himself silly.

CHAPTER NINETEEN

I T is a Saturday night and she stands at the balcony,
between the drapes lifting and falling in the breeze,
gazing out at the fortress silhouette of the city with the
summer sun sinking below the battlements. It gives her
a sad sweet pleasure to sense the never-ending cycle,
the death of a day and the dawning of another. But
when a cold lick in the breeze sends her shivering
back into the living room, she finds her father sitting
forward in his chair, and in front of him, in the middle
of the floor, a plain metal security box. 'I never did
get around to showing you these,' he says, turning the
key and flipping the lid. She watches, fascinated, as
he reaches inside and comes up with the pair of them

nestled still in cotton. She goes over and takes them from him. 'Where were these?' she asks and sinks down to the floor, cradling them as if they were living things. 'Don't laugh – they've been under my bed ever since they released them to me,' he says, mischievous and embarrassed at the same time.

'But, how come?'

'The auction. It turned out the hammer *did* come down before the policeman stopped everything. Your grandpa won! They had to be paid for out of his estate so, to cut a long story short, here they are.'

'I still don't get it. What about the Ruby Million thing?'

'That had nothing to do with it. We lost and that was that. It was all pledges anyway, so it was quits in the end.'

'And you just had them under your bed? But they must be worth . . .'

'Yeah, I know. I was told to put them safe away, but somehow I just . . . Anyhow, turns out they are no longer worth anything *like* that any more. So, anyway, whaddya say?'

'Like, what about?'

'Like, do you like them?'

'What, like, as if I could have them?'

'Maybe,' he says, smiling wistfully at her, wondering if she has any kind of feeling for the slippers. She considers: these shoes are gorgeous in their own way and wonderfully made, but are they in any way magical or fantastical to her? She picks up one of them, turns the rounded upper heel in her hand and sniffs at the kid-leather inner. It smells musty, although she can see that it is practically unused. In the end she speaks her mind, almost apologetic for it: 'Well, these are cool in their own way, but they don't do it for me. I never really got off on *The Wizard of Oz*. They would end up going mouldy under my bed instead of yours, which is kind of a waste of a million dollars or whatever. You could always give them to Mom to sell at the Newton Harbour Market.'

He laughs. 'You know, I had a funny feeling you would say something like that.'

'So what are you gonna do with them?'

'Well, up to now I wasn't too sure, but since you don't appear to want them, well, now I can do what I damn well like.'

'Meaning?'

'Meaning come on, let's go.'

■ ◆ ■

For the past few weeks he has been wondrous quiet. Aunt Crystal takes it for the grace of God, the scourging of the body leading to the elevation of the spirit. And in truth something cleansing has occurred in Harrison, as if the baser parts of him have been smelted down and purified. From the moment he stood up from his seat at the auction sale, once everything had gone crazy. There has been no satisfaction in what came after, no sweetness in his revenge and nothing come back to him that was good. He has seen the grocer and his wife, back in the deli, just going about their business; he has passed by his old friends Floyd and Dale on the other side of the street, unspeaking because he had shunned their company and become so secretive. And he has stood outside the Tabernacle, twice seeing his lovely girl go in and wondering if he could ever give himself to the bearded, white-robed white man in the old painting on the wall. It leaves him with the know-ledge that if he wants for something real in life, he has to change maybe and find something new inside himself. So when Crystal asks him if he would like to accompany her to Tabernacle again, he really does think twice before answering, 'Sure,' and a few days pass in which not once does he call her crazy or refuse her when she brings him cakes, and in which he goes out but once to take a hit.

They go the Tabernacle together. He walks in with her, slow and correct, and takes his place beside her. And when the minister calls on all who would shed their sins to come and receive the Holy Spirit, he consults what is in him and feels drawn to go, but then decides that the light is not truly in him. And so he stays in his place, keeps his eyes down and away from the lovely girl on the other side of the hall (not even allowing himself to know what colour dress she is wearing) and keeps quiet and inside himself, even when the chanting and wailing is like heaven and hell under one roof. And all the time he prays that maybe something good in him will show itself to her.

After the service he goes to the coffee place again. He has dreamed of looking into her shining face – it would be joy enough in itself – but now he cannot lift his eyes to hers. She, though, has her own questions: 'May I speak to you outside again, please?' she asks sternly, and he follows her dumbly to the street, not knowing if she will raise her hand to him again. But nothing of the kind awaits: 'Do you love God?' she asks.

'I want to,' he says.

'Do you wanna put aside money and possessions and everything of the kind?'

'I don't care about any of that no more.'

'And what about Jesus?'

'I don't really know Jesus.'

'You have to give yourself. Let go of everything – money, possessions, drugs, everything.'

'I know that. I can do that. I want to do that.'

'You don't know how hard that might be.'

'I wanna try.'

'Good,' she says. 'Good.'

She says this knowing everything he has already told her about himself. Deep down, she knows how it will go. In the span of a second. They will get together in all kinds of tricky ways, bringing heartache to both their families. She will see his good side and ignore the bad. They will love each other and be sufficient to each other for a time. And then some crazy, stupid thing will happen in some seemingly random way that has everything to do with him and nothing to do with her. He will be vulnerable again and get into all kinds of scrapes and will test her love to the limit and cause her pain. And she will be there to save him over and over, and he will love her and will swear on his life he will never let her down, and then go ahead and let her down. It will go on and on, the pain always growing and her never knowing which Harrison will be there for her. And even if he comes to know Jesus, he will just as easily fall away from him again.

And one day, even she will lose her saintly patience and tell him truths he does not wish to hear, and then, despite his adoration, he will hit her, like he has been hit himself so many times. He will hit her and be damned, and the more he is damned the more it will be her duty to save him. Because a bad person needs a good person to save them, and a good person has to have a bad person to save.

And so, because nature has created an undeniable attraction between them, and because her heart senses that it is meant to be, she denies what her head is telling her and tells him that she will see him again.

■ ◆ ■

Why has he brought her here, wonders Siobhan, tramping along at James's side, the streets becoming more cramped and gloomy with every step. He refuses, in a daddy-knows-best kind of way, to tell her where they are headed, and eventually they arrive outside the boarded-up store across from the Sunrise. She registers astonishment: 'I came here that first time,' which throws him a little, because he's been in charge of surprises up to this moment.

'Really? Then you met the guy that runs this store.'

'Sure I did.'

'Well, it was him who had the shoes in the first place.'

'Really?'

'You know, it just occurred to me that he could be long gone,' he goes on. 'I mean, he could've retired by now, on the money from the slippers – should've done if he had any sense.' His hand already on the door handle, James peers through, and there he is, Michael Marcinkus, his old friend. Siobhan recognizes the old man who had smiled when she asked such dumb questions, and offered her moutabubble or whatever he had called it.

When they step in the door to the same breezy ring of the bell, the shapes and colours and smells swarm all over James's senses to confirm that nothing has changed – except the old man himself, who is not in his customary place at the counter, but in the window sipping coffee; and who is not wearing his usual old

406

apron, but a rather snappy suit; and who is not chatting to customers, but sitting talking to a pretty little girl sitting on the stool alongside him, planted there like a kiddie's dolly. When he sees them enter, Michael jumps up, beaming magnanimously: 'James! How the devil are you?' he calls out.

'Good,' says James, meaning it, and stands back to fully take in Michael's transformation. 'You're looking pretty good, too.'

'Well,' says Michael, somewhat cryptically, 'who wouldn't, who wouldn't?'

When James introduces his lovely daughter, Michael greets her as a familiar face recognized. 'Well how about that,' he says, warmly. 'The girl who asked if we sold Chinese oranges and chewing gum.' She smiles sheepishly as he goes on: 'We still don't stock 'em, I'm afraid.' James looks at him a little nonplussed, so Michael moves things on. 'This is my granddaughter, Sylvie; her mother Jenny is out back somewhere.'

'I think we met already,' says James, a note of apology in his voice. He has a faint memory of this little cherub being in the Sunrise that dark time he had called on his way to the hospital.

Sylvie folds in on herself under James's uncertain gaze, but Siobhan brings her straight back out of her shell: 'Hi, beautiful,' she says, and produces, as if she has placed it there for the purpose, a lollipop from her pocket. Sylvie, at once alive to fresh-faced Siobhan, gives a gorgeous smile that instantly replicates itself on each watching face.

Michael signals to a young man standing over at the cash register – a chiselled man, smart and dark and together-seeming, in his own sharp suit. With a solemn nod back at Michael, he goes to the coffee machine, his hands fluttering deftly to conjure the perfect blend. James looks at him: a new employee, a manager, a relative perhaps? He turns back to Michael. 'So how you been all this time?'

'How many hours you got?' replies Michael. 'It's such a long and crazy story. How 'bout you?'

'That also is long and complicated,' says James. 'And how about Mrs Marcinkus?'

'Ah wonderful! In Miami at this very moment, and laying in the sun every hour God sends. She and our other two girls went together.'

The man arrives with a tray and quietly unloads it. James waits until he has moved away again. 'But listen,' he says, and swings up onto the window counter the security box he has carried all this time. He unlocks it and opens the lid, allowing the old man a glimpse inside and noticing a certain trepidation come over his face, which gives way to a sad smile. 'So they came to you,' he says wanly.

'Yes. My father died.'

'Oh, I'm sorry to hear it.'

'No, please, I'm over it now. To tell the truth,

Michael, we had our differences. But somehow it all came to me.'

'Good,' says Michael. 'These shoes were very special for me. I told you that much already.'

'You surely did. To tell you the truth, I envy you having such rich experiences to draw on.'

'Rich? Believe me, you don't. Memories like mine, they haunt you all your life, and if anything they squeeze you harder over time. Look what it brought me to . . .' He gestures vaguely at the shelves so that James is not entirely sure what Michael Marcinkus has been brought to, or how the acquisition of a million dollars might have made him suffer. Michael shrugs and drains his cup. 'But all that is over now.'

'So you decided to keep the place and stay on. I always thought that was on the cards.'

'Stay on?' exclaims Michael dramatically. 'God no, I got out. Look at me; what would I be doing in a suit? I don't work here no more, I just come here for coffee now and again. We sold out!' And he looks over and waves to bring the smart young man up to them: 'This is Marty – Marty Trabatore,' he explains. 'Marty, this is James and . . . and . . .'

And so Michael introduces James and the girl whose name he cannot grasp to the mystery man and explains how he and Grace had finally decided to throw in the towel on the business before it killed them both. 'Marty here is twice the businessman I ever was,' he points out generously. 'Money comes to him. My first partner was an Italian, did you know that? But the best thing about it, Marty loves the Sunrise just the way it is.'

'Ah,' says James, smiling approvingly at Marty, who takes his cue to wax Italian: 'I love the Sunrise; it is wonderful, a pleasure,' he enthuses, his accent thickening with his passion. 'How often you see a place so delightful, so traditional as this?'

'That's right,' says Michael, taking up the baton. 'Anyways, the deal is Marty takes on the business – for a consideration – so that it's his, all his, only he agrees to keep it exactly like it is, down to the last detail.'

'Down to the last detail,' echoes Marty with a flourish and, seeing a customer arriving at the counter, he bowls away.

'Terrific,' says James, smiling. 'Pretty neat, eh?' adds Michael. 'That's why we came over, me and Jenny – wherever she is – to show him the ropes, if you know what I mean.'

'Listen,' says James, 'we have to go soon, but I thought I should come over and drop these off with you.'

'Sorry?' says Michael.

Siobhan looks up, equally startled, as James continues, matter-of-fact: 'It's my decision. I want you to have them.'

'What? You can't do that. What would I do with them?'

'What you always wanted to do: put them in a case.'

410

'You don't understand. I let go of all that – and them. Sometimes you have to with dreams – let them go.'

'I think so, too,' says James. 'But out of interest, what *would* you do with them?'

'Well, if you have something good, it should go to the good.'

James takes Siobhan's hand in his and squeezes it: 'Anyway, please. Take them. They are yours – more than they really ever were mine. I can see they still mean a lot to you. Take it from me, these shoes are no longer worth anything like they were.'

'James!' Michael protests, troubled still. 'Truly. I wouldn't know what to do with them, not any more.'

'You could do whatever you like; you could throw them off the Empire State, or you could just you keep them somewhere. But I happen to think they would be better in your hands.'

The old man looks helplessly at Siobhan, who suggests, tongue in cheek: 'You could always float them down the river and let them go where they go.'

'Yeah, or tie them to a helium balloon and let them just fly away,' suggests James, also trying to keep things light.

'That is strange,' perks up Michael after a solemn pause. 'At one time I had thought that way myself – to take them to the East River and cut them loose. It would be madness, of course, and they would sink in seconds flat, and I would never really do it, but it's how

I see it in my mind's eye – to just cast them off and so they would float away on the current, bobbing up and down like so, until they came at last to the right deserving person.'

This seems to strike a chord with all three of them: Michael, James and Siobhan, standing there looking at a pair of shoes in a box, marvelling into the luminous expanse that Michael has imagined for them, and visualizing the ruby slippers, gliding and swirling, now apart, now together, waltzing on the waters until they are lost in the mist.

'So what's going on here!' A sharp voice rings out, startling them from their communal daydream. Jenny is standing there, looking them all up and down, more disdainful than puzzled. 'So who's all this standing here dreamin'?' But now her gaze switches from the newcomers to the slippers, her mouth turned down in distaste: 'And how in hell's name did *they* get here?' Michael looks up, smiling: so much like no-nonsense Jenny to be the party-pooper.

'Jenny, allow me to introduce my friends,' he says. But still she keeps her distance.

'No, no, no,' she says. 'First put *them* out of my sight.' Michael, James and Siobhan turn their backs to the counter, shielding the ruby slippers from Jenny's fiery gaze. 'I don't never wanna set eyes on them objects no more,' she says, then, realizing she has gone a little OTT, she adds, 'Sorry.'

Michael introduces Jenny to father and daughter, clumsily rehashing the tale of Chinese oranges and chewing gum, which leaves Jenny totally mystified. And it is while he is relating this that Siobhan hears something, glances behind her and gasps. Side by side on the floor are the ruby slippers, left and right. And Sylvie, who must somehow have slid the box down while no one was looking, has, with great concentration, slipped a little foot into one of them and is steadying herself against the counter in order to insert the other. 'Sylvie!' rasps Jenny, mortified. 'Someone get a picture of this,' says James, entranced. 'Beautiful, kiddo,' says the proud grandfather. And even Jenny is silenced then, because her lovely daughter looks up at the audience in raptures. Her head is high, her eyes are shining and a perfect smile is on her face.

Siobhan has it all in a flash: 'Oh, sweetie, you *shall* go to the ball!'

CHAPTER TWENTY

I T is odd how nobody really thought of the little girl
before when they were considering what to do with
the slippers. For who other than a child could hope to
love the shoes so fully, or be so absolute in their desire
for them, or gain so much pleasure from holding the
things they have longed to hold? Sylvie had always
been in the story in one way or another, starting with
all the times her momma brought her to the Sunrise.
Indeed, it had become a second home for her, a comforting and familiar place.

She loved to go and stand on the big green thing
they called the 'way-in machine'. Even though she
didn't know what it did, it was such fun to jump up

414

and down on the bouncy platform and see the needle leaping wildly every time. And then there was the fierce hiss and gurgle of the coffee machine that was like her mother somehow – the angry flush of steam and the delicious smell together. It thrilled her to hear the ring of the bell when the door opened, looking up eagerly to see the next customer walk in with the light. And always she copied down inside her mind the face that was on the person, staring hard at them from her safe place. And she learned their expressions and practised them, making her face fit to theirs, so she might try out what it was like to be them and they would never know.

And she loved the little surprises. Grampa was always feeding her scraps and goodies, though Mommy hated that and called it 'cupboard love', whatever that was, and scolded him he should know better. And when her mommy left her sitting in her little corner while she went off to do things, she let her mind wander and be sucked away into the tastes and the smells, and the colours and the sounds – like the meat slicer swishing fast, then swooping and falling heavy, when Grampa pushed the wodge of meat into it, with the skiddy ringing sound of it and the slices peeling off and the smell of meat creeping sour and sweet like sick, along the gloomy rows.

And Benjy suddenly jumping out in front of her, making her squeal with joy because he pretended to make eggs come out of her ears, and pulled faces and sang to her and chased her around the shop, Grampa laughing behind and for once not being horrible to him at all. So, she got all wild and excited and then went giddy and fell down, back into her quiet space and lost herself again. She made up stories for herself, trailing her hand among the bumps and swirls in the shiny wood floor – stories with different fairies living on different shelves; bright shiny fairies and dark dusty fairies, squidgy jelly ones and hard glassy ones. They flitted across the tip-tops, where only she could see them, and hid behind the cans and cartons, and once a teeny-weeny white pony slipped around the stands only a swishy tail ahead of her.

Benjy rolled his eyes and did a silly dance, crossing his eyes and swinging his arms across like a monkey and popped up and down at the same time, and she screamed out laughing. She did colouring-in when Mommy said to settle down. Mommy always gave her another colouring book for finishing the last colouring book, and sometimes little toys, but she only wanted sweeties. Grampa gave her sweeties without her doing anything, and they tasted so good, and even Grandma slipped her a chocolate candy now and then from her hidey place, but then Mommy said it was 'wrong and terrible giving candy to the kiddie like that'. But how could it be terrible, because it always tasted so sweet the whole world vanished until she chewed it to nothing? Her mommy never gave her sweeties, only another colouring book or puzzle book, and once a round thing called a yoyo which she couldn't do, although her mommy showed her how, and tied it on her finger and made her throw it down over and over till her finger was sore. It never whooshed the way it should, and in the end she got so mad she wiggled it off her finger and threw it on the floor, and her momma was mad and 'told her a thing or two', so she went into a sulk. But it always came out like her mommy said – she couldn't sulk for ever and sooner or later someone like Grampa did make her laugh, tickling her or making faces, and that was so delicious, even though she tried hard not to, because it made everybody smile and laugh as well, to see her go from down-face to up-face and not sulk no more.

At other times she was left with no one to make her laugh, so she just got bored and sat down and stuck out her legs and sucked her thumb, and her mind went away into the smell of warm bread and salami and olives and went into a dream of being in a sail-boat, with birds that could change their wings for legs and their beaks for mouths and say things just like real people, like, 'Ain't that the cat's pyjamas.'

Among all the days at the deli, the day she remembers best of all was when all the people were waving little green flags and being so friendly. She was at the front when Barrell went by the steamy window, then the old woman. It was like a cloud going over the sun.

Grampa went out and stood and stared at her to make her go away, and the stinky old woman turned with her face yellow like cheese with eyes in it, black like the black round things 'groan-ups' eat, and just for a moment she stared right into her and opened a special secret face just for her. She remembered it, and it stayed inside her, and she saw it again in dreams and when she thought of things that were strange about the world.

Then there was the time Grandma came over to stay the night and she came down the stairs grizzling; she was so tired but couldn't sleep, and Momma and Grandma were watching a movie that was all dark and shiny and fuzzy at the same time, with a man and a lady staring into their eyes and hers all sparkling and his hat pulled down. Mommy and Grandma had tears in their eyes, too. She squished in between them on the couch and got drowsy and nearly fell off to sleep, but jumped awake again when the music got loud at the end of the movie. The story ended when the man, who was good because he smiled when he wasn't being sad, shot with his gun another man who was bad – he never smiled and was mean to people. Then the beautiful lady went away in a silver airplane going up in the sky. And when Momma got up to make some tea she pretended to be asleep so they wouldn't send her straight to bed, and instead they let her stay there squidged between them. She heard them talking all quiet about

418

'damn fool slippers' and 'damn fool Poppa' and she didn't really know what they were talking about, but she did wonder why they were making such a worry over Grampa's slippers.

The next day they brought Grandma Grace back to the Sunrise in a taxi. Grampa was there but Mommy said he didn't look right – he was all tired and mumbling and being like he didn't belong to them. She was waiting for him to pick her up and hold her up to the ceiling like a plane flying and say, 'Look what the wind blew in,' like he always did, but instead he just looked old and tired and wiggled his fingers in her hair, not looking in her face, and then walked away and said nothing, wiping his hands. But then later he took her out to the alley and showed her the house they had made for Barrell the dog, and Barrell was at home in his house and Grampa said he had a TV in there. Then later she saw the squashed goldy box thing lying on the floor by the ice room. She bent down to pick it up and gave it to him, but Grampa snatched it away and she cried – not because he took it from her but because he was scary like he never was before. And then she cried again, and louder this time, because she saw her knee was cut on a tiny piece of glass. Mommy came running and was angry at her for not looking down first, but she was even angrier at Grampa. He said it was a 'little accident with the mop', but Momma just looked at him sideways, like she knew something was wrong.

She was there when Grampa and Grandma came round and all the family was there waiting and they pushed the tables together and ate dinner round the great big table and everyone chewed and chewed and said nothing, which was really strange because it was her who only said nothing all the days. And then they had apple pie and ice cream, but the 'groan-ups' made that go down so fast and then her daddy and Uncle Dan and Uncle Maurice suddenly shouted out, 'Go play, kids. Go do things. Watch TV.' And every time she came back they kept saying, 'Go in the back room and play with your cousins.' She went over to her mommy, but she just told her do what her daddy said (she never said that ever before). So she went over to Grampa, who looked just like a little boy staring at his feet. Then, after, she went and peeped around the door and saw all the 'groan-ups' staring at Grampa with angry eyes and red faces, like he should go stand in the corner.

She remembers it too when Grampa came round the other time and was mad, all shouting like she never saw before. She went and stood behind the couch and put her fingers in her ears. Her dad was drinking beer and watching TV, but then he got mad too and went red and stood up, looking down at Grampa. And then Grampa was riding on her daddy's back, just like playing pig-a-back. She saw they were having fun together, which was nice and happy because Grampa and Karl, her dad, didn't always be friendly. She thought it was a game, like silly old Grampa and silly old Daddy. Then Daddy started to make a noise like a bear – all rough and grunty out of his throat – and Grandma came running out of the kitchen and hit Grampa around the head with a frypan. And she was full of laughing until mommy got to screaming. Then she started screaming, too, because her mommy always knew what to do, but now she didn't, and that's what made it all so terrible.

After, when Grandma came and lived with them and Grampa didn't, she asked her mommy if he was dead, but she said he wasn't. And one day Mommy said, 'Listen, honey, how would you like to come with me and see the ruby slippers?' They walked all the way to the subway and sat up on the seats and everything fell away behind her and the train was full of people – all in lines and floppy like her cuddly toys with their eyes drooping down. When the train kept going she stopped staring at the people and just sat on Mommy's knee watching the shapes and shadows flying by and feeling small. But they were like giants going up the elevators and into the square and everything was up in the sky – lights and pictures flicking over like pages in a story-book. And they had gone around a high golden corner just when she was getting tired, and came near the big building which her mother called the 'sail room', and she sucked her thumb at the bigness of it all. On the outside it was like a grey castle, and as soon as they went in, it was all 'gorgeous' – that's what Mommy said.

421

They walked over squidgy carpets and she could feel the lights hot on her head, and they came into a great big humungous room where the walls and the carpets sucked all the talking out of everybody and the ruby slippers were up in a great big seashell thing. It was a bit like Santa's Grotto. She saw the shoes shining red, light spreading everywhere from them, and that was how she found out that the slippers were very, very special.

And Sylvie recalls the day Daddy said him and Mommy was going to the 'sail room' again, but she couldn't go. Auntie Suzy was being babysitter, but then Daddy came back and Mommy wasn't with him. He whispered to Auntie Suzy and her eyes opened wide like something terrible had happened, so she asked if Mommy was OK, but Daddy laughed and said, 'Oh she's fine, honey,' but then made a smile on his face like an egg all cracked, so she knew something was wrong. Suppertime, Mommy still wasn't home, so she sat around, picking at her food and moaning when Daddy took her to bed. Then when she woke up in the middle of the night, there was Mommy, and she felt happy again and decided not to make a 'song and dance' next time her mommy shouted at her or wasn't very nice, because it was much better than her not being there at all.

And of course she was there the day Grampa was in his new suit and they went to the Sunrise, which her mommy told her wasn't theirs any more. But when they got there, Grampa sat down drinking coffee, leaning back, young and happy like it was all still his. Then the door went *ding* so loud everybody turned to look who had come in. And it was the nice man with the sparkly face, the James man she remembered from before, and a pretty girl with orange curls flopping out of a blue hat. Her name was Ssh-bom and she had a lollipop just for her. Later James brought out the slippers, like magic, and put them on the counter, and they were so pretty, but not like when they were in the 'sail room', so she wasn't afraid to touch them. And they all stood around them and stared, and then Momma came over and said, 'Look at you all standing there dreaming.' And they started talking again and forgot she was there. So she reached up to the box and took one slipper, then the other, and put her foot into it – it would be so nice. Then Ssh-bom looked down pink and lovely and saw her and said, 'Sweetie, you shall go to the ball.' And all of them turned their eyes on her and smiled and she felt so happy, like lights came on all around her and inside, making her all glowing like the angel on the Christmas tree.

And the next time Mommy and her went round to see the 'old deers' – that's what Mommy and Daddy called them now – Grampa lifted her right up, up in the sky, just like he used to, and said, 'You want to play with the ruby slippers, Little Sylvie? You can, any time you come to see us. They are yours now. Yours. Yours. Yours.'

CHAPTER TWENTY-ONE

O F course, you might think of going there, to find
the place where all of this happened. And you
could just as easily do so, any day of the week: simply
follow your feet all the way down to the intersection of
99th and 2nd. There you would expect to come across
the perfectly preserved Sunrise Deli and Grocery
Store, kept just so since its heyday in the Twenties.
But disappointment would await you, because the
place is no longer there. Marty, the nice kind Italian
American who was so at home in Michael Marcinkus's
deli, was also very good at business and never missed a
trick. Long before he ever met Michael, he had known
that the city planners had ideas for a neighbourhood

development, and he knew people in property who thought often and much about this and had a gleam in their eye.

And for this reason, only a year after Michael had sold the lease to him, Marty received an offer to sell out and make a tidy sum, for which he was neither guilty nor apologetic. Money follows a man like this and, unlike Michael, a man like this never lost sleep over the making of it. The people who bought the lease from Marty also bought up the whole shambling block attached to the deli, and knocked it down and rebuilt the whole damn shebang.

On the corner where the Sunrise once stood is now a fried chicken outlet – not quite the real deal, but the owners managed to combine the letters K, F and C in the title and put up signs in orange and yellow. People were happy to stand in line and buy fast food from the place, which is open to this day, seven days in every week, so you could always drop in there if you were so inclined, as a kind of consolation once you had found the deli gone.

Michael and Grace, however, are not gone – either in the ground or in the head. They took an apartment, quiet and comfortable and at ground level, because both their sets of legs are going, as they discover whenever they walk out, which is less and less often these days. Their place is just around the corner from Karl and Jenny's in Brooklyn. (Karl lived to tell and retell to his own glory the tale of the crazy auction of the crazy shoes, his actions finally forgiven, though never quite forgotten.)

And neither was Barrell the dog forgotten. He was happy that summer in his house in the side alley. He loved being surprised by the different tasty morsels that would arrive in his bowl one day after the next. He enjoyed being walked twice a day, sometimes by Michael, sometimes by Benjy, and he made it through the fall, quite warm and comfortable in his cardboard kennel. But winter was a different thing, and the Sunrise was situated where the chill wind came down uninterrupted from the East River and could creep into your bones, which was never good if you were old and past your prime. In that respect it was a good thing that Barrell never had to endure the elements, and that other workings of time took their course instead. It was Sylvie who found him in mid-November, around about the time of her birthday. Grampa had sent her running round to the alley to see him, and as soon as she had come near to Barrell's house, she knew something was wrong, because by now they loved each other so well that the moment she came around the corner, he would always come padding out.

This was, for Sylvie, her first intimation of the cycle of things. Barrell's time had come. As for the ruby slippers, they never went into a display case, nor into the river; they did not find a home in the New

York Public Library or the City Museum, though they would, all the same, have commanded a respectable price. No, at this very moment the slippers are sitting pretty on a shelf in Michael's new living room. They are there behind his head whenever he and Grace watch TV, which is more and more these days, and in his vision whenever they sit and slowly take their meals together.

Michael remembers how Sylvie came and played with the shoes whenever Jenny brought her to see him and Grace in the new apartment; he recalls fondly how she would walk fine and high in them, and would throw a pink fluffy scarf over her shoulder to trail behind, which of course made everyone hug her and love her all the more. It gives him pleasure to think how, now that Sylvie has grown out of these things, others will follow. He receives comfort from the knowledge that, from time to time and generation to generation, there will be children to put the shoes on and experience the sensations that are somehow imprinted in them, there to be awakened and enjoyed anew.

Every now and then, Michael looks up at the ruby slippers and thinks how they meant so much to him when he was younger and how it is a wonder that once he was *that* but now is *this*. He thinks about Rosa, his mother, the remarkable woman who started it all when she placed these same shoes on the feet of a great star. It helps each year that goes by, his thoughts softening a little to an acceptance of who she was and who he is. Simply to feel better about things, little by little, over time. A shift here, a small step there.

And that surely approximates to happiness.